I07632922

Soft Parade

John Pansini

John Pansini
Publisher
Colorado Springs, Colorado

TITLE: SOFT PARADE

LCCN: 2021915832
ISBN: 978-1-7351873-7-2 (Hardback)
ISBN: 978-1-7351873-8-9 (Paperback)

Printed in the United States of America.

Cover & Interior design: John Pansini

First Edition: October 2021

10 9 8 7 6 5 4 3 2 1

Dedicated to the city of Colorado Springs.
Where my faith was rediscovered &
strengthened.

"How much sin (in ourselves) is kept hidden from us by God Himself in His mercy?" — Thomas Merton

Mt 7: 22-23: "On that day many will say to me, 'Lord, Lord, did we not prophesy in your name and do many great deeds in your name?' Then I will declare to them, 'I never knew you; go away from me you evildoers.' "

CHAPTER 1

Soft Parade

What a perverse thought to pop into the head of Reverend Lawrence Schmetterling at this moment of life and death — *his* life and *his* death. Over two thousand dollars worth of high end clothing and accessories were being ruined.

At two o'clock in the morning on Ash Wednesday a red Geo sat parked along a Grand Central Parkway service road in Queens, New York. A flood of biblical proportions cascaded down the pants legs of the pastor's *Giorgio Armani* midnight blue seersucker trousers. Hot urine soaked through finely woven black woolen socks and overflowed his *Prada Saffiano* black leather loafers. Rain had earlier slicked the grass; add to this the pastor's expanding puddle of piss beneath his Italian shoes. He felt like he was filling a small pond. The business end of a crazy woman's handgun stared him in the face; to be shot in the head was not how he expected Lent to begin or his life to end. He begged the woman to take his money, but the fierce look of murder that darkened her face told him that money had nothing to do with this.

What could he have done to this Daughter of Eve to make her hate him enough to kill him? He didn't even know her name! They were two strangers whose paths had crossed on Fat Tuesday in a jazz club on the Upper Eastside of Manhattan. He'd gotten into her little red Geo Metro because she was young and beautiful, and he desperately wanted to begat a multitude of sins with her. Pastor Larry truly believed he had always ordered his life according to Scripture. Did tonight's single trespass wash away all previous temptations he had so scrupulously avoided in the past? Is this why He of the uppercase had turned against him of the lower?

Lyrics from an old song by one of Pastor Larry's favorite rock bands jumped into the mix now tumbling in his head:

When I was back there in seminary school/ There was a person there/ Who put forth the proposition/ That you can petition the Lord with prayer...

Then lead singer Jim Morrison screamed: *You cannot petition the Lord with prayer!*

Were *The Doors* right and Pastor Larry's faith wrong?

Chapter 2

Nibbles Along the Edge?

An unmarked Caprice slowly entered the huge parking lot behind the massive Wallman's Shop-A-Lot on Queens Boulevard. The driver, Detective Frank Giavone, scanned the outer fringe looking for the perfect spot for their stake-out; i.e. a place to nap on the job. His partner, Detective Howard J. Goldberg, was already in dreamland, leaning up against the passenger-side door with his mouth hung open and emitting deep, guttural snores. Frank felt like he was sitting next to a Donkey Kong. It annoyed him that he did most of the driving while Howie did most of the deep "meditation."

Frank's sharp eyes finally spotted an enormous evergreen tree whose branches overhung an ideal patch of asphalt. He gunned the engine and roared towards it as if it was an oasis that might suddenly turn into a mirage. He backed the Caprice in between the faded yellow lines. As if he was wired to the ignition, as soon as Frank cut the engine, Howie woke up and rubbed the sleep out of his eyes with both fists. He looked around.

"Where are we? … Geez, Frank!" He pointed. "Is that Wallman's all the way the fuck over there?"

Frank had put them so far out that the mega-store didn't look quite so mega anymore.

"Might as well of parked us in Jersey." Then Howie folded his arms and nestled against the door and went into his *Do Not Disturb* mode. They had a couple of hours to kill before lunch.

Frank scrutinized his partner and grumbled, "Me and you, ain't exactly *Law & Order*."

Howie turned ever so slightly, opened an eye, and aimed it at Frank. Over his shoulder, "You watch too much TV."

Instead of tapping the snooze button on his brain, Frank gazed through the windshield at little specs: shoppers rushing to and from their SUVs. None of them bothered to glance in their direction. On the odd chance that one did, they'd have to wonder: *Did the great god of Chevrolet sneak all the way out there, squat and poop out a Caprice?* The unmarked car's peeling yellowish and green roof reminded Frank of the color of run-off from clogged nostrils. It had black-walled tires and a faded paint job that resembled a mud puddle. Hard to imagine this jalopy still ran; it looked more like it had been driven out there and left to rot back in the days when Clinton ruled.

Unseasonably mild for February, Frank rolled down the window; cross ventilation carried the fresh scents of trees and grass from outside inside. Birds chirped on this spring-like day. Frank wondered if God Himself had decided to bless the City of New York with some winter relief in honor of Ash Wednesday. On the drive to Wallman's, they had passed a Catholic church. A thought jumped into Frank's head: *Maybe I should stop for ashes?* And then, as he hung a U-turn and headed for the church, it rolled right out again: *Nah! Maybe next year.* A second U-ie sent them back towards Wallman's. Too bad, because a whole lot of *Maybe Next Year's* clogged Frank's head. A little over a month ago, on New Year's Eve, after yet another party of five that consisted of him, a pizza, a six-pack, a DVD, and the TV, Frank Giavone had resolved to power-flush all those *Maybe Next Years* out of his skull forever. A day or two later, though, he was back to the same old same old. Unlike with food where he preferred to bite off big chunks, when it came to changing his life, Frank preferred to nibble around the edges.

Frank scrutinized his reflection in the rearview mirror. At forty-four, he was still a good-looking guy. A woman meeting him for the first time would inevitably be drawn to Frank's high rent district, his north end: large dark eyes, a jutting jaw line that ended in a cleft chin, a touch of gray at the temples and a few sprinkles in a full-head of thick, wavy jet-black hair. Since Frank's scrutiny could go no further south than his squared off, broad shoulders, he tilted the mirror down. He admired his tight Pecs and powerful arms packed into the sleeves of a blue blazer. When he tilted down some more, he smirked. Almost from out of nowhere up popped his main issue: Mt. Jelly Belly. At six-foot one-inch tall, he topped off at around two-hundred-forty pounds; all of it massed a cut above a low-riding beltway. For Frank, heaps and heaps of food did double duty. It filled an empty tummy along with an empty life. That was why he liked partnering with Howie, a guy who made him feel like a slim Jim. Two years younger, Howie packed two-hundred-fifty pounds into a five-foot six-inch frame. Short and squat and with a barrel chest and arms a gorilla would envy, Howie had a cheery smile, curly light brown hair, and happy eyes. He looked more like one of Santa's elves than a cop. Never mind that this elfin could crush a man's skull just as easily as he did walnuts in his palms. And like Frank, Howie was also partial to fast food and slow motions.

Frank and Howie's "stake-out" was about to be interrupted by a call to Frank's cell. He pressed the receive button with his thumb. "Giavone … Yeah … Yeah … OK. Bye." He turned to Howie. "We got a shooting off the Grand Central at Little Neck Parkway. Ferro and Dankanich are on scene. The vic's on his way to Queens General."

Howie yawned and stretched his arms high over his head. "Good. Maybe them two hot shots will close the case by the time we get there."

For most of his career, Frank's enthusiasm for *the job* rested on a bottom shelf right next to Howie's. They'd been partners for seven years, growing older, fatter, and lazier together. A lot of dust had collected on Frank's ambition. He passed through life like a ghost. Frank worried that the day might come when old, worn out, and still alone, he would put a bullet in his head just to relieve the boredom. And now this: a shooting off Little Neck Parkway. Nothing *ever* happened in that neighborhood. Was this a sign? What if God had decided to bless Frank with a special event, some poor slob's murder?

Frank turned the ignition to get the Caprice moving. The Snot Rocket, as they called their fossilized relic from the late '90s, coughed, growled and finally kicked over. The steel beast had a Hemi engine and could really zoom; but only when it had a mind to. Like the two cops it hauled, the capricious Caprice was predisposed to nod off whenever it felt like it. But it did have great tires.

The Snot Rocket headed north on Little Neck Parkway. When it crossed Union Turnpike, the next mile was uphill. As the grade steepened, the automatic transmission slipped into a lower gear. The engine growled, easily power-lifting 3,700 lbs. of vehicle and another almost five hundred pounds of New York's finest to the summit. When the Snot Rocket got going, nothing could stop her. At the top of the hill, just before reaching the massive stone bridge that carried the GCP over Little Neck Parkway, Frank veered the Caprice to the right. They were now on a service road that lay about twenty feet down an embankment from the Grand Central. To the right of the service road stretched a forty foot wide patch of gently sloping grass that ended at a seven-foot high fence. The fence was spotted with trees and shrubbery. It separated the service road from a development of high-end ranch-style homes. The fence served as both a sight and sound barrier. People with big bucks do demand peace and quiet. Not today. The service road had been blocked off and jammed with police and emergency vehicles. He glanced at his watch. It read 8:38 a.m.

Grinning, "Think we're gonna disturb somebody's breakfast," noted Frank.

"Yeah," grumbled Howie, "ours."

Directing uniformed police officers and CSU techs, a petite brunette in a navy pants suit and cream colored blouse stood in the middle of an area marked off by yellow crime tape. With short hair, big green eyes and a trim, athletic body, Detective Susan Ferro was the girl every cop at the One-O-Five wanted to take to the prom. Frank included. But he couldn't even get up the nerve to ask her to have a beer after a shift. As he and Howie ducked under the yellow tape, Frank called to her. She turned, surprised to see two senior detectives on scene, especially two senior detectives no one ever saw anywhere except seated at their desks stuffing their faces with pizza or Chinese take-out.

Detective Ferro walked towards them, her hand extended. "Frank," she said. He got a handshake and nice smile; Howie a cool nod. "Detective Goldberg."

Detective Susan Ferro and her partner, Detective Ralph Dankanich, were both young (late 20s for her, early 30s for him) and college graduates. Captain William Graham, commander of the One-O-Five, held these two up and comers in high esteem. As for Frank and Howie, he cursed their ancestry back seven generations.

"Where's Danky?" Howie casually asked Detective Ferro.

"*Detective Dankanich*," she said with emphasis, shooting Howie an angry side-glance, "has taken a few uniforms with him to canvass the neighborhood."

When Frank asked what they had so far, Detective Ferro began to read from her iPad: "Vic Reverend Lawrence Schmetterling of Colorado Springs, Colorado; white male, age thirty-two; medium height, build; found 8:13 by man walking dog; money and ID untouched; robbery not a motive." Then she tapped and swiped the tablet to show several crime scene photos to Frank.

"Vic was shot once between the eyes," she said, adding, "He was lying on his back, head pointed towards the fence."

Frank asked Susan if they found anything useful. She replied that their priority was to get the victim to the hospital. All they found so far was a shell casing from a .32.

"And that." She pointed to a light colored topcoat. It had been laid out neatly on the damp grass, inside down. Its good side was face-up like a small rug.

Howie, a bit of a neat freak to begin with, said to Frank: "Like he didn't want it to be ruined? Maybe he figured he was walking away from this."

Susan added, "It's a Giorgio Armani. Color, viscose plaid; lists for two grand."

That sure smacked some *Wow!* on Frank's and Howie's faces.

"Wristwatch a Rolex," Susan said, "and the rest of his ensemble looked expensive, too."

Frank, who shopped in a bargain basement, said to Howie, "Looks like the Rev's got some spare change. Must be good money doing the God-thing."

Noted Howie, "So what's a preacher doing all the way out here in the middle of the night, dressed to the nines?"

"I'm sure it wasn't to give the Sermon on the Mount," Detective Ferro quipped. "I'll go help Ralph canvass."

Frank nodded, and then he nudged Howie. "Let's me and you take a look around."

"No, you do the ground search. Lemme do the thinking."

A proper division of labor: Frank's eyes were fine-tuned instruments capable of spotting a nickel in a haystack. Pennies he ignored unless they were face-up. So Frank stalked the grass where he figured the shooter was while the CSU techs concentrated on the areas where the vic had been found and where the topcoat had been laid out. Howie headed back to the Snot Rocket to get his coffee thermos. Caffeine, and plenty of it, stoked the brain of Detective Goldberg.

"Hey, Frank," he called as he poured, "it's for sure our preacher didn't walk all the way out here. So whose car do you think he came in, his or the perp's?"

"You tell me, Sherlock."

"He was from out of town, so maybe he rented a car. Maybe our preacher passes by and sees somebody broken down in the middle of the night. Being Mr. Good Deeds, he stops to help and gets jacked. We run his credit cards, maybe we'll catch something."

Frank nodded.

"Got just the guy for the job," said Howie. "That kid in uniform, Officer Daniel George."

"Two Names," said Frank. "Yeah, I know 'im."

P.O. Daniel George (a.k.a Two Names) came from a pool of cheap labor that Frank and Howie had exploited many times before: young uniforms who thought that assisting the Double G's, Detectives Giavone and Goldberg, would benefit their careers. Schmucks.

Frank's eyes continued to pound the ground. And then, like an eagle zeroing in on a mouse from a thousand feet, he spotted something. With all the grace of a heavily-laden camel, Frank dropped to his knees and picked at the grass.

Howie, still holding onto his coffee cup, came over. "Whadda ya got there?"

Frank had found a tiny half-moon shaped piece of rubber. He held it up. "What's this look like to you?"

Howie squatted, careful not to get any green on his gray slacks or spill his coffee.

From behind them, a nasal voice boomed, "Found something, Frank?"

Frank turned his head. A grinning Detective Ralph Dankanich stood next to Susan. "Looks like the Double Gs are scrounging for lunch money again," he said to her.

Frank and Howie were notorious in the One-O-Five for having wallets tighter than a specific part of Captain Graham's anatomy. Not that Frank appreciated being reminded of it, especially by Danky. He despised the guy for many reasons: Detective Dankanich was young, educated, had a bright future with the NYPD, and was partnered with Susan Ferro.

She shot him a *Stop It, Ralph* look. Then, "What do you have, Frank?"

He handed her the piece of rubber.

Danky said, "It's a piece of rubber, Frank, not a quarter. That won't even get you a cup of coffee. You could leave it for a tip, though."

A particular witticism Danky should have saved for a private moment with his partner. Just being in close proximity to this clown was enough to make all the buttons on Frank's console blink red; but that last remark short-circuited the whole system. Frank stood up, clenching and unclenching his right fist. Should Danky let loose another surge of snark, Frank was ready to force-feed the guy his own teeth and gums.

Danky waved his hands in mock surrender and backed away. "Whoa, big guy, you don't have to leave a tip if you don't want to."

When Frank took a step towards Danky, Susan quickly moved between them. "I'll bag this for the lab, Frank. Thanks." She gave him a calming smile that gently guided Frank's animal instinct back into its cage.

Frank told Detective Ferro, "Me and Howie are gonna head over to Queens General. You and Numb-Nuts stay here and supervise."

"*Does he mean me?*" Danky faked hurt like he'd just been told his breath stunk.

***

At the hospital, Frank and Howie pulled out their badges for the young woman at reception and stated their business. She told them she'd page the doctor. While they waited, he and Howie walked over to a snack machine, dropped in a few quarters, and sat down to polish off some goodies.

Howie, about to chomp down on a chocolate bar, asked, "So, you think they're doing the nasty or what?"

Frank popped a white, sugar-coated mini donut in his mouth, chewed and gulped. "Whadda ya talking about, Howie?"

Mush-mouthed: "Danky." He licked his fingers, "Think him and Ferro are getting it on?"

Frank burped. "Pardon me… That would be very unprofessional. Besides, Danky's married."

Howie shot his partner a snarky grin. "What pumpkin patch did you just pop out of? Since when did that ever stop anybody from doing anything?" Carrying that thought a bit further, "Tell ya what. If he ain't, then he's gotta be gay."

"She ain't that kinda girl, Howie."

Howie nodded in the direction of a short, pot-bellied and prematurely gray haired man approaching at a brisk pace. "Must be the doctor." He rolled up the candy wrapper and, not seeing a garbage can nearby, tossed it under the seat.

"Don't do that," said Frank. "This is a hospital! You're spreading germs."

Howie stood up. "Hey, germs gotta eat too."

Smirking at his partner, Frank stuffed the donut wrapper into his Styrofoam coffee cup and looked around. He spotted a can about thirty feet away. May as well have been thirty miles. No way was Frank going to lug two-hundred-thirty pounds that distance. Still sitting, he discretely placed the cup on the floor behind his shoe. Then he gently guided it under the seat with his heel.

Dr. Alan Bloom, Director of Neuro-Trauma and attending physician to the Reverend Lawrence Schmetterling, growled at the receptionist that she should have sent the detectives to his office instead of making him "slepp" all the way down to reception. After humbling the underling, he turned to Frank and Howie.

A none-too-friendly: "What can I do for you?"

"I'm Detective Giavone and this is my partner Detective Goldberg. We'd like to have a look at Reverend Schmetterling if you don't mind."

"I *do* mind. The man is comatose, Detective, so he won't be answering any questions. Now if you'll excuse me." He started to walk passed.

Frank's arm shot up, just short of the little man's chest. "You're not excused. We got some questions for you, too."

The doctor cleared his throat with a deep growl: "Follow me."

Frank did not expect to suddenly be struck so claustrophobic when he stepped behind the curtains in the trauma ward. The hospital bed seemed to fill the space like a huge, white continent. An image of Antarctica popped into Frank's mind; he'd watched a *National Geographic* special on that land mass a couple of weeks ago. Surrounding the bed on both sides, only the foot was clear, were panels with blinking lights and instruments with wires connected to the vic. The narrow aisles on either side only accepted visitors in single file. Schmetterling, covered with a white sheet, lay flat on his back. A drip fed fluids into an arm via a long tube.

Howie glanced down at the vic's bare arms. "Look at that, Frank. The guy's got goose pimples. Is he cold or what?" he asked the doctor.

"I'll tell the nurse to turn up the heat a little," said Dr. Bloom. Then he squeezed his ample self bedside. He bent over to examine his patient more closely. To the detectives crammed together across from him the doctor said, "This man should not be alive."

"A bullet between the eyes? No kidding," was Frank's dry comment.

Howie leaned in for a closer look at the vic's face. "Think this guy is actually thinking things, Doc?"

"We really don't know for sure what goes on inside the mind of a comatose patient. If there's consciousness in this man, it's not at a level we can reach."

"Any chance he might come out of it?" Frank said.

Dr. Bloom mellowed, but only a little. "All we can do for the patient right now is provide him with intravenous feeding and monitor his vitals. But the bullet, which is still lodged in his brain by the way, has done severe neurological damage."

Frank stepped a little too far backwards and almost toppled an entire row of rather expensive medical devices.

"Careful, Detective, or we'll be garnisheeing your pay for the next 10,000 years."

The doctor cleared his throat. A long lecture was about to begin: "When the brain is injured it has a tendency to swell." Looking directly at Frank and Howie, the doctor clasped his hands tightly together for emphasis. "There's little room inside the confines of a skull to accommodate much in the way of brain swelling."

The doctor shot them a look that Frank read as: *Bet there's a whole lotta room inside your skulls, though.*

Bloom continued, "When a brain swells, its outer layers press against the cranium. This causes damage. In this patient's case, although the brain swelling has subsided, severe damage has already occurred. Add to this the destruction caused by the bullet and, without going into details, this patient's prognosis is poor."

"How come he's still breathing, then?" Frank asked the doctor.

"The brain swelling that followed Mr. Schmetterling's injury was not severe enough to damage the brain stem. That's the most primitive part of the brain. It controls all our life functions: breathing, heart rate, temperature, etc."

"How long can he stay like this?" Howie asked.

Dr. Bloom removed his eyeglasses and rubbed the bridge of his nose. He had the weary look of a man whose days ran twenty-four/seven. "Mr. Schmetterling's brain swelling has subsided; for now. But the bullet might cause an infection that might, in turn, cause the brain to swell again. If that happens, then it will eventually kill both the cortex and the brain stem. Then he'll be put on a respirator and remain in his current state indefinitely."

"What if he gets better?" asked Frank.

"He won't, but even if he does regain consciousness, we're fairly certain that the bullet has left him permanently blind, deaf and paralyzed from the neck down. For him to regain consciousness would be like dropping a working mind down a black hole. This man would be trapped inside himself until the day he dies."

Frank grappled with the harsh truths as told by the attending physician. He knew damn well that living didn't always mean being alive. For the Reverend Lawrence Schmetterling to regain consciousness, to see, to hear or to move even a finger ever again would take a miracle. Frank had never put much faith in miracles, although the very fact that Reverend Schmetterling still lived was, by Bloom's own admission, miraculous.

In the Snot Rocket on their way back to the precinct, Howie suggested they dump this one back on Ferro and Danky. Frank figured differently. He'd had enough of nibbling around the edges. The

Schmetterling shooting would be his big bite and big gulp.

CHAPTER 3

Words Without Meaning

Larry … Is … Awake …

Where am I?

He remembers the lunatic who shot him; he remembers the bullet that drilled into his face releasing jets of white hot gas into his skull; and he remembers the excruciating pain of his brains boiling. Now it's gone. But the numbness he feels tells him his body is gone too. So is the light and so is sound. He is in a place of such complete nothingness that he thinks back to a conversation he once had with a young woman who had been blind since birth. She was with a member of his congregation. She came to him for counsel in regards to whether her upcoming marriage to a sighted person would work.

"Do you love him," Pastor Larry asked, "and does he love you?" When she replied, yes, he said, "Then I wish you both a long and happy life together. And may the Lord bless you with many, many children." And then he was moved to pity because the girl would grow old and die without ever having seen anything as inspiring as a purple sunset crowning Pikes Peak or as awesome as a smile on her child's face.

So he said, "It must be terrible to see only darkness. I can't even begin to imagine what that must be like."

She chuckled. "Pastor Larry, I don't *see* anything. Light, dark, colors, *to see*; to me they're words with no meaning. They describe experiences I've never had." Then, without ever having seen a smile, she gave him one. "And you're right, you can't begin to imagine."

He can now.

Memories are Pastor Larry's only companions inside his black hole. And he knows exactly which one to pluck that might help explain what has happened and, maybe, where he is.

He remembers flying from Colorado Springs to New York on the Friday before Ash Wednesday. On that flight, he sat reclined in a first-class seat. He felt like Jesus riding into Jerusalem, not on an ass, but a Boeing 737. New York was his hometown, a city he had not been to in ten years.

He grinned: *Prepare the fatted calf, Mom, Dad. Your prodigal has returned in glory!*

The next morning, on Saturday, he signed a contract with The Lord's Broadcasting Network (LBN). The deal meant that Larry's longtime dream of being a televangelist superstar would begin with the new fall season. He would spread the Word, stir the masses, and bring in the sheaves. Glory, adoration, and silver, plenty of silver, would overflow his baskets. He knew that serving the Lord while also serving oneself was not only crass but a sin. So what? Although Larry was as flawed as any man, he had some-One special: Jesus the Christ was his personal Lord and Savior. He not only loved him but forgave him his trespasses.

Larry chuckled, thinking about the welcome home his parents would give him. For sure there would be no feasting on roasted bovine. His mother's culinary skills extended only as far as macaroni and cheese, beans and franks, tuna casserole, corn beef and cabbage, and potatoes. Although he loved his family, Larry did not look forward to seeing them again. Childhood held no fond memories for him. He'd felt nothing but the burden of everyone else's great expectations. When he had left seminary at Notre Dame, he had severely disappointed his Catholic-to-the core family. Pastor Larry did not look forward to finally telling them about his new religious calling and conversion to Evangelical Protestantism.

He took a sip of club soda and smiled. Savoring its tiny bubbles, he held the glass aside and set an admiring gaze on the symbols of the Lord's love for him: a blue *Canali* herringbone suit; and also new, highly polished black *Bottega Veneta York Leather Brogues* on his feet. The suit had set his congregation back $2,000 and the shoes added another $900. Pastor Larry wore a solid white Ike Behar dress shirt and blueberry silk tie. As he took another sip a pesky quote from Luke pried open the lid and jumped into his head. It began to kick at all the glad tidings he given unto himself:

Luke 9:3: He said to them, "Take nothing for your journey, no staff, nor bag, nor bread, nor money – not even an extra tunic."

Jesus held *His* disciples to a strict carry-on policy. But a lot had changed since the days of sandals, sack-cloths, and travel by donkey. In today's world to preach a Gospel of Prosperity one needed to appear blessed by the Lord Himself. Wealth, success, and confidence were powerful sales tools; therefore, Pastor Larry felt no obligation to observe ancient travel restrictions. Dealing with the TSA was more suffering than even the most saintly saint should have to endure.

Larry claimed Fat Tuesday, a night of debauchery the day before Lent begins, for himself; sans the debauchery of course. A jazz club on the Upper Eastside was not a field Pastor Larry normally tilled on behalf of the Lord. And the ultra cool folk gathered within sure weren't lilies. He found an empty table and ordered his first Long Island ice tea. Then he sat back to observe the heathens engaged in their heathen rituals. One day he would introduce these people to the Light and the Way. At that very moment, another light and another way sauntered in through the front door. A black or Hispanic woman, tall as a fashion model and just as elegant, found an unoccupied seat at the bar. Her body language announced to all: *I am here!* She removed her cream colored jacket and folded it into her lap. She wore a flowing yellow dress and black high-heeled sandals. Even Larry recognized that she was dressed out of season.

Larry stood five-feet ten-inches. Although a bit stocky, his frame did carry clothes well. With short-cropped, dirty blond hair, he was reasonably good-looking, at least as judged by those who set their clocks by Mountain Standard Time. But despite the success that would soon be flowing his way, Larry's fragile ego threw the covers over its head. Instead of picking up his drink and going over to introduce himself, he stayed put. This was New York City where a goddess like her should only be served by the high priests of Wall Street, Broadway, and Yankee Stadium. And they did come: a steady procession of upscale men presented themselves unto her. And like a herd of swine infected with demons she cast them, one by one, into the sea.

He flagged a passing waitress and ordered his second Long Island ice tea. Then he checked his *Rolex*: 11:33 p.m., an hour and a half past his normal bedtime. When he finished his drink, he paid the waitress for the drinks and gave her a generous tip. About to leave, he made the same wretched mistake Lot's wife did: he turned around and looked at the woman one more time. She was still alone. He watched her take a sip of her drink that looked to be club soda. With an elbow resting on the bar, a thumb beneath her chin and an index finger running alongside her cheek, she looked straight at him.

Was that a smile! Did she just smile at me?

Larry's eyes immediately ducked for cover. He quickly turned away. Then another glance over his shoulder: she *still* stared at him. Although never the best judge of nuances in women, her eyes seemed to say, *What are you waiting for*? Larry took a deep breath and prepared to go over and introduce himself. Then a hard truth hit him in his most vulnerable: despite professing to be a man of faith he knew he'd gladly hand over the head of the Baptist to spend one night with her.

Time to petition: *I'm weak, Lord, and a bit tipsy. Please give me the strength.*

Some-One was not listening. Instead of heading for the door and a night of watching Animal Planet reruns on cable, he headed straight for the woman. "Excuse me. Mind if I join you?" He extended his right hand, and said, "My name is—"

She cut him off with another smile. "Not at all, sit, please."

The ease with which they exchanged pick-up chatter surprised and relaxed him. Odd though, she never bothered to give her name. When asked, she acted as if she did not hear. This bothered Larry, a man with far more family values woven into his fabric than he cared to admit. But he was also human, a man who generously accepted his limitations. His confidence began to grow. Soon women like her would throw themselves him. He would resist of course — most of the time, anyway. If he'd known chatting up women in bars would be so easy, he'd have done it a lot sooner and a lot more often.

Her smile radiated, but its glow shown inward on a secret page only she could read. Although she didn't say much, her body language spoke loud and clear: when she paused to seductively sip her drink and moisten her full, red lips; when she laughed at his wit; when she appeared sufficiently awed by his charm; and when she seemed mesmerized by Larry's powerful intellect. Never before had he connected so effortlessly with a woman. He glanced at his *Rolex*: it read 12:26 a.m. Three more Long Island ice teas conspired with a soaring ego to emboldened Larry to go for it.

Before he could invite her back to his hotel room, she said, "Let's go back to my place." Then she gracefully slid off her stool. "We'll take my car. Looks like you've had one too many." She slipped on her cream colored jacket. Larry's eyes followed her swaying hips as she sauntered towards the front door. He dropped money on the bar and followed. But in his haste, he had made a serious omission: a visit to the lavatory.

Riding in her car, one-too-many Long Island ice teas drip, drip, dripped into his bladder.

Whenever her little red Geo-Metro hit a bump in the road, he groaned. He glanced out the window just as they passed the exit sign for 168th Street. The Queens/Nassau border that separated the outer borough from the rest of Long Island was only a few miles away. Since the woman had said she lived in Babylon, this meant they had a long way to putt-putt before he got to a toilet. He begged the Lord to help him hold it in.

Larry looked at his companion and wondered what had come over her. The beautiful and supremely confident young woman he'd met in the bar drove with the fanatical intensity of an eighty-six-year-old expecting something terrible to pop up in front of her any second. Her shoulders were hunched, and she leaned so far forward that her chin nearly touched the steering wheel. She squinted as if she couldn't see well. Gosh darn-it! There was nothing to see, the road was empty!

Another bump, another groan; "Please stop that!" she said sharply. "Please stop moaning while I drive. It's distracting."

Larry gritted his teeth. *You call this driving!*

In bars on the Upper Eastside anonymity hung as amorphous as idle chatter. But here in *her* car on their way back to *her* place, Larry believed he had the right to know *her* name. "How come back in the club you wouldn't tell me your name?"

She snickered. "You didn't ask. You were too busy talking about yourself. Remember?"

About himself? He'd told her nothing about himself. Not that he was an ordained minister and not that he would soon be a huge televangelist superstar. Nothing! "Well, I'm asking now. What's your name?"

"I'll tell you."

"When?"

She shot him a predatory smile. "When I'm ready;" then she squinted and turned her attention back to the empty road.

"By the way, my name is Larry Schmetterling in case you're interested," he snarked.

Another bump, but instead of a groan, Larry shot her an angry look. *She did that on purpose!* The Geo crawled along the parkway. These tiny bug-mobiles magnified every bump by a factor of ten. The limit posted in New York was fifty-five. Larry guessed they were rattling along at least ten m.p.h. below the limit. Prayers to the Almighty aside, Larry knew that deliverance for a bladder that was slowly calcifying into a rock lay on the horizontal and not the vertical plain.

"Uh…?" *Think you can coax a little more speed out of this lawn mower?* "Think you can drive a bit faster? It's one o'clock in the morning. No one's on the road."

"My, my, in *such* a hurry." Her teasing smile said: *Patience. We'll get there. And when we do, I'm all yours.*

Stupid woman! The first thing Larry was going to do when they got to her place was pee!

The highway lamps rolled light across her face in deepening shades of black, white and gray; they gave her a sinister look. She left her lightweight jacket unbuttoned. Larry caught a glimpse of breast as she hunched over the wheel. Her smooth coffee-colored skin glistened in the semi-darkness. Thoughts of her dark, naked body entwined with his pale, naked body, and then *Bang! Bang!* the Lord's silver hammer did smote Larry on the head.

What if He's testing me?

Like a giant sequoia, Pastor Larry had always thought himself a righteous man firmly rooted in morality and self-control. No wind, no matter how strong, could blow him over — until tonight when alcohol had flooded his moral plain and poisoned his roots. But to be human is to be wicked by nature, so says the Bible. For too long Larry had denied his humanity. No more! Tonight he could revel in it because he had a personal Savior who loved him and would forgive him. After spending the night with her, Pastor Larry would pray for forgiveness in the morning. Maybe he could even convince this mystery woman to join him in prayer. What if he could turn her around and bring her to Jesus? Then making love to her would be a bad means to a good end.

Larry reached down and turned on the radio. This was *her* car and *her* radio; so why had it been preset to a Christian music station? He pushed another button, then another, and then another. All had been preset to Christian music, Christian talk, or FOX News.

Larry frowned. "Are you a Christian?"

She shot him a wry grin; then she turned off the radio. "It's distracting."

Since she had given him nothing of herself, Larry found himself fixated on what he could see: a face of near perfection but for one tiny imperfection; a mole high on her right left cheek just below the corner of her eye. Why hadn't he noticed it before? That mole struck him as vaguely familiar, like he'd seen one in the same location but on a different face. Whose? Who did she remind him of?

Where did all the sunshine go? Unease now loomed inside of Larry like angry clouds threatening to dump buckets of rain ready to squelch his lust. Who was this enigma in a yellow dress, and where was she taking him? Like another televangelist, Jim Bakker, had he fallen into the clutches of another Long Island Lolita? If so, what to do? To jump out of a car traveling at 45 m.p.h. was *not* an option. He closed his eyes. Maybe a short nap would take his mind off guilt, apprehension, and a bloated bladder. Then a horn blasted behind them, so loud it sounded like it was riding in the back seat.

"What the heck!" Larry said, opening his eyes just as a SUV roar passed. The man in the vehicle threw them *the finger.* The woman glared out the windshield at the other driver and mumbled something along the lines of cretin and compared him to a specific part of the lower bowels.

Larry rubbed his eyes. "What just happened?"

"I suppose it *was* my fault," she replied angrily. "I might've drifted into his lane. But there was no call for that!" A pause, and then she added in a chastened tone, "I'm not a good driver. And I don't see very well at night."

Oh, geez! That's encouraging. But at least she had finally given him a small piece of herself. "If you ask me, that guy was driving way too fast."

She smiled and softly said, "Thank you."

And then — *Praise the Lord!* — the woman eased the Geo onto the exit ramp at Little Neck Parkway.

"Why are we getting off here? Thought you live in Babylon?"

"I do. We're going to make a quick stop. I thought you might like to stretch your legs and get some fresh air." There was neither a hint of kindness nor concern in her voice.

The car slowed as they approached a red light at the intersection of the service road and Little Neck Parkway. When it came to a stop, she glanced in both directions; the night was so quiet Larry could hear the hum of the traffic controller's halogen lamps. Then she ran the light. They continued along the deserted service road. They pulled off to the side and stopped. With the engine running, she said, "Let's go for a walk."

Larry hesitated before getting out. "Ok, but first — I'm a little embarrassed, you being a lady and all."

She smiled as if she could read *his* secret pages. "Why don't you just walk over to that fence? I promise I won't peek."

Only steps away from the fence he could hear her steps crunching the gravel and then tread onto the wet grass. Larry stopped and did a quick 180, a little too quickly given his blood alcohol level. He nearly toppled over. Dizzy, it took him a second to focus on the film noir he'd suddenly been thrust into. With the service road and the lights of the Grand Central on the hill behind her, the woman stood in silhouette. A breeze tossed her hair and dress to the side. She stood with her feet spread and arms dangling in front of her in a V. She gripped something in both hands. Then slowly and with great deliberation, she raised her arms to eye level and laid him dead in her sights. A stream of hot urine exploded from his bladder and began to run down his leg. He begged her to take his money but please don't shoot him.

"This isn't about money, fool!"

"What then! Why do you want to hurt me?"

In a playful voice like adult speaking to a child, "I don't want *to hurt you*, Pastor Larry, I want *to kill you*."

She called him *Pastor* Larry? He never told her his calling!

"Are you peeing in your pants, you filthy pig?"

A barely audible: "Yes." Larry felt shamed by the squeaky panic in his voice and his weak bladder. And then he remembered something. He grasped at the one last straw that might save his life. "It's the first day of Lent! You can't kill me on Ash Wednesday! It's a sin!"

"Oh, please. You're not Catholic anymore."

How did she know *that*? How did she know so much about him? Did they meet by chance or was this part of a plan? Whose plan? Who hated Pastor Larry enough to murder him? As the inevitable slowly coiled around him like a death shroud, Pastor Larry felt compelled to pray. He *was* a man of faith, and even if the Lord did not spare his life, this was *not* how a man of faith died! Bad enough the police would find him with pee soaked pants.

A song began to play in Larry's mind — *The Soft Parade*. That was when Larry decided that The Doors were right petitioning the Lord with prayer would not save him.

OK, so You're abandoning me, Lord, but I will never abandon You!

He took a step toward her. She stepped back. The ground upon which he was about to drop to his knees was cold and damp, so he removed his two-thousand dollar topcoat and spread it out in front of him. Even in these last few moments of life to kneel on wet grass would be uncomfortable.

When he looked the death merchant in the eyes he saw she seemed confused, like she'd lost control of the situation. As good a time as any to make a final request:

"Please allow me one last—"

Suddenly, Larry's black hole fills with a burst of light and a sharp *pop!* When his mind's eye clears, Larry is no longer remembering he's reliving! Once again he shares time and space with the crazy woman who shot him! Time slows to a crawl. He sees the bullet corkscrew round and round headed straight for his face. Larry's head, neck and body freeze so he can't even duck or turn away. When the bullet hits, it sends him reeling backwards. Once again a jet of hot flame ignites in his head. Larry feels like a free-floating particle of dust being carried aloft by gentle thermals; ashes to ashes and all that. Suddenly something massive slams into his back, knocking the wind out of him. Larry has collided with terra firma. He struggles to catch his breath. His head is cradled in the soft, wet grass; wet with rain and his own blood? The area centered by his nose and eyes feels pulpy. His chest rises and falls as he desperately sucks in air. He can even hear the grass: the breeze that drifts through it and footsteps that compress it. The steps come closer and closer; then a snap like something, maybe a twig, breaks.

"Damn these cheap Chinese shoes," the shooter growls. "Just bought them!"

Her footsteps continue, but there is a change in cadence. Instead of the steady step, step, step of a person walking, the tempo is asymmetrical, like someone favoring one foot over the other. Larry senses her presence hovering over him. He can hear her garments stretch and slide against bare skin as she bends down and presses her fingers to his neck to feel for a pulse. He smells the scent of her perfume

Her tone mocks him: "Not dead yet? Oh well. I suppose it's my Christian duty to end your suffering."

Larry moans and grits his teeth; he expects more pain and a final shot that will blow out his candles — again! But instead there is a pause.

"Bullets cost money, and I'm not rich," the lunatic says to herself out loud. "I'll let the Lord finish you when He's ready. Rot in Hell, Larry!"

Larry hears her cackles fade away.

His theater of mind goes dark again. He is back in his black hole. Pastor Larry has been born-again, all right, into a new galaxy of consciousness. To be shot in the face — not once but twice! — and then to fall back into nothingness can only mean one thing: yes, Larry is dead and this black hole is Hell. Death and damnation are his new eternity. Fear and terror leave him feeling like a soft and vulnerable creature held so tightly in predatory jaws that he can barely breathe.

Then, *Wait a minute! But I am. Breathing!*

And his heart, he feels it's thumping pulse as if it's still part of him. How can this be! How can a mind still receive sensations from a body that should be lying in the morgue? One moment a chill sweeps over him, and the next he feels embraced in warmth as if a blanket has been thrown over him.

Since when does Hell have climate control? That's not in Scripture.

What about the voices? It's not so much he can hear them, it's more an awareness of male voices speaking *about* him. Baal, Belial and Dantalion; and Ariel, Gabriel and Michael; he knows who they are. But who are Frank, Howie and Doc?

Angels or demons?

The gravitation that has kept Larry's galaxy of consciousness a coherent whole begins to weaken. Reverend Lawrence Schmetterling knows he is slipping away — slipping away from what to where?

Like that blind girl he counseled long ago, oblivion is just a word, a word with no meaning.

Chapter 4

A Purpose Driven Life

After "dropping" off an annoying passenger at Little Neck Parkway, and also ridding the human race of one more evildoer, Tracy Millen pulled her red Geo into the driveway of her split-level home in Babylon, Long Island. She turned off the radio that had been playing Christian music. She glanced at the digital clock on the dashboard; it read 2:23 in the morning, Eastern Standard Time; that meant it was 12:23 Mountain Standard Time. A certain person in Colorado would be awake and eager for news.

Tracy went upstairs to her bedroom and sat down on the bed. She dialed an ancient pink, rotary princess phone. The phone rang only once.

"Hello?" The other person sounded anxious, but not in a good way.

"It's done," she said. The chilly finality in Tracy's tone caused the other person to moan. Tracy held the receiver under her chin and examined the .32. "No, I didn't dispose of the gun. You worry too much." Tracy had an intimacy with the weapon: how comfortable it felt in her hand, the security, and power she felt when she wielded it; no way would she ever part with such a precious object. Besides, the Lord would protect her from the police, so why worry about holding on to evidence?

"Don't be getting all weepy on me. This was your idea, remember? Huh? … We've cleansed the temple. You should feel good about it. I do … How did he die? If you're asking if he died like a man of faith…" Tracy had different degrees of laughter depending on her mood. At the top of the scale, when she found something truly ironic, she cackled. "No, he wet his damn pants!"

She cackled into the receiver.

"You hate it when I laugh like the Wicked Witch of the West? You've been saying that since we were children. Well, I'm not in the west, you are. Guess that makes you the wicked one!" More cackling.

A shot to the head should've meant a quick death; it had worked that way once before. That the evildoer's immortal soul might still be clinging hopelessly to its earthly remains hardly mattered: ashes unto ashes; dust unto dust; and the damned unto damnation. Not that the other person needed to know that when she left the scene Pastor Larry was still alive.

"*Don't. Lecture. Me!* You know how mercurial I am." Tracy reached over and put the .32 in the drawer of her night table. Then she lowered the receiver onto her lap, closed her eyes, and slowed her breathing to let the bile settle. Putting the receiver to her mouth again, "Just before I shot him, he did the strangest thing. He took off his topcoat and laid it out on the grass in front of him. Like a prayer mat." She snickered, "Not that he had the chance. I shot him before he — what? Why? Because! That's why! Don't waste your pity on a man like him. Not everyone is entitled to a last prayer. He has the rest of eternity to pray for forgiveness, not that he'll be getting any. Huh? … I'm tired, and you're beginning to annoy me."

Tracy let out another sigh. Then she took off her shoe to examine the broken heel.

Last time I'll wear stilettos. Imports! They better give me my money back!

As the person in Colorado continued to weep and wail and moan about poor Pastor Larry, the mercury on Tracy's mood scale made a steady climb towards the red zone. Being the Lord's Holy Avenger was burden enough, but why did He afflict her with weak-willed people? "It's late. If you don't mind, I'd like to get some sleep. I have to be at work in a few hours. Bye."

After hanging up, Tracy slipped into a black nightgown and headed downstairs: to the basement; to her special room; to do penance; and, hopefully, to be forgiven.

When she awoke again, Tracy had no idea how long she had laid face-down in an excruciating position, a horizontal crucifixion of sorts. When she prostrated herself before the Lord, she lost all sense of time. Tracy Millen had to seek His forgiveness because she was the Lord's Avenger; as such her duty had to be performed coldly and without passion. The Lord demanded that she always colored her book in black, white, and gray. He would not permit her to paint in rainbows. Thus she had to atone, not shooting the evildoer, but rather for taking such pleasure in tormenting the miserable creature before she exterminated him.

The cold, bare, concrete floor left her with no feeling in her forehead, her shoulders, breasts, knees, and feet ached. Adding to her woes, she had to pee. She cackled remembering that Pastor Larry's last living act was to wet his pants.

The 15'x18' room in Tracy's basement was where she performed her acts of contrition. Befitting such a sacred space, black velvet curtains covered small casement windows near the ceiling, two on either side of the room. The overhead fluorescent lamps were seldom lit. Most of the room's illumination came from a metal matrix of red-cupped candles. The candelabra had been special ordered and modeled after those she'd seen in Catholic churches. Smokey fingers of burning incense clawed upwards leaving black stains on the dropdown ceiling. To the matrix's immediate left, and up against the far wall, was a makeshift altar where statutes of suffering saints and the Blessed Mother stood; all had been purchased from a store that sold *Santeria* icons. At the altar's epicenter was a picture of a sad Jesus, His eyes frozen in a pitying stare. With grey walls and a grey floor the room had all the good cheer of a tomb. Light and freshness from outside were not permitted inside.

Every joint in Tracy's cranky body felt locked in place. Slowly, she rolled onto her back, looked at the ceiling to focus her eyes, and then sat up. With her long legs stretched in front of her she massaged some feeling back into her knees and flexed her toes. Tracy stretched her arms high above her head. Then she rotated her neck and heard it crack. She rubbed her forehead; it felt like frozen tissue. As she began to stand she again was reminded of her shoes. Tracy hugged herself tight to smother a building rage. Rage in Tracy was easily lit and could quickly grow into a firestorm that would consume everyone and everything around her — including herself.

She hit the off button on the CD player that lay on the floor. It radiated heat. It must have been running for many hours. A spiritual eclectic, Tracy had no problem borrowing from other faiths. Buddhist chants had been looping over and over, non-stop. The deep guttural, almost inhuman voices of the monks accurately reflected God's anger with her.

As she ascended the stairs, Tracy felt an octogenarian rather than a woman who had been alive for only twenty-nine years. In the kitchen, the clock on the wall read 6:32 a.m. She turned on the radio, pre-set to the Lord's Broadcasting Network. LBN confirmed what she already suspected: it was Thursday morning. Tracy had been laying face-down like a corpse for over twenty-four hours. That meant that she'd missed an entire day's work as floor manager at the local Wallman's Shop-A-Lot. She had not been able to call in sick because she had slept through all of Wednesday. If they fired her, so be it. She hated the job anyway. A prayer burned in her heart:

One day, O Lord, if You are truly pleased with me, Your humble daughter, then deliver me unto Saks or Target.

The Bible said, "Ask and you shall receive." Was a job in a better store for a few more dollars more an hour too much to ask? Tracy was unsure. *Her* God was an angry, harsh, and demanding father. Although she knew He loved her, no matter how hard she tried, He always found fault with her, sometimes over the most trivial things. He was nothing like Tracy's biological dad. A kind and gentle man, he always told his young daughter how good she was, how happy she made him, and how beautiful she was. He referred to her as his pretty, little butterfly. That was long ago. Memories of childhood in Tracy Millen had been relegated so far back in time that only their fossilized bones remained. Back then, she might have been like a butterfly: lithe, delicate and innocent. No more! Life had yanked Tracy's wings out by the roots. Ugly and painful stumps now scarred her psyche. Unlike a butterfly that agonized in silence when torn apart, Tracy *could* scream her fury. And she could act-out like she did on the Reverend Lawrence Schmetterling. Tracy had targeted the shot so that the bullet would penetrate the pastor's skull right between the eyes. She wanted him to get a good look at what was coming: the cessation of life followed by eternal damnation.

Dead in her sights, the evildoer had trembled with the consistency of standing *Jell-O*. She smirked when she heard him wetting himself. She noticed a growing pool of urine spreading on the ground. The kind thing to do was to wait until he finished peeing before killing him, but Tracy felt no kindness towards the man. Then she noticed his shoes. They must have cost hundreds of dollars while she, the chosen one, wore cheap Chinese imports. As the creeping puddle of urine grew larger and showed no sign of letting up, Tracy felt every bit the spider to the evildoers' fly. She watched as her venom slowly worked its way through his system, paralyzing him with fear. In no hurry to rip *his* wings off, she preferred instead to pull them out one ligament at a time. What need did he have for wings anyway? The man was no angel.

Tracy believed that her mission was Justice not Mercy. The Lord would dispense His benevolence upon whom He wished. When the time had come to put an end to him, her finger began to apply deadly pressure to the trigger. And then, quite unexpectedly, this particular slug decided to crawl out of the primal muck of its own fear. Pastor Larry began to walk towards her holding his hands out in supplication. What trickery was this? Tracy stepped backwards; she felt her resolve weaken. She could not let this happen. For the good of many, this bad man had to die. Then he stopped, only yards away, and took off his expensive topcoat and spread it in front of him on the damp grass. He clasped his hands together. In a voice that gripped his doom more firmly as she did the gun, he was about to ask her for one last prayer. How dare him! Abomination! He was worried about getting his knees wet! Before he could finish his sentence she squeezed off a shot, and thus did she blow the creepy-crawler off his high branch.

The Pastor's body lay with his arms were splayed out at his sides as if in a bizarre crucifixion; his head pointed down the slope towards the barrier fence. Tracy took in a deep breath of cool, moist air, held it, and then exhaled. She listened: nothing stirred from the homes on the other side of the fence; and no sirens off in the far distance. Not even a car passed on the parkway behind her.

Dead silence, she thought, and snickered at the irony.

From between the V of the soles of Pastor Larry's *luxurious* shoes she could see his chin, his nostrils, and a thin plume of vapor that rose from the hole between his eyes. His breathing, though shallow, had not yet ceased. As she stepped towards him her heel caught in a rut. She heard a s*nap!*

"I just bought these!" *This is your fault, Larry! Oh, how I hate you!*

Tracy hovered, ready to put a final round into the evildoer's pulpy face. Then she remembered a promise she had made. "It would be *so* unkind of me. And I did promise to tell you when I'm ready. Well, I'm ready. My name is Tracy Millen, pleased to meecha!" And then the dung heap lying at her feet moaned. Tracy let up on the trigger. Bullets cost money.

Tracy couldn't help herself, she cackled with delight as she turned around and headed back to the little red Geo.

When she arrived for work at Wallmans on Thursday morning, "I'm so sorry, Mrs. Schubel," she told her supervisor, "but there was a terrible emergency yesterday. I didn't have a chance to call in."

A model employee who rarely missed a day and worked overtime whenever asked, Mrs. Schubel easily forgave Tracy.

Tracy's happy mood swung to the other pole less than an hour later in Women's Shoes. Evenly, "What do you mean, I can't have my money back!" Tracy snarled at the sales associate behind the courtesy desk.

Meekly, "I'm sorry, ma'am, but the heel's broken. And they look like they've been worn in the rain," the girl said.

"Damp grass!" Calmer, "And I've worn them only once. A new heel should not break so easily."

The associate looked to be around twenty and new to the job. Tracy decided she shouldn't take an attitude with this girl. To get so worked up over a twenty dollar pair of shoes was a sin. The girl relented, but she still appeared to be stressed over the situation. "I want to do the right thing, Miss Millen. Please don't say anything to my supervisor."

"I know her. Mrs. Schubel. She's nice. No need to worry. I'm sorry if I spoke harshly to you. Things have been rather stressful to say the least — *I shot someone the other night* — so please forgive me."

The girl smiled. "No problem, Miss Millen. I'll just ask you to fill out this form."

Tracy put the shoes back into the box. "Let's forget the whole thing. I'll simply have the heel fixed. Have a nice day, Miss."

With fifteen minutes left on her lunch hour, Tracy headed to Home Furnishings to price a new carpet, one with soft, deep piles. Surely to suffer for the Lord was a great privilege, but to wake up on the floor in her special room with aching knees and a forehead that felt like a pancake was to suffer the trivial. And Tracy had never been one to endure trivialities.

CHAPTER 5

Rubber Sole

Desk Sergeant Tony Benvenuto made a face like toxic waste just oozed into the One-O-Five. It was Thursday, 3:07 p.m.

"Captain wants to see youse two," said Benvenuto to the Double Gs, detectives Frank Giavone and Howie Goldberg.

Without acknowledging Benny the Low's existence — their term of *non-endearment* for one of the toadiest of Captain Graham's toadies — they headed for Fearless Leader's office. Frank rapped on the glass door. Not bothering to wait for an *Open sez me*, he and Howie lumbered in. Graham's office was neat, clean, and squared away. It reflected the Captain's belief that he should personally spare the City of New York all unnecessary costs. In Frank's opinion, though, Graham was an uptight jerk who was cheaper than he and Howie put together.

The Double Gs pulled up chairs and made themselves comfortable. "You wanna see us?" Frank asked, sounding like a guy with an impatient mind's eye on the clock. In fifty-three more minutes he expected to be back in the Snot Rocket and he and Howie would be on their way to a pre-dinner feast; a little something to hold them over until they got home. In between, they were supposed to interview Reverend

Schmetterling's parents.

Frank and Howie knew that the Captain despised the ground they walked on and the air they breathed. Once, an old biddy with nothing better to do than stare out her window all day, had spotted the Double Gs taking a shady rest in their cruiser parked under a tree. She called the precinct to complain, and ever since then Captain Graham considered them blotches on his permanent record. But they were both seventeen-year veterans and in tight with the union. That made their stains indelible.

Seated behind a desk more suited to a file clerk than a high ranking police official, Graham said, "Nice of you two Buddhas to show up. Hope I didn't disturb your meditations."

Howie shot Frank a *What's He Talking About?* look.

Frank leaned over to explain: "Ever see them statues of that fat Chink sitting under a tree in his underpants smiling all the time?"

"Oh, that guy."

Frank's knowledge of Zen and its Eight Paths to Enlightenment came to him during a particularly bad stretch on a long, rocky road: the early days of his marriage. While still a rookie in Jackson Heights, he'd had a brief affair with a woman named Mona. The forty-two-year-old ex-flower child ran a sushi bar. He often stopped by for lunch although the only taste Frank ever developed for raw fish was its low cost; i.e. no cost. Back in those days Frank had a young wife who nagged at him for being lazy and lacking ambition. But Mona accepted him for what he was: a master practitioner of the art of just getting by. As for the Zen-thing, that was the pry bar with which Mona tried to open his closed mind. Frank finally told her the truth: "The only way you'll catch me on one 'a them eight paths is if every one of 'em ends in an eight course meal."

No more free lunches for Frank. No more Mona either.

Memories of Mona reminded him just how far off the path he *had* strayed. His life was now like a walk in the woods on a bleak, November day: cold and lonely.

Suddenly, the growling voice of Captain Graham leaped out at Frank like a dog hiding in the bushes. "Where have you two been all day? Have you questioned the family? Have you contacted Colorado?"

Frank said, "We were just about to hit the phones. And we're meeting the vic's parents tonight at 7:30."

"Why didn't you do that yesterday?" the boss demanded.

A quick thinking Howie said, "Cause they were visiting the hospital."

Graham flicked these two lazy pests away. "Get outta here."

Back at desks that faced each other, the top half of Howie's body leaned out into the aisle. "Here comes my boy. And by the look of 'im, I'd say he's got good news."

A smiling Police Officer Daniel George, Two Names, carried a computer printout in his hand. Howie pulled up a chair for his protégé.

Two Names sat down. "I don't think Sergeant Benvenuto likes you guys. When I came in this morning and asked where you were, he said, 'On a stakeout.' When I asked when you'd be back, he said, 'Whenever they wake up.' "

"Ignore 'im," said Howie. "You stick with us kid, and you'll learn something."

Two Names grinned. A short, barrel-chested, kid built like a rock and just as hard, he looked more like a New York cop than the two packages of 70% chuck chopped seated with him — until he put on that shy smile of his. With curly black hair and dark eyes, Officer George could be charming or, like Howie his mentor, kick the crap out of a skel. But today, the twenty-four year-old was all smiles.

"Whadda ya got for us, Two? And make it quick cause we're outta here in 40 minutes," said a yawning Detective Giavone.

"I ran the vic's credit cards beginning 1, February, and, as I expected, he did rent a car. From Hertz. They said the car hasn't been returned yet."

"No surprise there," mumbled Frank.

"And then I thought to myself: the doctors said the guy's blood alcohol level was high: point zero-eight. So I'm thinking maybe he played the good citizen and didn't drink and drive. Maybe he left his car somewhere and drove with the shooter? It was a long shot, but I looked at all the records for abandoned cars beginning one, February. I matched them with the same parameters. A late model green Taurus was rented by the vic and left in a garage on East 76th Street."

Howie reached over and grabbed the kid's shoulder. "You did real good, Two. Now we got a starting point, the garage, and an ending point, the Grand Central. All we gotta do is figure out what happened in between."

"I know the area," said Two Names. "A lotta bars and clubs around there. Plenty upscale, too."

Howie said, "You canvass the area with the vic's picture and see if anyone remembers seeing him — maybe with a woman." The lab report on that piece of rubber that Frank had found came back this morning. It was the heel tip of a woman's shoe, a stiletto.

"Not an expensive shoe, either," the crime tech had told Frank and Howie. "The type you can buy at any Wallmans."

Detective Ferro said she'd been in flats that day, so that tiny piece of rubber sole was not hers. Frank theorized to Howie and Two Names: "Maybe it went down like this: our preacher drives to the Upper Eastside looking for some action. He meets a woman. Maybe he knows her, maybe he don't. He has a little too much to drink, and being a man of the cloth, figures drinking 'n driving is a sin. So they leave in her car. Since he's registered at a hotel in Midtown, they musta been headed for her place. Then they pull off at the Little Neck Parkway exit, and she whacks 'im."

Howie and Two Names nodded. Frank's theory fit the known facts. Then Howie added, "Maybe our preacher ain't the only one prowling the bar scene. Maybe Little Miss Shooter is too. Maybe we got a nut job who likes picking up guys and shooting 'em. Hey! Maybe we got us a serial killer, a Daughter of Sam."

That put some rev in Frank's engine. "We solve this case and we're on the six o'clock news." Then to P.O. George, "Run the MO through the computer. See if we got any other shootings or killings matching this one. And run a financial check on Reverend *Likes-The-Chicks-A-Lot.* He still coulda been whacked by someone he knows."

Howie chuckled. "Yeah, like, Tony Soprano's wife really got it in for them preachers."

Frank said to Two Names, "Do his credit cards, bank accounts, stocks, bonds —"

"He knows the drill, Frank," said Howie. Then he pulled out a thermos and refilled his mug with coffee. "You guys want some?"

"No thanks," said Two Names. "I only drink coffee when I'm at the computer. Keeps me focused."

"Then get yourself a whole damn pot," said Frank. "We're gonna question the parents tonight. I want something by six."

***

On Ash Wednesday, someone — possibly a woman — put a bullet in the face of Lawrence Schmetterling. Tonight, Thursday, Frank and Howie were in the home of the reverend's parents in Queens Village. A familiar cooking smell drifted into the living room. Although Frank's Catholicism had lapsed a long time ago, the aroma of tuna casserole triggered childhood memories in him: fish for Lent.

He and Howie made themselves comfortable on the sofa. Across from them on a worn but comfortable upholstered chair from the 1950s sat Mr. Mike Schmetterling. His wife, Toby, sat on the chair's armrest and laid an arm across its backrest. Frank noted that even in this time of extreme anguish there was little physical contact between the Schmetterlings. Mrs. Schmetterling was a double-breasted mountain of a woman who towered over her scrawny, 5'4" husband. Schmetterling the elder was bald except for the curly red ring of hair that circled his head. An unkind thought snuck into Frank's head that almost worked a grin onto his face:

Bozo the Clown and the Bride of Frankenstein.

The aroma of tuna casserole fired those neurons in Frank's brain that were in a perpetual state of famine. *Feed us!* they demanded. He sniffed the air. "Smells good, Mrs. Schmetterling. I remember my mother used to make tuna casseroles for Lent."

The mother did her best to smile and remain cordial despite the awful circumstance. "Oh, it's just something I put together before we go to the hospital to see Larry. There's plenty left. Would you and Detective Goldberg like a plate?"

Before either Frank or Howie could reply, *Yes, yes, hell yes!* Mr. Schmetterling spoke: "They're busy men, Toby. They came here to do a job not eat." The man's face was locked into a perpetual scowl that said he hated the world and everyone in it.

"How's your son doing, Mrs. Schmetterling?" Frank asked. The mother he liked.

"He's been moved to a private room. I've been playing show tunes for him. He loves them. Especially *Cats.* The song *Memories* is his favorite."

"Enough with the memories, Toby!" Mr. Schmetterling turned to the detectives. "My son's no fag. He likes lot'sa different kinds 'a music."

Ignoring her husband, "I talk to him," Toby continued, "and I know he hears me."

"I grew up in Queens Village, too," Howie began. "My parents lived over on 217th."

"Yeah, we got a few Jews on this block, too," the father remarked absently, sounding like fewer the better. "And more and more Blacks, Spics, Chinks and them Sand Niggers are moving in all the time."

Even Frank, not known to celebrate diversity, was taken aback. He wondered how far the apple now laying in Queens General had fallen from this dumb-ass tree.

The father added, "We're German. Schmetterling means butterfly in German."

Frank had nothing against homosexuals. Live and let live had always been his motto. While he questioned the parents, Howie's job was to make mental notes about the cocoon from which Reverend Butterfly emerged. The Double Gs believed that they learned a lot about people by examining their sources. On the outside, the house itself had pale green vinyl siding and white trim. It was a typical two-story, Queens Village walk-through, topped off by a roof with dark green shingles. These single-family homes, jammed together had tiny front yards and only slightly larger backyards. *Ugly!* was Frank's first impression when he and Howie had first pulled up in front of the house.

A chain-link fence set the Land of Schmetterling apart from its neighbors. A narrow driveway on the right-hand side of the house led to a one-car garage. The home's innards were dull and drab and at the moment smelled of tuna. Heavy drapes on the windows kept certain things like light, noise, Jews, Blacks, Spics, Chinks and Sand Niggers on the outside from getting inside. The furniture, though old and most likely bought when the Schmetterlings were first married, was tidy and well kept. As for all the Catholic icons strategically scattered throughout the downstairs, Frank wondered: *Bet they got a whole cathedral in the basement.*

"Who do you think shot my Larry, Detective Giavone?" Mrs. Schmetterling asked, near tears.

Before he could respond, the angry voice of Mr. Schmetterling boomed: "Probably some illegal alien out to rip somebody off! You wait, Trump's gonna kick 'em all out."

"We're fairly sure, sir, that robbery was not the motive," Howie calmly replied. "It's even possible that he was shot by somebody he knows."

"Who the hell does he know 'round here anymore!" the father snapped. "My son hasn't been in New York for ten years."

"What about Colorado?" Frank asked Mrs. Schmetterling. "Who does your son know back in Colorado?"

The Schmetterlings were at a loss. Obviously they didn't know much about their son's life out West. Then Mrs. Schmetterling remembered something. She shot her husband a quick glance as if for confirmation. He nodded.

"The woman who called this morning, Karen Stone," she said once again looking to the dumb-ass tree she was hitched to. "She told me she worked with Larry; she called to ask why Larry hasn't gotten back yet."

"What did you tell her?" asked Frank.

"I told her everything. I did the right thing, right?"

"Yes ma'am, you did. How'd she take it?"

"Real bad. I think my son and this woman are more than just friends."

The father shot Frank and Howie a *Told Ya My Son's No Fag* look.

"I have her phone number," Toby continued. "Would you like it?"

"We already know how to find Karen Stone," Howie said.

"Told ya these guys were good," Mr. Schmetterling said to his wife. "They're gonna get the bum who did this." He shot the Double Gs a big smiley-face.

A second first impression began to formulate in Frank's mind: *Maybe this guy ain't so bad after all.*

"What can you tell us about your son's work?" asked Howie.

Again the parents looked at one another for an answer. Finally, the father said, "All we know was that our son manages a bookstore in Colorado."

"A Catholic bookstore," the mother added, bowing her head, closing her eyes, and crossing herself.

Frank glanced up from his note taking just long enough to shoot Howie a *They Don't Know Squat* look.

Frank asked, "What personal details can you give us about your son? If we can get a sense of who he is that'll help us find out who shot 'im."

"He's no fag," Mr. Schmetterling grumbled. "He likes all kind'sa music."

"We know that, sir," said Howie. "Thanks."

Frank could see the father had annoyed Howie, too. The only hate in his partner's heart was for anyone who threatened his food supply.

Mrs. Schmetterling gave the Double Gs a proud mommy's smile. "My son wanted to be a priest since he was six-years-old. He had a full scholarship to Notre Dame."

Howie: "What happened?"

The smile dropped off her face, hit the floor, and rolled under a chair. Mr. Schmetterling answered for his wife: "He left! He up and quit in less than a year! Can you believe that?"

Given what the ex-Catholic turned Protestant preacher might've been up to the night he was shot Frank found it hard to believe the guy had ever considered the priesthood. He wouldn't be surprised if it turned out the guy *was* a fag.

"When was the last time you saw your son?" Howie asked.

Toby answered: "Sunday night. He came for dinner Sunday night."

"Yeah," the father grumbled, "and he couldn't wait to get outta here, either."

"Did he tell you what he was doing in New York?" Howie asked.

"Something about mixing business with pleasure," said the father.

Frank snapped his notepad shut. "That'll be it for now, Mr., Mrs. Schmetterling." He handed his card to the mother. "If ya can think 'a something else, please let us know."

"Of course. And please call me, Toby."

"And call me Mike," the father said, standing. He smiled and vigorously shook both detectives' hands.

The way Frank figured it, the parents were so grieved that they looked to him and Howie as saviors. It felt good to be worshipped for a change.

"We got a coupla angles we're gonna work on over the weekend," Frank told them, "and on Monday we're gonna talk with your other son, Matthew."

Those angles were a Knicks' game with his two sons on Saturday night and a big Italian dinner at Mom's on Sunday. As for Howie, his quality time with the family probably meant watching TV with his wife while stuffing himself with high carbs.

Back in the Snot Rocket, Frank said to Howie, "Looks like we got us a vic with a secret life nobody knows nothing about."

"Sure would like to know what business Reverend Butterfly was mixing with what pleasure."

Chapter 6

Cats!

Matthew Schmetterling, the victim's brother, met Frank and Howie at the door of a two-story Tudor in Whitestone, Queens. The guy looked like he had a whole field of wheat growing on top of his head: stalks a barber had mowed into a flat-top. The only times Frank had ever seen a haircut like that was in old films from the fifties or when a Jehovah's Witness knocked on the door. The way he figured it, the guy was either a religious whack-job or an ex-marine.

The physical similarities between the Schmetterling in the hospital and the one standing here were striking except this one came in a larger package: six-foot two-inches, around two-hundred-fifty pounds. The Reverend might be stocky, but his brother was a wall. Frank envied the wide flatness of the man, no middle-aged bulge on this guy. The Double G's followed Matthew from the front door towards the living room. Frank, a pro football fan, noticed the man's tightness, like anger and self-control ran through the poor guy's head, scrimmaging in his soft tissue with their cleats on.

As they passed the stairway, Matthew stopped and called up to his wife: "*Michelle. They're here.*" Then he told the detectives, "She's putting the boys to bed."

"How many kids you got, Mr. Schmetterling?" Frank figured talking about family might give this guy a timeout.

Schmetterling leaned into the banister, his anxious eyes still looking up the stairs. "Two," he replied absently.

"How old?" asked Howie.

"Huh? What? Oh. Three and five… Michelle!"

A sweet voice that carried melodies of angels and harps called down from above: "In a minute, Matthew."

In the living room, Frank and Howie plopped themselves down on the sofa. Schmetterling sat at the very edge of his seat on a matching chair across from them. When he finished cracking his knuckles, he let his hands hang between his knees.

Frank zeroed in the guy's rolling thumbs. "Where do you work, Mr. Schmetterling?"

"I teach math at the Bronx High School of Science." Schmetterling closed his eyes and began massaging his temples.

Howie asked, "Like your job, Mr. Schmetterling?"

"Yes I do. Unlike most teachers in the public school system, my students are bright and motivated. Makes my job much easier."

Frank heard footsteps descending the stairs. Mrs. Michele Schmetterling entered the living room with a soft smile on her face, thus confirming his angelic image of her. The only things this petite, blue-eyed blonde in her early thirties lacked were wings and a halo. She joined them, and Frank immediately noticed that she positioned herself exactly as the older Mrs. Schmetterling had: on the armrest of her husband's chair, except she entwined her arm with her husband's. She said that she'd taught elementary school for two years before marrying Matthew.

"Sometimes I miss the children," she added wistfully, "but now I have two of my own to take care of… My mother-in-law insisted I take good care of you, detectives. I'd be happy to put on a fresh pot of coffee if you'd like."

"That won't be necessary, Michelle," the chip off that other stubborn block said.

"These men are here to help us, Matt," she said, gently.

"These men are here to do a job, Michelle!"

She shot him a disapproving look as if he was a bad boy in one of her classes. "We're Christian, Matt, and it's the Christian thing to do." She headed for the kitchen.

A defeated Matthew Schmetterling slumped back in the chair, arched his brows, and ran his hands down the sides of his face to recompose. A brief pause, then, "My mother phoned. Thanks for treating my parents so kindly. My Dad can be a bit of a, uh" – searching for the right word before settling on – "jerk. He's really a decent guy. He's just upset that's all."

"We understand," said Frank, and Howie nodded.

Michelle called everyone into the dining room.

Into the Schmetterling's most sacred space rode the Five Hundred: the Double G's as measured in pounds. The detectives took seats around a solid oak table that must've cost grand or more. Clearly this piece of furniture, recently polished and well maintained, was the pride and joy of the Schmetterling's homestead. That made Frank uneasy. He knew that by the time he and his partner were done eating it might look like a brigade of light cavalry had charged across the table's gleaming surface. Despite placemats and doilies, a slaughter of crumbs, a bloodbath of spills, and dirty napkins would litter the table like corpses; the only thing missing would be hoof prints. Frank decided to politely refuse Michelle's offer. But when she entered from the kitchen carrying a tray of goodies, he figured he'd rather be careful than hungry.

"Geez, Frank!" Howie would later remark back in the Snot Rocket. "Them brownies were fucking fantastic! And did ya getta loada them cute little sandwiches, all cut into little squares. She even cut the crusts off. Shit, if I wasn't married, and she wasn't married, I'd fucking marry 'er."

As Frank always knew the path to Howie's heart led straight down his esophagus.

Although Frank tried to keep his mess confined, spillage was inevitable; so were the crawling crumbs that crept further and further from his placemat. But compared to his partner, Frank was being downright dainty. Howie ate like a caveman devouring a Bronto-burger off a slab of rock. Shock and awe on the woman's face as food bits littered and puddles of spilt coffee soaked the surface of her precious table. When an event occurred, either he or Howie would apologize profusely as Michelle swept in to mop up.

"That's OK, Detective," would be her reply. But with each new incident her gentle nature thinned like the layers of polish she must've rubbed into its flat oak. By the time Frank and Howie finished their serious chomping and moved on to nibbling, she stood grim-faced beside her husband with a *Handi-Wipe*. Frank wondered if she slept with the damn thing.

"Tell us about Larry," Frank said. "Your parents said he wanted to be a priest."

"Yes, he had a full scholarship to Notre Dame." Matthew's tone was boastful, not jealous. No sibling rivalry there.

"When was the last time you saw your brother?" Howie asked.

Deflated, he replied, "Haven't seen him in years, but we talk on the phone. A lot."

"And we get a card every Christmas," his wife added, her weak smile apologetic.

"Your parents said they had supper with him..." Frank paused to flip through his notes. "Sunday night, February 3rd."

"A week ago, Sunday, that's right."

"He was supposed to visit us that Thursday for dinner," Michelle added, "but he called to cancel. Something to do with business had come up."

"Was he gonna meet someone?" asked Frank.

"He didn't say." Michelle shot her husband a puzzled look. "Do you know, Matt?"

He shook his head.

"Your mother mentioned that your brother wanted to be a priest since he was a kid," said Frank. "Why would a little kid wanna do something like that?"

A question that finally pushed the needle on Michelle's *Pissed Off Scale* into the red zone. Sharply, "What on earth does that have to do with Larry's being shot, Detective?"

"Please stop interrupting, Michelle! Let them do their jobs!"

Matthew was about to explain his brother's childhood dreams, when the phone in the kitchen rang. With her thin veneer of civility finally stripped away and her prickly nature exposed, a tight-mouthed Michelle left to answer it. She took the *Handi-Wipe* with her. Out of the corner of his eye Frank saw her throw it into the sink.

"It all began with a nun, Sister Victoria," said Matthew. "She was probably the one who first filled his head with that nonsense, reinforced by the hopes and dreams of my parents of course." Schmetterling looked pained when he admitted, "Larry was a strange kid."

Michelle called from the kitchen: "*Matthew. It's your mother.* She's at the hospital. She wants to know when we'll be there."

"When I'm finished with the detectives!"

Frank nodded sympathetically. His ex-wife was well-practiced in annoying the shit out of him. "Tell us about when your brother was a kid, and why he left the seminary."

***

What am I doing here again? Is this some kind of bizarre resurrection: die, wake up, die, wake up; over and over and over? And where's that music coming from? Is that… Cats! *?*

The crypt where Larry's consciousness now lies in state, why is he suddenly aware of a song from a soundtrack long forgotten?

Memories… all alone in the moonlight…

It's as if an unknown force has hit a metaphysical play button allowing Larry's soul to spiral in a double helix with its beautiful melody and lyrics. Not only is he enchanted by the music, but he is grateful for this small blessing.

… how happy we were then, with the memories…

In life Larry had a special affinity for show tunes, songs that propelled the story and took him to wonderful places. He remembers that his mother shared the same passion, and her favorite was the soundtrack of *Cats!*. But woe to him who likes the same music as his mother; add to that that Larry wanted to be a priest, didn't do sports, and didn't date girls. Thus, he had to constantly defend his manhood to the ignorant and misinformed; his father being the Offender-in-Chief. After years of suffering the man's suspicious stares and innuendoes, Larry exploded the very day he left for seminary.

"I'm not gay, Dad, if that's what you think!"

"Oh no, son, I never thought that," was his father's text. But the man's subtext was readable on his face: *I want to believe you, Larry, I really do, but you'll never get a girlfriend if you go to the seminary.*

His father's doubts about him do not matter anymore. *Memories* from *Cats!* and memories from life are all Larry has left. His mind's eye is looking down a long corridor of time with doors on either side. Each door opens into a different room and each room holds a choice made or not made, a path taken or not taken. At the very end of the corridor, where Larry's formative years are stored, he finds what he's looking for: a door marked, "Sister Victoria."

He opens it and steps inside.

***

When Larry was six and studying catechism for his first holy communion, he overheard his young teacher, Sister Victoria, telling his mother, "You have such a bright little boy, Mrs. Schmetterling. Father James and I believe he has the calling."

From then on, the sister made it *her* holy obligation to guide little Larry along a righteous path towards *his* holy obligation. As she explained it little Larry, "A very long time ago, when the country was still young, a lot of people left their homes in places like New York and headed west. They rode in wagon trains. How do you think they found their way across this big country of ours?"

"Roads? Like when my daddy drives us in his car?"

"Very good, Larry. They followed the same roads that all the wagon trains that went before them did." She hugged him. Then she laid a hand on each shoulder and looked deep into his eyes. "Do you know how you can make God happy, Larry?"

"How, Sister?"

"By following trails left behind by others who also wanted to please Him." According to Sister Victoria this was all he needed to do to put a big smiley face on the Lord God Almighty.

Little Larry welcomed Sister's special devotion to him. She was pretty, and she had an ode to joy in her voice that lifted his spirit. The other nuns at his school were old and always dressed in black. But Sister Victoria wore a sky blue habit that matched her sparkling eyes. She carried with her a fragrance of roses and talc.

Larry told his big brother that he loved her and wanted to marry her when he was all grown up.

Matty arched his brows. "She's a piece 'a work, but that can't happen. Nuns can't get married. Sorry, Lars."

When the Apostle-To-Be stood before Sister Victoria, ready to be tested, she sat in a chair. Instead of a habit, she wore a short blue skirt, white blouse and black pumps. With one pale-hosed leg crossed over the other, she held a catechism in her lap. "Who made you, Larry?"

"God made me."

"And why did God make you?"

"To know Him, love Him and serve Him. And to be happy in Heaven with Him in the next life!" Little Larry announced, clapping and hopping up and down.

"Very good, Larry!" She pulled him to her and gave him another hug.

When little Larry asked her how He made him, the Sister shifted uncomfortably in her seat and coughed into her hand. "Ask your parents." Putting a shine back on her face, "Let's continue."

When Larry got home, he asked his big brother the same question. Eleven-year-old Matthew was happy to provide Larry with all the gory details and misconceptions.

Larry grimaced. "Sounds icky, Matty."

Matty grinned. "Yeah, but it's fun, too."

"How do you know!"

"Because I'm going on twelve, almost a teenager, ya little shit!"

Six more years of Catholic education left Larry still following in the righteous ruts left by the saints. As for Sister Victoria, she turned out to be a major disappointment. She and Father James rejected their callings, ran off, and got married.

"She wasn't supposed to do that, Matty," a stricken pre-teen Larry groaned to his big brother. "She took a vow!"

"Vows can be broken, Lars." Then he smirked. "Guess she got called in another direction. A body like that should *not* be wasted on a nun anyway."

His immature mind had practically beatified the woman. What kind of saint would debase her own purity like that? As for sex, by this time Larry understood at least its mechanics if not its depth of feelings. Imagining Sister Slut moaning, her legs wrapped around Father Hump, as brother Matty often referred to the happy couple, was almost as disgusting as the time he'd inadvertently walked in on his parents. Seeing those two mismatched bodies going at it had been enough of a blinding abomination to cause Larry to run into the bathroom and vomit.

From first grade all the through high school, for 12 long years, the Holy Mother Church poured Her teachings into Larry. His mind had turned into a collecting basin, acquiring and holding commands that came to him in uninterrupted flows. By the time he graduated high school, however, he began to reconsider. Maybe the Church's dogma covered his mind like a thick layer of silt blocking the light from penetrating into his depths. Finally, in college a steady stream of wonderful new ideas began to wash all the muck away. For the first time, Larry had an inkling that maybe like Sister Victoria his calling might lie in another direction.

***

"My brother told me a whole new world of ideas opened up to him in college," Matthew told Frank and Howie. "That's my best guess as to why he left the seminary."

Frank's pen hovered above the page where he'd just scribbled: "cathlic school then collage…" The rest was blank. Frank's mind was stuck in its own mud hole: how best to summarize all of this?

"My parents never understood," Matthew continued, "but I think that leaving seminary was a wise decision. And I told him so." He shrugged his broad shoulders. "I suppose he simply outgrew his faith. Happens sometimes." Matthew spoke like a man who knew about such things.

Frank finally managed to extract his mind from the muck; he wrote: "Vic figured girls are better than all that praying crap."

"When did your brother leave the seminary?" Howie asked.

"My brother left Notre Dame about ten years ago. Then he lived in California for a short time. He moved to Colorado Springs two years after leaving seminary."

"What did he do in California?"

"Uh?... I really don't know."

"What does he do in Colorado?" asked Howie.

"He owns a Catholic bookstore," said Michele. She was standing in the kitchen doorway leaning up against the jamb, her arms folded across her chest.

"No he doesn't," Frank began. "We looked at your brother-in-law's tax records. He's the pastor of a fundamentalist church, His Holy Tabernacle, in Monument, Colorado."

Mr. Schmetterling's eyes widened and his lower jaw practically dropped into his lap. Mrs. Schmetterling looked as if she was about to gag on a *Handi-Wipe.*

Said Howie to the Schmetterlings, "Your brother never mentioned that he's—" thumping a fist to his chest to suppress a burp — "pardon me, a preacher?"

Not hard for Frank to read what must be going through the mind of Matthew Schmetterling right now:

You mean to tell me that my pious, Catholic-to-the-core brother has been shepherding a bunch of backwoods, inbred, buck-toothed hicks in some little outhouse of a church on the prairie?

Frank arched a brow at Howie. "Strange he never mentioned it to his family." In truth, it was not strange at all, not with a mother and sister-in-law who were religious whack-jobs.

Moving along, "Did your brother have any friends here in New York that he might've contacted?" Howie asked.

"No. Like I said before, he hasn't been back in ten years. And even before that he never had any friends here."

"Not even an old girlfriend, maybe?" Howie asked.

"Larry didn't date much here. I can only hope that he bloomed *after* he left seminary."

"What about this Karen Stone, the woman who called from Colorado," said Howie. "Has your brother ever mentioned her to you?"

Michelle took that one: "No, Detective, but my mother-in-law believes they have a special relationship." She stood alongside her husband. "Matthew, it's getting late. Visiting hours end at nine."

He nodded. "Is there anything else?"

Frank gathered up his pen and notepad. "Nope, that's it." Then he thanked Mrs. Schmetterling for everything.

She forced a smile through her teeth.

***

As soon as Matthew and Michelle walked into the hospital room, Larry's mother clicked off the CD player taking away *Memories* and *Cats!*

An angry father said to his wife, "Tomorrow, it's Elvis!"

CHAPTER 7

The Anomaly

Conscious once again, Larry suspects that a mystery force has pulled his disparate particles of spirit to press them into a coherent whole. This time, he finds himself in a place so breathtaking and so wondrous, like the interior of a magnificent cathedral, that Pastor Larry thinks maybe that black hole was his purgatory — never mind that, in life, Larry never believed in Purgatory or indulgences. To him, they have always been a fund raising and marketing gimmicks of a corrupt institution; besides being completely non-Scriptural. But none of that matters now. He has found Heaven. Soon, Reverend Lawrence Schmetterling, a Christian who has dedicated his life to spreading the Word will be in His holy presence. Pastor Larry will finally meet his Maker.

He feels his soul floating, carried on a wavelength of light as magnificent and as blue as the sky. Gleaming marble, white as clouds and supported by twelve massive white columns, form complex patterns across a clerestory ceiling. Just below the point where the ceiling begins its sloping curve are eight enormous stained glass windows depicting scenes from the New Testament. Their colors are purple, red, green, and white on a pale blue background. And below the archivolt — an ornamental molding that follows along the elliptical circumference of the clerestory — there are ten more blue tinted, stained glass windows. At the rear of the cathedral behind the altar are smaller and narrower stained glass windows. It's as if the roof has been rolled back to let the sky in. Being in this new place Pastor Larry's joy cannot be contained. It's ready to burst through the clerestory ceiling and into the infinite bliss that lies beyond.

As his mind's eye begins its descent from above, Larry sees rows and rows of brown pews filled with worshipers; a long line shuffles along the center aisle towards an altar. And then Larry sees himself on that line! And now he remembers where he is — or, more precisely, where he was.

THIS ISN'T HEAVEN!

His spirit is crushed. He remembers.

Larry flew into New York City on a Friday. The next day, he signed a contract with *The Lord's Broadcasting Network*. On Sunday, he went to Mass at Roman Catholicism's holiest of holies in the Big Apple, St. Patrick's Cathedral. Then the Holy Spirit moved Larry to leave the pew and join the faithful in their pious march up the center aisle to receive:

"The Body of Christ… The Body of Christ…" said the priest as he held up and dispensed the Eucharist into each pair of cupped hands.

Considering Larry's Catholicism lapsed a long time ago, through what mystery of faith had he suddenly decide to join the Eucharistic parade? He knew that since he was no longer in communion with the Church of Rome, he was committing, at least according to Church's teaching, a mortal sin. Accumulate enough of these grave transgressions and not only would God's smiley face turn upside down, but He'd bare His teeth as well.

Still progressing up the aisle, and despite the elegant grandeur of this interior space, Larry's mind declared this high holy cavern a relic from a dead past. In mainline Catholic and Protestant churches prayers murmured and songs echoed. Not like in some of today's mega-mart Evangelical churches. In these palaces of glass and steel, praise and worship were glorious blasts of sound offered up in high fidelity. Did worshippers have to be loud for Him to hear?

When Larry finally stood before the priest, he folded his arms across his chest: Catholic for, *Thanks but no thanks.* As he walked away from the altar, Larry reminded himself that his personal Savior was not a presence kneaded into a razor-thin slice of stale-as-cardboard bread. He turned at a side aisle that led out of the Cathedral. After making such a bold statement by refusing the Eucharist, Larry felt as if a glaring spotlight had been cast upon him that would follow him all the way to the doors. But when he glanced into the pews, only one pair of eyes met his. They belonged to a slim, frumpy woman who kneeled alone in a pew. Even from behind her dark glasses, Larry could feel her stare bore into him like a drill. What was *her* problem?

The clothing she wore seemed more suited for disguise than church: a plaid topcoat buttoned all the way to the collar; a white scarf was wrapped around her head like a turban so that not even her ears showed. And the sunglasses that bridged her nose had large, black lenses that gave her the look of one of those bug-creatures from a low-budget 50s horror flick.

The way Larry figured it: *You're a horror already, lady. Ditch the glasses.*

When he reached the rear of the church, he turned around and glanced into the pews again. The woman turned around and lowered her dark glasses just enough to reveal scowling eyes.

Why, because I'm leaving Mass early? Judge not lest you be judged, you old frump!

The woman was a mystery Larry had no interest in solving. Through St. Pat's massive doors, he stepped out onto 5th Avenue on an unseasonably warm, sunny Sunday morning. He admired the secular world. Larry took a deep breath, letting the City's air fill him. And then he coughed. This city-Eden's hellish fumes hacked at his lungs.

Nonetheless, the Big Apple shined like a beacon that had finally called him home. How Larry missed its vitality, its mass anonymity, and its uncaring pursuit of its own ends. He might even move back here; after all, New York is the media capital of the world. Unfortunately, though, Larry had only three days left in Sodom on the Hudson as the simpletons back home referred to New York. In reply to their hayseed wit, he would always wink and say, "No, that's Jersey."

In a blink of his mind's eye, Larry finds himself back in the black hole. The grandeur of St. Patrick's Cathedral, the lights, the smell of incense, the music, all gone. What kind of Supreme Being would allow Larry's hopes to soar to such dizzying heights only to bring down His mighty fist to smash his soul? What had he done in life to be tortured like this in death? Nothing! Not a damn thing! Larry's God is a cruel God! That brief interlude, that tease of Heaven is like a drop of water on the tongue of a man dying of thirst. Larry's soul is about to collapse in on itself, and then he remembers his murderer's face. His mind's eye focuses on the only visible clue he remembers about her: the mole on her cheek.

I know I've seen that on someone else. Who? The frump in St. Pat's?

Why should a woman he only saw once in church dwell in his mind like a timorous mass? It would take a miracle that only occurs in National Geographic, or perhaps a million makeovers, to lift the caterpillar in St. Pat's to the level of moth let alone the exquisite creature who once sat next to him on a bar stool. And then, as his mind stumbles away from her, he trips over another memory: he distinctly remembers that he asked his murderer while she drove the little red Geo if she'd ever been to St. Patrick's Cathedral.

She replied that she wasn't Catholic. Not really much of an answer, but he didn't bother to press her further. Now he wishes he had. Looking back from a point in infinity, he thinks that maybe the murderer and the old frump in St. Pats were the same person. He'll never know. Not in one infinity, not in two, three, four infinities, not in a million times billion times trillion infinities. How different it would have been had he recognized that evil Daughter of Eve in the bar as the old Frump in St. Pat's. He never would have gotten in her car. And he'd still be alive.

Larry's soul has become like a stagnant puddle lying at the bottom of the bottomless pit. Suddenly, he becomes aware that something else has settled alongside him. Its weight and its mass are tangible. It's as if a pebble has been dropped into his soul. Suddenly, searing, white hot pain boils up and fills his black hole. And all that Larry is now is agony. Even though he does not know what the mysterious object is, he knows that's where the pain comes from. He fears he might have to endure this agony for all eternity. Larry feels a pull on his consciousness. That mysterious force is at work again, but this time when it pulls the coherent whole of his mind apart, he does not fight it. To sleep the sleep of the dead and not feel this awful pain is a blessing.

Larry fades away.

***

Monday, 8:23 p.m., Dr. Alan Bloom could smell the pot roast as soon as he entered the door of his home in Yonkers. His favorite dish put a smile on his otherwise grumpy face. For the doctor this had been another long and exhausting day in an endless series of long and exhausting days. He was looking forward to a late dinner with his wife and two teenage sons. What a lucky man he was to have married a woman who could not only cook, but who also knew how to navigate the treacherous seas of her husband's moody moods.

"Hey honey, I'm home!" he called. This was a private joke between the doctor and his family. It meant the mercurial doctor's mercurial mood would be *Home with the Cleavers* tonight.

His eldest son said to the younger: "Hey, Beav, Dad's home."

And the younger replied, "Yeah, Wally, now we can eat. I'm starved."

The Blooms were enjoying their dinner and conversation, when the doctor's beeper went off. Bloom pulled his phone off his belt and growled, "It's the hospital!" Rather than throw the damn phone out the window, he read the text message. It said:

"Anomaly at 8:46."

Five days ago, on Ash Wednesday, shooting victim Lawrence Schmetterling had been rushed into emergency surgery. Because of the bullet's location in the victim's brain, the surgeon thought it best not to remove it. After the patient had been stabilized, he was admitted to Neuro-Trama where the director himself, Dr. Bloom, and a small staff of specialists and interns took over. To further evaluate the full extent of the patient's brain damage he was given an EEG. An electroencephalogram (EEG) tests and detects electrical activity in the brain by attaching electrodes to the scalp. Among various other functions, EEGs can be used to confirm brain death in a patient. And that was exactly what Dr. Bloom was about to do, declare Reverend Schmetterling's brain dead.

And then, "What the—!" exclaimed the intern monitoring the patient's EEG flat line rolling across the computer screen. The intern had almost dropped the F-Bomb in front of his boss. As everyone in Queens General knew, Dr. Bloom did not appreciate foul language. Although thirty-one-years-old the intern looked like a teenager; so everyone called him Dr. Doogie.

"Sir," said Doogie, raising his voice to an almost adolescent pitch, "we have an anomaly."

The anomaly was one that none of the attending physicians had ever seen before: a spike in amplitude that exploded up off the patient's flat line. It lasted for only a micro-second before the patient's brainwaves flattened out again. Bloom and the rest of the medical team were stunned. That spike was 189 micro-volts in amplitude. Such amplitudes are associated with an adult's brain that was awake. Because of that fortuitous spike, Dr. Bloom had not declared the Reverend brain dead.

He also did not suggest to the family that the patient be taken off life support.

After that first spike, Dr. Bloom had ordered his staff to constantly monitor his patient's EEG and inform him immediately should another spike occur.

There had been a second spike the next night, on Thursday, when the family had been playing a CD for the patient.

"Excuse me," the doctor told his family. "I have to call the hospital. I'll be right back." Bloom smiled again. This was wonderful news. For almost a week he'd questioned his decision not to declare Reverend Schmetterling brain dead. He had not told the family about the spikes, either, because he did not want to give them false hope.

All self doubts were gone. He called the hospital and spoke with Doogie. Dr. Doogie told Bloom the spike occurred at 8:46. He added that its amplitude began low at 23. Such a number was associated with a person awake and at rest.

"But then it immediately shot up to 383," said the intern.

"Interesting," said Dr. Bloom.

Interesting indeed; a radical theory began to formulate in Dr. Alan Bloom's mind: an alpha, brain wave amplitude of 23 indicates a conscious person in ordinary circumstance; for it to suddenly shoot up to 383 means a brain under serious stress; therefore, was his patient experiencing an extreme emotion when that spike occurred?

"Let me know immediately should there be any more anomalies," Bloom ordered the intern.

When he rejoined his family he was in a festive mood — Dr. Bloom might soon publish a paper about Reverend Lawrence Schmetterling! — which in itself was an anomaly. He hated writing papers.

Chapter 8

King of the Planet of the Apes

Tracy pulled her red Geo into the driveway and shut the ignition. Tuesday afternoon, she'd left work early to meet the cable man. She recently purchased a high-definition TV from Wallmans, and it needed to be hooked up. As she stepped out of the car, she noticed little Larry Devito, her next door neighbor's son, in his backyard. He sat on a swing fastened to an overhead tree branch. Only six-years-old, sorrow hung on the boy like chain mail; its weight caused the boy's shoulders to droop, put a slouch in his walk, and hung his head. Something had to be especially wrong today because he didn't notice Tracy drive up. Little Larry always had a smile for her, one she welcomed even if it was the kind of smile a person only sees in people who had been beaten down by life for forty years.

Tracy got out of the car and waved to the boy. "No school today?" she called.

He looked up and called back, "I got a tummy ache this morning. Mommy let me stay home."

With black hair and dark brown eyes, Larry was short, overweight, and not athletically inclined. Tracy knew what it was like to be an outcast child. No doubt for a boy like little Larry, school was a place of constant torment. If Tracy had been his mother she would have home-schooled him. Unfortunately, little Larry's mother, Christine Devito, was a vile creature more demon than human who cohabitated with someone even more wicked, John Panfino. He was not her spouse. Fornication! And the way they both neglected the child, Tracy prayed that one day the Lord would set His vengeance upon both of them, using her as His instrument of course.

Christine and John lived in a large two-story big box of a house that had two false gothic columns by the front entrance. Two huge evergreen trees shaded the front yard, and an elm, with the swing attached, occupied the backyard. The house was white stucco, with white gutters, black trim, and a black shingled roof. Tracy's split-level with yellow siding, white gutters, white trim, and a white shingled roof, squatted to the right of the Devito mini-mansion. Tracy's home was neat and well kept, while Christine's homestead, which Tracy derisively referred to as *Guinea Gothic* because wicked Italians lived inside, was the finest on the block. Twice a week John sat atop his *El Toro* mower steering in ever collapsing rectangles across both the front and backyards. When he cut the grass on weekends the noise did upset the delicate balance of Tracy's psyche. She did appreciate, however, that the shrubbery that lined the Devito property on three sides was perfectly aligned and well pruned by John. Soon a beautiful flower garden would accent the front of their home. The man did have a green thumb.

The Millen and Devito driveways were side-by-side, the only part of the Devito property that lay open and not cutoff from neighbors like a great barrier reef of shrubs. While Tracy's driveway was asphalt, brick paved the way to Christine's two-car garage. A stone path led to the front door. Every time she backed out of her driveway and passed the abomination, Tracy was reminded how much she loathed Christine and John: the black jockey on their front lawn.

Living next door to these people for over two years, Tracy knew that the shine outside could not hide the emotional squalor inside. On this particular Tuesday afternoon, the muffled sounds of screams and shouts, and large objects being tossed about came from inside the house. It was only a little past two, early in the day for one of Christine and John's drunken brawls. And why was the woman home so early on a weekday afternoon?

Tracy crossed the brick driveway onto the manicured lawn and into the backyard where Larry sat on his swing. "You know, when my brother and I were young, we had a tree house," she said. Then Tracy moved behind the child and gave him a gentle push. "Not as nice as your swing, though."

Little Larry brightened. Then wistfully, "Wish I had a tree house."

Tracy paused to consider — *So much sadness in this poor child's life.* — and then she came to a decision. "I can't build you a tree house, Larry, but how does a play-set sound? You can climb up a ladder and slide down into a sandbox."

That lit the boy up. "Could you, Tracy, could you really?"

"Yes" — *with His help* — "I can do anything."

"Push me higher, Tracy, push me higher!"

"Weeee!" she said, pulling him further back, and then letting go of the swing.

Wallmans sold backyard play sets for $500, a lot of money for someone who worked there at a floor manager's salary. But Tracy decided to charge it to her credit card, and then pray for lots of overtime. She would buy it tomorrow and have John haul it over in his pickup. He was a roofer who sometimes worked but most times didn't. He and Christine lived off of her legal secretary's salary and his unemployment checks. At the moment, John was in one of his mid-winter down times. Tracy guessed that must've initiated their latest battle; so putting together a play-set would give him something to do instead of to pick on little

Larry. Although she'd never seen any evidence of physical abuse on the boy, John's pounding words left invisible welts on the child's not-yet-fully-formed psyche. Fastening a swing to that tree had been the only kind thing he'd ever done for the boy. Tracy swore that if she ever saw a mark on that precious child, with or without His blessing, she'd do Panfino and his slut too!

"Hungry, Larry? I baked an apple pie yesterday. Would you like a piece?"

"Ooh, yes, yes!... Tracy? Can I have some ice cream, too, please?"

"Of course you can." She held out her hand. "Shall we go, little man?"

Larry jumped off the swing, and they headed hand-in-hand to her house. Inside her kitchen the boy finished off a scoop of chocolate ice cream and a small piece of pie. Little Larry was already chubby, and Tracy fretted about packing any more pounds onto his round little frame; although he'd get plenty of exercise once he got his new play set.

Tracy wiped a dab of ice cream off the tip little Larry's nose. Then she noticed that sadness had once again melted the child's joy. It lay like a puddle at the bottom of a dish. "Aren't you looking forward to playing on your new play set?" She could hear the chirp in her tone; she hated when she sounded like a damn tweety bird!

He forced a smile: "Yes. And thank you so much Tracy. Wish I had someone to play with." By now he was near tears. "Only you and my mom love me."

She reached across the table and gently enveloped his tiny hand in hers. "God loves you, Larry. He loves you so very, very much. Does your mom take you to church?"

He shook his head, no.

Inside, Tracy's guts churned, but outside, "That doesn't matter, Larry," she said sweetly. "I hardly ever go to church, but God still loves me. You love Him, too, don't you Larry?"

He shrugged. "Yeah, I guess. Don't even know who God is."

Tracy was shocked. What kind of a parent didn't teach her child about God? "Do you know about the Bible, Larry?"

Again he shook his head, no.

Suddenly the commotion inside the Devito house moved outside: a man and a woman were screaming at each other in their driveway. Then a car door slammed, an engine roared, and tires screeched. Tracy looked out the window and caught a glance of John's pickup truck back out of the driveway at speed. Then she saw Christine walking back to her house, crying.

"Excuse me, Larry. I'll be right back." She walked out the side door and called to Christine, "Miss Devito. Larry is in my house. We're having some ice cream."

A weak smile, and in a choking voice, she said, "Thank you very much. I apologize for… all… this, Miss Millen."

Tracy went back inside and took out her Bible. She sat on the sofa with Larry snuggled against her. "Before we begin, Larry, I want you to promise me this will be our secret. Don't tell anyone we're reading the Bible together. Not yet, OK?"

Larry nodded. "You're still going to buy me a play set, right?"

She held him close and kissed him on top of his head. "Of course, sweetheart, didn't I promise you? I never break a promise."

***

The next day, Wednesday, Tracy stood in the middle of Women's Wear with a cell phone to her ear while she waited for a non-digitized person to come on the line.

"For English, please press or say one," chirped the pre-recorded woman.

Tracy wanted to reach through the phone to snap this tweety bird's neck; instead, she poked, *One*, so hard she broke a nail.

"Please enter or say your telephone number, including the area code."

Tracy entered her phone number, including the area code.

"Please listen carefully to the following options…"

Tracy listened carefully all the while daydreaming about going postal on every living creature at Simulcast.

"… To speak with a representative, please press or say zero."

"Zee roh!" yelled Tracy, drawing the attention of nearby shoppers. She held up her phone and said, "Cable company." The shoppers understood.

"All representatives are busy assisting other customers. Thank you for your patience."

Patience! What patience! I'm not Job!

On Monday, she had called the cable company. After finally getting through to one of Simulcast's minions, that person assured her an installer would be over to hook up her new TV on Tuesday. He never showed. Tracy's Christian love lay upon her like a finely woven, delicate, white cloth. It would not withstand harsh treatment. Three days of dealing with Simulcast, and with every pour on her body oozing acid, her Christian love began to fray. Finally, when another cable demon came on the line, Tracy let him have it:

"I keep taking time off from work and your people never show!"

The fiend assured her that someone would definitely be there tomorrow, after two.

"He better!" She shut the phone off.

The next day, Thursday, Tracy left work at 1:30 p.m. As she pulled into the driveway she saw little Larry's mother loping across the front lawn calling, smiling, and waving. Then the woman fell flat on her face, a precipitous fall and prelude to the bottomless pit she would one day topple into for all eternity. Tracy assumed another liquid lunch had caused the stupid woman to trip on a blade of grass; such were the treacheries of suburbia. Too bad, though, that she hadn't cracked her skull on that awful lawn jockey. When Tracy noticed Christine was slow to get up, she knew it was her Christian obligation to go help the drunken slut.

Sweet Jesus! Why me? And why today?

Tracy arrived as Christine, embarrassed, regained her footing. From the clear look in eyes and no smell of alcohol on her, little Larry's mom had definitely *not* been drinking.

"Are you OK, Miss Devito?" said Tracy, with as much empathy as if she'd accidentally brushed shoulders with someone in passing.

"I'm fine. Thank you, Miss Millen. You must think me an awful clod."

She smiled. "Of course not," *I think you're just plain awful.*

Larry's mom's pressed blue jeans were immaculate, except for two clumps of turf now attached to each knee. She brushed them off. "I told that son of mine not to dig on the front lawn!" She examined her white sweater, now stained brown and green along the forearms. "Look at me! I'm a mess!" she screeched as if struck by tragedy. She flicked and swatted at her clothes as if they were infested with fleas. Christine's slippers lay behind her scattered on the grass. Tracy went over to retrieve them. She was reminded of a patient at the hospital who was also obsessed that her hospital gown always be as pure white as an angel's wings. One day, just for fun, Tracy accidentally-on-purpose spilled a can of Coke on her. The woman began to shriek and tear at her hair before attendants could straightjacket her.

Christine apparently shared the same neurosis as this woman, which made Tracy think: *Not all loonies are in the bin.*

Annoyed, Tracy held out the slippers. "You look fine, Miss Devito."

Christine grabbed them, and then she turned and shouted in the direction of the back yard, "Damn you, Larry!"

The woman had just blasphemed her own child! Fearing what terrible vengeance this lunatic might extract on little Larry, she invited Miss Devito to her home for a cup of coffee. The invitation pulled a plug, and the woman's rage drained away. She smiled pleasantly. "Please call me Christine."

"Please call me Tracy."

"I'd love to have coffee with you, Tracy."

Sitting in a dentist's chair and having sharp instruments poking around inside her mouth would be preferable to sitting at her kitchen table sipping coffee and listening to this stupid woman prattle on and on about she and John. Not once did Christine suggest they switch to something with a little more bite to it. Occasionally, Christine paused to scrutinize details of her hostess' plain tastes. Tracy felt violated.

Christine was a short, heavyset woman in her early 30s. She had dark, neatly combed short hair, big brown eyes, and beautiful, long lashes. Her smile was radiant. There was no hint of a liquor dependency in those eyes, or in her speech or on her smooth, clear complexion. When Tracy tactfully broached the subject of alcohol, Christine said, "Oh, no, John and I are tea-totallers. There's no liquor in our house."

Have I misjudged this woman? "I don't drink either. For a short period in my life, after the… I used to drink heavily."

"After what?"

Tracy had no intention of getting into *after what*. But Christine would not so easily let go. Finally, Tracy curtly told her that she'd rather not talk about it.

Since Tracy would not elaborate on her life, Christine went back to a recital of *My Life With A Loser*. Then she finally admitted that she suspected John was having an affair.

Tracy, who knew a thing or two about infidelity, replied, "Men are like that."

"Don't know why another woman would want him anyway. He can't hold a job. He's been sponging off me for three years. And I don't like the way he's always belittling my son!"

Got that right! "If I were in your shoes, Christine, I'd throw him out." *Not without first putting a hole in his face.*

Christine's face showed signs of a violent struggle taking place inside her as both her love for and her hatred of John tore into each other like animals fighting over a carcass. No surprise when this side finally emerged victorious:

"But I love him so very, very much," Christine admitted.

Not the least bit interested in hearing more about Christine's woeful relationship with John, Tracy suspected it was a book with 1000 chapters, "If you don't mind me asking, Christine, I see you've been home from work the past few days. Are you ill?"

"Actually, I'm out of work at the moment, lost my job last week."

Since the woman was out of work and needed help, the Christian thing to do was, "I'm a floor manager at Wallmans Shot-A-Lot. I think I can get you a job there."

Christine laughed off the kind offer. "*Wallmans*. Oh dear. I hope it never comes to that. I'm a paralegal. I make well over a hundred thousand a year."

Then why can't you buy your son a damn play set!

"Almost forgot: I want to tell you that as soon as I find another job I'm going to repay you for that play set." Christine gazed upon Tracy as if she had the heart of Mother Theresa, the beauty of the Virgin Mary, and the financial assets of Oprah. "I do appreciate the job offer, though. And don't worry, I'll get something soon."

Those words, that look, and being wrong about Christine and John being heavy drinkers, confused Tracy. Suddenly a scream of pain and the wailing of a small child coming from the Devito's backyard had Tracy ready to jump up and rush to the rescue.

Christine held up her hand. "It's OK. I'll handle it." She walked over to the double-hung window that faced her own backyard and opened it. "How many times have I told you not to do that, Larry?" Turning to Tracy, "He likes to go head-first down the slide." Then she repeated to her son, "How many times, Larry?"

"But Ma!" he called back.

"But Ma nothing! Get in here! Play time is over!" Then she told Larry to go home and wait for her in the bathroom. "I'll clean those scrapes."

Anxious to be alone again, Tracy told Christine, "Maybe you should go tend to him."

Christine sighed, "It's hard raising a son on your own. That's why I need John." The woman seemed about to turn to a new page in her storybook without end. Tracy had to get her out of here. She could feel her darker impulses pressing up against its Christian shielding.

"I really should be tidying up a bit before the cable man arrives," she told Christine, "and thanks so much for coming over."

"Anytime you'd like to stop by my home, please do. We've been living next to each other for three years. Why has it taken so long for us to become friends?"

"Closer to two years, and I'm a private person, Christine."

"Larry sure loves you."

That put a smile on Tracy's face. She carried it with her all the way as she walked Christine to the front door.

Christine said, "You've been so kind to my son, if there's anything I can ever do for you Tracy." Her eyes were pleading.

Ask and you shall receive. "There is one thing," Tracy said, and pointed at the lawn jockey. "Him. He really annoys me."

Christine put a hand to her mouth and she reddened as if she'd just passed gas in public. "Oh, my! I had no idea! Please forgive me. I can assure you no racial slur was ever intended. I'll ask John to paint his face white tomorrow."

Tracy's mind sighed: *Getting rid of him would be better, dear.*

***

Curses, screams and the sound of a scuffle coming from Women's Wear snapped Tracy's head in that direction. As manager it was her job to deal with disorder, and disorder always had the potential to roll back the stone on Tracy's hidden rage. Today was Saturday, the second day of Wallmans pre-Spring weekend sale. A ruckus was taking place next to a dressing room. Tony Magee, a security guard, was struggling with an unkempt blonde woman. From a distance, the woman appeared to be in her fifties. Tony had her arms pinned behind her shoulders. Despite the fact that he was young, fit and a foot taller than her, he looked like a man trying to stuff a wildcat into a bag.

"Get your hands off me!" the woman screamed.

Quickening her pace, Tracy arrived just as two more guards had come up and grabbed hold of the wretch. With three pairs of hands ready, willing, and able to plant the woman's head into the vinyl floor, she stopped fighting. Her chest heaved and perspiration dotted her reddened face. She looked up at Tracy.

"Please make them stop! They're hurting me!" the woman pleaded.

Tony still had her arms pinned behind her while the other two guards pushed down on her shoulders with their combined weight. If Tracy didn't do something soon, Wallmans might have the indelible stain of this woman's face on its floor. Forcing a mantra into her mind, *In His image in His image in His image…,* Tracy commanded, "Enough!" With her eyes, she ordered the guards to ease up.

Upon closer examination, the woman was clearly a substance abuser and probably a lot younger than she looked. The woman was strung out. Tracy knew she just could not let her go. She said a silent prayer asking for the Lord's guidance. The woman was wearing a ratty full-length coat the color of dirty snow. It was bursting at the buttons. Although she appeared to be packing at least one-hundred-sixty pounds beneath her outer garment — Tracy guessed her to be about five foot-three — her face was that of a thin, frail woman.

Tracy had a pretty good idea what had happened even before she asked, "What's going on here, Mr. Magee?"

Mr. Magee said he'd seen her disappear into a dressing room carrying an armful of garments only to re-emerge several minutes later, "Looking like the dang Pillsbury Dough-Girl!"

"Ma'am," Tracy said in a calming tone, "I'm afraid we can't let you leave the store until you unbutton your coat for us."

"You think you're better 'n me, doncha, Miss Uppity?" the woman yelled. Then she invited Tracy to go perform a sexual act with herself.

This had been a particularly bad week for Tracy Millen, and her fuse was already burning too close to the powder. Wallmans annual pre-Spring clearance sale always brought with it some of the most obnoxious, ill-mannered and ill-tempered beings the Good Lord ever created. Through it all, Tracy had managed to maintain a saint's patience. And now, this snotty little woman had dropped the F-bomb on Tracy. Tracy was reminded of an old song about a woman who let pity and kindness take her too close to the snake. It bit her, and she died. Instead of taking the wretch to the office to discuss drug counseling and offering the woman a job if she cleaned up her act: *You've given me Your answer, Lord: not everyone is worthy of redemption.* Tracy ordered the guards to take the woman to her office and call the police.

As she turned to walk away, Mr. Magee touched her arm. "Hold on a minute, Miss Millen." He smiled. "I done good, didn't I? How 'bout you 'n me having dinner sometime?"

Tony Magee, a good ole boy from Mississippi, was tall and blond and handsome. Tracy knew he'd taken a fancy to her. A lot of men did, but her beauty was both a blessing and a curse. She could use it for good (to serve His divine will) or evil (to serve her own sinful nature). A constant struggle within her, so lest Tracy give in to her base instincts, she shunned all romantic attachments.

"You *did* well, Mr. Magee. As for dinner, I don't socialize much. Sorry. Have a nice day." She began to walk away; then she stopped, turned, and gave him a smile. "I do thank you for the invitation, Mr. Magee." She hoped this would soothe his ego. Men were such fragile creatures.

When Tracy pulled into the sanctity of her own driveway, she believed that the trials and tribulations of a long day were finally over. As she got out of her Geo, a husky voice spiced with a heavy dose of testosterone, called to her, "Yo, Tracy Millen. How-ya-doin' ?"

The voice belonged to John Panfino, Christine's live-in boyfriend. He was in his driveway hosing down his black Ford pickup, paid for, no doubt, by Christine's highly inflated *God Forbid I Should Ever Work at Wallmans* salary. He turned off the hose, dropped it, and walked towards her. The weary tone in her voice when she replied to his call of the wild should have warned him, *Do Not Disturb.* But the man was either clueless or just plain dumb.

Five foot-six at the most, Tracy gazed down upon John. He had a rain forest of black hair spilling out of a white, sleeveless T-shirt. It was chilly but not cold enough to deter this imbecile from showing off his weightlifter's upper body. With thick patches of pubic hair covering his powerful arms and shoulders, and sticking out of his nose and ears, should the apes ever take over this planet they would surely proclaim John their king.

"What's with the Mista?" he said in a Jersey-mobster accent. "We're neighbors, call me John."

I think Chimpanfino would be far more appropriate.

His grin accentuated the lustful thoughts that lay inside the tiny confines of his misshapen simian skull. He gestured towards his backyard. "Little chub-o sure loves his play set."

"You did an excellent job putting it together. Thank you, John. Now if you'll excuse me."

"How 'bout joining me for a cup of coffee? I'll put on a fresh pot."

Tracy suspected that neither Christine nor little Larry were home. "I've had a very long day, perhaps another time."

Chimpanfino stepped into the tight circle marking Tracy's *Enter At Your Own Risk* zone.

"You're a very beautiful woman," he said, his close-set, coal black eyes beckoning.

A single fingertip pressed into his matted, jungle-haired chest was enough to halt his forward progress. "You really don't know who you're dealing with, do you? Get lost!"

John looked every bit the dumbstruck ape as his brain grappled with how to respond. The best he could come up with was, "I'm dealin' with a snot who thinks she's better 'n everybody! And tomorrow I'm paintin' that nigga statue back the right color!"

True to his word, Chewbacca must been busy last night, because the next morning as she backed the Geo out of her driveway the lawn jockey was black-faced again.

Tracy came to a decision: *He's gotta go.*

CHAPTER 9

What If the Son of Man Was One of Us?

Matthew and Michelle, and their two sons Mark and Luke, arrived at the hospital on Thursday evening at a little passed seven. When they entered Room 1313, Matthew was taken aback by how haggard his parents looked. They must have been at his brother's side all day.

His father gave Matthew a tired smile. "Glad you brought the boys."

Matthew wasn't. They were too young to see their uncle laid out like a corpse, but he and Michele couldn't find a sitter.

Mark, the oldest, said, "Uncle Lars looks like he's sleeping."

"He is, honey," replied Michelle, smiling. "He's having peaceful, beautiful dreams."

Matthew turned away and gritted his teeth. *He's not having any dreams, Michelle! Peaceful or otherwise!*

"Tonight, when you say your prayers, boys," she continued in a preachy tone based on a faith that grated Matthew's sense of logic, "ask God to wake Uncle Lars up soon."

How dare she fill their children's heads with such garbage! Matthew knew the truth: his brother was like a husk after all its guts had been ripped out. Larry would never wake up! The real battle — three against him — would be when the time came to decide whether or not to pull the plug.

Michelle and his mother went for a walk outside; the poor woman needed a break and some fresh air. February's warm snap continued. It was like spring outside, but the women took their coats anyway. After they left, Matthew's said he wanted to step outside also for a smoke. He asked if he could take the boys with him. Matthew readily agreed; he wanted to spend some quality time alone with his brother.

Matthew sat forward on a chair next to his brother's bed. In his heart he knew Larry would never be coming back. Matthew bowed his head, closed his eyes, and laid a gentle hand on his brother's rising and falling chest.

I might not always have been nice to you, but know I will always love you, Lars. The big man began to weep. Suddenly, a flaming rage swept inside him. The sorrow and despair he'd been feeling ignited like dried brush. He wanted to kill the man who'd done this with his bare hands. Punch his face into pulp, stomp his guts out, and then kick his body until every bone in the man's wretched carcass was smashed.

"Oh geez, Lars," he said, choking on grief that felt like a rock in his throat, "all you ever wanted to do was make the world a better place." Then he felt a strong impulse to slam a fist into the wall: "What kind of God let's something like this happen to someone like you?" The answer roiled inside him, words he dared not speak aloud even though no one else would hear him:

There is no God, Lars! You've spent your whole life serving a myth!

Matthew knew he had better regain his composure before the women returned. "Don't know whether you can hear this or not." He reached down into the bag Michelle had brought along and took out his own personal CD player. He gently placed the earphones around Larry's head. Then he popped one of Larry's favorites into the player.

"This one's for you, Lars, wherever you are." He hit *Play.*

***

Larry can't believe what he's seeing: daylight! And what he's hearing: the steady rumble of an engine. And what he's feeling: legs moving beneath him. In the blink of his mind's eye, he has awakened on a bus!

What am I doing on a bus? Haven't ridden one in years.

Putting that particular jolt to his class consciousness aside, the sensations he now feels are tangible. His chest expands as he sucks up every cubic centimeter of air that can be crammed into his lungs. He holds; and holds; and holds. To have breath inside him once again is to be alive once again. Straining, straining, straining to hold on, feeling like he's going to burst, and then — *Whooshhh!* — he lets the air out for the sheer joy of taking more in. Then he closes and opens his eyes. He's still on the bus, he's breathing normally, and he's still alive. Fantastic!

Strange though, the air has that piney, septic smell associated with a hospital and not the diesel fumes of a bus. And what about this bus, is it a Greyhound? Is it taking him back to Colorado Springs? What happened to his airline ticket? Did he lose it? Is this why he's riding with the unwashed masses? He hasn't been on a bus since high school when he used catch the Q-43A that ran along Union Turnpike. Larry decides not to dwell on the negative but delight in the positive. Thank the Lord, he's alive and this nightmare is finally over. An exhilarated Reverend Schmetterling walks up the aisle, nodding and smiling at his fellow passengers; but none of them have discernible faces. Their features are as blurred as the outside greenery that whizzes passed the windows. Whether these people are young, old, male or female, he does not know. He decides not to sweat the details.

Continuing up the aisle, he spots an empty seat next to a scruffy man in his early thirties. The man's right arm rests on the sill, and he's staring peacefully out the window. His complexion is ruddy, like he's spent a lot of time outdoors. His attire is rough-cut and unpretentious: a red flannel shirt, sleeves cutoff at the elbows and with only two buttons fastened at the midriff (no T-shirt and no hair on his chest), faded blue jeans, and work boots. Larry finds it odd that of all the passengers on the bus only this man has clarity. With shoulder-length brown hair, a long, narrow face that ends in a pointy beard, the man looks like an anachronism from the 1960s. This being a strange ride indeed, Larry checks the man's hands for holes.

There are none. Larry asks, "Is this seat free?"

The man looks up and smiles. "Sit, friend."

"Thanks," says Larry. "My name is Reverend Larry Schmetterling. I'm pastor of a small congregation in Colorado Springs." Ordinarily Larry prefers to keep his calling to himself, but he feels the need to make it known that *he* is also a holy man and worthy to be seated on the stranger's right. He also feels the need to tell the man about the founding of *his* church, His Holy Tabernacle. Humility aside, Larry is justly proud of what he has accomplished.

***

The Lord who Pastor Larry worshipped was born above a stable. The humble origins of His Holy Tabernacle took place in an even more obscure setting: a small office above a bar on Tejon Street in downtown Colorado Springs. The space itself was enough to depress any man's soul: a desk and a matching chair, two folding chairs stored in the closet, a thrift store sofa against the wall to the immediate right of the entrance. An overhead light with an attached fan and a cross and a painting of a smiling Jesus hung on oak-colored paneled walls. The stale odor of beer permeated everything permeable. Because of all the above, the founding members of the HHT spent as little time as possible in this "rattrap," as Larry called it.

Pastor Larry, then age twenty-eight, and cofounders, twenty-six-year-old Karen Stone and thirty-one-year-old Curtis Frothe, gathered to discuss a mission statement for their new church. As the only ordained minister, Larry led the discussion. He sat on a chair behind the $169 *K-Mart* desk. Curtis and Karen sat directly across from him on the sofa.

"We should reach out to those whose spiritual needs are not being met," Larry began.

"I agree," seconded Curtis. "Despite all the churches in town, I'll bet there are still plenty of people who drift from congregation to congregation."

"I'm not just speaking about church folk, Curtis," Larry said.

The smallness of Curtis' mind shown on his face: a puzzled look that Karen happily sunk her fangs into. "He's also talking about bikers, cowboys and gays, Curtis."

"Bikers and cowboys I have no problem with. But gays!" Curtis looked as if he'd been asked to swallow a can of creepy crawlers along with the muck they slept in. "I'm sorry, Larry, but I'll only accept gays and lesbians if they're willing to repent and seek counseling."

Karen snickered. "That's mighty Christian of you, Mr. Frothe. There was a time not that long ago when people like you weren't welcome in certain churches."

"It's not the same, Karen. My race is not an abomination in the sight of—"

"To some people it is!" she shot back.

"... the Lord. Who, by the way, is not a blue-eyed, Wasp from Pittsburgh!"

"I know, Curtis! He was a Jew with a big nose!"

These two had been hurling stones at each other ever since they'd all struck out on their own; Larry, Karen and Curtis had only recently left a local evangelical organization named *Focus on God's Grace* (FoGG). As much as he'd like to, Pastor Larry could not simply cast them both into the sea. Karen and Curtis were critical to the success of His Holy Tabernacle. CFO Curtis kept the church's cash flowing smoothly and uninterrupted. And Karen, his current girlfriend and Curtis' ex, kept his own life's blood flowing smoothly and uninterrupted.

Larry declared, "Enough! All are welcome at His Holy Tabernacle regardless of race, social status or sexual orientation."

"Then we may as well be Unitarians!" Curtis threw up his hands, bounced off the sofa, and began to pace the room.

"Please sit down, Curtis." In soothing tones, Larry added, "This is the Lord's feast. Our church's mission is to offer people *His* bounty. We are the wait staff. It's not our place to say who can or cannot sit at the Lord's table."

Karen nodded. "I like that. Let's use it in our pitch."

Larry's argument knocked the halo on Mr. Frothe's self-righteous head askew. A begrudging, "I still have problems with it, but I'll pray that the Lord will open my heart."

Larry smiled. "That's all I ask, Curtis."

Unexpectedly, it was Karen who threw the next rock. "Maybe Curtis has a point. While people like us, progressives like you and me, Larry, have no problem with LGBTQ people others might not be so tolerant."

"LG…Q…T — what?" Curtis, who still sheltered in the grotto of his own ignorance, threw up his hands and looked at Larry. "Where does she come up with this stuff?"

"LGBQT means Lesbian, Gay, Bi-sexual, Transsexual, Queer — Curtis. Something most well-informed people already know. Even wingnuts."

Said Curtis to Larry: "By *wingnuts* she means people like us, who follow Scripture."

Ignoring him, Karen continued: "If we adopt a policy that's too open, we might turn some people away." Then Karen reminded them both that the rightwing, hateful types also happened to be the people most generous with their tithes. "We need them if our church is going to prosper."

"No, no, absolutely not!" Larry said, pounding the desk. It swayed a little. "I'll never have a church like that."

Meekly, "Ok, ok. It was merely a suggestion," Karen said.

Curtis aimed a snarky look at her. "Don't worry about her, Larry. She knows it's you who brings in the sheaves."

"I thought it was sheep?" said Karen. "What's a sheave?"

Larry ignored the woman's Scriptural and agricultural ignorance. He paused a moment and lowered his gaze. With elbows resting on the desktop, his hands formed a steeple that rested just below his bottom lip. This was how Pastor Larry liked to project contemplation. Then he let loose a deep thought: "I want this added to our mission statement." He took another dramatic pause, then, "Saint or sinner, our church will never turn anyone away from His Holy Table — I mean, Tabernacle."

Both Karen and Curtis seconded the statement, but Curtis suggested it needed to be expanded. And then it came to Pastor Larry like the *Bong!* of a cathedral's bell; a conservative congregation he once worked for in California addressed the very same issue.

"How about we say something like this: 'God loves each and every one of us exactly as we are. But He also loves us too much to let us stay that way. Our church will always choose the lost over the saved.'"

"How about we lay some guilt on them," Karen added. "We say, 'If a saved person chooses to attend another church because we prioritize the lost, then we will be saddened, but we will not change our mission.'"

Curtis looked puzzled: "Why should we say something like that, Karen?"

"Because," Karen replied, "it lets certain people hold onto their sense of superiority. Christians like you, Curtis, need that," she snarked.

"No, Karen," Larry said. "It shows leadership, commitment, and clear direction. We'll also add that saved people should rejoice in serving the lost."

"That'll work." Then she paused to add, "How do we deal with gay marriage?"

Pastor Larry reminded his girlfriend that His Holy Tabernacle followed Scripture. There would be no ceremonies joining same sex couples in *his* church.

All proposals were adopted. As it turned out, the good people of their growing congregation were far more tolerant and eager to serve the lost than even Larry had imagined. Curtis gave credit to the Holy Spirit working in their hearts. Karen, speaking of the congregants, had to admit, "Maybe they're not so bad after all."

And Larry, while his mouth offered up hosannas unto the Lord, in his heart he happily sung praises unto himself.

***

"My preaching opened their hearts," he tells the scruffy man seated on his right. Larry's smile is so radiant it lights up the entire bus.

The scruffy man nods, and then goes back to staring out the window.

"Is this bus headed for Colorado?" Larry asks.

The man turns to face him again. Smiling warmly, "This bus will take you home, Larry."

"Now?"

"No, you're not ready yet. But soon, I promise."

Not exactly sure where *home* is or how much he wants to go back, Larry is about to speak; then he notices something else odd about this trip. There is no sensation of movement; it's as if the bus is at a dead stop and it's the world outside that flies by at sixty m.p.h.

"Excuse me, sir. I didn't catch your name."

The man grins. "Who do you say I am, Larry?"

"Uh, excuse me, please," says Larry, his voice rising octave by octave, "but this is too weird. I'm frightened."

"Don't be afraid, Larry," says the man, "for I am always with you." He smiles and lays a gentle hand on Larry's left arm. Larry sees the hand but can't feel any pressure.

"I ask you again, sir," Larry says more forcefully this time. "Who are you?"

"Verily I ask you again, Larry: Who do you say I am?"

"Uh… The Christ?" Larry's laugh is as weak as his joke.

Instead of a thundering voice and lightning bolts flying from his fingertips that would make Larry jump back into his black hole for cover, the stranger's laugh is kind. He grabs Larry behind the neck, and gently rocks him in a most friendly manner. Larry can't figure any of this. If the man is the Messiah, then He sits at the right hand of the Father and will judge the living and the dead; so Larry figures it's best to be on His good side.

"How shall I call You, then? Lord?"

"Call me Sonny; pleased to meet you, Larry."

They shake. Sonny's grip is firm, but his hand is cold and smooth like polished marble. Despite the man's earthy appearance, Larry feels as if he's just shaken hands with a statue.

"Is this a dream?" Larry asks tentatively.

Bluntly, "Yes it is, Larry."

"Jesus! No, excuse me, I mean — never mind. If this is a dream, no offense, Sonny, but why couldn't you be a woman?"

"No offense taken, Larry, and no offense intended, but, if you recall, wasn't it a woman who put you here in the first place?"

"May I ask you a question, Sonny?"

"Sure, Larry, shoot."

Larry winces.

"Sorry," says Sonny.

"I *was* shot, wasn't I?"

"Afraid so."

"So I am dead, then… Is this Hell?"

"No, it's a bus."

A flash of anger: "Please don't patronize me, Sonny."

"I do apologize, Larry. Please forgive me. And I will answer you this way: Verily I say to you, Pastor Schmetterling: Matthew 7:22-23."

"What has that got to do with anything?"

"It's everything, Larry. I'm quoting Scripture, the word of God."

"I know! I used to be a minister, remember! What does it say?"

Sonny shoots him a smart-aleck grin. "Since you used to be well versed in Scripture, why don't you tell me?" Then Larry notices that Sonny looks past him.

"And speaking of women, Larry, look who just got on the bus. An old friend of yours."

Larry's eyes trace Sonny's line of sight to a woman walking up the aisle. Unlike everyone else on this bus of the damned, she *has* clarity. Larry is stunned. His lower jaw hangs suspended; he is unable to speak. When mind and mouth are finally in sync again:

"Oh… my… God. How did *she* get here?"

Bérénice Sans-Tache, the only woman he has ever loved, is walking towards him. Her eyes and her smile are as loving as he remembers. Bérénice taught art history at St. Mary's College back when Larry was an instructor of philosophy there.

St. Mary's is a small women's college attached to Notre Dame.

A burst of joy explodes in his heart as he stands to greet her. As for

Sonny and everyone else on this bus, they are meaningless figments of his imagination. Larry's mind's eye has been rendered tunnel vision: just Bérénice, her arms outstretched ready welcome him.

Oh, to hold her in his arms once more, to kiss her sweet mouth, to feel her hot cheek pressed to his, to take in the scent of her hair, her body, to feel her warm, moist breath on the nape of his neck, to…

To nothing! Larry feels the gravitational force that binds his mind into a coherent whole rapidly weakening. And then, as if someone has hit a stop button, consciousness is gone.

***

When Michelle and his mother returned, Matthew glanced at his watch. They'd only been gone minutes. Michelle said it was a bit chilly outside.

Then surprised and delighted, "Matthew! You're playing music for your brother, how wonderful!" His mother turned to Michelle and said, "He can hear it, I know he can."

Michelle nodded. Then she asked Matthew, "What CD is this?"

"Joan Osborne."

Taken aback, his mother asked, "Ozzie's wife?"

Michelle gently patted her mother-in-law's arm. "No, no, it's worse than that, Mom. She's a lesbian."

"Dear Lord!"

Matthew rolled his eyes towards the ceiling; then he hit the stop button.

***

Dr. Doogie, once again assigned to monitor patient Schmetterling's EEG, made note of another micro-spike. Then he paged his boss, Dr. Bloom.

CHAPTER 10

Relativity of Perception

Detective Howie Goldberg pushed another donut into a mush mouth and swallowed. Then, "*Burp!*... I dunno, Frank, you really think Fearless Leader is gonna go for it?"

Thursday morning, February 14th, Frank and Howie were at their desks shuffling papers while fueling up on coffee and donuts. Frank paused his own chomping, swallowed, and wiped his mouth with a napkin. He said, "We'll take Two Names with us."

Howie nearly upped his chuck. "To Colorado?"

"No, Captain Willy's office. Fearless Leader likes the kid. Thinks he's smart. And he's the one that dug up all that financial stuff on the HHT. Let him explain it."

Forty-five minutes later, Frank, Howie and Two Names were in the boss' office. By the time Frank finished explaining why the Captain should approve their field trip to Colorado Springs, Graham was staring at them from above the rim of his bifocals; a bad sign.

"Tell me what you found, Officer George," said Captain Graham.

Two Names cleared his throat and shot a quick glance at Howie who nodded, *Go 'wan, Tell 'im.* "I looked in both the Colorado and federal tax databases for His Holy Tabernacle—"

"Wait 'a minute," Graham interrupted, "whose holy tabernacle?"

Frank snickered. "Schmetterling's."

Two Names continued, "His as in God, sir. Anyway, I didn't find a bookstore — the parents and the brother had mentioned one — but I did find a HHT Holding Group. It's listed as a non-profit, religious organization."

The Captain smiled. "Good work Officer George. What's their angle?"

Howie answered: "They're supposed to be doing some kinda overseas preaching stuff."

Two Names added, "Their cash on hand doesn't amount to much, like around forty, fifty grand at any given time."

Graham snickered. "Not going to convert many heathens for that kind of money."

"Tell 'im who runs it, Two," said Frank.

"The Chairman, CEO and CFO of the HHT Holding Group are Lawrence Schmetterling, Karen Stone and a guy named Curtis Frothe respectively. The three of 'em are also the board of directors. And get this: they're listed as officers for His Holy Tabernacle, the church that Schmetterling runs."

"And that's why we think we should go out to Colorado and question both Stone and Frothe," Frank added.

Countered Captain *I-Run-A-Tight-Budget* Graham: "At this point, I think it's best if we let the local PD handle the preliminary questioning."

"With all due respect, sir," said Howie, "who would you rather have question the only suspects we got, me and Frank or Marshal Dillon and Festus?"

"You have a point, Goldberg."

Frank took it from there: "Two ran credit checks on Schmetterling, Stone, and Frothe, whose salaries, by the way, are listed at forty-five, forty, and forty-two grand a year. According to their credit card receipts, they're living *way* large."

Captain Graham arched his brows. "So the woman makes less money. How progressive," he snickered. "She might be resentful. We can use that."

"And like, you should see the cars they drive," said Two Names. "Schmetterling owns a brand new Mercedes XL, Stone a late model BMW and Frothe a Lexus *and* a Ford Explorer."

Added Frank, "If there's one thing I know about churches, sir, they're cash cows. A lot of green in the collection plates, and not too many receipts, know what I mean?"

The Captain was now in full agreement. "As much as I hate giving you two Buddhas what amounts to a vacation, you can go." Then he issued the following warning: "Try not to eat *all* the food out there. Leave some *grub* behind for the cowboys and Indians."

***

Dr. Bloom snapped his fingers. He wished he could get these four people out of his office as easy as that. Thursday night, and the doctor was in a hurry to take his wife to their favorite Italian restaurant for a special Valentine's Day dinner. But he had called the family in before visiting hours; the time had come to tell them about the patient's anomalies.

"Your son's brain activity lasts even less than a snap of my fingers. Less than the blink of an eye; but we now suspect there might be some level of consciousness in the patient; especially when the patient is exposed to outside stimuli. Like last night when he reacted to music."

Joy and hope from the mother: "His brother played one of Larry's favorite CDs and he heard; a mother knows these things," said Toby Schmetterling. Then she turned on her husband: "I told you, Mike!"

The father, Mike Schmetterling, hesitated to take hope in something he did not understand. "Larry's awake only for the blink of an eye? What's that, Tobie?"

Despite a dislike to Mr. Mike Schmetterling, a man Dr. Bloom considered an ignorant bigot, he sympathized with his pain and confusion. And sympathy was something the doctor carefully rationed when it came to dealing with patients and their families. Besides, the younger Schmetterlings, Michelle and Matthew, he liked them. They were educated people.

"I understand the mathematics of waves, Dr. Bloom," said the brother, "amplitude and length. Are you telling us that Larry's brain activity is, like…" he paused, rolling his right hand as if trying to churn up the right word, "… spikes?"

Dr. Bloom nodded; he noticed that the father and mother were still confused. "Mr., Mrs. Schmetterling," he said to the parents, "think of these episodes as micro-bursts of consciousness."

"Not a whole lot," said the father, sadness hanging on his face like a deadweight.

"Think of it this way, Dad," said the brother. "Time perception is relative. What seems like micro-seconds to us might be minutes, hours, and days in Lars' mind."

The father looked to Bloom. The doctor nodded. Even he hadn't considered the relativity of perception. The brother had impressed him.

And then the father asked, "What if Larry is in pain?"

A *whoosh!* sucked all the oxygen out of the room.

***

The next day, Friday, Frank and Howie were back in the Captain's office getting their final instructions from Graham: "The local PD will provide a liaison detective while you're in Colorado. Her name is Karla Libbee."

"Karla Libbee, hmm," said Howie. "Bet she looks like that bull dyke on TV, what's'er name? You know the one you got the hots for, Frank."

"Her name's Xena," said Frank, "and she ain't no dyke!"

Frank's fantasies had been aroused. He smiled inside, but some of that inner glow must've passed through his lampshade, because Captain Graham gave him and Howie the following warning: "Don't let me hear that you two have behaved in anything less than a professional manner. I swear if you bring disgrace on my department, I'll have your pensions."

After getting off the phones, and before digging into the smoking hot pizza that just arrived, an angry Frank noted, "Can you believe that? Only the rector — whatever that is — can release information on Schmetterling. And he's on a sabba-dabba-badda-dickle — on vacation."

Detective Goldberg bit off another humongous chunk of pizza. Then, speaking with his mouth full: "Give it to Two Names. Bet he even knows what a rector is."

Said Frank, "The poor kid must be tired of canvassing the neighborhood where we found the car. Think maybe we should give him a hand?"

After another swig of *Diet Coke*, Howie burped, and then patted his chest with a closed fist. "He doesn't need our help. He gets to club all over the Upper Eastside and deduct it from his taxes." He stopped short. Howie looked like 1040 pounds of taxes just dropped onto his head. "Church?... Cash?... Deductions?... You thinking what I'm thinking, Frank?"

Frank's eyes went from, *What're you talking about?* to *Now I can see the light!* "Let's take a closer look at them tax records."

It would be nice to have all the info before they headed out to Colorado; they were scheduled to catch a flight tonight at eight. Instead, the Double G's had to reschedule their flight for Saturday because Frank and Howie still couldn't follow the money trail as left behind by the HHT Holding Group. At five o'clock, Saturday, with the finances of the HHT Holding Group still in the shade, Two Names dropped the Double Gs off at La Guardia Airport.

"Don't forget about the vic's friend, that Wicker guy," Frank said to Two Names as he got out of the car.

Two Names had finally spoken to the rector, Monsignor Hanifen. Hanifen had said that Schmetterling had only one close friend at the seminary, a man named Paul Wicker. Wicker had served as a priest for a few years before leaving the priesthood altogether. The Monsignor said he believed Wicker was now a big shot living on Long Island.

When the plane was safely off the ground, a flight attendant pushed a cart full of sodas and sandwiches up the aisle. Frank and Howie had to dip into their own pockets for money.

Howie took a first bite and made a face. "Uggh! This ham and cheese tastes like it's made of wet cardboard. Can't believe I just spent five bucks for this crap!" Regardless of the true age of the sandwich, that didn't save it from disappearing into Detective Goldberg — in three bites.

Examining his own sickly gray luncheon meat, Frank decided to get his money's worth by nibbling. When he finished eating, he asked Howie, "Wonder what business our preacher was up to in New York?"

"Bet it had something to do with all that money them people at the HHT was raking in. Hey, New York's got Wall Street. Maybe he came here to invest it?"

"He could'a done that over the phone," Frank said.

"Maybe he was gonna invest in something shady."

Frank nodded, and then took out his notepad. "This is what we got so far: Schmetterling arrives in New York on Friday afternoon, February 1st. He checks into a hotel in Midtown and rents a car. The rest of Friday and all of Saturday, we don't know where he was or what he did. Sunday night, the third, he has dinner with his parents, then leaves. OK, so Monday night, he's supposed to have dinner with his brother, but he cancels. Tuesday night, as near as we can figure, he's on the Upper Eastside, bar-hopping maybe. And maybe he meets a broad, and she shoots him Tuesday night or early Wednesday morning. That's all we got." He snapped the pad shut.

Three hours later, the pilot's voice came on the speaker to say that the plane was on its final approach into the Colorado Springs airport. An infrequent flyer, Frank hated soaring at 30,000 feet, but he hated landing even more. Each time the plane dropped while on its approach, so did Frank's insides. He closed his eyes; they would not reopen until this big bird was taxing on terra firma. He dug his fingers into the armrests. The plane descended from the north. To the west stretched the great Rocky Mountains, a long corridor of shadowy giants with halos of gold and violet that seemed to explode off their peaks as the sun dipped behind them on its westward-ho to the Pacific.

Howie had the window seat. "Geez, Frank, look-it that sunset! Look-it them mountains!"

Frank's jaw tightened; for him, the grandeur of the moment slipped past. Images of a fiery crash and thoughts of inhaling flames flared in his mind. Frank wondered if maybe his life before the Schmetterling case wasn't so bad after all. Routine could also be a shelter, a comfortable place where he could always lay his head and take a nap.

"Hope you ain't gonna have to change your underwear when we land, Frank." Mimicking Captain Graham, "Don't you bring disgrace on me and the NYPD by crapping in your pants, Detective Giavone!"

Bump! Bump! Bump! And then the plane began its smooth cruise on pavement. Frank could breathe again.

After some speculation on their part while deplaning, Frank and Howie had come to a conclusion regarding Detective Libbee: the woman meeting them at the Colorado Springs airport would be a warrior princess with a badge and gun. When fact finally met fiction, a fine looking, shapely woman approached them as they waited by Gate 3. She fit nicely into a navy business suit worn over a V-necked pink blouse. And she looked tough. Thirty-something Detective Libbee was at least five-foot eleven-inches tall (six-two in the heels she wore). She had dark hair, bright blue eyes, and a cheery smile that locked onto Frank.

Howie nudged his partner. "She likes you."

Frank could hear her high heels *clack, clack, clacking* on the vinyl tiled floor. The sound of women walking in heels, along with their swiveling hips, was a turn-on for Frank.

After introductions, she asked if the NYPD detectives were hungry. She must've known that the quickest way into the hearts of two hefty bags like the Double Gs was to stuff 'em.

"Hell yeah! I mean, yes ma'am," replied an enthusiastic Detective Goldberg.

Frank said, "It was a three hour flight from New York and all I got was a lousy ham & cheese on white."

"Well I c'n offer you boys a lot more 'n just a sandwich. I'm gonna cook y'all a mighty fine dinner. But first, since the three of us will be working together so closely…"

Something about the way her eyes roamed the range when she looked at Frank both frightened and aroused him. Although an imposing figure, there was nothing mannish about Detective Karla Libbee. She was all woman all right. She just happened to come in a larger package than those sticks that pranced the catwalk.

"How 'bout you fellas call me Karla, and I'll call you Frank and Howard."

"Howie, call me Howie."

"OK, Frank and Howie, so how 'bout it? I'm from New Mexico, and

I cook some mighty fine Tex-Mex. You boys like it hot 'n spicy?" she asked.

"We sure do, Karla," said Howie, answering for both of them.

"And after we finish discussing the case, you boys can fill me in about life in New York City. *Seinfeld* is my favorite show. I have every dang episode on DVD."

Howie nudged Frank as if to say, *And she's intellectual.*

While Karla waited with their luggage, Frank and Howie excused themselves to the big boy's room. After finishing his business at the urinal, Frank flushed and walked over to the sink to wash his hands. Looking at his partner's back in the mirror, "I dunno, Howie, something's not right about this Detective Libbee. Taking us to her house, feeding us, what's up with that?"

"She likes us." Howie flushed and joined Frank at the sink. "Especially you," he added, throwing Frank a wink.

Karla's modest two-bedroom home lay west of Interstate 25 in a quaint neighborhood aptly called the Westside. Working class people lived there, and Karla was definitely a working class family of one. She told the Double Gs that she and her ex-husband had bought the place when they were stationed together at Fort Carson, an army base just outside of Colorado Springs. Back in New York, Frank lived in a dingy apartment in the basement of someone else's house in Syosset. On those infrequent occasions when Howie stopped by, he always referred to Frank's place as, "The Home of the Cave Bear."

Frank had felt such shame that he never ever invited anyone else over. But sitting next to Howie in Karla's immaculate living room decorated in the soft, warm colors of the Southwest, Frank had a peaceful easy feeling. "This is a really nice place," he called to the kitchen where Karla was reheating a casserole in the microwave.

"That's mighty nice of you to say, Frank," she called back.

When she returned to the living room, Howie shoved himself over to make room for her to sit between them.

"So, Karla," Howie began, "no kids?"

"No, thank God. My ex was an alcoholic, so drunk most of the time that he hardly ever got his soldiers in formation. He still comes by from time to time begging to get back together."

The bell on the microwave tinkled. "You boys will excuse me while I serve. I fixed a casserole this afternoon. Figured y'all be hungrier 'n badgers." She headed back into the kitchen.

"A badger — is that that that thing that stinks like a skunk?" Howie whispered to Frank.

"How should I know what a badger smells like," hissed Frank.

"Come and get it!" Karla called from a small dining area that was just off the kitchen, behind the sofa.

The spicy aroma of Tex-Mex casserole drifted into the living room. It was like a forklift grabbed onto Frank's nostrils and lifted him off the sofa and dropped him into a chair at a round table. The Double G's eyes went wide with wonder: heaping helpings of casserole filled three china plates. Three place settings with white cloth napkins, rolled in wooden bows, along with three bottles of Dos Equis beer and three tall, frosted glasses lay in front of them. In the presence of a fine lady, and not to bring shame on Captain Graham's NYPD, both he and Howie curbed their enthusiasm and ate like human beings for a change. Karla had one serving while the double Gs had three each, with Karla filling their plates until there was none left. When the Double Gs told Karla that this was the best meal they ever had, that sure put a smile on her face. Then the three detectives turned to the matter of The Church of His Holy Tabernacle and the HHT Holding Group, Ltd. Karla suggested they visit the church on Sunday to confront their suspects.

"That'll really catch 'em off guard," said Frank, feeling a lot more comfortable now that his belly was topped-off. "It'll throw 'em that we found out about their little HHT scam."

"Exactly," said Karla. "That'll have them wondering what else we know."

Karla drove the Double Gs back to their motel in her personal car, a late model, light blue SUV. She glanced at her wristwatch. "It's half-passed ten." She looked at Frank and asked, "Is it true what they say about New York, the city that never sleeps? How 'bout I let you fellas buy me a beer?"

Frank, whose first impulse had always been never to act on impulse, acted impulsively. "*Sure,*" he said. Then he shot his partner in the back seat a *Just Me and Her* look.

"Well, this New Yorker sure needs his sleep," Howie said, catching Frank's drift.

When they got to the motel, Howie got out and slammed the rear door shut. "Don't stay out too late; we got church in the morning." He winked at Frank.

No sooner had Karla pulled out of the motel's parking lot than Frank's impulse control, accompanied by a heavy dose of insecurity, kicked in.

What am I getting into? This is like a — no, not like a date, this IS a date! Why is a good looking broad like her coming on to fat, ole me? She's playing me.

They rode in silence, making a series of lefts on side streets with no lighting. There were no signs of life inside any of the single family homes that flanked the roads. Frank wondered if the whole town was asleep. Finally, they rolled up to a well lit thoroughfare. Karla pulled into the left turn lane to wait for the green arrow. When it came, she swung the white SUV onto Academy Boulevard.

"Like Country & Western, Frank?" Then she pressed down on the accelerator and ripped passed a string of slower moving vehicles.

Frank had been raised listening to his parent's favorite Italian crooners: Sinatra, Bennett and Jerry Vale. His idea of C&W was a cowboy singing to his horse on *Hee Haw.* A less than enthusiastic, "Yeah, country music is OK."

Karla did not catch the shrug in his tone. "Good! I know a club where we can go. It's called Cowboys. Now how 'bout that!" With a teasing wiggle of her upper body, she added, "Ya feel like doing some line dancing, Detective Frank Giavone of New York City?"

Again his voice shrugged: "Yeah, sure."

Until they'd turned onto Academy Boulevard, Karla's face had been hidden in shadows. Now the street lighting and the headlights of cars coming from the opposite direction lit her up. There was strength and character etched into every line on her face; an attractive face with a narrow chin and high cheekbones in perfect triangular symmetry. No doubt in Frank's mind, by the way she drove the vehicle with a single thumb wrapped around the bottom of the steering wheel, and the way she easily maneuvered him into this accepting her invitation that this was a woman who figured she was in control.

Many years and many pounds ago, when Frank's ego was in full bloom, he would've been far less suspicious of attention from a quality chick like Karla. Now, given the number of long, cold winters his ego had endured, it had lost more than its fair share of petals. If he wasn't careful, a woman like her could easily pluck what few he had left.

"I dunno what's happening to me, Karla," Frank said rubbing his eyes for effect, "but all of sudden I'm exhausted. Not up for dancing tonight. Sorry."

With both hands now riding atop the steering wheel, she shot him a surprised look. "Thought New York was the city that never slept?"

Sounding a lot more apologetic than he intended, "I'm from Long Island."

"OK, Frank, how about we go somewhere and talk?"

So that was it! She wanted to pump him for information. Knowing how secretive and untrusting Captain Graham could be, Frank knew his boss would tell the CSPD only what he figured they needed to know. That made him wonder what the locals might also be holding back.

"Yeah, Ok. There's a coupla things we can go over about the case."

"*The case?* It's Saturday night and all you wanna do is talk about *the job?* Sorry, Frank," she said coolly, "but I punched out a coupla hours ago. We c'n go over that stuff tomorrow morning. How 'bout I just take you on back to the motel?"

Without waiting for a reply, Karla whipped the SUV into a hard U-turn. The headlights of oncoming cars flashed in Frank's eyes. Then she accelerated far ahead of the rest of the herd. Driving with Karla was like driving with Daisy Duke!

Happy to still be alive instead of sticking out of somebody's grill, once again Frank's old life wasn't looking so bad at the moment. The way he figured it, the grass was always greener in another yard, until you hopped the fence and landed in a pile of dog poop. Frank had built himself a private patio with routine as its planking. With routine, he always knew what came next. This Detective Libbee was too full of surprises. Frank had better be real careful before he jumped into her backyard; not just poop but the whole dog might be hiding there. With big teeth!

Chapter 11

Bullets Over Babylon

Saturday night found Dr. Bloom home with his sons watching a Knicks game on TV. The cell phone next to him on the end table beeped. He'd been keeping it close for good reason. In came a text message from one of his interns monitoring Schmetterling's EEG: "Another anomaly." The message went on to say its period — its duration — was eight micro-seconds.

***

Like leaves blowing in through an open window, particles of Larry's consciousness swirl and gust, round and round, into his black hole. When an unknown gravitation sweeps them into a pile, his mind is whole once again. He wonders:

What great sin have I committed to be forever damned? Does God hate me because I left seminary?

Larry remembers that day in the office of Monsignor Richard Hanifen, Rector of the seminary at Notre Dame.

***

"I'm leaving, Father," he told a stunned monsignor.

Larry liked and respected the man despite the fact that his ostentatious office would be the envy of the pope himself. Hanifen stared at him for a moment in quiet contemplation; his elbows rested on the desk and his fingertips touched in a steeple. Then, "I see. Your grades are excellent, Larry. Several of your teachers have told me that you have the makings of an outstanding theologian. The Church would hate to lose someone with your gifts, but..."

Eager to be over and done with this unpleasantness, Larry stood and offered his hand. "Thank you, Father, but I've prayed long and hard about this."

Hanifen motioned for Larry to sit a moment longer. "The Church recognizes that the priesthood is not for everyone. While I'm not going to try to dissuade you, may I ask why?"

Larry shifted uncomfortably, reluctant to state his true feelings.

"Be frank, Larry. Is it a woman?"

"No, it's not a woman, although marriage is an option I might wish to pursue some day."

Hanifen nodded. "I understand. You know, Larry, there are still plenty of opportunities within the Church for a lay person. One can serve God and Man in many ways. I sense you're deeply troubled over this matter. Talk to me, Larry."

How to tell a man you admire that he had wasted his life serving an institution no longer relevant in the modern world. As far as Larry was concerned, the Roman Church was too deeply rooted in the middle ages, when even kings knelt in the snow to beg forgiveness. For example, today, despite all the encyclicals and condemnations issued by previous popes, the vast majority of married Catholics practiced birth-control. Once heirs to St. Peter the Church's hierarchy had now become as stiff-necked as the Sanhedrin.

Instead of the truth, Larry told the monsignor, "There's a quote — I forget by whom — that goes: 'I've been so heavenly minded that I've become no earthly good.' " Then Larry stood again and offered his hand; he asked Hanifen for his blessing.

The monsignor arose from his own chair, leaned across a vast expanse of mahogany, and clasped Larry's hand in both of his. "May God's love always be with you, Larry."

When he walked out of Hanifen's office that day, it was as if he had crawled out from under a heavy load. Breathing would be so much easier now that the crushing weight of other peoples' great expectations had finally been lifted off him. Larry felt exhilarated, for the first time *he* was the captain of his own soul, *he* would chart his own course towards new and exciting waters where he could explore life in all its complexity.

Larry's roommate at Notre Dame was a fellow seminarian named Paul Wicker, a man more than twice Larry's age. Wicker told Larry that he had converted to Catholicism twenty-six-years ago when he married his wife. A widower of four years when he entered seminary, Wicker had a Master's Degree in Nuclear Engineering. Before taking up his new calling, he'd been an engineering vice president at the Indian Point nuclear power plant in Buchanan, N.Y.

"Providing power to the masses for the boob tube, video games, and neon lights did not energize my soul anymore," Paul had said. "With my wife gone and my two daughters married with children of their own, I sought a new meaning in life. Like you, Larry, I felt called to serve God, His church, and Man." Then he chuckled. "Pardon the pun, but I want to electrify the people and enlighten their paths to our Lord, Jesus Christ."

Larry grinned. "You still think in kilowatts, don't you, Paul?"

The stream of fresh ideas that had begun to flow when Larry was an undergrad turned into a great flood under Wicker's tutelage. Paul poured out everything he knew about the physical world and how perfectly harmonious it is because its Creator is so perfectly harmonious.

"Time and space and matter, everything in the universe is connected to everything else, Larry. And it's all connected to God."

On the day he left Notre Dame, Paul helped him pack. "For what it's worth, Larry, I think you've made the right decision."

Larry smiled and nodded at those kind words. But, "This is gonna kill my parents."

Paul laid a comforting hand on Larry's shoulder. "I'm also a parent, so I doubt that very much; we parents are a lot more resilient than you kids think."

The first challenge Larry faced in his new life was to find meaningful employment. What could he do with a B.A. in Religious Studies and an M.A. in Ethics? Working for Microsoft, where there was no god but the Gates god was out. So, too, Wall Street, where the theology of "Greed is good" ruled. Thus, with all of his training in religion and philosophy, it seemed he would be yoked to them for the rest of his adult life.

His first job was a teaching position at a private, ultra-conservative, fundamentalist high school in Irvine, California. He was promptly fired after only one semester. The school didn't take kindly to a nervy New Yorker suggesting to impressionable young minds that the story of Adam and Eve was a creation myth of the Israelites. But what really sealed his fate were his assertions that since human beings and chimpanzees shared 99% of their chromosomes that meant a common ancestor.

"Do you really think Adam and Eve were monkeys, Schmetterling?" his irate principal demanded to know. "As one of their descendants, do you see me covered with hair like a damn hippie?" Other than what grew out of his nose and ears, the man was hair-impaired; his bald head was as empty on the outside as his skull was on the inside. Even his eyebrows were sparse.

Larry smiled. "We can agree to disagree, sir."

"Feel free to disagree with me anytime, Schmetterling, but you can't argue with Scripture."

People like his principal, who refused to open their hearts or their minds, Larry mocked them behind their backs. As far as he was concerned, these primitives on the far right of the religious spectrum had much more of the ape in their genome than the general population. They were abominations even unto all Chimp-dom. Great savannahs of enlightenment stretched before them, but these fearful creatures refused to climb down from the trees. Instead they clung to the upper branches, howling and casting their dung down upon those who dared walk upright.

After being fired from that school, it didn't take long for Larry to hit turbulent seas. With no job, no money, and no health insurance, he knew he was steaming full-speed ahead towards the twin Isles of Poverty and Despair. Terrified, he prayed that the Lord would point him towards a new North Star. And He did. Two days before Larry was scheduled to be interviewed for food stamps, he received a phone call from his former teacher and old friend, Monsignor Hanifen. The Monsignor told Larry that an instructor's position had opened up at St. Mary's College.

St. Mary's was a woman's college attached to Notre Dame. Larry feared he was headed into temptation.

"I've already spoken to the selection committee, Larry. It's yours if you want it."

He most definitely did *not* want it. But dead broke and about to crash onto the rocks, Larry faced two awful choices: take a job at St. Mary's or ask his parents for money.

Larry never had a girlfriend in high school; for that reason he didn't go to his senior prom. In college, he "dated" only one girl. Her name was Kristen. Although rather plain — she was short, a bit overweight, and had a poor complexion — it was her gentle nature and kind heart that melted his. Twenty-year-old Lawrence Schmetterling was in love. Unfortunately, what Larry mistook for a serious relationship she took for just hanging out. Reality was about to clunk him on the head. He invited her home during spring-break to meet the parents. His father was ecstatic. Pulling his son aside and nudging Larry in the ribs, "She's got a nice tits… I'm so proud of you, son. So…?" His father's proud smile widened, "You getting any?"

His father's crude reference to Kristen's breasts genuinely offended Larry. But daddy-dearest's question truly flumoxed him. "Any what, Dad?"

"You know," his father said, pumping his fist twice, "Any action?"

A novice back in those days, it took a beat for him to catch on. "Oh… Dad! That's gross! We've decided to wait."

"Wait? For what? You ain't no priest yet! Enjoy yourself."

"What if I *enjoy* girls so much I leave the seminary?" Larry snarked.

"Then your mother will kill herself."

Speaking of his Catholic-to-the-core mom, she had been rather frosty to Kristen from the moment the girl first walked in the door. Now, as she waited in the car for Larry to drive them back to school, it was his mother's turn to pull him aside. Adjusting his jacket, she said, "Kristen's a nice girl, Larry, but you can do better." She kissed him on the cheek and bade him farewell.

Larry was terribly confused. As far as he was concerned Kristen was perfect. When he had finally summoned up the courage to tell her how he felt, she informed him, "You're a really nice guy, Larry, but I'm afraid we'll never be more than friends."

In those days, Larry had always taken the opinions of others far too seriously; this girl had vaporized his fragile male ego with the atomic f-bomb: "Friends." For the next two years he never asked another co-ed for a date.

Larry boarded a bus headed for South Bend, Indiana. Hidden among his carry-on luggage was a dirty little secret: like any other normal twenty-three year-old male, Larry more than liked girls — *"I'm not gay, Dad!"* — he lusted after them. Unlike other men his age, though, he had never actually *known* one. He had lied to his father when he pompously proclaimed that he and Kristen were *waiting*. He sure as heck wasn't! If she had invited him into her bed he would have jumped right in. There was no holy angel that sat on one shoulder whispering in his ear: *Be proud! You have resisted temptation! You have pleased the Lord!* Instead, on the other shoulder sat his true self. It said: *Admit that you're just too damn scared to even talk to a woman!*

It was not an aggrandized sense of piety that kept Larry's sinful nature in check, it was fear. Girls scared the hell out of him. The ride from California to Indiana was a long one and the panic inside him grew and festered with each passing mile. His final destination, St. Mary's College, was a school for young women. Instead, he knew his fear of women and the fragility of his own ego would not keep him safe from the clutches of so many Daughters of Eve.

Thinks Larry of the black hole: *Daughters of Eve? Why was I so medieval back in those days?*

When the bus finally arrived in South Bend, it took all his strength not to jump right back on again.

The year Larry had spent at St. Mary's turned out to be the happiest of his life. For the very first time, Larry fell in true-love. Her name was Bérénice Sans-Tache, and she was an instructor of art history. She had been born in France, and to Larry of Queens Village, that made her exotic.

"You are a very kind, very gentle, very patient man," she said in a French accent that all by itself was enough to make him swoon. "That is why I love you, Larry."

Except for his mother, no woman had ever told him that before. But memories of Bérénice Sans-Tache later turned out to be too painful. She used their love as a test of her own devotion. Best to skip passed that dark chapter. Larry's mind's eye opens onto events that occurred immediately after he left St. Mary's College. He remembers packing up his broken-heart and hauling an empty shell of himself back to California.

Out West he found a job at one of the many evangelical organizations that had sprouted across Southern California like lilies of the field. His biblical knowledge was impressive. He believed his talent was truly a gift from God. And such talent was being wasted sitting behind a desk opening envelopes stuffed with cash and taking phone calls to console the troubled. Only occasionally was he allowed to address a congregation. Larry wanted to preach the Good News. To gain the necessary credentials he enrolled at a Bible college run by the Church of the Nazarene. After completing his coursework in record time, and armed with a divinity degree, he sent out resumes to various churches. Larry held fast to a belief that he could spread salvation among the unwashed, unthinking, and unquestioning masses. He saw himself as their savior, although Larry vowed never to allow himself to be hung on a cross for *their* sins. But the religious market was a tough one to crack; too many preachers chasing too few pulpits.

And then He intervened. In what could only be interpreted as the Lord at work in His mysterious ways, Larry was hired on as pastor to a congregation in the small farming community in the Simi Valley. In his very first sermon, he boldly announced to the people, "I will lead you to a richer, fuller and happier life in communion with Jesus the Christ!"

Instead of a wave of awe and inspiration, a wash of bewilderment overflowed the pews. After the service, while greeting the congregants, more than one of them came up to him and said, "You meant Jesus Christ, not Jesus the Christ, right Reverend?"

Larry assumed the bumpkins were being polite. To themselves they must've been thinking: *How c'n we trust a fella who don't even know God's last name?*

Eventually the waters between Larry and this flock did part. Twice hired, twice fired, and he heard his father's voice remind him:

"Schmuck! Stick to the script. Remember, only what they wanna hear."

Larry would not give up. A new crop of fundamentalist organizations were sprouting up in the fertile fields around Colorado Springs; so he let his living waters flow from the Pacific to the Rocky Mountains. But once there, it wasn't an Egyptian princess who fished the prophet of Queens Village out of troubled waters. It was a peasant girl from Pittsburgh.

A woman he would come to *know* but would never love: Karen Stone.

***

Tracy Millen opened the drawer of her night table and took out the always loaded .32. This killing would be premeditated. A quick glance at the clock: its digital readout said 3:11 a.m. Early Sunday morning, the street would be dead asleep. Dressed in a white robe and pink bunny slippers, she walked out the side door. The night frost chilled her. She wanted to get this over with, so she could get back into her warm bed. As expected no lights shown in any of the other homes and not a car could be heard in the distance. The eternal peace and quiet of God's own universe reigned on this little block in Babylon.

The silence was broken by a *crack!* from Tracy's little .32.

She scampered back into her house; then up the stairs and out of her robe and slippers, and back under the cozy covers. Tracy smiled. This one had been for her. She didn't think the Lord would judge her too harshly for what she'd done. The poor boy, he just had to go.

Like a secret lover come to call did the first light of day sneak through the pink lace curtains of Tracy's bedroom window. It kissed her eyelids; it caressed her face. She awoke at 6:23 a.m. on a glorious Sunday morning to the sounds of waking birds beginning to chirp. Throwing off the quilt, Tracy swung her legs over and sat up on the side of the bed. She stretched her arms high above her head. Her mood inside matched the splendid conditions outside. She put on her old but comfy white terrycloth robe, slid her feet into her pink bunny slippers, and headed downstairs to the kitchen. Most mornings were a mad dash to get out of the house and get to work on time; not today. This day belonged to only her. She'd enjoy every precious minute of it, beginning with a breakfast of ham and eggs (sunny side up), coffee, and fresh squeezed orange juice with the pulp strained away. (No impurities for Tracy.) Then she'd soak in the tub for twenty or thirty minutes.

What to do the rest of the day? Read from her Bible? Pray in her special room? Not today. Go to church? Unlikely. Tracy praised the Lord seven days a week; Sunday was just another day to her. Besides, she didn't like being jammed in with God's lesser children, those who would never be her equal when it came to sacrifice and devotion. Should she clean the house? No, it was clean enough. Take a walk? Why not? To waste such a gorgeous day would be sacrilegious. So after a hearty breakfast — more than Tracy normally ate in an entire day — and a bubble-bath, she put on black jeans, white tennis shoes and a pink sweater and headed out the door at 7:45. She got back a little passed ten.

Tracy dozed on the sofa with her Bible laid open across her chest. A frantic series of *Ding-dong! Ding-dong! Ding-dong!* chimed her bells. Then followed a series of *Pound! Pound! Pounding!* on the front door. Someone outside sure wanted to get inside in a big hurry. Tracy figured it had to be monkey man beating on her door in a blind monkey rage, and jumping up and down and screeching.

Make my day, John. Make my day, she thought as she got off the sofa to answer.

Tracy opened the door and there stood an outraged John looking like someone had stolen all of his bananas. Christine stood behind him looking scared and fearful of what her crazy live-in might do. If she only knew what Tracy was capable of she'd run back into her house and leave the hairy beast to his own fate.

Christine spoke first: "Sorry to bother you, Tracy, but—"

"Shut up, Chris!" To Tracy, "It was you, wasn't it?

"Me? What are you talking about, John?"

"My jockey! His damn head is smashed to pieces!"

True. Twenty yards from where Tracy had fired the fatal shot, a lawn jockey stood with his head blasted to bits.

"Don't talk to her like that, John," Christine said. "She's a lady."

"Lady? She's no lady!" He turned to Tracy: "What did you do? Bash it in with a bat?"

If you only knew. "I don't own a bat. Sorry John."

John Panfino was beginning to take on the color of an eggplant. The calmer Tracy was the more deeply purple he got.

"It must've been kids from the neighborhood," Christine pleaded with John.

"No, it was her!" he replied, pointing a hairy knuckled finger in Tracy's face.

"I'm truly sorry for your tragic loss, John," Tracy said, savoring the phony sweetness in her voice. She began to close the door, but John's hand and foot impeded its progress.

If you ever expect to climb a tree again — "You'd be wise to remove yourself from my door step, John."

"Whadda ya gonna do about it?"

Tracy's right foot shot straight up, catching John in his pill box. Eyes wide, mouth hung open, and holding his precious pouch, John coughed, groaned, and fell onto his side.

Stunned, Christine looked down at John, then at Tracy, and then back at John.

"I *did* warn him." Then she added, "Have a blessed day, Christine." A smiling Tracy closed the door.

Christine Devito and John Panfino were ready for an early start to the next Halloween. They had a headless jockey; now all they needed was a matching headless horseman. Perhaps a headless horseman riding an El Toro lawn mower?

Chapter 12

Prayers From Hell

Larry's consciousness awakens amid a swirl of bright colors: red, green, blue, silver and gold. In the background he hears merriment, festivity, and Christmas carols, all in surround-sound. It's a party! Larry Schmetterling finds himself at a birthday party for the Lord! He feels like a little boy again; his spirit is aglow. He has always loved Christmas and celebrated both its religious and secular aspects: joy to the world and jingle bells; Santa and toys; the most wonderful time of the year. He thinks back to Matty's electric trains running around a tree and many presents covered in beautiful gift wrap.

Like that bus ride with Sonny the sensations he feels are tangible. But unlike the ride where he was *on* the bus, Larry isn't *in* the party; he's an observer, an observer watching his living self. It's like watching a movie he's seen before: the sights and sounds of this gala have been taken from an actual event that comes from Larry's past. To experience it again, even as a watcher, is a blessing.

The buffet served at the Focus on God's Grace (FoGG) for the staff's annual Christmas party is plentiful and excellent. But there's no liquor being served, not that that matters to Larry's living self. What does rile Larry of the Black Hole, though, is when the soundtrack changes. Christmas carols have been replaced by bland religious music blasting glory to God on a CD and sung by those who can't make it in the real recording industry. Whenever forced to listen to this dreck Larry would imagine Jesus, seated at the right of the Father, with a finger in each ear telling His Dad,

"This is more painful than crucifixion."

Larry remembers that later the supreme beings of FoGG went back to playing really good Christmas songs.

Larry sees the flesh and bone of his former self standing near the buffet table sipping a fruit punch. It pleases him that he's dressed for some serious mingling in a black, herringbone double-breasted suit and white crew neck sweater. As for the rest of the crowd of about a hundred people, the men folk are all in suits and ties: a lot of browns, grays and plaids. For the women it's high-necked blouses, long skirts and low heels. No reds or pinks or floral patterns, nothing that would enhance their appearance. Maidens dressed like old maids. It's not that the single women here, Larry the Living's main interest, are unattractive; quite to the contrary. These women are young, intelligent and deeply spiritual. Their problem is a misplaced sense of guilt and piety that has compelled them to adorn themselves in such a way as to repel male advances rather than encourage them.

Could have used a few daughters of Eve at this party, thinks Larry of the Black Hole.

A little over two years have passed in Larry's post-seminary self. He is now living in Colorado Springs. As manager of FoGG's bookstore his presence at this function is a holy obligation. Larry of the Black Hole watches himself scour this patch of barren ground hoping to spot a rose among the weeds. Then a blip flickers on Larry the Living's radar screen: she's standing by the dais nibbling from a plate of delicacies. Short, a bit chunky, and with long, cinnamon hair that highlights a small, oval face, he guesses her to be somewhere in her mid twenties. Everything stands in relation to everything else, and this girl definitely stands out. She's wearing a black, strapless evening gown that wraps around her curves as tightly as a second skin. The gown's neckline plunges just far enough to remain safely within bounds of what FoGG considers good taste.

Not surprising that high art like her would attract attention. She's surrounded by a pack of the holy hounds from Hell: Larry's male colleagues. The poor woman has become the main course in their feeding frenzy. The FoGG dogs are practically climbing all over each other battling to show how charming, how witty and how full of the Holy Spirit they are. Even from across the room Larry can see polite indifference on the woman's face; too bad those closest to the action have eyes yet cannot see. Larry's living self decides to hang back. When the pack moves on, he'll move in. Unfortunately, as soon as one hound drops off the chase, another takes his place. Looks like the poor girl will carry an entourage all night.

Larry watches his living self toss his plastic cup into the trash. *This is where I'm about to make my move — with a little help from a friend.*

Instead of the hounds from Hell being scooped up in the hands of the Almighty and cast into the sea, Larry the Living's silent prayer, the most uptight and un-cool black man he has ever known, Curtis Frothe, joins the fray. Although Larry is friendly with nearly everyone at FoGG, he has only one real friend there: fellow New Yorker Curtis. When the girl spots Curtis it's as if she's found a personal savior. She slips her arm into his. Now that the territory has been clearly marked, one by one, the FoGG dogs slink away until it's only Curtis and the girl.

Larry resumes his forward progress. Walking towards them with his hand extended in greeting, Larry says in his friendliest New York accent, "Curtis, how'a'ya?"

After exchanging pleasantries, Curtis smiles and says, "Larry, I'd like you to meet my, uh — Karen Stone." Curtis' hesitation speaks volumes:

the man is unsure of the exact nature of his relationship with this woman, a good sign.

The woman offers her fingertips to Larry as if too much physical contact between herself and the people at this party will infect her with religious cooties. Instead, Larry wraps both of his hands around hers: "Pleased to meet you, Karen."

"Nice to meet you, too," she says, slipping free. Larry gets the same polite indifference she gave the low-dogs. Before he can say anything charming, Karen whines to Curtis, "Can we leave now? Please?"

"In'a minute." Then he tells Larry, "Karen has just been laid off from Safeway. She's looking for a job. Didn't you tell me you have an opening at the bookstore?"

"Yes we do." An opening provided by Mr. Frothe that Larry slinks through. "Here's my card, Karen. Why don't you give me a call, and we'll set up an interview."

Another polite smile followed by a flaccid, "Thank you."

Suddenly the bright lights of Christmas Past go out. The party might be gone but Larry's consciousness remains. Then the stage lights comeback on, and the black hole has been reconfigured into a tiny, windowless room; his office in the rear of FoGG's bookstore. Jammed into this cramped space are a gray metal desk and two matching chairs. Larry of the Black Hole sees himself seated with his back squeezed up against an off-white wall. Karen sits across from him her back to the door. Her body language says that she is in a hurry to be somewhere else. On either side of the desk are olive green metal bookshelves. To Larry's left, unopened cartons of books are piled one on top of the other, rendering the aisle impassable.

Spent over a year in that hellhole; guess it was a prelude to spending all eternity in this hellhole.

Karen Stone and Larry are chatting, but their voices are muted. Then

Larry of the Black Hole hears himself clearly ask, "So Miss Stone, where do you see yourself in five years?"

An unimaginative question that rolls Karen's eyes in their sockets: "Certainly not here, Mr. Schmetterling. Sorry to be so blunt, because I really do appreciate this interview, but I don't feel I'm the right person for the job." She stands and extends a small delicate hand.

Her hands were the only soft thing about her.

Instead, Larry motions for her to sit another minute. "I appreciate your honesty, Miss Stone." He lowers his tone: "A rare quality around here." Upping the volume again, "Curtis tells me that you really need the job, so why don't you just accept the position until something better comes along? And I promise I won't allow anyone to attempt to convert you."

"How much does the job pay, Mr. Schmetterling?"

"$10.00 an hour."

"Geez! How are people expected to live on that?"

"The people, who pay these wages, Miss Stone, don't particularly care; building up treasures in Heaven and all that."

"There is no Heaven," she says, staring him straight in the eyes, almost daring him to proselytize.

"I myself only make a few dollars more than that, and I'm the manager." Larry's frustration with FoGG extends far beyond a minimal wage.

Obviously, Ms. Stone senses this because she asks, "Where do *you* see yourself in five years, Mr. Schmetterling?"

He grins. "Like you, Miss Stone, I expect it will not be here."

"In that case, I'll be happy to take the job. And thank you, Mr. Schmetterling."

"Good! Please call me Larry."

"OK, Larry. You can call me Karen."

Sealing the deal, they shake on it; this time he gets an entire hand to clasp instead of merely fingers.

"I don't mean to pry, Karen, and it certainly has no bearing on your work here, but you're an atheist, aren't you?"

"Yes. I don't believe in God or religion. If you began with the first two Stones swimming in the primordial soup and totaled the religious fervor in every generation since, I doubt if you'd have enough to fill a thimble."

Larry laughs. "Then why the close friendship with Curtis?"

"Because he's a kind and sweet man… When can I start?"

They agree on the next day.

"One more thing," Larry says. "You're not from New York, are you?"

"No, I'm from Pittsburgh. People make that mistake all the time." A puzzled look, then she adds, "I don't know why."

You had a certain attitude, dear, thinks Larry of the Black Hole.

Suddenly the stage lights in Larry's theater of mind go dark. Alone once again, he feels a searing, white-hot pain. In desperation, he conjures up memories of Karen Stone and Curtis Frothe hoping to relieve the agony.

Larry remembers how carefully he had observed the unfolding Frothe-Stone drama from a discreet distance. Whenever a forlorn Curtis would come to him and complain that he just didn't understand women, Larry would say, "They're a mystery, Curtis."

I'm dead, and they're still a mystery to me, not that it matters anymore.

Then Curtis confessed, "We've been sleeping together for months. Then one day she tells me we're getting too involved. What the heck is that supposed to mean? We're sleeping together! How more involved can two people be?"

Guess I liked him so much because he kind of reminded me of me — or rather how I used to be.

After an inability to imagine Mr. Spreadsheets and Miss Hard As A Petrified Rock as a couple, Larry told his naive friend, "For some people sex doesn't always have to have a deep spiritual meaning."

"Does for me! I know this is going to sound absurd, Larry, me being a guy and all that, but I feel used."

Larry could only commiserate with his friend. As for Miss Stone, clearly she and Curtis could never be a serious item.

"You think she has commitment issues, Larry?"

"I don't know her well enough to say, Curtis. My suggestion is that you confront her once and for all and tell her how you really feel."

And so Curtis did. Soon thereafter the curtain finally fell on the Frothe-Stone soap opera.

"I'm going back to Long Island," a depressed Curtis told Larry. "I'm gonna stay with my… I'm gonna stay there for a while."

Curtis' leave of absence filled all the young old maids who tilled the barren fields of FoGG on behalf of the Lord with both hope and sadness. Sadness that he'd be leaving and might never come back, and hope that if the tall, dark and handsome Mr. Frothe did return, he'd be eligible again.

Working closely together every day at the bookstore Larry's lust for this woman grew. She often wore skirts to work, which would prompt him to ask, "Karen, would you mind putting these books on the top shelf?"

With a teasing smile, she would say, "Of course not, Larry." Then she would carefully ascend the stepladder and, balanced on one foot, she would stretch, allowing his hungry eyes a leisurely stroll along every angle on her fully extended five-foot three-inch body.

Certain naughty thoughts regarding him must have filled her dance card as well, because, when her eyes waltzed with his, she'd say, "Larry, would you mind putting this box in the corner. *It's so heavy*."

Broadening himself, "Of course not, Karen." Then, no matter how heavy, or how low his testicles dropped, he'd try to lift the box as if it was a feather.

Haunted by his love for Bérénice, instead in Karen Stone Larry would find exactly what he needed in a woman: looks, an ttitude, and all for the short haul.

Curtis' trip back home lasted a full six weeks. Despite Larry's pledge not to, he and Karen had become one flesh in practice if not in fully sanctified theory: secretly, the happy couple had set up good housekeeping together in a tiny apartment off Nevada Avenue.

Finally, Mr. Columns & Rows found out about their unholy living arrangements. So did everyone else, by the way, a fact the righteous pragmatists of FoGG chose to ignore. Why jeopardize their cheap labor supply because of the sin of fornication? Curtis kept his anger inside, but not hidden so deep that Larry and Karen did not notice his bottle cap fizz whenever they approached. Curtis appeared to dive deeper into his accounting work, all the while trying to balance his own books. He spoke to the two people who had betrayed him only when necessary.

Months passed, and then one day Larry approached Curtis with an offer: "Karen and I are going off on our own to establish a new church, Curtis. We need a Chief Financial Officer. We'd like that CFO to be you. We're offering you an equal partnership. So whadda'ya say?" Larry offered his hand.

Curtis stared for a moment. Then they shook on it. "Jesus tells us to forgive, Larry. I forgive you and" — a far more begrudging — "*her*."

The pain that has filled Larry's black hole is finally gone. This leaves him in a more charitable mood; instead of blaming his eternal damnation on them — after all Karen had corrupted his body, and Curtis had given him a bite of the poison fruit from the Tree of Greed — Larry prays for their souls:

Hope You turned their lives around, Lord, and they did not end up in a place like this.

As Larry fades away again, he wonders: *Does the Lord hear prayers from Hell?*

CHAPTER 13

A Midnight Cowboy Comes to Call

First one up, first one in: on this particular Sunday morning that meant Howie had first crack at the bathroom. While he waited, Frank took out the preliminary report Karla had written up about Karen Stone and Curtis Frothe, the two most likely to succeed should the Reverend Schmetterling fly away to heaven.

Frothe's driver's license photo showed a mousy accountant: age thirty-three; height six-foot one-inch, weight one-fifty-five; and eyes, hair and complexion, all brown; mixed race no doubt. As for Stone, she looked kind of cute. A bright eyed and perky smile, she looked like getting her picture taken at Motor Vehicles had been the highlight of her day. With cinnamon hair and bronze streaks ala Ms. Clairol, at twenty-nine, short and a wee bit plump, she looked more like a sidekick than a statuesque leading lady.

A flushing sound thundered from the bathroom. Howie came out fully clothed and carrying folded pajamas under his arm. He walked over to the bureau and deposited them in the top drawer. He sat down on his neatly made-up bed with crisp navy corners.

"Where you wanna go for breakfast?" Frank asked.

Howie thought for a second. "Pancakes at IHOP."

"OK." Frank tossed the reports onto Howie's bed and gathered up his own toiletries. "Safe to go in there?"

Howie grinned, but Frank went in anyway. Howie had left behind a foul cloud of Tex-Mex that could choke a colony of cockroaches. Holding his nose, Frank turned on the fan and sprayed the tiny room with air freshener. Then he opened the window to let the stink out. When he came out of the bathroom to wait while the smell-be-gone worked, he saw Howie propped up against the headboard with one leg crossed over the other. He was reading Karla's report.

Frank sat down on the edge of his own bed. "What do you think of this lady detective? I think she's up to something. Broads like that don't go all out for guys like me."

Howie shrugged. "Maybe she's got no taste. That ex-husband of hers sounds like a real piece 'a work. You gotta be an improvement on that clown."

Came a tap, tap, tapping on the front door.

"Get that, will ya," Frank said, as he headed for the bathroom. After last night's wimp-out, he needed a few minutes alone to compose himself before facing Karla again. From inside the bathroom, he heard the front door open and Howie greet Detective Libbee.

"You figure them for our main suspects, too, huh?" said Howie.

Before Karla could answer, Frank burst out of the bathroom. "Did you check their whereabouts at the time of the shooting?"

"I verified that both of 'em were in town when Pastor Larry got shot."

The brows in Frank's mind's eye furrowed: *She called him Pastor Larry not Reverend Schmetterling or the vic. Does she know him?*

Howie said, "Still doesn't mean nothing. Could'a been a hit for hire; we get a lot of 'em back in New York."

“We get ‘em here, too, but I bet they cost a lot less.”

If she was still pissed about last night, it didn’t show. Her body language suggested she was more disappointed than angry. Karla must’ve been one of those women whose outer layer had been case-hardened by a whole string of inadequate men. The way Frank figured it, that made it a little easier for him to get away with acting like a wimp last night.

Frank said, “Read your report on Stone and Frothe, Karla. You’re gonna be a big help to us out here.”

She smiled, then, “Let’s get going. I was brought up not to be late for church.”

“OK, but me and Howie haven’t had breakfast yet. Let’s grab something on the way.”

When Howie mentioned IHOP, Karla said there was one on the way. When Frank announced that breakfast was on him, that sure snapped some wide in Howie’s eyes.

Karla drove them north on I-25. The cool, dry, piney-peppery-sage air that blew in from the open car windows smelled a hell of a lot better than the car stink of Queens. Frank rode upfront with Karla in a clean white CSPD cruiser with blue trim and lettering. Unlike on the plane out here, he was enjoying the sights. To the left stretched an unbroken string of gray, jagged snow-capped peaks, and to the right lay a vast flatness dotted with patches of upscale housing developments and fenced in rangeland sprinkled with brown cows. They were headed for Monument, a town about 20 miles north of Colorado Springs. There lay the home of His Holy Tabernacle.

When Karla pulled into a parking lot of a three-store shopping mall, Frank expected to see a steeple. “So where’s this church?” he asked.

Karla nodded towards the mini-mall. “It’s in the basement.”

“You gotta be kidding,” he mumbled, getting out of the cruiser.

Karla glanced at her watch. “Service should be just about starting.

Shall we?"

"I'll wait in the car," Howie said.

They headed towards the mall and Karla asked, "What's with your bud?"

"He's Jewish. He takes them things very seriously. He'll only set foot in a church for a funeral or a wedding."

"I see. When was the last time you went to church, Detective Giavone?"

"When I got married, about twenty years ago; didn't know Howie then, so he wasn't there." He noticed that all three stores in the mini-mall were closed. "So how do we get to the basement?"

"There's a stairway 'round back. Follow me."

As they clanked down the metal stairs, Karla had to walk carefully to avoid catching her spike heels in the wire mesh. Following discreetly behind her, Frank noticed that those heels, though probably uncomfortable, sure did fine tune her calves. Although raised in the tradition of stone cathedrals named St. Something-Or-Other, Frank knew he shouldn't be thinking these things in a church, even one squirreled away in a basement below a Pizza Hut, a hair salon and a feed store. He did his best to corral those naughty thoughts regarding Karla, but like stallions on the prairie, they free-ranged in his mind.

They were both dressed in their Sunday best: Karla in a tight, gray flannel suit with a short skirt; and Frank in a navy sports jacket, a yellow dress shirt and a blue knit tie, and gray slacks. At the front door, he stretched to reach over the top of Karla to hold it open for her. In heels, she was taller than him. She smiled at the gesture. Inside, it was standing room only. He and Karla took up positions by the door.

From the pulpit, Karen Stone said, "Instead of a service, and because of the absence of our beloved Pastor Larry, Mr. Frothe has suggested that we offer up silent prayers for his recovery. Let Him hear our prayers," she implored, her short arms reaching out to those assembled, "so He will give Pastor Larry back to us."

Rolling her eyes, Karla whispered to Frank, "Spare me."

"When was the last time you were in a church, Detective Libbee?"

"A week ago, right here."

"Feel any closer to God?"

"Not in this place."

Someone shushed them.

"Howie's not gonna be happy," Frank whispered to Karla. "The pizza place is closed."

"He sure eats like a horse. Maybe he should try the feed store."

"It's closed, remember?"

Karla stifled a giggle.

Meanwhile, an emotional Karen told the congregation they could stay as long as they liked. She and Mr. Frothe would wait outside. Karen and Curtis walked up the center aisle. As they passed Karla made a move to follow, but Frank stopped her. "Hold up. Let's wait until more parishioners are outside. I wanna put the grab on them in front of their people."

Twenty minutes later the pews began to empty. At first a trickle, like no one wanted to be the first to leave. Then a flood of bodies poured through the gray metal, double-doors and up the stairway. Frank and Karla let themselves be carried along with the tide. They headed back to the front of the stores and woke up a snoring Howie in the cruiser. Karla drove them around back to within twenty feet of where Karen shared condolences with the rest of the congregation. Curtis Frothe stood solemnly at her side, head bowed. When Frank, Karla and Howie got out of their vehicle, they drew nervous stares from Stone and Frothe, and curious ones from everyone else. Rather than hanging around,

Karen and Curtis headed for her cherry red BMW. As they were about to get in, the detectives made their move; Karla led the way. She walked up to Karen and flashed her badge in the other woman's face. Then she introduced Detectives Giavone and Goldberg. Curtis stood on the other side of the car, waiting for Karen to hit the power locks. Howie, meanwhile, moved behind him and placed his hand firmly against the small of Curtis' back. The guy's eyes widened and the color in his face grew paler and paler. He looked like a cup of java filling too fast with too much cream.

A small, angry crowd gathered about twenty yards away. The people started to move closer, but Karla imposed her imposing self between Karen, Curtis, and the faithful. "Police business, people, move along."

The mob headed back to their assorted SUVs, pickups, mini-vans, and Cowboy Caddies.

"We know this is a bad place to talk, Ms. Stone, Mr. Frothe," Frank the charmer began, "but we got some routine questions we'd like to ask. We'd rather do this in your office at the Antlers Doubletree tomorrow morning at nine. Is that a problem?" Not much of an inflection at the tail end of Frank's sentence, so it hardly qualified as a question.

"Uh — I have an appointment tomorrow morning. Perhaps we could, uh…" Then Stone pushed out one of her perky smiles: "Perhaps we could meet later in the afternoon?"

The detectives decided that was not acceptable. Karla suggested to Frank and Howie, "Maybe we should just take 'em in right now?"

Judging from Frothe's pinched-vise expression, being questioned in a police station by three big, mean detectives put him in a crack. "I think you should cancel your appointment, Karen." Then he began to rub the mole on his left cheek, just below the corner of his eye. Running his fingers over it must've given Frothe a sense of security.

Karen, who showed an intimate knowledge of Mr. Frothe's body language, reluctantly agreed.

In the car on their way back to Colorado Springs, Frank noted, "That Frothe guy, did ya see how pale he got when Karla shoved that badge in their faces. Didn't know a black guy could turn so white so fast."

"He's the weak link," Karla added. "I say we lean on him. He'll talk."

***

Monday morning, across town in an omelet parlor, Frank and Howie were polishing off a hefty breakfast of steak, eggs, and pancakes. Karla had a bowl of granola and a grapefruit. The two NYPD detectives had already decided that they should all be deliberately late for their appointment with the primary suspects. Unlike steaks, which tended to get tougher the longer they cooked, with people the opposite was true. Time was on their side, so even after Frank and Howie had finished inhaling their food, the Double G's just sat back and relaxed.

Karla shook her head and grinned. "You boys from New York *are* bad. How would y'all like to come over to my place for dinner tonight? We c'n watch my *Seinfeld* DVDs."

"My favorite show," Frank replied. Turning to his partner, "We'd love to, wouldn't we, Howie?" The way Frank figured it, Detective Libbee was up to something, and he wanted Howie there to help him get a read on her; two heads better and all that. But this time, Howie missed his partner's drift. He politely declined. Damn!

A little past noon, the detectives finally arrived at the office suites of the HHT Holding Group. Frank took the blame for them being late. Then, recognizing the suspects East Coast accents, he played up their common roots. That seemed to relax Curtis, who mentioned he was from Babylon on Long Island. All that down home, folksy chat did nothing to smooth Ms. Stone; she held her sharp edge. When she sat down behind her desk, she invited the detectives to pull up chairs. Only Frank and Howie, with big loads on their feet, did. Karla remained standing; so did Curtis. Nervous once again, he began to sway from side to side and rub the mole on his cheek.

"So what is it you want from us, detectives?" Karen said, her tone impatiently hostile.

Frank looked around the room, slowly taking in the decor. The suite held two other offices that belonged to the HHT Holding Group. This one, though, clearly had been the territory of the head honcho himself, Pastor Larry. It had a deep pile beige carpet, a huge cherry wood desk and an oak computer work station pushed up against the wall. He thought it weird that in the office of a preacher there were no crosses or holy pictures on the walls.

Howie said, "Real plush, you people must be doing real good."

Added Frank: "Didn't know there was so much money in religion." To Howie and Karla, "Think we're in the wrong business." Then he began a series of easy questions that the suspects skated through.

Then Howie served up the meat: "Did Mr. Schmetterling have any enemies?"

Karen looked to Curtis for reassurance before answering. "Yes, he did. Colonel Stephen Fryd, that's F-R-Y-D. It's pronounced 'fried' as in fried fish. He's a hyper-conservative member of our congregation who has contributed large sums of money to the Church."

Karla, busy taking notes, absently asked, "Why should Colonel Fryd and Pastor Larry be enemies?"

Frank's mind sat up and took notice again. Karla must've been concentrating on writing so hard that she'd dropped her guard for the moment. Once more she referred to Schmetterling as "Pastor Larry." Was Colorado Springs so damn small he figured everybody knew everybody else? He shot a quick glance over at Howie. His partner had to be thinking the same thing.

"The Colonel is retired military," Karen continued, "army I believe. Am I right, Curtis?"

Curtis nodded. Clearly this retired army colonel evoked a degree of discomfort in both Ms. Stone and Mr. Frothe; therefore, it was at the weakest link that Frank aimed the same question: "Mr. Frothe? Why would they be enemies?"

"They disagreed on certain church policies."

"What policies?" asked Howie.

Karen and Curtis shut down, so Karla had decided to kick-start their motors again: "Right now we have a fella who was shot over 1,500 miles from here, and the only people with possible motives are you folks."

That sure put some rev in Karen: "That's ridiculous! Why would we want to harm Larry?"

Frank looked at Curtis, whose color had gone to light coffee just like yesterday. *This guy is hiding something.* A quick look at his partner: Howie was thinking the same thing.

Bluffed Karla: "We know all about the little scam you're running." The detectives strongly suspected a scam, but at this point they could only guess at what it might involve. "To tell you the truth, we're not interested in your business practices. All we care about is who shot Schmetterling. So if you have another suspect…"

Karen and Curtis exchanged glances. Then Karen answered, "Larry and the Colonel had strong disagreements over the direction the Church had taken. The Colonel thought we were leaning too far left, whereas Larry thought the Colonel was to the far right of FoGG."

"FoGG?" asked Frank.

"Focus on God's Grace," Karla replied, "the main competition, right, Miss Stone?"

Karen shot the other woman a snarky, "There's no competition, Detective. We're all here to serve the Lord."

Karla smirked. "If you say so."

Curtis added, "We had two strong willed men, each with a different vision. Larry wanted a church of love whereas Colonel Fryd wanted a church of law. Since the Colonel was the largest contributor to our church and—"

"The entire mall belongs to him," Karen cut in. "We lease space from him… There are those who agreed with the Colonel's position. With their help he mounted an organized effort to have Larry removed as pastor."

"How many agreed with the Colonel, Ms. Stone?" Karla asked.

Curtis answered instead, "We have over 1,500 members. I would guess about a hundred hold beliefs similar to the Colonel's. Of those, only a handful actively supported Colonel Fryd."

"I gather, then, that the Colonel's effort to remove Reverend Schmetterling was unsuccessful?" Karla asked.

No Pastor Larry this time. The way Frank figured it: *She's back in the saddle again.*

"Yes," Curtis replied. "The Colonel may have held the purse strings, but Pastor Larry held the hearts and minds of our people. Please believe me when I say the majority in our congregation are decent, honest, and hard working folk."

"How would you categorize Colonel Fryd as in fish, Ms. Stone?" Karla asked.

"A gun loving, self-righteous, wing nut, Detective Libbee," Karen replied. "I'm sure you already know that the Springs has more than its fair share of these crackpots. Many of them moved here from California to escape crime, pollution and the brown tide."

Said Karla, "Are you saying the Colonel is a bigot?"

"Yes I am, Detective Libby," was Karen's to-the-point reply. "People like the Colonel celebrate diversity in whiter shades of pale."

Looking at Curtis, Howie asked, "So how'd you feel about that, Mr. Frothe?"

Curtis' terse reply: "My father was black, my mother white. The Colonel and I were hardly friends, but I wouldn't go so far as to call him a racist."

"Thanks for your help, Ms. Stone, Mr. Frothe. We'll be in touch," said Karla, looking like she'd made up her mind about something.

Thinking the worst was over, Karen and Curtis visibly relaxed. They showed the detectives back to the elevator. *Ping!* went the doors, opening. The three detectives stepped inside. Then Howie stopped the doors from closing with his hand:

"One more thing: do either of you know a guy named Paul Wicker?"

Frothe admitted the name sounded familiar, but he wasn't sure who he was. Karen said she thought she remembered Larry telling her that Wicker was an old friend from the seminary.

Again the doors started to close; this time it was Frank whose hand halted their progress. "We have it from reliable sources that Mr. Schmetterling was in New York on business. What kinda business?"

Both Stone and Frothe insisted that Larry went to New York to visit friends and relatives. "If Larry had business in New York," Karen coolly assured them, "he didn't tell us."

***

That night at Karla's place, she and Frank had just finished dinner. Frank sat on the sofa in the living room across from the TV.

Karla cleared the dining room table and stacked the dirty dishes in the sink. "I'll wash these after I drop you off at your motel," she said. She came in and sat down next to him. "Let's watch TV," she said, patting his hand and smiling.

Instant hard-on — Frank tried re-arranging himself so she would not see. But they were sitting so close, and she was such sharp cop, how could she not notice? The ball was now in her court. How would she play it? To cover his obvious naughty bit, he was about to ask her why she had called the vic Pastor Larry and did she know him, and then her cell phone rang. Karla picked it up off the end table and read the caller ID. Then she excused herself and went into the kitchen.

He leaned to listen, but all he could hear was mumbling. And then, "Oh no!" When she came back into the living room, she looked like she wanted to rip somebody's head off. "That was my captain. My drunken ex is in the hospital." A flash of fury, "And your partner put 'im there!"

When Karla dropped Frank off at the motel, her tired smile said, *I've been through this stuff with my ex before.* And then she added, "How 'about we try again tomorrow night?"

"Sure."

"I'll pick you up in front at six. I'd rather not have to deal with your partner 'til I'm in a more Christian frame of mind."

Back in their room, Frank told Howie, "What did you do, Howie? I was just about to question her about calling the vic Pastor Larry, and then she gets a call from her captain. If you got an explanation, it better be good."

A relaxed, "It is, so sit and take a load off," he told Frank.

***

Sometime around ten there came a *Thud! Thud! Thudding!* on the motel door. Definitely not a raven; it sounded like some moron was outside pounding the door with the palms of both hands. Interrupting Howie during a *Baywatch* rerun was bad enough. But he had laid all the snacks and goodies he'd been munching on the night table next to the bed. To disturb Detective Goldberg when he was eating was like poking a lion while it feasted. Someone might get mauled. He lumbered to the front door. When he opened up, a tall, lanky man in jeans, boots, a cowboy shirt and cowboy hat glared down at him. It looked like the guy's brain was floating in a skull filled with pure alcohol.

"Hey, pal," said Howie in a none-too-friendly tone, "I think maybe you got the wrong door. Get lost." He was about to close the door but the guy's foot was in the way.

"Ain't neither," slurred the urban cowpoke with the glassy red eyes. "Y'all stay the hell away from my woman, ya hear me, fat boy!"

A balled fist then headed straight for the middle of Howie's face. A fist he easily intercepted. Quickly hooking the guy's right arm behind his back, and then placing his own left forearm in back of the guy's neck, Howie smashed the skel's face into the wall — one, two, three times. Then Howie walked calmly back to the night table, got his cuffs, and shackled the cowpoke, hands behind his back. Standing over the thrashed pile, "I take it you're Mr. Bobby Lee Schwimm, Karla's ex-husband."

The pile groaned.

"Nice to metcha!" said Howie. He kicked the midnight cowboy hard in the ribs. Then he called 911. Let them come and shovel this load of manure the hell out of *his* room.

CHAPTER 14

High Hopes

Like a jet of gas that ignites a roaring furnace, Larry's consciousness blasts into its black hole. Is something new about to be forged? Is his soul the fuel? Is his agony its byproduct?

MAKE IT STOP! MAKE IT STOP! he begs the Lord. Then slowly, the fury inside him begins to burn itself out. It smolders until all that is left are its wisps.

The pain is gone, but a new scene has been forged in Larry's black hole. He finds himself standing at a podium in a brightly lit ballroom. This time he is not an observer observing himself. With his own eyes he sees *his* people! Pastor Larry is about to preach to the assembled body of Christ, the good folks of His Holy Tabernacle. The images are so clearly defined, right down to a stray thread hanging from the tip of his red, white, and blue flag tie. If Pastor Larry is once again in a state of hyper-reality, why is he wearing such a hideous tie? In military towns like the Springs, anything with a flag on it, and especially when worn in conjunction with a cross, proclaims, *I love America! I'm for family values! I'm a warrior for Jesus!*

Larry has always believed wearing one's faith and patriotism on one's sleeve — in this case around one's neck — is tacky and beneath him. That's why he always hated that awful tie. Then he remembers that as soon as he proved himself to his congregation as a true-blue American that tie went to *GoodWill.* But why has this cheap piece of fabric made in China been resurrected to hang around his neck now? Then he examines his attire more closely: a plain tweed sports jacket in blends of brown, tan, and green. His dress pants are khaki; his footwear deck shoes from Wallmans-Shop-A-Lot!

Why am I dressed like a dog from FoGG? My mother wouldn't even dress me like this! I'd rather ride naked on a horse on Academy Boulevard than be seen in public in these clothes!

Is he a paper cutout, a plaything the Lord has pasted these awful clothes on? Has He inflicted on him an especially ugly form of penance? But that can't be. There are no penitents in Hell. There is no hope in Hell.

"Abandon all hope, ye who enter here." Dante's Canto III. I read it in college. In Italian!

So Larry the scholar agrees with Dante, there is no hope for the damned. But what if this hell hole is not Hell? Again Pastor Larry is drawn back to the possibility that his soul is in Purgatory. But there is no Purgatory! He thought he had flushed all that non-Scriptural Catholic nonsense out of his head a long time ago. But if he's wrong, then there's a chance he can get out of here. Maybe if he gives these people something akin to The Sermon on the Mount, the Lord will shine His mercy down unto him? Pastor Larry takes in a deep breath. He holds and releases. Then he looks out onto those assembled. Larry will draw strength from these people. He will deliver the greatest sermon ever told, one that will save his immortal soul.

Directly in front of him is a section of seating: twelve metal folding chairs in each row, ten rows deep. Two aisles of red carpeting — Larry sees the intricate patterns of black, white and gold woven into its rich fabric — separate the center section from two cater cornered sections. The side sections are eight by eight matrices of chairs. Larry estimates seating for over two hundred people. There are even standees against both walls. He has drawn a full house. Narrowing his focus from a crowd in general to individuals in particular, he begins to pick out specific faces. He spots his nemesis, Colonel Fryd, seated in the left rear, side section. He looks the same — well almost. Instead of the sour look he usually aims at Larry, Fryd appears anticipatory like he expects something wonderful to happen.

And it will, Colonel, it will. I promise.

Larry also sees a military couple; both are army and stationed at Fort Carson. The husband is a tall, lanky, good-natured guy who drinks too much. His wife is a large athletic woman. Sullen and cynical, and according to her physically weaker spouse, she hasn't hesitated to lay a few knocks on him from time to time. They once came to him for marriage counseling. After only a few sessions, he told them the truth: irreconcilable differences. Whether they took his advice he doesn't know because they left the church soon thereafter. But they're back now, and Larry is happy to welcome them.

Amazed at the grandeur that surrounds him, Larry smiles; and then he wonders what has happened to the HHT's bargain basement church in Monument? In this new space, colonnades of glowing lamps jut out from terra cotta walls. In the middle of a recessed white ceiling are two monstrous crystal chandeliers. At the back of the room are two sets of floor to ceiling, ornate wooden doors. The room seems better suited for a waltz of bodies moving in syncopation rather than a church service. Yet these souls are gathered here to await the good news as proclaimed by their pastor, the Reverend Lawrence Schmetterling.

No more stalling. Pastor Larry is ready to confess his sins to all. He coughs into his fist. His throat feels as dry and scratchy as Colorado's high plains baked in the sun. Before he says anything, he must first quench a parched throat. He looks to his right and sees Curtis about ten feet away sitting in a chair, a guitar laid across his lap. Curtis will provide today's music, accompanied by two of Colonel Fryd's three daughters: a tall blonde and her shorter, dark-haired sister. Karen calls them The Nasalettes. She stands directly behind Curtis and his backup singers. She's smiling too, but Larry knows that her joy does not come from the spirit. Karen's mind is counting the house and calculating collection baskets stuffed with cash.

Larry coughs into his fist again. Curtis immediately stands up, walks over to a small table and fills a glass with water. He brings it to Larry. Larry thanks him and reaches for the glass; rather than feeling its cool, smooth surface, he feels nothing. He drinks the water. Larry gulps down the liquid but his throat is still dry. He can't taste the water nor can he feel its refreshing coolness in his mouth or flowing down his gullet.

Wait a minute. Something's not right.

Then full out panic seizes Larry when he hears himself speaking words that are in complete disconnect from his mind. Some unknown force has rendered him a woofer and a tweeter listening to a recorded message of himself. And then he remembers that this is not the present, it's the past! The service that's about to begin took place in a rented ballroom in the Antlers Double Tree Hotel in downtown Colorado Springs. He's having another flashback!

A plug is pulled. Larry's high hopes of getting out of this hole swirls down the drain.

"On behalf of His Holy Tabernacle," he hears himself say, "I'd like to welcome you all to our inaugural Sunday service." No longer in control of his body, a force turns his head to where Curtis and Karen stand. "I'd like to introduce our staff: Mr. Curtis Frothe and Ms. Karen Stone."

Polite clapping and smiles from the congregation, a cautious gathering not yet won over. This must be why he is wearing that corny flag tie.

"Inside your welcome packets you were given is the form you need to fill out to receive two free tickets to Mel Gibson's *Passion of the Christ.* A word of caution: While the movie is an incredibly moving experience that no Christian should miss, it's also incredibly violent and may not be suitable for young children."

As pastor of a church that has not yet fully come to pass, Larry has made a huge leap of faith when he personally laid out the money for those tickets: 500 tickets @ $5.50 = $2,750 charged to his personal credit card. But as Larry told his partners, "We're doing God's work. I put my faith in Him, so I'm not worried. Doesn't the Bible say that our offerings will multiply tenfold?"

To which Curtis replied, "I still think free tickets to a movie is tacky, Larry."

Karen's response: "As long as it's his money, Curtis, I think it's a wonderful idea."

My money, my vision, my church! I did everything, Lord, and this is how You repay me!

Larry remembers applying for loans and grants, but his requests for seed money from religious organizations like the Free Methodists and the Assemblies of God came with controlling strings that stretched all the way back to the benefactors. Larry would not cede his vision to outside forces; so the considerable startup costs associated with founding even a small church, $65,319 to be exact, was also charged to his many credit cards.

That's faith, Lord, my faith!

Next came something even more hideous than the clothing he wore that day: the croaking of the Curtis Frothe Trio singing bland praises unto their Heavenly Father.

Now I remember! Curtis and the blonde, they had the hots for each other. That's what pissed her daddy off. I got caught in the middle. Why should I be blamed for their sins?

Pastor Larry can't take it anymore. He must escape from this service, this ballroom, this flashback. By the sheer force of his will the scene is gone; this hole is dark again; but his consciousness still hovers. And then a new torture begins with a song.

***

Far, far away in Larry's latest EEG spike, music played in another level of awareness: *Once there was a silly old ant/ thought he'd move a rubber tree plant/ everyone knows an ant can't/move a rubber tree plant/ but he has high hopes…*

When Larry's father, Mike, entered hospital room 1313, his mother, Tobie, turned down the volume on the CD player.

"Show music again! Geez, Tobie. He can't hear!"

"Yes, he can, Mike! I know he can." Pumping up the volume again, "It's from *A Hole in the Head*, one of Larry's favorite movies."

Mike looked at his wife as if she'd just passed gas in public. "A hole in the head? What's wrong with you Tobie?"

It took her a beat to catch on. "Oh my!" She clicked the player off.

***

Creeping, crawling, they scurry to and fro across the rolling folds of his remains in a single-minded devotion to the task at hand: eating Larry! A new torment infests his black hole: a swarm of ants have somehow breeched his coffin. He feels the stings of tiny jaws multiplied by tens of thousands; the ants have come to take him apart, piece by piece, and carry him off in chunks to feast upon as if he's nothing more than a pile of compost left to rot for *their* benefit. How can this be? Larry is a human being, the most noble of God's creations; only to be murdered, buried, eaten, and finally reduced to excrement out of an ant's butt?

He has always believed that ants (along with honey bees) are the marvels of the animal planet. God so loves the ants that should He ever get so irritated by those made in His image — "Enough with these fools!

Let me scrape them off my plate!" — Humanity will be dumped into the Divine Garbage Disposal and the Garden given over to the ants, the bees and the butterflies. Thereafter, not only would life on earth survive but thrive as well. But here in death, these hideous little creatures have come to deliver unto Larry a terrible vengeance. Thousands of buggers have come to eat of Larry's rotted flesh as if he be a perverse eucharis. What mad theology of the body is this?

Larry's admiration for ants increased one Saturday afternoon at a barbeque in Joel Koyster's backyard. With his jaws working over a hamburger, Larry happened to glance down and see an ant dragging a crumb of bread twice its size across the pavement.

Ants are neither happy nor sad; they simply are. They struggle to survive, not to find meaning in life. Quite different from the complex, uptight church folk now gathered here. Joel and his Japanese wife, Youki, lived in a one hundred year-old house on Wood Avenue. Wood Avenue and its immediate vicinity drew the old money of Colorado Springs. Grand homes on wide, tree-lined streets: it was as if a small piece of the lush northeast had been transplanted to an arid, southwestern town.

Joel, a retired air force general and the father of three boys, had met his wife while stationed in Okinawa. Although an executive V.P. at FoGG, Joel could always be counted on to come through when His Holy Tabernacle needed an infusion of new funds, no questions asked. And every year in late August, the Koysters held a garden party where only the select were invited; including Colonel Fryd, his family, and a few others who shared Fryd's opinions. Year after year, barbeque after barbeque, these people voiced the same complaints about how Pastor Larry led *his* flock. Like the topsoil in the Koyster's English garden, did Larry's tolerance of these CINOs (Christians in Name Only) erode.

Jesus spoke of peace; these people believed their Lord would one day return brandishing a sword. Jesus spoke of justice for the poor; these people believed that the poor were poor because they were too damn lazy to be rich. Jesus spoke of community, that each should have only what was necessary; these people hated socialism and wanted it all. Jesus said that all were God's people; these folk believed that only they had been specially chosen. Thus, after each party, the only time of the year when all the malcontents gathered in one place, it took Larry long sessions of thoughtful prayer before his fertile fields of Christian love could regenerate. These awful people would've turned Job into a psycho-killer. Coincidently, the year of the Great Ant Revelation also happened to be a particularly tense time at His Holy Tabernacle. Fryd had been whining about where church funds were going. He threatened to go to the IRS.

"Go ahead, Mr. Fryd," Larry had coolly informed him. "I have nothing to hide."

Problems with the Colonel paled in comparison to what he was going through with Karen. Pastor Larry was too tied up doing the Lord's work to be tied down to a pessimist like her. The really laborious task would be how to convince Karen that the time had come for her to pack up her rakes, hoes, and other digging implements and leave his garden for good.

Larry was off by himself seated near the grill; around him knots of the faithful congregated in small clusters. Karen stood by the Koyster's Koi pond chatting up an elderly couple she had known when she worked at FoGG's bookstore. Curtis sat on the grass strumming his guitar and singing with two of Fryd's three daughters, the same Nasalettes who always sang with him in church. The short, darker daughter resembled her dad and also shared the same prickliness towards Larry the Colonel did. The tall blonde favored her mother, mother who, no doubt, must be off somewhere sipping rice wine with Youki. As a church sponsored event, imbibing was always done out of sight. Nothing was ever overt in evangelical Christian circles.

Larry sat on a folding chair, arms resting on spread knees and a glass of ice tea on the sidewalk at his feet. He watched the tiny black ant struggling. He picked up the ice tea, sipped, and then chuckled. *You go for it, little girl!* Larry had watched enough nature specials to know that worker ants were all female. The ant appeared to be headed towards a large rectangular cement box where plants grew. The cement planter sat on the ground up against the seven foot high wooden fence that surrounded the backyard.

The Koyster's English garden was carefully organized. Joel had plants in pots, plants on trellises as well as growing things rooted in the earth proper. The grill stood in the middle of a paved area next to the house. A sidewalk extended from the paved area, bisected the backyard and led to a door in the rear fence. Off to the right at mid-yard was the fish pond. Lily pads floated on the dark green surface while beneath, like ghostly shadows, Koi swam.

Sitting by himself at the party's fringe, Larry reveled in his solitude: just him and the ant, who, by this time, had reached a joint in the pavement that, to her, must've seemed like a crevasse. As the ant attempted to drag the crumb across, it fell in and became wedged. To haul it free would take great effort. Was the ant up to it?

Larry was about the reach down to pick the bread out when, "Mind if I join you, Pastor?" The voice belonged to Cindy Fryd; the Colonel's other blonde darling. She was *not* part of the Curtis Frothe Trio. She was the middle child and a junior at Colorado Christian University.

Smiling, "Not at all, Miss Fryd," Larry replied, pulling up a chair for her.

"Cindy, please."

"OK, and please call me Larry. Today, I'm just another guest at Joel's party."

Her smile glowed. She had big blue eyes, high cheekbones and a face that sparkled with the brightness of youth, a refreshing change from that other face he had to look at every morning. Karen's face had become more and more hard set, undoubtedly stoked by the anti-theism that roiled within her. Even her smile was angry.

Cindy scanned the ground. "What are you looking at Larry?"

"Oh, nothing. How's school?"

Cindy, a nursing student, said she'd be graduating next June. After that she intended to do missionary work in Africa. This fine young woman was like an invigorating summer breeze blowing through a stuffy garden party where only those deeply into themselves dared take root. Speaking of which, here came a grand sequoia, Joel to check the grill. His foot was dangerously close to trampling the poor little ant still trying to extract the crumb.

Larry burst off his chair. "Whoa! Careful Joel. Watch your step, please."

Joel looked down and around, confused.

"An ant, she's trying to drag a piece of bread back to her nest. You almost stepped on her."

Joel, never the Buddhist, scrutinized his pastor with unspoken words: *It's just an ant.* "Of course," Joel said, flipping the burgers, oblivious to the ant and its travails.

"That's so sweet," said Cindy, her hand to her heart. Looking down at the ant, "The crumb is stuck in the crack. We should do something."

Larry smiled. Kindness, especially for its own sake, always touched him. "We better not. Ants are delicate. In trying to help it, we might crush it. The best thing we can do is watch and hope it makes it on its own."

The ant continued to struggle unaware that two omniscient beings looked down upon it and admired its valiant efforts.

Joel gestured at the ground with the spatula and said, "Please watch over the meats with the same concern you show for bugs, Pastor."

After Koyster left, the ant finally managed to yank the crumb out of the crevice. Larry and Cindy exchanged knowing smiles. He was deeply touched by a sweet girl and her kind thoughts towards a creature that most people trampled daily with no thought at all. Such a delightful young woman, and then he remembered: *She's Fryd's daughter! His twenty-one year-old daughter! How will it look?*

Not good judging from the hard looks the Colonel now sent his way. But Larry would not be intimidated; he locked eyes with his nemesis. Fryd broke contact first. He turned his glare in the direction of Curtis singing with his other two daughters. Seeing all three of his girls in the company of misters Schmetterling and Frothe soured the Colonel's face like a man whose cherished roses were being doggy doo-ed.

Ms. Stone was none-too-happy either. Her expression sent Larry a text message: *She's too young for you, jerk!*

Not wishing to play any head games with Karen because he knew he'd lose, "Cindy, would you mind fixing me another iced tea?"

The empty deck chair next to him had not even cooled before another butt occupied the space. When Cindy returned holding two ice teas, one for him and one for her, Karen smiled at her and said, "Oh! Is this your seat?"

"No, no, Miss Stone. It's OK." After handing Larry his drink, "See ya, Pastor" she said, and left to join her father.

Karen nodded in Fryd's direction. "The last thing we need is more trouble with *him*. And you'd better say something to Curtis. I don't think the Colonel appreciates his other two daughters taking up with a mulatto."

"Karen!" he replied, his face showed the disgust he felt. "Please don't talk like that."

Adroitly changing the subject, "What were you two looking at?"

"We're watching that ant." He pointed, "See her dragging that piece of bread? They're very good for the garden. Without ants nothing would grow."

"Thank you, Mr. *National Geographic*."

He knew she hated when he watched all those nature programs, and he hated when she watched *Jeopardy* and *Dancing With the Stars*; irreconcilable differences. Meanwhile, the ant had managed to drag the chunk to the base of the cement flower box.

Karen sipped her ice tea and looked down at the ant again. "Why doesn't someone just step on it?"

"It struggles to stay alive, Karen! Why do you want to kill it?"

"To put it out of its misery?" Then she chuckled.

"That ant is more content with its life than most human beings are with theirs," said Larry. "It knows its purpose and how to go about it. How many people can say the same thing? God made us complex. Sometimes we're just too darn complicated for out own good."

"Well that you, Lord," she snarked." To the ant, "You go, little fella!"

"It's a worker ant, Karen. It's a girl."

"You go, girl! You're right about one thing, though, ants *are* a lot like us. Women do all the work while men sit around and yak."

The little lady's nest must have been buried in the potted plant's soil. So, with the crumb locked firmly in her jaws, up the smooth, white concrete surface the ant climbed. About a third of the way up, she lost her grip and the crumb fell. Down she went and took hold of the bread again. And up she went — again. No more successful in her second attempt, she lost her grip and the crumb tumbled down.

"It's too heavy," said Larry. "You should break it into smaller pieces."

"Speak louder," Karen snickered, "I don't think she hears you."

A third, a fourth, and a fifth try with the same results. But the ant would not give up.

"If you'll excuse me, I have a $1,000 contribution from the Wards to attend to," Karen said, referring to an elderly couple, David and Charlene, she'd been chatting up at the Koi pond. "Time to close the deal."

When she left, careful not to injure, Larry separated the ant from its bread. Then he placed the crumb on the top ledge of the flower box. In himself was he well-pleased. But pity the poor ant. She ran in circles, with no understanding of where her daily bread had gone. That a divine hand had reached down to help was well beyond her comprehension. Larry took the crumb off the ledge and placed it back on the ground in front of the ant, which promptly turned and ran away in the other direction.

That was when Larry had his epiphany: *Maybe that's how it is with us? God reaches down to help and we haven't a clue.*

Suddenly a jet of fire blasts into Larry's black hole setting his soul ablaze like an eastern Colorado praire fire. After what feels to him like an eternity of agony — MAKE IT STOP! MAKE IT STOP! — it finally burns off every last trace of his consciousness. All that is left are charred remains.

He is at peace again, at peace in the deep sleep of nothing.

CHAPTER 15

The Voice

Seven billion human souls packed onto this snot-ball called Earth while it spun aimlessly through space and the Holy Spirit spoke only to Tracy Millen? This was what she truly believed, but she dared not tell anyone, not even her brother, Curtis. The world had its own way of dealing with prophets. In ancient times they were pressed to death beneath the stones of ignorance, intolerance and fear. In today's technologically advanced societies, anyone who spoke His truths and carried out His will had to be crushed under the full weight of the psychiatric profession. They were stamped with the Mark of the Beast — *Insane* — and then cast into the dungeons of the damned — *asylums.*

God's latest revelation came to Tracy in early March, when the Holy Spirit had said, *Remember, Daughter, you must love thy neighbor as thyself; thou must bear witness unto them for they are my children, too; show them that my love, forgiveness and salvation is a grace given unto all.*

What about John? Tracy asked, referring to next door neighbor and ape man John Panfino. *Even him?*

No answer.

What of Pastor Larry? He was lost. Did he see the light?

No answer again.

Tell me, please! When I shot Pastor Larry, did I do the right thing? Was it Your will?

Nothing.

Yes, the Holy Spirit did speak to Tracy, but only when *She* felt like it.

***

Tracy loped across Christine's freshly cut lawn careful not to snap another heel. She shot a sly grin at the headless jockey, and then she glanced at her wristwatch before knocking on the DeVito's front door. A smiling Christine opened it. She wore an elegant black pants suit, high heels, and a radiant white jacket.

She looks absolutely beautiful, inside and outside. Thank You, Lord Jesus. She'll find You and maybe I'll finally have a friend.

Turning, Christine called, "Larry, honey. Tracy's here." To Tracy, "He's so excited."

Tracy heard the approaching sound of little feet thudding on the carpeted floor boards; then an excited six-year-old jumped right next to his mom. Christine said, "Maybe we can talk to the priest about getting Larry baptized?"

Tracy smiled a correction: "The pastor not priest. I don't know him personally, but I'm sure that won't be a problem. We'll have it done today, right after the service. Is John coming?"

A disgusted, "No, he's eating popcorn and watching basketball."

Tracy shrugged, imagining John a crackling kernel in Hell's fire with his lidless eyes set in an eternal stare at Satan's big screen TV.

"Sorry to say, Christine, but some people are beyond our help."

Sharply, "That doesn't mean we should give up on them, Tracy."

"You're right, Christine. I'll pray for him." *That he chokes on his popcorn.*

Little Larry walked between his two favorite women holding each one by the hand. They headed for Tracy's little red Geo. After the service, Tracy went up to Pastor Carl to ask if Christine's son could be baptized immediately. He readily agreed. They all went back inside the church where Pastor Carl anointed the boy with oil and water. Afterwards, Little Larry would not let his mother towel him off. He was proud to be a brand new Christian.

As the boy hurled himself into the back seat, Christine wiped a tear from her eye. "Thank you so much for all you've done for my son and me. We love you, Tracy. Don't we, Larry?"

"Yep."

Tracy had never seen the boy so full of joy. She vowed to protect him from all harms to the point of laying down her own life if necessary. He had become part of her. She wondered if the spirit of her unborn child now dwelt in little Larry DeVito. And as she loved the son, she also loved the mother. Woe to any who dared to bring hurt or unhappiness upon this woman.

And that means you, Chimpanfino!

Little Larry would not stop talking about Pastor Carl, a man in his late 50s. Then, with the enthusiasm and determination only a six-year-old could muster, he boldly announced, "I wanna be a minister like Pastor Carl when I grow up, Mommy."

"Of course, honey," his mother said, reaching behind her into the back seat to pat her son's knee. "You'll be a great priest — I mean pastor. You have such a *good* heart."

Unexpectedly, the adoration in Christine's eyes when she looked at her son was like a razor slicing off pieces of Tracy's heart. She thought about another little Larry, a man now but once an innocent child. Had he said the same thing to his mother so many years ago? Had she looked upon *her* son with the same loving pride? Now, as Pastor Larry lay in Death's waiting room, what torment did his poor mother suffer? As if it was walking past a graveyard on the deepest, darkest night of Halloween, Tracy's aching heart dared not stop, look, and listen. Demons lurked ready to pouch and jab at her conscience with pitchforks of guilt and pity.

On Monday, Tracy stalked the floors of *Women's Wear* feeling like a caged animal. Guilt was poking its sharp stick at her through the bars. Uncertainty rattled her usually steely conviction. She'd never doubted her calling before, but then, she'd never been commanded to kill before. Yes, she'd taken lives — her late husband and her unborn child — but those crimes had been driven by the evil that once dwelled within her, an evil she thought she'd left far behind. But when she saw Pastor Larry's terror, hadn't she taken perverse pleasure in that? Feeling her finger on the trigger and knowing she could snuff him out with a squeeze, hadn't that made her feel powerful? Refusing his request for a final prayer, hadn't that made her feel like a god? And when the bullet ripped into his skull and he crumpled, hadn't that felt orgasmic?

Tracy dropped to her knees, closed her eyes, and flung her arms out. "YES!" she screamed.

Late afternoon in the middle of *Women's Wear* was not the best place for an epiphany. People stared. Shoppers slowly began to spread away from her in concentric circles. Knowing the evil was still her shadow companion, she begged the Lord to take it away. And then she felt a gentle hand on her shoulder.

A hushed voice asked, "You OK, Miss Millen?" It was security guard Tony Magee.

He helped her to her feet. She stood up and brushed the dust off the knees of her sky blue pantsuit. Too ashamed to look Tony in the eye, with neither a word nor a glance Tracy walked to the back storage area and punched out early.

When she pulled into her driveway, she saw John waxing his Grand Cherokee. The man treated that damn car better than Christine and her son. He pointed to the headless lawn jockey and called out to her, "I know it was you! He's gonna stay that way, too, to remind you of what you done."

In her bedroom, and before bothering to shed her work clothes, she immediately called Curtis to ask about Pastor Larry.

"There's no change," Curtis said. Then his true feelings exploded in her ear: "I never should've let you talk me into this, Tracy!"

"Me! How dare you!"

When her brother was on the swim team back in high school, the back-stroke had been his specialty. Apparently he'd not forgotten: "No, no, that's not what I mean." Curtis sounded like a man who knew he was about to be caught in the undertow of Tracy's rage.

"I know exactly what you meant, Curtis!" she yelled into the phone. "You were the one who passed judgment. You were the one who said he was evil. I didn't even know the man!"

"I'm sorry. I'm as upset about this as you are. I didn't know what I was saying. Forgive me."

"You mean everything you say, Curtis!" She slammed the receiver down.

Nothing was ever his fault! The whole world conspired against *him*, tempted *him* into evil! Christians like Curtis and Larry were all cut from the same sack cloths. Let the Lord deal with them in His own way. Tracy retreated to the sanctity of her special room. Here the Lord would speak to her. Here He would tell her if she'd done wrong. Tracy laid flat on her back, the cold hardness of the concrete floor pressed on the back of her skull and the heels of her feet. She had not yet bought a soft carpet. Tracy wanted to suffer; she needed to take onto herself the pain she had caused Pastor Larry's mother. Then she remembered that truly penitent Hindus slept on a bed of nails. Tracy, ever the borrower from other faiths, figured if she asked John Panfino to build her one, no doubt he'd be happy to.

How many hours had she stared at the ceiling hoping it would miraculously open and a light from heaven would descend unto her? Tracy felt like an infected wound that needed to be cleansed. All night she prayed and all night she waited for His voice to come unto her and say, *Fear not, daughter. I will never abandon you.*

When those soothing words did *not* come, she finally ascended the basement stairs. In the sanctity of her bedroom, she might be granted a few hours of sleep before she had to endure another day at Wallmans. But the disease in her soul would not let her sleep. It drained guilt for what she'd put Pastor Larry's mother through like puss.

Please Jesus, let me take on that poor woman's suffering that her burden may be eased.

***

You claim he approached you in the bar, a Voice did say, *with lust in his heart.*

Tracy shot straight up in bed. She glanced to her right to the digital clock on the night table, the same table where the little .32 hid. It read 5:47 a.m. All night she waited to hear Her voice. But it wasn't the Holy Spirit who finally spoke to her. It was a voice she'd never heard before, one so foreign and so strange that she could not tell whether it was male or female, devil or angel.

Of his own free will, the Voice continued, *he could've just as easily avoided temptation — are these lies you tell yourself?*

"Who are you?" Tracy yelled out loud.

Isn't it also true that in the car Larry was beginning to have second thoughts? You can't deny that, can you? The man was as conflicted about his sins then as you are about yours now.

"Yes, but he could've told me to stop and let him out. I would've. I would've driven him all the way back to Manhattan and nothing would've happened!"

The Voice laughed. *I don't think so, Tracy. You beg God to have mercy on you, but did you show him mercy? No! He asked you for one last prayer, and you shot him instead. And don't tell me you didn't enjoy the whole thing, either. I know you too well.*

"He tried to trick me!"

Again the Voice laughed. *You speak of tricks. Here's one for you: Pastor Larry still lives. Truly, the Lord works in mysterious ways.*

"Who are you?" she screamed.

You shot a man and there will be consequences, for you and for Curtis.

Tracy grabbed her head. A demon had put a chisel to it, split it open, and jumped inside her most private space. The demon kicked and pounded against her walls. Tracy hurled herself out of bed and ran into the bathroom. Fumbling for the bottle of aspirins, she took two out and gulped down some water. Then, still in her nightgown, she sat in the empty bathtub and wept.

***

From the start, Tuesday had been a bad day. In the morning, before she'd left for work, she called her brother Curtis: a call made at 7:30 her time was 5:30 his time. Groggily he answered. She told him about the strange voice she heard and that she feared she was losing her mind. She knew that although her brother loved her, as far as he was concerned, her mind had escaped the confines of sanity long ago.

"That's nonsense, Tracy," he said. "What voices?"

"Not voices, Curtis, a voice. It implied that what we did was wrong."

"We've both been under a lot of stress. The voice you heard was your conscience. Mine torments me, too. Larry's in God's hands now, Tracy. Just have faith."

"Don't you *ever* question my faith Curtis Frothe!" She slammed the receiver down. "Thanks for nothing!"

The strange Voice followed Tracy to work: *You've given up so much for*

God, dedicated your life to Him, and all you ever asked for in return is for Him to give you a loving heart.

It was Wallmans pre-Easter sale, and Tracy began picking up blouses, jeans and skirts, still on their hangers, from the floor. She moved like the fog through the frenzied shoppers viciously attacking the racks in *Women's Wear.* Lions ripping at a warthog's carcass apart were more delicate. Despite the high-pitched voices surrounding her, all she could hear was that androgynous thing telling her what a mess she'd made of her life.

It's always been within you, Tracy. You're in control. You have to find the goodness that's in you, the love that's in you. Don't expect a higher power to do it for you.

"I don't want Him to do it for me, just help me!" she said, a bit too loud; but when she looked around, shoppers were going about the mad business of skirmishing for bargains.

No one paid attention to her suffering. No sooner had she placed a skirt back on the rack in its proper place, when another hand yanked it away again. The woman, at least two sizes larger than the garment itself, held it up to her torso. She looked at the price tag, and then flipped it back across the top of the rack. Tracy's intent to morph into a new and loving being would be seriously tested today. If she could get through a Wallmans' sale without killing a shopper, then she might just turn into the butterfly her dad had always believed she was.

You've been dead inside for so long you've forgotten what it means to be alive.

Then she saw Tony Magee approaching. The security guard had been spending so much time in Tracy's domain that the staff had begun to talk. Why couldn't those vacant minds she worked with confine their silly chatter to *American Idol* or *Who Wants to Marry My Damn Dad*? Why did they insist on lifting the lid and peeking into her private business?

Eyes down and stare inward, Mr. Magee wore the expression of a man whose thoughts raced through his mind like tiny NASCARs headed for a wreck. When he looked up and saw her, he gave her an insecure smile.

"Uh, Miss Millen... Uh... I was wonderin' if, ma'am, if you'd, uh." He paused, summoning up all the fortitude he could muster before letting the words burst out: "Would ya like to have lunch with me?"

He likes you, is that so awful? the Voice said. *He's a decent man. You could do worse. Damn, girl! You have done worse, a lot worse.*

"Thank you very much Mr. Magee," Tracy said, "but I'll most likely skip lunch today. I'm not feeling well."

"Sorry Miss Millen." Almost bowing, he covered a hasty retreat with, "Y'all take care now, hear?"

"Enjoy your lunch, Tony," she called after him. "And please call me Tracy."

He nodded but still would not turn around to look at her.

Being nice to someone, being considerate of another's feelings, that wasn't so hard? the Voice said. *What's hard is to take a chance. When are you going to take a chance, Tracy?*

As Tony walked away in his long strides, Tracy thought: *A nice man. Tall, trim, fit.* Then she caught herself and shoved those dirty thoughts out of her head: *No, no! Lust is sinful.*

True, Tracy, but how about love? That's what you need, to love and feel love again. Forget God! He's abandoned you!

"You're right," Tracy said.

"Excuse me?" A woman pushing a cart filled with kids and merchandise came up behind her.

"Wasn't talking to you lady!" Then she scurried up the aisle after Mr. Magee and called to the still retreating security guard. When she caught up to him she said, "If that invitation is still open, yes, I'd love to have lunch with you."

Although she'd never seen him wearing one, Tony Magee's face lit up like he'd just stumbled onto a sign that read 90% off all MAGA hats.

Chapter 16

Where the Buffalo Roam

The next morning, Karla came by the motel to pick up the Double Gs. Frank quickly noticed that apparently a night's sleep did nothing to Christianize her mood towards Howie. After a grudging apology for her ex's after hours visit, she did not turn the other cheek. "Dang, Detective Goldberg, did you have to beat on him like that? You cracked his dang ribs!"

Howie, not Christian to begin with, shot back, "A skel throws a punch at me, don't expect me to be nice, Detective Libbee. And he's lucky I didn't crack his skull."

They followed her out to a borrowed CSPD cruiser. Detective Libbee had arranged for a driver. She introduced him as Officer Barry Knuppel, a twenty-something body-builder with a blond crew cut and a big smile. Frank and his partner rode in back while Karla sat up front and chatted with the kiddy cop.

Heading north on I-25, Frank, careful not to be overheard, grumbled to Howie, "That schmuck looks about as tough as the Good Humor man. Wouldn't last two minutes in New York." As far as he was concerned, weight lifters — up, down, up, down, up, down — jerked more than dumbbells.

"I think he's boffing 'er, Frank," murmured Howie. "You got some heavy competition."

When the cruiser pulled into the driveway of the enormous ranch of Colonel S.J. Fryd, U.S. Army, Ret., Frank ordered Officer Larkin, "Stay with the car, kid."

On the front porch stood two pimple-faced teenagers wearing brown T-shirts, camouflaged pants suited for Iraq, and desert boots. They had shaved cue-ball heads, slack jaws, and dull eyes. They appeared to be related. Frank's guess: the Ozark Mountain boys. One held the door open for the detectives while the other led the way to Fryd's office.

Howie leaned closer to Frank and in a low voice, "Betcha mammy and pappy was brother and sister. Didn't affect them much, huh?"

"Give 'em banjos and they're good to go," Frank said out of the side of his mouth.

Through the sliding doors and into a study that seemed as big as a cow pasture stepped Karla followed by Frank and Howie. They had entered the Land-O-Man's-Man, especially in that man's own mind. The study was every bit as grand as the combined offices of the HHT Holding Group; but whereas the HHT's offices favored nouveau riche, Colonel Fryd's tastes ran more along the lines of a military museum. The only piece missing was a knight in shining armor. Standing Army-proud behind a large, cherry wood desk, a smiling Fryd gestured for them to, "Have a seat, please, detectives."

Karla remained on her feet. In the car on the way north, she had insisted on taking the lead in questioning this particular suspect. Without telling Karla, both NYPD detectives had already decided to let her have her shining moment. As far as the Double Gs were concerned, Fryd was *not* a serious suspect.

Although short, five-six at the most, Fryd *did* look impressive sitting there all spit and polish behind a neatly compiled desk. Two flagpoles flanked it. One carried the cloth of the Great State of Colorado, the other the great United States of America.

The Colonel sent a squinty-eyed look in Karla's direction. "Excuse me, ma'am, have we met?"

"No. How would you categorize your relationship with Reverend Schmetterling?"

"Strained; especially of late. I'm afraid I was — excuse me — *am* no longer able to place my trust in our pastor."

The way the Colonel kept eyeballing Karla as he talked, like he couldn't quite place her, left no doubt in Frank's mind: *This guy knows her.*

Bored with Karla's line of questioning, Frank let his mind and eyes poke around in Fryd's office. Slung along the paneled walls were an AK-47, an AR-15 and a Chinese carbine. Also adorning the Colonel's ramparts like objects of worship were photos of Jesus, President Donald J. Trump — who Frank loved and Howie hated — and the Reverend Jerry Falwell. Directly beneath the photos was an Associate's Degree mounted on a plaque from the Nazarene Bible College of Colorado Springs. It was dated June 1963. A Bachelor's from another Bible college in Denver, this one dated June 1965, hung next to it.

When Karla paused just long enough to flip a page in her notepad, Frank jumped in: "That's a really nice collection you got over there, Col. Fryd." Frank pointed to a large glass display case up against the wall and to the right of the desk. In it were a small arsenal of military handguns along with a finely crafted model of a tank and three vintage hand grenades. Most of the other memorabilia were from the Vietnam War era.

"Thanks, Detective, been collecting for years."

"Guess you were quite a soldier, huh, Colonel?" said Howie.

"I did two tours of 'Nam, Detective," Fryd replied. He appeared eager to give one and all a blow-by-blow account of the horrors of war, but Karla, obviously pissed-off at the Double Gs' interruption, interrupted:

"Ever been to New York City, Colonel?"

"Once. On my honeymoon. We flew down from Niagara Falls." To the New York detectives, "We spent about a week there. We had a wonderful time, my wife and I."

"Been there recently, Colonel?" Karla asked.

He chuckled. "Haven't been there since 1988. And if you mean to imply that I had anything to do with—"

"Know anyone in New York, sir?" Karla would not be sidetracked.

"No."

For a guy who claimed he spent so much time in "Nam", there were no photographs of the Colonel taken during his supposed tours of duty. The only picture in the room with the Colonel in it sat on his desk. Next to him in the photo stood a forty-something blonde: tall, well-bred and showing about as much life as a store mannequin. She was flanked by two twenty-something replications of herself, and one shorter, darker and rounder teenage girl. Not only had this last daughter inherited her father's looks, but his warm smile as well.

Thought Frank: *Cinderella.*

"Am I a suspect, ma'am?" Fryd calmly inquired.

"I ask the questions, Colonel, you supply the answers."

"Why doncha tell us about the war, Colonel?" Howie said.

"Yeah, all me and Howie know about Vietnam is what we've seen in the movies."

Karla snapped her notepad shut and dropped into a seat. Crossing one long, shapely leg over the other, Karla's blue-gray skirt was hemmed a cut above her knees. When she sat, the skirt inched up along a smooth thigh.

"Glad to, Detectives," began the Colonel, easing forward in his chair and letting his eyes drop for a sneak peek at Karla's legs. "It was nothing like the movies, I c'n tell ya that much."

While the Colonel blabbered about the horrors of war as he imagined them, Frank figured not all the bullshit on this ranch was confined to Fryd's barns. He and Howie knew a hell of a lot more about the Colonel than they had shared with Detective Libbee. After Two Names had run an extensive background check on Fryd, Frank had dubbed him Col. Kentucky Fried as in chicken. A good laugh was had at the Colonel's expense. Fryd was a retired Colonel, but not from the regular army. He was a retired Colonel from the Colorado National Guard. He never fired a shot at, nor had he ever been fired upon, by foes of the United States of America. As a matter of fact, the Colonel had joined the National Guard back in 1969 in order to keep his butt safely planted on the high plains of Colorado rather than put it at risk in the rice paddies of Vietnam. Back in the mid-sixties two honorable ways of avoiding the draft were a college deferment — the Colonel had already graduated, so his was gone — or by joining the National Guard. A good cop like Karla must've already known all this, so why hadn't she bothered to tell Frank? And what else wasn't she sharing?

Just as Colonel Kentucky Fried was finishing up his personal account of twenty-six months in hell, came a knock at the door. "Enter," he barked in his command voice.

One of the genetic mutations from the front porch walked in and stood at attention.

"Detectives, would you and Miss Libbee care for some coffee?" Fryd asked.

Before Frank or Howie could answer in the affirmative, Karla glared at Frank and Howie as she answered *for* both of them: "Thank you, but that won't be necessary, Colonel. And please call me Detective Libbee.

And please call these men Detectives Giavone and Goldberg."

"My apologies, ma'am." To the mutant, "That will be all;" then to Howie, "Goldberg? You wouldn't be of the Jewish persuasion, would you, Detective?"

A relaxed, "I'm of the Jewish conviction, Colonel."

Equally relaxed, Fryd smiled and said, "I'll bet there are a lot of Jews in New York City. I'll bet there are more Jews in New York than there are in Israel."

"Yeah," said Howie, "and we all know each other."

Howie's snark passed right over Fryd. "I've always been a strong supporter and great admirer of the State of Israel, Detective Goldberg."

"We all appreciate that."

Karla shot an angry look at the Double Gs, and then she asked, "Colonel, we've been told that you and Reverend Schmetterling had strong disagreements over the church's direction."

"I think I know where you heard that, Detective. I can assure you my disagreement with Pastor Schmetterling had nothing to do with church policy."

"It's been alleged, sir, that you tried to seize control of the church. Is that true?"

"That's nonsense, Detective. You make it sound like I was planning a coup." The Colonel snickered, then, "I hate to speak ill of the dead — pardon me, should not have said that — but frankly, Pastor Schmetterling was a crook. And I'll wager his unholy partner is, too."

"Which unholy partner, sir?" asked Karla.

"Miss Stone. For a long time I've suspected, but have been unable to prove conclusively, that she and Larry have been siphoning off church funds."

"Did you ever confront Reverend Schmetterling about your

suspicions?"

"Yes."

"His reaction?"

"He accused me of being an extremist! Darn near called me a bigot, and said I was trying to take over *his* church. Then he pretty much invited me to leave."

"His office?"

"No. The church!"

"Did you?"

"Hell no! Excuse me Detective Libbee, ma'am. I refused to leave the church. I've been with His Holy Tabernacle from the very beginning, and..." Suddenly the Colonel's face lit up and he slapped the desk. "Now I know where we've met, Detective Libbee! At the church. In the beginning. You and your husband were members."

Karla's pale face flushed pink. Then she cleared her throat and asked, "Yes, we were. You were about to say, Colonel?"

"I was about to say that nobody's gonna run me off! Sometimes our pastor acted like he was a dang pope. Suppose that's his Catholic upbringing rearing its ugly head. You were a member of the congregation. Surely you know what kind of man he was — I mean is. I discussed the matter with other members of the congregation who also shared my suspicions. Someone suggested we contact the IRS."

"And did you?"

"Yes, Detective Libbee, we sure did. From them we learned about the existence of the HHT Holding Group, Ltd, something that Pastor Schmetterling never bothered to mention to the congregation. Tell ya something else, Detective." Leaning closer, "If the pastor ever awakes from his coma, he better jump right back in again because the government will be coming for him and Stone."

"Can you give me a name from the IRS to collaborate your statements?"

"IRS Agent Ms. Laurie W. Ballman. She will verify everything I've told you."

"Tell me more about Stone and Frothe?" Karla asked.

"In my opinion, the Stone woman is probably even more crooked than Pastor Schmetterling. She might even have been the Eve who gave him the first bite of the apple."

"And Frothe?"

"A quiet fella," was all he had to say. Clearly Colonel S.J. Fryd did not care for Frothe either. That *might* merit further investigation, but not right now. Frank was getting hungry. Same with Howie; his partner shot him a *Let's Gedadda Here* look.

"Thank you, sir," said Frank, "you've been very helpful."

That not only took the Colonel by surprise, but Karla too. There was a deep intake of breath like she was about to heap a string of curses on the Double Gs, but instead she gripped the seat of her chair, and let out a low grumbling sound. Frank and the other two males in the office found this quite scary. Then, without a word or a backward glance, she stormed out of the room.

Colonel Fryd arched brows, "I live in a house of women, Detectives, so I think her mood swings are biological."

Frank did not appreciate Kentucky Fried's snark regarding Karla. H replied, "I'll be sure to mention your interest, sir."

Without bothering to thank the Colonel for his time, the Double Gs left.

Outside, Howie said, "Even I think that guy's a fucking pig."

"You're evolving, Howe. Maybe me, too."

They paused to let a tractor pass. "I've seen one 'a them things on

The Dukes of Hazard!" he told Frank, who was distracted by watching Karla lope across the gravel driveway in high heels.

"That's some tight skirt she's wearing," Howie mumbled. "Looking good, huh?"

Frank nodded then, "Yeah, good and mad."

As they approached the cruiser, Karla's moody mood turned to excitment. She said, "Tell them what you just told me, Barry."

"I questioned several people, and—"

"In a minute, kid," replied Frank. Then, without breaking stride, he gently guided Karla off to the side and out of earshot of the others. "We gotta talk."

They stood side-by-side about twenty feet away with their backs to the others. "How come you never mentioned that you were a member of that church?" Outside Frank was all business. Inside: *She's been playing me! Making like she likes fat, ole me!*

"It was a while ago," she said, as her eyes searched the ground for a rock to crawl under. "I wasn't a member for very long. Guess I should've mentioned it. Sorry."

Frank, still Catholic enough to remember The Act of Contrition, found hers unconvincing.

"And what were ya'll trying to pull in there?" she suddenly fired back.

"We were done."

"I wasn't! He's our guy. I'm more convinced than ever he had something to do with the shooting."

"Why do you say that? What else you got that you're not telling?"

"I have nothing more to say." She whirled on her heels and stalked back to the car.

***

The next morning, Frank awoke early, even before Howie. Still angry that Karla had held back that she was a member of His Holy Tabernacle, an antsy Frank walked to a nearby convenience store to get a newspaper. Back at the motel lobby sipping coffee and snacking on three packs of Twinkies, he laughed out loud when he opened to the first page of the *Gazette Telegraph's* Metro Section. In it was a photo and story about two buffalos standing in the street, staring at the curb. The mini-herd had escaped from a local meatpacker. Instead of making their way back onto the high plains and freedom, they'd taken a wrong turn and ended up on busy Colorado Avenue, a main drag on the Westside of Colorado Springs. Should they mount the curb and take a dump on the sidewalk or run wild in the streets with the SUVs? The hairy humps were too slow making a decision; the cops came and shot the two fugitives from Pattie Land dead.

Frank sympathized, but only to an extent. He preferred to think that all meat-creatures came pre-packaged in tightly wrapped plastic. How they got that way was not his concern. What was his concern, however, was an article on the front page. When he got back to the room, he felt like putting his fist through the wall. He had let a cowgirl from New Mexico play him, play him good. Howie was a large mound still in bed. His head was covered and he lay on his side facing away from Frank.

"Get a load 'a this!" Frank said, smacking his partner's butt with the folded up metro section.

Howie's crawl back to full consciousness was slow. After rubbing some awake back into his eyes, he sat up and glared at Frank. The curly brown hair on top of his head spiraled upwards in such a way that,

"Hey, horny, read this," said Frank.

The headline he referred to read: "Still No Clues in Shooting of Pastor."

Hundreds of people get shot in New York every day. In a city that didn't give damn about a preacher, religion, or Jesus, what was no news there was big news in this dinky little town where the buffalo still roamed.

"This is why she's trying to steal our case," said Frank. "I don't like being played."

Howie said that was what happened when Frank thought with that certain organ on the down-low instead of his head. Then he stood up and stretched. Before heading into the bathroom, he told Frank, "She played you, now you play her. Call her. Take her to dinner tonight. Flatter her, and then pump her, Frank, pump her hard."

"No way I'm having sex with that broad!"

"I said, *pump* not *hump*."

"Same thing, Howie, same thing."

CHAPTER 17

An Irreconcilable Movie Review

"But the Good Lord, He forgave them that crucified Him," said Mr. Tony Magee.

Doing her best to keep the safety on her easily triggered temper locked, Tracy replied, "He's perfect… I'm not."

"You been cured, right?"

Tracy leaned back in her seat, sipped from her coffee, and leveled a gaze at Tony that quickly caused him to drop eye contact. "The doctors say I am."

At lunch, they sat in the booth of a nearby diner. Tracy had just given Mr. Magee a chunk of herself large enough to make most men to seek the Heimlich maneuver. If he bolted out the door never to be seen again, so be it. There'd be one less complication in her life. A pause while his simple mind wrestled with a fact far above him in weight class. Then, Tony rolled back in his seat and flapped his hands.

Laughing, "You must think I'm 'a dumb ole redneck, Tracy. I'm supposed to think that a pretty gal like you done shot your husband?"

"He was an evil man," she said. "He treated me terribly. It was because of him that…" Tracy could not bring herself to say the word abortion. "I was a very disturbed young woman back then."

Tony nodded and took in a deep breath. Then he closed his eyes as if in silent prayer. This poor soul sought guidance, but as Tracy well knew none would be coming from the Almighty. She would have to do it.

"I committed a great sin against God, Tony," she freely admitted. The murder of her husband was done according to her will not His. "And for that I truly repent. But it's difficult for me to forgive the man and forget what he made me do."

"What?" When she refused to answer, then more to himself than to her, "At least you say you're sorry for what you done."

That was *not* what she said, not at all. The man had ears but could not hear.

"If Jesus c'n forgive them that nailed Him to the Cross, who am I to cast the last stone?"

Tracy felt her jaw tighten and her teeth grinding: another one of these so called Christians who no matter how many times they were born again would never understand that their "Good Lord" was not here to make their lives any easier. He never did it for her, why should He do it for them?

When the waitress returned with the check, Tracy said, "Let me get this, Tony."

"No ma'am. I said it's on me, so it's on me."

Tracy Millen knew the more deeply involved she and Mr. Tony Magee became the more danger to both their immortal souls.

The next day, after her shift and Wallmans' pre-Easter sale ended without Tracy shedding blood, Tony Magee offered to walk her to her car. "It's late, Miss Millen. Ain't such a nice neighborhood 'round here, ma'am."

The neighborhood was quite safe else Wallmans Shop-A-Lot would never have located there. It wasn't late, and she'd parked her car just outside the mega-store's yawning doors that swallowed shoppers, and then spit them out twenty-four hours a day, seven days a week.

She gave him a smile that shined inward and in a kindly tone, "Thank you, Tony, that's so sweet of you."

As they walked together towards her car, his shift was over too, the engine that fed words to Tony's mouth sputtered. On the verge of stalling, he struggled to ask her something. Tracy sensed in him a simplicity that she found quite refreshing. She wished the Lord had blessed her with such an uncomplicated life.

When they got to her little red Geo, he finally said, "Uh, Tracy-ma'am, maybe me and you…" He abruptly stopped, closed his eyes and pushed the correct grammar out: "Maybe you and I c'n have dinner sometime?" When he opened his eyes again, he anxiously searched her face for clues. She would not give him any, so he forged ahead, "I know a nice I-talian restaurant, *Da Vinci*, not far from here. Maybe we c'n have dinner tonight?"

"That sounds like a wonderful idea." Tracy suspected that *The Da Vinci* might be too pricey for a man who subsisted on Wallmans' wages. "But since you paid for lunch, how about letting me pay for dinner?"

Although Tracy knew that a woman picking up the check did not sit well with the traditional Mr. Magee, she insisted. And no one resisted when Tracy insisted.

He held the door as she got in. Then Tracy had an idea: "After dinner, there's somewhere I'd like to take you."

***

Tracy had the target locked in her sights. Then she squeezed the trigger: *Crack!*

"Dang, woman!" said Tony Magee. "Never knew a gal who could shoot like that."

Lowering her weapon, Tracy turned her head and offered him a wry grin. "I've had lots of practice. Remember?"

That last remark ripped the smile right off of his face. She'd invited him to her gun club for some target shooting. For Tracy this was business mixed with pleasure: pleasure to be in the company of the tall and handsome Mr. Magee, and business because she had to keep her shooting skills honed on the chance that she might have to carry out His will again. Then she asked Tony if he wanted to fire off a few rounds with her *target pistol*— Tracy would never let anyone touch something as personal as her little .32 that she kept hidden in the night table next to her bed. But her lust for this man was growing, so the time might come when she'd grant him access to both her .32 and her bedroom.

"No thanks. Don't like guns."

"Thought all of you…" she stopped herself.

"You thought all us good ole boys like guns? No, ma'am. Not me."

"Then why'd you come?"

He shrugged. "Just like spending time with y' all."

Out of curiosity, she asked if he was a Trump supporter. He said no, but he didn't vote for Hillary either. "I just stayed home."

Tracy knew she had severely misjudged this man. When she fired off another round, he flinched. Then he asked, "You've made peace with the Lord Jesus Christ, didn't ya? You're saved, right, Tracy?"

She laid her weapon down, took her protective eye and ear pieces off, and looked at him through dead eyes: "Mr. Magee, I'm closer to our Lord than you'll ever know."

The next evening after work, "I think I'm falling in love with you, Tracy," Tony told her as he walked her to her car for the second night in a row. To his evangelical mind, being in love must've made the lust in his heart less of an abomination in the sight of the Lord. Not so in hers. Lest Tracy ever forget, sex, even as practiced within the sanctity of the marital bed, had for her led only to despair, guilt and ultimately death.

In that cauldron of emotions that stirred in Tony Magee's heart, only their steamy wisps seemed to escape his mouth: "I wanna be with you, Tracy."

By *be with you* she suspected he did not mean kneeling side-by-side and praying together. Tracy certainly had her own share of conflicting emotions that sexual desire caused in those who tried to lead a holy life.

"Sssh," she said, looking into his eyes and placing a finger gently to his lips. "Don't worry. I'll be strong for the sake of both our souls."

He might have agreed with her in spirit but not in practice. She could tell that Mr. Tony Magee was anxious to slip into fornication, and in his simplicity of mind, if the Lord could forgive Tracy murdering her husband, then of course He would forgive him for having sex with a woman he thought he was in love with.

That weekend, she invited him to her home in Babylon on Saturday night for dinner and a movie. Other than her brother on his occasional visits back East, no one had set foot inside her house for many years. Her nerves, normally packed in ice, prickled just beneath her skin. What picture would Tony draw of her in his mind after this? Should she show him her special room? Would he think she looked pretty tonight? Would her cooking please him?

"I don't go to the movies often, Tony. What do you recommend?"

He said he'd bring his personal DVD of Mel Gibson's, *The Passion of the Christ.* "Can't get enough of that movie." Then he admitted that he'd seen it at least five times already.

The dinner turned out to be a complete success: Southern fried chicken and sweet potatoes, corn-on-the-cob, and her special homemade buttermilk biscuits.

"My father's grandmother, my great-grandmother, was from Mississippi," she said. That sure enough put a smile on Mr. Magee's, a Mississippi native's, face. Tracy, however, felt no special affinity for the repressive lands that lay behind the Cotton Curtain. "The recipes for the chicken and biscuits were hers, been in our family for years."

Patting a belly-full of high carbs, "Best I ever ate. What about your momma? Where was she from?"

Flatly, "The Bronx." The finality in her tone suggested that the pale branch of her family tree be of little consequence.

"Tracy, I mean, after all, uh… You are half, uh… white. Sometimes you sound like you don't much care for white folk."

Confusion, "You think I'm a racist?" that quickly turned to anger: "Maybe my mother and I just weren't close!"

"Honor thy parents, remember?"

The simpleton believed he'd one-upped her with a Bible quote. She was about to make a reply that would be like a dagger plunged into his soft under-belly. Instead, she held back her anger and said nothing.

"I know nothing about your family 'cepting that you shot your husband and your parents are both dead. Any brothers? Sisters? Nieces, nephews, cousins you wanna tell me about?"

Mimicking his good ole boy accent: "Not 'a one worth mentioning, y'all."

A hurt, "I may not be the smartest tack in the box, but you got no call making fun 'a me like that."

The look on his face ripped her heart out of her chest and stepped on it. "I'm sorry," she said, wrapping her arms around him and drawing him closer. With her forehead against his chest, she added, "My temper is my burden. I pray for strength every day." Looking up and smiling again, "Let's talk about something else."

"Now how 'bout that movie!" he said, stomping and slapping his knee, a habit that grated on Tracy. "Great, huh?"

Alas, Tracy could not, and would not, lie. This would be the first and last time she'd ever bear witness to such a gruesome flick. "It's a horrid movie, Tony. The violence is far more graphic than need be."

Surprised that she didn't share his reverence for the Gibson's *Passion*, "Thought you said you're a Christian? Don'cha see? It shows how much the Good Lord loves us. How he suffered for our sins."

"Yes, but it said nothing about His life, His teaching."

"Dang woman! Sometimes I just don't getcha!"

That last remark inched Tracy closer to her hot zone. "I don't need to watch a Jesus snuff flick to remind me that He died for our sins. I've so totally committed my life to God even to the point of risking it for Him." *And killing when He so commands!*

Tracy loathed fundamentalists and their warped creed. They were abominations unto Him. These hypocrites who believed themselves God-centric were in fact self-centric. Tracy remembered a woman named Melissa whom she'd known at the hospital. The woman claimed to have found Jesus, thereby recovering her sanity.

Tracy knew insanity when she saw it, and Melissa still played in that sandbox.

"When I've done something truly pleasing in Jesus' sight," Melissa had once confided to Tracy with a giggle, "know what He does?" She closed her eyes, and then with a look that resembled sexual gratification, she added, "Like manna from Heaven He rains chocolate brownies down upon me."

Given Melissa's strange ecstasy, Tracy had to wonder about the ingredients of those brownies. Skeptically, "You mean they fall from… the… *sky*?"

Melissa's eyes popped open. "No stupid! He rewards me by making the cooks put brownies on our dessert menu." With a dreamy smile, Melissa floated back from whence she came: somewhere over the rainbow.

A condescending, "I see." *And they say I'm nuts. Like to put a hole in her face.*

People like Melissa and Tony, and especially dark angels like Pastor Larry Schmetterling, their minds reduced God to nothing more than a man-servant. A wizard hiding behind the curtain called upon to fulfill all their petty needs. All they had to do is tap their red ruby slippers together three times and say, "Jesus Christ is my Lord and Savior; Jesus Christ is my Lord and Savior; Jesus Christ is my Lord and Savior."

As for Melissa, one afternoon, she ran down the hall trying to escape attendants armed with medication not baked into brownies. Thanks to Tracy's foot, down she went. *Crack!* went her head into a wall. That scrambled her eggs even more. Also, *snap!* went her collar bone.

"I stopped her for you," Tracy told the astonished attendants.

Melissa had paid a heavy price for merely being a mere irritant. What if Mr. Tony Magee turned out to be something more? He could inflict a major disaster upon Tracy's soul. What might she do to him then?

She would not let her thoughts meander any further down that path.

CHAPTER 18

Frank's Ladder

Karla had agreed to meet him for dinner tonight. At the restaurant dark feelings lay hidden on the flip-side of Frank's happy face. They were at a cozy booth in a steakhouse off a main drag called Academy Boulevard. Karla sat across from him, sipping a lite beer while staring out the plate glass window at traffic that whizzed by. Either she was on the lookout for escaped buffalo or guilt kept her eyes from holding his. The waitress came to take their orders. Frank asked for a New York cut, rare. When Karla ordered a buffalo steak and lobster, Frank suggested, "How 'bout a cow steak instead?"

Karla smirked. "Guess you read the papers this morning. Despite what you might think, buffalo are dangerous animals, Frank, and we do what we have to protect the public. Besides, things like this are rare; that's why it made the news." She grinned. "Only the Good Lord knows what kinda critters roam the streets of New York."

"We call 'em skels, and they got two legs not four."

Karla cracked a smile.

"By the way, I gotta tell you, you were looking hot this morning. You even had Howie's motor running, and he don't even look at other women 'cause he's scared shitless of his wife."

Karla chuckled, and fanning herself, "My, my, Frankie Giavone all the way from New York City, you *do* have a way with words. I might swoon right here." Serious again, "Why are you and Howie so quick to cross the Colonel off the list? Excuse me, but did you notice the man has an arsenal? He's a dang gun nut."

"Yeah, but did you also notice he's got no stuffed heads on the walls."

"Beg pardon?"

"No dead animals. This guy's big on the outdoors. Camping, fishing, all that stuff. And he's also into trophies big time. So why no dead heads hanging on his walls? Because the guy's not into hunting, that's why. He's never even applied for a hunting license. All guns registered to him are military. And he's a member of a shooting club, an expert marksman, and—"

" — quite capable of drilling Pastor Larry between the eyes."

"The only thing this guy's ever shot is a lotta bull; which leaves us our two original suspects, Stone and Frothe. And did you notice how they tried to pin it on Fryd."

Calmer: "I'm still not giving up on Fryd."

"OK. If there's something there, you'll find it. You're not only a helluva woman, but you're a good cop, too."

"I've been told I was tenacious."

Laughing, "Hey, Karla, don't be using none of them three-dollar words on me. I'm just a dumb New York cop, remember?"

"No you're not. And neither is your partner. You fellas are a lot smarter than you let on. So how about leveling with this li'l ole country gal: what's so dang important that you need to wine and dine me tonight?"

Evenly, "You tell me."

She leaned forward, and with her palms flat on the table, she looked him straight in the eyes and said, "I take orders, Frank, just like you."

"You saying your *boss* ordered you to steal our case?"

Her expression said that he was so far off base as to be sitting in the bleachers. "Course not. I'm supposed to give you and Howie every professional courtesy."

"Yeah, to be helpful but not too helpful." Frank lifted his cop's mask and let his true contempt for the CSPD show. *And Graham was worried about me and Howie being unprofessional.* "What kinda Mickey Mouse operation you people running out here?"

Her eyes were furious, but her voice remained calm: "My Captain told me your Captain was condescending on the phone."

"Boo—hoo! So what? What's that got to do with us? And what's your connection to Schmetterling?"

"Guess I owe you that much. It's no biggie anyway. While we were still in the army, Bobby Lee and I briefly attended His Holy Tabernacle. At my instigation, we went to Pastor Schmetterling for counseling. That's all of it, Frank, except that Schmetterling acted like a total a-hole taking my husband's side."

"What about the Colonel? Why are you guys so hot for the guy?"

"Like you read in the papers, this is a big case out here. Captain Whitley told me that since Schmetterling was one of our most solid citizens, and we have the primary suspect, Colonel Fryd, why should we let the NYPD take all the credit?"

Frank agreed that the shooting of Reverend Schmetterling had its seeds planted here. But not where Karla and the CSPD were digging.

"Me and Howie wasn't gonna cut you out, Karla. You gotta believe me."

"I do but…"

"When you've been a cop as long as I have, Karla, you learn to trust your gut. And my fat gut's telling me Fryd is a dead end. Me and Howie still like Stone and Frothe, but we ain't gonna nail 'em without your help. You with us or not?"

Karla looked torn. "I shouldn't be telling you this, because if Captain Whitley ever finds out, it could mean my job."

"I sure as hell ain't gonna be telling that guy nothing!"

"Keep it down, Frank," she said in a low voice. "This is Colorado Springs not New York City. We're civilized here… Captain Whitley and his family are also members of His Holy Tabernacle."

That sure put an arch in Frank's brow. He reached into the breast pocket of his blue corduroy jacket and pulled out a notepad. Karla eyed it as if it was a dirty diary onto which her secrets were about to be indelibly marked. "So that's why you wanted to wine and dine me tonight."

Frank's motives were far more complex than that. A good looking woman had tricked him into believing he was good looking too. She held the ladder from which he had climbed out of a dark hole and back into the bright lights of feeling alive again. Trouble was she could kick it out from under him anytime she wanted. All this was too complex for Frank's simple mind to put into words, so he gave her the most obvious truth: "Yeah."

Karla hesitated, but only for a moment. When her words began to fly, Frank's pen was hard pressed to keep up with the flow.

"Pastor Larry had an affair with a silly girl who thought he walked on the water," Karla began.

That tied into something he had not mentioned to Karla: the piece of high heel sole they'd found at the scene, and NYPD's theory that Schmetterling might've been with a woman the night he was shot.

"Pastor Larry spent last Labor Day weekend with one of the Colonel's daughters, a girl named Cindy Fryd. He took her to a resort in Keystone, and then, at the last minute, his conscience kicks in, and he tells her they shouldn't do what they'd gone there to do."

"I can see where that would piss her off," said Frank, "but—"

"There's more. They ended up doing their dirty business anyway. His terrible sin was as soon as they get back to the Springs he tells her he can't see her anymore. He doesn't call and makes like the whole thing never happened. So she gets mad and tells daddy." According to Karla, Kentucky Fried pulled Pastor Larry aside after a Sunday service and confronted him. Although no one overheard the words exchanged, several witnesses saw the Colonel beat on the Reverend.

"Captain Whitley was one of 'em who had to pull Fryd off."

When Frank asked if Schmetterling pressed charges, Karla said, no. Everyone at His Holy Tabernacle figured the fight had to do with their ongoing feud about the church's direction. By not allowing the police in, the flock admired Pastor Larry as a man who lived his faith. "The congregation blamed Fryd," she added.

Frank smirked. "People are morons."

"Amen."

Said Frank, "And then Schmetterling gets shot in New York and—"

"My captain starts digging and comes up with the dirt about the pastor and the daughter."

Since she'd been so open with him, Frank told her about the heel sole and that Schmetterling might've been with a woman when he was shot. "Did you check the whereabouts of Fryd's daughter at the time of the shooting?"

A smile began a slow crawl across Karla's face. "She said she was off camping. By herself. Convenient, isn't it?"

A skeptical: "In winter?"

"She said she camped in Florida."

"Who goes to Florida to pitch a tent when they can stay in Disney

Land?"

"World, Frank; it's Disney World."

"When did she go, and how long was she gone?"

Three weeks," said Karla. "And the dates fit the time frame."

"Did you run her credit card receipts?"

"Yep. Plenty of receipts between Colorado and Florida," she said, "but isn't it a one day drive from Florida to New York?"

"We did it once when we were married," said Frank, "twenty four hours of straight driving, yeah. When did you question her?"

"About a week before you got here. We didn't say anything to her dad, though. Captain Whitley is gonna jump on Fryd himself once you fellas leave town."

"Me and Howie are heading home tomorrow night. I wanna question Cindy Fryd before we leave."

Reluctant at first, "This could get me in big trouble with my captain," before she finally agreed: "I'll set it up."

Business concluded Frank had something to ask. But vestiges of his old self, a frail ego that still huddled in a far corner of his mind: *A woman like her: smart, good looking, great cook, gives guys in their twenties the hots — what made me think she'd go for me?*

Then the new Frank jumped up and marched into the open: "The dinner at your place, going out dancing…"

"We never danced, Frank, remember? You want to know if I came on to you to throw you off the case."

Frank let his face answer.

"No, Frank. I like you."

That was when he noticed her left hand laying on the table all by its lonesome. Was she meeting him halfway? If he didn't act now, he never would. For the rest of his life he'd be asking himself, *What if*? Clever, winning words were not coming. So acting on impulse for the second time with this woman, he sent out a feeler. He reached across the table and covered her hand with his.

She slipped away. "But not in that way. Sorry if I gave you the wrong idea."

Frank's ego collapsed and scurried back into its safe place.

The next day, based on the photograph he'd seen on the Colonel's desk, and given his frame of mind regarding women in general, Frank expected Miss Cindy Fryd to be a stuck up snot. He, Howie, and Karla were questioning her in one of CSPD's interrogation rooms. After observing how the young woman reacted under Detective Libbee's intense grilling, his opinions did a one-eighty. She struck him as a caring, humble and honest person; qualities he'd rarely seen in women her age, women hot enough and young enough to think they owned the whole fucking world. Easy to see why Pastor Larry had crumbled to her charms. What Frank did not understand, though, was why Karla clung so stubbornly to her boss' soap opera theory that Fryd had gotten even with the man who'd done his baby wrong. Especially after what Karla had told him and Howie earlier in the day: that IRS Agent Laurie Ballman confirmed everything Fryd had said. Ballman added that part of the ranch serves wayward youths. The Colonel tried to instill some military discipline in them. According to Agent Ballman, "Fryd is a fine fella."

Cindy told them that her affair with her pastor was foolish and childish, but she had no regrets. "We all make mistakes, detectives. I try to learn from mine."

Regarding Larry's preaching, she said, "Sometimes he sounds more like a man trying to close a deal than someone speaking from the heart. It's like he's afraid to challenge his congregation because he's afraid he might lose us. I think Pastor Larry has plenty of room to grow as a

Christian."

Honey, his growing days are over, thought Frank. "What can you tell us about Miss Stone and Mr. Frothe?"

"Ms. Stone I don't know very well."

"And Frothe?"

Cindy was like a runner stuck in the block. Finally, "I shouldn't be telling you this but — my sister Margaret had a brief affair with him. She never told Dad."

That sure put an arch in Karla's brow. "Which sister is that?"

"My older sister," she replied, referring to Fryd's other blonde beauty.

"And how do you think your father would've reacted had he known she was dating Mr. Frothe?" Karla asked.

Cindy snickered. "Are you implying my father is racist, Detective Libbee?" A vehement, "Well he's not! He wouldn't have liked the idea of their dating no matter what color Mr. Frothe is."

When Karla asked her to explain her camping trip to Florida, Cindy said the affair at Keystone had not gone well and had taken a toll on her spiritually. "So like our Lord, I went to the wilderness to pray and meditate."

Karla pressed, and Cindy admitted that both she and Reverend Schmetterling had been so racked with guilt that night that they just could not get-it-on sexually — an entirely different story than Karla had first told to him. He wondered what Detective Libbee thought of this new version of events. As for Frank, he believed Cindy Fryd.

To Frank and Howie, "As Detective Libbee will tell you," turning a glance to Karla: "yes, Detective, I remember you and your husband Bobby Lee from His Holy Tabernacle." Back at the Double Gs, "Evangelical churches like ours preach heavy doses of guilt and shame. It's emotionally crippling, especially for women."

Frank looked at Karla. He just had an epiphany: *That's why she won't sleep with me! I feel better now.*

After Cindy left, Frank said to Karla, "If your captain still wants to waste his time with her, that's his business. What about you?"

Her jaw tightened; Karla exercised her right to remain silent. Then she excused herself to go attend to some local police business.

"Maybe there're some more buffalo on the loose," said Howie, grinning. "So? You bang her last night or what?"

Frank exercised *his* right to remain silent.

Chapter 19

Good/Evil...God/Devil...Same/ Different Name

After interviewing Cindy Fryd on Thursday, February 22nd, Frank and Howie left Colorado. The next morning, Friday, Frank told Captain Graham: "We've narrowed it down to two suspects: Karen Stone and Curtis Frothe, Schmetterling's business partners."

Another two weeks went by, two weeks where nothing happened except, as regular as a bowel movement, came one phone call after another from Matthew Schmetterling, the brother. None of which were returned; not by Frank or by Howie or by Officer George. Reap and sow and all that stuff: Frank's repeated phone calls to Notre Dame for Paul Wicker's address weren't being returned either. And then came a piece of good news:

Officer Daniel George to Detectives Giavone and Goldberg: "I've been going over the phone logs of the HHT people. It seems that on Friday, February 1st — the day Schmetterling arrived in New York — Curtis Frothe made a long distance call to a woman named Tracy Millen of Babylon. Also, while you guys were in Colorado, they were calling back and forth almost every day."

Detective Giavone to Officer George: "Get us all you can on this woman, Two."

An hour later came the big letdown: "She's his sister," said Two Names.

Detective Goldberg to Officer Daniel George: "Then forgedda'boudit." And with no intention of laying his wallet where his mouth was: "Go order us a pizza, will ya, Two?"

The next day, with time to kill before punching out, Howie said maybe they should go to the hospital to check out the vic. "Losing my motivation, Frank."

At the hospital, they met Dr. Bloom. For this guy, where every day was a bad day, today must've been one of his worst. "I just spent eight hours digging a tumor out of the head of a forty-three-year-old father of four. The operation was a complete success, so I left closure to my assisting surgeons. Then I went to the cafeteria to unwind. And then terrible news." Bloom removed his glasses, closed his eyes tight, leaned his head as far back as his neck could go, and rubbed the bridge of his nose.

The doctor straightened up and let out a long sigh. "The patient inexplicably died."

"We understand, Doc," said Howie. "We just wanna take another look at Schmetterling. We won't stay long, promise."

The doctor motioned for them to follow. Bloom spoke over his shoulder to the trailing detectives as they all entered Room 1313: "A guy that shouldn't have died did, and a guy who shouldn't be alive is." Clearly the delicate balance of the nutty neurosurgeon's universe had been knocked out of whack.

Inside the room, the detectives met the parents again. Frank asked if he and Howie could be alone with their son for a few minutes. Mrs. Schmetterling gave them an adoring smile. "See, Mike, they do care. They haven't given up."

Mr. Schmetterling's smile, although not as bright as his wife's, was every bit as grateful. The poor guy looked completely exhausted. A nod to Frank and Howie, and then to his wife, "Let's get something to eat, Tobie."

After they left, "He looks kinda peaceful, don't he, Frank?" said Howie.

"Yeah, like he's sleeping or something."

Dr. Bloom asked, "Seen enough?"

Frank spoke his frustration directly to the victim: "Let's hope your pal Paul Wicker has something for us."

The detectives and the doctor turned to leave the room, and then…

***

Larry erupts into his black hole with his mind screams its excruciating pain. Flames rage through his soul consuming all. This hell into which he has been damned is far worse than anything the cruelest medieval mind could have conjured. Even enlightened men like Dante and Milton, and Dickens and Marley in their Christmas Carol could never have imagined such horror. How long must Pastor Larry endure such torment? The Lord forgave those who spit on Him, who scourged His flesh, and who crucified Him.

So why can't You forgive me? You died for my sins, too!

And He who is the alpha, the omega, the first in creation, says nothing.

ANSWER ME!

Why does He, the most Supreme Being on high, whom Larry has served, praised, and loved all his life refuse to show His face? Could it be that He is not the loving, compassionate and merciful God Larry has been taught to believe in? Is He the trickster, a cruel deity who hides in the shadows while inflicting grief, despair, and brutality on those pitiful creatures He made in His image?

Come out! Show Yourself! YOU ARE THE EVIL ONE!!!

As the pain increases exponentially Larry carpet bombs his black hole with a string of obscenities, heaping curses and abominations upon God Almighty Himself.

There is no devil, it's You just You! It's always been You. You are the author of Man's suffering! I CURSE YOU!!!

Not even such blasphemies can bring Him out of hiding. Larry's fury rips through his black hole with trillions of joules of pure hatred! He wants to explode in the face of his God and rip His eyes out.

"ARRGGHHARRGGHHARRGGHH…"

CHAPTER 20

The Hunchbacks of Notre Dame

"ARRGGHHARRGGHHARRGGHH..."

The supposed lifeless lump just shrieked! The Double Gs, Dr. Bloom heard it!

"Jesus!" exclaimed Frank, jumping back.

Then Reverend Schmetterling arched his back, kicked his feet, and batted his arms in raking motions like he was clawing at a monster only he could see. Howie snapped at the doctor,

"Thought you said this fucking guy is a fucking Mr. Potato Head!"

Bloom's dark pupils filled the entire space behind thick lenses. "The medical term is..."

"I don't care what the fuck you call it! You said this guy can't talk!" said Howie, about to fling more f-bombs at Bloom. "So how come he's fucking screaming, then, huh!" To Frank, "This is one 'a them What-the-Fuck moments."

"No shit!" Frank seconded.

"Uh?" was Bloom's dazed reply.

"You said he's paralyzed from the neck down," Frank added, "so how did he do that?"

It took a few beats for an astonished Bloom to find his voice again:

"He is paralyzed. He can't even relieve himself without help from a nurse."

The initial shock of seeing his comatose patient kicking and screaming as if this coma was a sack he'd been thrown into passed in a New York minute. Dr. Bloom sprang to action. He called for the nurses and said to the detectives, "I think the patient's brain is swelling. This might be the end of the line for this poor man. Now get the hell outta here!" To the nurses who had just rolled a gurney in: "Get this man to op, right now!"

Out in the hallway, Howie said to Frank, "If Reverend Butterfly kicks it, we'll have the bullet that's still in his head."

"I'll call Susan and Danky and have 'em standby."

Later, Detective Susan Ferro called from the hospital to give Frank the news: "Schmetterling's brain did swell. Dr. Bloom was about to go in and remove the bullet, but then the swelling suddenly subsided. Geez, Frank, it's a miracle."

"So what's his condition?"

"Dr. Bloom said it was touch and go for awhile. He thinks a high fever caused the convulsions and the scream you heard was reflex pushing air out of the vic's lungs."

"No way! I know what I saw, what I heard, Susan. No way that was reflexes. When the parents came running in, I thought the old lady was gonna faint and the old man have a heart attack."

"I'm sure the whole thing was awful, but since I wasn't there, I won't speculate. The good news is Schmetterling is going to make it. He refuses to let go. Life holds on for all it's worth."

Back at the precinct, Frank looked at Howie, seated on his side of their co-joined desks, and said, "Let's get the hell outta here. Let's go get a drink."

"I don't drink and neither do you."

"Let's go eat, then. I need to talk."

Howie grinned. "You buying or crying, Frank?"

Frank glared at his partner.

Making motions of small surrender with his hands: "Ok, Ok, just kidding." Arching his brows: "Guess this is serious."

Frank's idea of comfort food — a hamburger smothered in onions, a large order of French fries, and a beer, light — might fill his belly but not his soul. With his appetite reduced to medium-high, the assault began: one burger gone, one large order of fries half-gone, and one light beer gone with another on the way. He and Howie were in a Greek diner on Northern Boulevard. While Frank's eating machinery moved slower than usual, Howie's happy, hefty meal had already been devoured.

"What'sa matter Frank? Ain't you hungry?"

"It's the case, Howie." He paused to nod his thanks to the waitress as she set a second beer on the table. "It's just too weird. It's creeping me out."

"Me too." Then to the waitress: "Miss… Can I have an apple pie ala mode with chocolate ice cream, please?" Then back at Frank: "Did you hear that guy scream? Like he was in pain or something. But Dr. Jolly tells us he ain't supposed to feel nothing."

"Sounded more like agony to me; if this guy is really suffering that bad then he's better off dead."

"Yeah, and we'd have the bullet."

"It's almost a month already, and we still got nothing. I'd hate to disappoint the parents."

"We're this close," Howie said, holding up a tiny space between his thumb and index finger. "Geez! Can you imagine what Fearless Leader will do for us if we solve this one? Forget the Snot Rocket, it'll go to the crusher, and we'll get new wheels."

Frank nodded. "OK, Howie, you motivated me." And he dug in to what was left of his meal.

When the waitress returned with Howie's pie ala mode, he asked for the check. To Frank, "It's on me."

"Thanks, Howie." Then to the waitress, "Can you bring me one 'a them, too, please."

Howie's stare narrowed its focus. "You're taking advantage of my generosity, Frank."

The next morning, Frank's rolling fingers drummed impatiently on the desk. On hold with Notre Dame, he imagined the scene on the other end of the line: a large, dark room with its high ceiling supported by stone pillars. Deep in the bowels of one of the college's monastic buildings, chants, the kind he remembered as a kid when his mother used to drag him to High Latin Masses on Christmas and Easter, played in the background. Rows of sour-faced monks — round, soft, with humped backs and suffering from permanent constipation — sat bent over tiny desks. Each desk was lit by a single candle. They scratched meticulous notes into dusty ledgers with quilt-tip pens. On one of those yellowed pages inside a musty old book lay the information Frank needed regarding Mr. Paul Wicker. These were the humpy monks who had been ordered by Monsignor Hanifen himself to cooperate with the NYPD detectives.

The Monsignor just got back from sabbatical. He said he's been on retreat in a monastery and totally cutoff from the outside world. When Frank had told him about Schmetterling being shot, Hanifen had been stricken.

"This is terrible. I'll pray for him, Detective Giavone."

Ain't gonna help, Padre. "Wicker's address will be even better, Father." Frank was not one for all that praying stuff; people had been praying to God for thousands of years with little or no results. Either He wasn't listening or He didn't give a rat's ass.

The monsignor had given Frank the name of the head hunchback to contact, and then he said he had a call to make to a woman Larry was particularly close with when he taught at St. Mary's College. Her name was Bérénice Sans-Tache. After he hung up, Howie perked and said, "Here comes Two. And he's smiling."

Despite certain disbelief, Frank figured that maybe a silent prayer was about to be answered. Two Names said that his personal canvass of the Upper Eastside finally paid off. Two bartenders had positively ID'ed Schmetterling. They'd said they saw the pastor sitting with a tall Hispanic or a light-skinned black woman. She'd been sitting at the bar by herself for nearly half an hour, shooting down every guy who dared approach her.

Added Two Names, "One of the bartenders said that she looked way out of Schmetterling's league, but they ended up leaving together anyway."

Howie smiled. "Good work, Two."

Frank looked at his partner: "A tall Hispanic or a light-skinned black woman. Catch my drift, Howie?"

Howie quickly pulled his own boat alongside: "Frothe's sister, maybe?"

Frank, Howie, and Two Names huddled around Frank's and Howie's joined desks. The three of them gulped coffee, downed donuts, read printouts, and made guesses. Frank strongly suspected they had the perps, Frothe and his sister, but the double G's still needed a motive.

Howie to Two Names, "Go back as far as you can with the phone logs, I wanna know who's been calling who."

An hour later, Officer George came back with the information. "No calls from the Schmetterling to the sister. Then I checked her phone logs. No calls from her to the vic. The only Colorado calls she made were to her brother, Frothe."

Howie's conclusion: "So the vic and the sister probably didn't know each other."

"Here's something else interesting," said Two Names. "Other than to her brother, she made no long distance calls. And other than work, she made no calls to anyone. Doesn't even own an iPhone." Two names made a face like Ms. Tracy Millen was a creature from out of the Dark Ages.

"Sounds like she had no life and no friends," added Frank.

Two Names continued: "On Wednesday, the morning of the shooting, she calls Frothe at 2:19 a.m. How 'bout this?" Two Names held up a single finger as if testing for prevailing winds. "Schmetterling is coming to New York, so Frothe tells him, 'Why don't you give my sister a call?' They meet up at that bar, and then she drives them out to her place. But she pulls off at Little Neck Parkway and shoots 'im."

That became the consensus. But Howie put voice to a question that had been rattling around in Frank's skull like loose peanuts: "Why?"

"It's gotta have something to do with the money the church rakes in," said Frank.

"About that whacko sister," added Two Names. "She's got a juvenile record. Wish I could get at it."

"Don'worry'bout it, Two," Frank said. "I know somebody who knows somebody who knows somebody else. I'll get you them records, no problem."

The next day, the gloom and doom that had attached itself to this case finally took a hike. In the stratosphere where Frank's dreams soared a jet stream of happy feelings propelled him through the rest of a glorious Friday. He and Howie had just gotten back from Jersey where they'd questioned the vic's old seminary buddy, Paul Wicker. And Two Names had completed a check on Frothe's whacko sister, Tracy Millen; now they had her. As Frank was about to key in the number of a local pizzeria, he felt a soft breeze rustle against him. Detective Susan Ferro had sidled up to his desk. She carried with her the fragrance of a meadow of wildflowers. Frank looked up and smiled at her thinking: I just might finally ask her out.

But she looked worried. "Captain Graham's been looking for you all day, Frank. He's really pissed. I wouldn't keep him waiting if I were you."

"You ain't us, so don-worry-bout-it," was Howie's casual snark.

"Did you question Wicker yet?" she asked Frank, ignoring his partner, the Humpty Dumpty who sat on a wall waiting for his smoking hot pizza.

"Yeah, we just got back from Jersey. That guy Father Hanifen was a big help."

Eagerly, "So tell me. What happened in Jersey?"

"Hate to tell it twice, Sue. After me and Howie make a coupla calls…

"And finish eating," Howie was quick to add.

"…meet us in Graham's office." She walked away. "And bring Two Names with you," he called, eyeing her tight butt until she turned the corner.

"Don't even think about it," Howie warned. "She's way outta your league."

"Maybe not."

Big Head Frank, followed by Howie, Susan and Two Names — superstars do need their entourage — was so full of himself that he needed a forklift to carry his ego into Graham's office. The Captain stared at his two least favorite detectives from above the rim of his bifocals.

"Mrs. Schmetterling, the vic's sister-in-law, called me this morning. She complained that you two have been less than diligent in returning phone calls. And now we have a new problem: she said her husband hops a plane for Colorado on Monday. I've already put in a call to the local PD. They're gonna intercept him up at the airport."

"Good. Guy's got a mean streak," noted Frank. Time to spread the good news to the boss: "We just got back from Jersey, had a little talk with Paul Wicker. He lives in North Bergen."

"You gotta see this guy," said Howie, laughing. "He looks like Sanny Klaus."

"I don't care what he looks like," said Graham, "just tell me what happened."

Frank filled the boss in about Schmetterling's February 2nd meeting with Wicker. Then he told him that Wicker said Karen Stone had called him the day after Larry was supposed to return to Colorado. She asked if he knew where Larry was. Wicker told her he didn't know.

"So Stone lied to us. She did know Wicker," said Graham.

"Yeah, and so did Frothe, only he's a bigger liar," Frank added. "Wicker told us he called the offices of the HHT about a week after the shooting." Looking at his notepad, "That would be Thursday, February 14th. He spoke with Frothe, and Frothe told him that Schmetterling had gone off on a retreat somewhere."

"OK," said Graham, "so they're both liars."

"There's more," said Howie. "Wicker called the HHT again on Tuesday the 20th, the day me and Frank went out to Fryd's ranch. This time he spoke with Stone. She was the one who told him that Schmetterling had been shot. We figure the finger points more to Frothe than Stone."

Frank smirked. "CSPD's still chasing after that Colonel guy."

"So let 'em," said Graham.

Frank exchanged grins with Howie. The best they'd saved for last. "We got our shooter," he told the Captain.

"Yeah," added Howie. "It's the sister, Tracy Millen. She did time in Mattawan for killing her husband," he added, referring to Mattawan State Hospital for the Criminally Insane.

"Shot 'im right between the eyes," said Frank. "Real coincidence, huh?"

Captain Graham removed his glasses. "Tell me more."

CHAPTER 21

Heartbreak Ridge

Sister Bernice, formerly Bérénice Sans-Tache, had a jumble of thoughts and prayers on spin cycle in her head. She pulled into a rest stop just across the Pennsylvania/New Jersey state line. She was on the final leg of an eastbound, eight hundred plus mile drive from South Bend, Indiana to Queens General Hospital in New York City. She parked the black Lexus SUV and entered the restaurant. These were modern times and Sister Bernice seldom wore a habit.

In her mind, Bérénice referred back to one of her favorite old movies: *I'm a thoroughly modern Millie, not a penguin.*

Everything had moved so fast beginning with a phone call yesterday evening from Monsignor Hanifen. He told her that the only man she'd ever loved had been shot and was now in a coma. He knew she did not own a car so the Monsignor had offered her the use of his personal vehicle for the trip. He also gave her the use of one of the seminary's charge cards for expenses. The man was a saint.

"I'll pay you back as soon as I can, Father," she'd told him. She'd get the money from her parents back in France.

Bérénice Sans-Tache had left South Bend a little past eight p.m. Driving all night, the only stops she made along I-80 East was for gas to fuel the SUV, coffee to fuel her, and use of the restroom. It was early in the morning and the sun had just begun to rise in the east. The Monsignor's Lexus needed a hearty breakfast of premium gasoline. As for Bérénice, her breakfast consisted of a cheese omelet, a fresh fruit salad, and two cups of coffee. Across the table from her sat her constant companion: Guilt. Not only was Larry Schmetterling her first love, but his was the only heart she'd ever broken — smashed actually.

Oh, Larry, please forgive me, her heart wailed. *I used you, and then I left you!*

Bérénice made the Sign of the Cross to thank the Lord for getting her this far. GPS might be her guide, but He was her way.

Thirty minutes later, refreshed and energized, she drove out of the rest stop. Back on I-80, the closer she got to the George Washington Bridge, a main artery that fed cars into the heart of New York City, the denser the traffic grew. Stuck in stop and go traffic — she had to crawl through the morning rush hour — fatigue had finally fogged her mind. Her eyelids felt like lead weights were attached to them. More than once she had to shake herself awake.

She finally reached Queens General in mid-morning. After paying an outrageous fee to park the Lexus in the hospital's lot, Bérénice asked for directions to Larry Schmetterling's private room. As she approached Room 1313, she saw a large man seated on a bench just outside. Given a similarity of features, she knew instantly that this man must be Larry's brother, Matthew. Larry had spoken of him many times. He clearly loved and admired his big brother. She wondered what Larry had told Matthew about her, the woman he had once asked to marry him. To Sister Bernice, though, that all seemed so very, very long ago. Not that she ever stopped thinking about him or praying for him. Although she'd never meant to hurt him, she had used him as a test before taking her final vows. Larry had her love; but in the end, it was God who had her love *and* her devotion.

When she saw anguish and anger battling for supremacy on the Larry's brother's face, trepidation slowed Bérénice's steps. She had seen that very same look only once before — on Larry when she said she would not marry him.

"You will always hold my heart, Larry," she'd said. "I still love you, and I always will, but my life belongs to God. I know that now."

He stared at her, a man destroyed, a man whose spirit glowed hot with hate not love. Tapping her breast with her tiny fist, "Hate me, Larry, hate me! Not God. The choice has been mine. Free will, a grace He gives us all."

She could see tears well up in his eyes as he abruptly turned and walked away. A very sad chapter in both their lives had come to an end, and she had never expected to see him again.

***

Matthew sensed someone approaching. When he looked up, he saw a rather plain woman, petite like his wife Michelle; she had mousy brown hair cut short, and round dark, doe-like eyes. Even without much makeup, they were by far her finest feature. He knew immediately who this woman was: Bérénice Sans-Tache; in French *sans-tache* meant without blemish.

Not exactly without blemish anymore, are you, Bérénice? You and my brother did the nasty many, many, too many times! You used him to test your faith! You should not be here! You ruined my brother's life! If it wasn't for you, everything could've been so different!

He stood up and glared down at this awful woman. She stopped dead in her tracks. He saw in her face that her will to proceed had hit a wall. She turned and began to walk away. Then she stopped, took a deep breath, turned around and continued forward.

"My name is Bérénice Sans-Tache," she said with a slight French accent. "I am an old friend of Larry's. How is he?"

Flatly, "I know who you are Miss Sans-Tache. My wife and mother are inside with Larry. They're praying. I'm sure they will be delighted to see you — *Sister.*"

"*Merci.*" She passed without looking him in the eyes.

***

Someone meekly tapped on the door as if it was marked, "Do Not Disturb." Michelle wondered if perhaps it was a new nurse afraid to intrude while she and her mother-in-law, Tobie, prayed at Larry's bedside.

"Matthew?" Tobie called to the closed door. Then she turned to Michelle and mumbled, "That can't be Matthew. Why would he knock?"

"Please come in," Michelle called.

A woman a few years younger than Michelle entered and smiled shyly. She was dressed in a plaid suit jacket and matching skirt, a white, high collar sweater and black pumps. She primped at bit at her straight light brown hair cut short, just below her chin. She had bangs, large, brown eyes and thick eyebrows. The woman was more cute than pretty. Michelle took an instant liking to her. Her mother-in-law was delighted; obviously this woman was a close friend of her son. She looked a bit haggard like she had made a long, hard trip to be here with Larry.

"Pardon me, madams, my name is Bérénice Sans-Tache," she said in a French accent that caused the senior Mrs. Schmetterling's face glow with pride. "I apologize for my appearance but I have been driving all night from South Bend — I am afraid to fly. As soon as I heard what had happened to Larry, I had to come immediately." Then she noticed the Rosary beads in Michelle and her mother-in-law's. "Oh! I am so sorry to be disturbing your prayers."

"Oh, no," said Tobie, "would you like to join us?"

Smiling brightly, "I am quite delighted," said Bérénice. She reached into her shoulder bag and pulled out an expensive set of silver Rosary beads. "Is a special gift from my parents when I — was given to me a long time ago."

Michelle immediately recognized that there was more to this

Bérénice Sans-Tache, but there would be plenty of time to question her after they all finished praying together. Michelle brought another chair over for Bérénice and set it next to hers. Michelle inhaled and smiled. "That's a nice scent, Bérénice. What is it?"

"Is nothing really. I just freshened up a bit in the ladies room before coming to be with Larry. Is strawberry and mint body wash. It has always been Larry's favorite on me." She smiled wistfully, and then the olive skin on her face flushed deep red like a woman who had released an intimate detail.

She might have been my sister-in-law, thought Michelle. *Maybe there's still a chance? Oh please, Jesus, give him back to us!*

***

A soft murmur of prayer seeps into Larry's black hole. It carries with it a familiar scent of strawberries and mint. Memories of Bérénice Sans-Tache are with him once again. How many eons have passed since he'd kneeled by her side as she lifted her devotions unto the Lord? How many eons have passed since he'd inhaled her scent, as fresh and alive as a mountain meadow of wild flowers in spring? And how many eons in time have passed since he'd felt her warm body entwined with his?

A longing for a phantom he once loved is a new torment inflicted on him by a Supreme Being whose cruelty is as limitless as it is eternal. There is no doubt in Larry's mind how much better his life would've been if the Lord had freed Bérénice Sans-Tache and allowed her to marry him. The good Catholics that they were, they would have raised six, seven kids.

For Larry of the Black Hole, memories of Bérénice lead his mind along a bumpy road all the way back to Heartbreak Ridge. From that height he will clearly see what was and what might have been.

***

Larry had left the seminary at Notre Dame exhilarated. Now he was finally free to charter his *own* course. He pointed his sextant in a direction that would take him far, far away from church and religion. As for God Almighty Himself, Larry had carefully stored Him in the hold, to be called back on deck only if Larry found himself in danger of floundering.

Larry knew he was brilliant: he could read Greek, Latin and Hebrew; he spoke fluent German and French; so he felt confident he could easily master computer coding in any number of languages or even the intricacies of accounting; both bedrocks of the business world. Business management did not interest him, though, because then he'd have to deal with people. He remembered how cruel human beings could be. No, Larry preferred the logic of numbers to the illogic of people.

Still Larry would rather study an ancient piece of Scripture looking for new meaning. Not only was that where the action was intellectually, but it was far more fulfilling to Larry's spirit. But a career in programming and accounting was not to be.

Sorry, Dad, but this son will never be rich.

And neither would Mike Schmetterling's other son, Larry's big brother Matthew. A brilliant student of applied math and computer science at Columbia University's School of Engineering, unlike Larry, Matthew was offered many high paying positions right out of college. But he decided to go for a Master's at Columbia's teaching college. Matthew also wanted to make a difference. At first, Matthew came out the better for his choice: he met his future wife Michelle who was also going for a degree at Columbia Teachers. Larry, on the other hand, had he remained at Notre Dame his life as a priest would have been all laid out. Yes, he'd never be rich, but he'd always have a job and people who needed him.

When Larry was fired from his job as a teacher after only one semester by that naked ape principal in Irvine, California, that majestic ship he expected would carry him to new lands had dropped him off on a deserted island instead. Not only was he broke and about to apply for food stamps, but he felt abandoned by God. And then He worked in one of His mysterious ways: Monsignor Hanifen called to tell Larry that an instructor's position had opened up at St. Mary's College.

"It's yours if you want it, Larry," the monsignor said.

What happened next should have re-chartered Larry's new course towards true love; but instead the Eternal Constant had pulled a fast one: He and His church stole Bérénice from him.

You took her from me and despite this I still loved and served You. And how do You repay my devotion? By dumping me in this hole.

Fuck You with a capital F!!!

***

Prayers finished and Rosary beads stowed away until the next time, Bérénice said, "I am quite tired. Now I will find a hotel. I must sleep, please."

The intensity with which she prayed had exhausted her to the point where she could barely keep her eyes open. But neither Schmetterling woman would hear of such a thing. Michelle immediately volunteered to drive Bérénice back to her home in Whitestone.

"You can sleep in my sons' room. They can sleep in our room. The boys love their sleeping bags. It will be like an adventure for them."

Bérénice was just too darn tired to argue. She left with Michelle.

To be in New York indefinitely praying for Larry to recover would be Bérénice's penance. Shame and guilt over how she had used him to test her devotion to God was testimony to her own sinful nature. And what if he woke up — Lord willing — and he saw her face again?

Does he still hate me?

How could he not? From what Monsignor Hanifen had told her, "He's a bitter man, Bérénice. He thinks the Church has let him down."

"Not the Church, Father, I let him down."

Bérénice had given him a bite of the apple, and then snatched it away. She was truly a daughter of Eve, a term she hated but Larry was quite fond of. When Michelle told her that Larry had left the Catholic faith to become an evangelical minister, she felt acid roiled inside her as if it would consume her very soul. As for Larry's immortal soul, Bérénice truly believed no one could receive salvation without being in communion with the Church of Rome. In her mind, ex-Catholic Larry's immortal soul now suffered in Purgatory. It could only be received into Heaven after much prayer by her and others who loved him. Bérénice knew that although she was a modern, enlightened woman, she still held fast to an ancient belief in Purgatory.

Was that another one of her many failings as a person?

With visiting hours ended and prayers over, Bérénice and Larry's mother and sister-in-law stowed away their Rosary beads. She noticed once again the other women eyed hers as if they were somehow more holy simply because they cost a lot of money. Bérénice hated that other people naturally assumed that because she came from privilege that somehow her becoming a nun made her sacrifice even greater.

"You gave all that up to serve our Lord and His people," others would say.

"I'm a sinner, same as everyone else," was her standard reply. And for sure, she knew this was true.

Bérénice was the youngest child and only daughter of the Sans-Taches. She had three older brothers and the youngest of them was seven years her senior; therefore, all the Sans-Taches sheltered this shy little girl as if she were a jewel that must be carefully stored in a case — only to be taken out for special occasions. To them, such an innocent who showed quiet love and trust in everyone and everything was too good for this wicked world. Because her family shielded her, she never experienced the toil and tribulations growing up that other young girls did. Then came the day that fourteen-year-old Bérénice finally wanted out of that jewel case; she announced that she wanted to serve God, His church, and Man as a nun. Her father and brothers were delighted. But her mother, who knew Bérénice better than anyone, did *not* approve. Madame Sans-Tache thought her daughter far too young to set her life's course.

When Bérénice asked why, Madame Sans-Tache told her: "You've already been cloistered by your papa and brothers. You must be quite sure you want to be a nun. Once you take your final vow, Bérénice, to change your mind later will be a slap in the face to God and His church."

That thought horrified Bérénice. She promised her mother she would never do such a thing. "When I become a nun I will be a bride to Christ — forever."

"You will always love God, Bérénice, I have no doubt. But first you might want to find out if you can love a very special man one day."

A compromise was reached: her parents would pay for Bérénice's higher education; she would study art history. Upon graduation, they would also pay an advanced teaching degree. Then, and only then, if she still wanted to enter a convent,

"With two degrees, Bérénice," said Madame Sans-Tache, "there isn't a convent in France that would refuse you. You will serve God by teaching His children."

When she turned eighteen, Bérénice realized that before leaving the world, however briefly, she must first engage with it; but in a safe way.

"Mama, Papa," she announced, "I want to study at Notre Dame in Indiana, America. It is a wonderful Catholic institution — and named for our Blessed Mother!"

Her parents and brothers were delighted, especially Madame Sans-Tache: "Americans are *so* much nicer than the French. I know how shy you are, Bérénice, but do try and make new friends — a boyfriend, perhaps?"

Bérénice smiled, lowered her eyes, and blushed. *Ce qui sera, sera..*

Chapter 22

A Snake in Her Garden

True to his word, when Frank said, *Open sez me*, the walls of Tracy Frothe's juvenile records did fall. And so did the court records of her trial along with psychiatric testimony and police interviews with her deceased parents; some of the testimony at trial also included that of Ms. Millen, herself.

In Graham's office, a nervous Two Names cleared his throat about to tell the boss about the trial. After an encouraging nod from Detective Goldberg and a smile from Detective Ferro, he began to read from his notes. Frank sat quietly. He dare not show how anxious he was to be on the six o'clock news.

According to Officer George, tall and gangly and strange, Tracy Frothe had suffered through a childhood of teasing and abuse from other kids. But one tormentor stood above all the rest; a pimpled-faced, little buck-toothed brat named Stevie Chimkin. One Saturday afternoon, eight year-old Tracy invited classmate Stevie to come up and see her brother's tree house.

"Somehow," noted Two Names, "poor Stevie went over the rails." He made a downward motion with his left hand. "Tracy is reported to have said, 'Stupid Stevie. He musta thought he was a bird.' Stevie Chimkin claimed she tripped him."

The authorities investigated but did nothing. Stevie's parents, with a son who had fractures in both wrists as he had extended them to break his fall, told Tracy's parents that their daughter was sick and should get help before she hurt another kid. When the parents took Tracy for counseling, the child psychologist warned them that they might have a sociopath on their hands. Tracy's mother said that she and her husband had better watch their daughter more closely, but the father insisted Tracy was just a little high strung and that she'd grow out of it.

Tracy's parents did their best to put a collar on their daughter's aggressive behavior, and there was only one other *incident.* It had occurred when Tracy was twelve. A dog had bitten Curtis. A few months later the animal was found poisoned to death.

"Curtis Frothe insisted that he didn't do it," said Two Names, "that it was Tracy. He said she'd been throwing food over the fence for weeks on her way home from school."

"Yeah, blame the girl," snarked Detective Susan Ferro.

When Tracy reached young-adulthood she had grown taller, ganglier and more moody. She did not have many dates through high school. By the time she entered college, however, she had blossomed into a statuesque, beautiful young woman. But the young men who came to call didn't stay long. Word spread among the male student body at Stony Brook that Tracy Frothe might be gorgeous, but she was also, "One creepy chick." The more mature males on campus were not so easily intimidated. Tracy began a series of short affairs with a short order of professors and associate professors. And then she met Elmore Millen, professor of Ethics and Religion, a man twenty nine years her senior. When they married soon after her graduation, neither of Tracy's parents objected even though the groom was a couple of years older than they were.

"Guess they figured she was *his* problem now," quipped Detective Susan Ferro.

Tracy admitted that the first year of her marriage to Elmo was the only time in her young life that she was truly happy; a time made even happier when she became pregnant: joy to the world for Tracy, not so for old Elmo. Already providing for two ex-wives, four children and six grandchildren, he did not need another drain on his meager resources. Neither did he look forward to dirty diapers and sleepless nights listening to the wailing of the latest twig on his family tree.

"Finances aside," said Two Names, "there was another matter of even greater concern to him. According to the testimony of a colleague, old Elmo had said, 'What if my young sapling turns out as twisted as its mother?' "

"A distinct possibility," noted Graham.

"That's when old Elmo told his wife to get an abortion." Two Names hung that one out there, letting it stink up the room. Then, he quoted Professor Millen directly, " 'I don't want you to have this baby, Tracy,' the old guy tells his young wife. And she says, 'An abortion? How can you ask me to do this, Elmo? You're a professor of religion!' Then get a load of what Millen tells her: 'I'm a scholar, Tracy. I teach the philosophy of religion. That doesn't mean I let other peoples' dogma run my life. I won't let them run yours either.' "

According to Tracy's own testimony, her husband's nagging eventually wore her down. Reluctantly, she ended the pregnancy. But the abortion had left her devastated. Guilty and full of self-loathing, she tried to put it behind her. And she might have succeeded, too, had it not been for her husband's flip-flop.

"Guess what the husband says next? 'We've committed a terrible sin when we killed our own child, Tracy. Now I think it's God's will that we atone for it by living in chaste marriage. If we refuse to give in to our fleshly urges, we can mend our wounded spirits.'"

Shaking her head, a grim Detective Ferro said, "I feel sorry for her."

Two Names continued to read from Tracy's testimony at trial: "'I thought you didn't believe in God, Elmo!'

'I didn't say that. You misunderstood me, Babe. What I said was that I don't believe in religion. I *do* believe in God, however.'"

Up to now, Frank had not dropped his two cents into the piggy bank. But since he was the senior detective on the case, his input was vital. Only Detective Ferro noticed. With her eyes, she asked, *What's wrong, Frank?*

He made no reply, neither with his eyes nor his mouth. The sad, lonely, and tragic life of Ms. Tracy Millen as being laid out by P.O. George gnawed at Detective Giavone. Like a mighty oak tree, Frank's professional detachment was being sawed off at its base.

Two Names went on with the story: somehow Tracy managed to live by the new commandment as laid down by her lord and master. Not that her husband resided on the same tablet. Two new laws had been chiseled onto Elmore's heart of stone: 1) I no longer lust for my wife; and 2) I must conserve my energy. Old Elmo's fire didn't burn as hot as it used to. Now reduced to smoldering embers, he decided to save what few sparks he had left for the occasional coed who might pass through one of his classes.

Finally Frank's professional detachment tore free: "Whatta piece 'a work! Think I woulda shot the fuck, too!"

Tracy had been born crazy — there wasn't much she could do about that — but as to her naiveté, she soon grew out of it. It took only a few months for her to discover her husband's infidelity. When she confronted him, he denied everything.

"Tracy testified that, 'Calm settled over me when I told him I don't believe you, Elmo.' Then he said, 'That's all in the past, Babe. I love you. Can't you see that? Please forgive me, Tracy.'

'I do Elmo, I truly do.'"

The consensus among the cops was: *Yeah right!*

Old Elmo should not have taken a lunatic at her word. Unknown to him, Tracy took up a new sport: target shooting. She had told her court appointed psychiatrist that she liked the power she felt when she held a weapon in her hands and fired it. Tracy kept a target pistol at the range and an unlicensed .32 at home. She told her mother that since Elmo was always working late or going to conferences and leaving her home alone, she kept the gun for protection. Tracy said there was evil out there; it was all around her.

Poor old Elmo, professor of Ethics and Religion, dispenser of wisdom, molder of young minds, and debaucher of young bodies never saw it coming. Came the day and, *Bang!,* out went his lights.

Tracy turned herself in to the police. She was found innocent by reason of insanity, and most likely jury sympathy, and sent to Mattawan State Hospital for the Criminally Insane. There a miracle occurred. What couldn't be accomplished in the first twenty-six years of Tracy's life — sanity — her doctors accomplished in eighteen months; they declared Tracy no longer a threat to herself or society. She was released. Tracy told her father that the doctors could claim whatever credit they wished, but she knew the truth: she had found Jesus while at Mattawan. He had cured her.

"Good work, Officer George." In himself was Captain Graham pleased. He smiled. "Knew you guys would come through." Then he reminded everyone that physical evidence tying Frothe's sister to the shooting would be a big help.

"Waidda minute!" Howie interrupted, holding an index finger up for emphasis. "That gun she used to kill her husband, the paperwork says it was a .32 caliber. What if she did 'em both with the same gun?"

"By now it's probably in the ocean," was Frank's dry comment. He was the senior detective on the Schmetterling shooting and no way was he going to let Howie implant a brown nose up the Captain's butt.

Howie's face lit up. "We don't need the gun because we got the bullet! They dug it right out of Elmo's head. So all we gotta do is match the ballistics of that slug with the one from Schmetterling. There's our physical evidence. We can arrest 'er this afternoon, then grab Frothe tomorrow and be home by Friday."

Captain Graham shined his lights on Howie. "Good thinking, Goldberg."

Then Two Names dumped the cold wash of reality on everyone by reminding them, "The bullet's still in the vic's head."

Captain Graham's smile did not dim; instead it boldly announced: *This is why I make the big bucks and you don't.* "The Millen woman, *she* doesn't know the bullet's still in Schmetterling."

Still an implant, "That's right! Think I know where you're going with this, sir," said Howie.

"This is what I want you guys to do when you question her," Graham said. "She must've shot Schmetterling with the same gun she used on her husband." Snapping his fingers, "What's the guy's name?"

"Elmo, sir," Howie replied.

"Yeah, Elmo. I want you two to tell her that we're waiting for the ballistics report to come back to us. And when we get a match, the next time we come to visit it'll be to slap the cuffs on her. When we light that fire under her butt, let's see how high she jumps."

Graham began to bark out more orders: "Frank, before you and Goldberg go out to Babylon and question the Millen woman, I want you to call that lady detective out there in Hooterville. Tell her to make sure that Schmetterling's brother doesn't do anything to screw this up." He looked at his watch. "Today's Friday the 14th. You have the weekend to get it together. I want this case closed no later than next Friday."

"Next Friday is Good Friday," Detective Ferro reminded everyone.

"Not to me," said Howie.

Graham let that one pass over him. "Make my Easter a happy one, guys."

When Frank got back to his desk, there was a little pink slip waiting for him. It was a phone message from Karla. It read: "Important. Call me."

This was a long distance call Frank was eager to make, but he needed a private place to make it because Howie had his antenna up. So he stepped outside the precinct and thumbed Karla's number into his cell phone.

When she picked up on the second ring, he joked, "Whadda ya sitting on the phone or what?"

She laughed. "Yep, that's me. I have some news, Frank. You mentioned a motive. Try this one on: Frothe and Stone were once lovers — until Pastor Larry came along."

"No kidding! How'd ya find out?"

"She told me."

"How'd ya manage that?"

"Just some girl-talk; it was easy, really. The woman has been disappointed by so many men so many times that I had no trouble establishing a bond with her."

"Think Stone had anything to do with the shooting?"

"I spent a coupla hours with her, Frank, and, no, I don't."

Frank's turn to deliver even bigger news: he told her about Frothe's twisted sister and that she had shot her husband right between the eyes. "We're going out there to question 'er."

"Y'all be careful now. If she's as crazy as ya'll say, she's dangerous."

Frank assured her not to worry that he and Howie knew what they were doing.

"Don't be so damn glib, Frank."

He had no idea what glib meant.

"I've had a lotta experience dealing with crazies," she added, "so promise me you'll be careful."

"Yeah-yeah, OK, Karla." It annoyed him that she would talk to a detective with years of seniority as if he was a rookie. Now with a firmer grasp of exactly what glib meant, he glibly added, "This'll make you happy. We'll take a young uniform with us for protection. He's a plenty tough kid."

"Call me when you get back, Frank."

He smirked, "Bye, Karla," and hung up.

Chapter 23

The Sound of Music Fades

A loud scream, "POOP!" by Bérénice Sans-Tache emptied her lungs of all breath while she slammed the palm of her right hand again and again against the steering wheel so hard it left a bruise. She was lucky not to break a bone. In her limited and narrowly defined lexicon of obscenities, "poop" was the foulest. It ranked even higher than "damn". As for "G-damn", that word was far too blasphemous to even allow entry into her pious mind let alone out her *Thou Shalt Not* mouth.

On Palm Sunday in the early evening, Sister Bernice was doing 90 m.p.h. on I-80 West; but she could not outrun her feelings: she had left Larry when he needed her most; she had lied to his family; and she had failed in her calling as a nun. She had to get back to her safe place, South Bend, Indiana, the sooner the better.

To his family, to the doctors and to the police, her beloved was a victim and an empty vessel. They could see no further than his body. But Bérénice had seen his soul. She had sensed his torment until she could take no more. That made her a selfish coward.

After Mass she had said goodbye to Michelle and Tobie Schmetterling with many tears and much hugs and hope. But she had lied to them, telling them she had to get back to Indiana to prepare for a trip back to France for Easter.

"I haven't been able to celebrate the Resurrection of our Lord with my family for many years." That much was true, but her next trip to France would be in the summer when she holidayed with her parents in Montpelier; she did this every year.

Bérénice felt her heart flutters when Larry's mother thanked her for being here for her son. "I know he knows you're with him," Tobie said, putting on a brave smile and clasping her hand.

After listening to Larry constantly complain about a mother who pushed him in a direction she wanted but he did not, Bérénice had always resented her. That she had been so quick to pass judgment on a woman she had never met made her feel like an even bigger pile of poop.

"God bless you and peace be with you," said Michelle, a woman her age and who she felt genuine affection for.

We could have been like sisters, Bérénice thought sadly, *but I am so unworthy.*

She was glad for one thing, however; Larry's older brother Matthew, a most awful poop, had left for Colorado last night. He felt the local police were doing nothing.

"I feel so useless just sitting here waiting for something to happen," she'd overheard him tell his wife. "I'm taking a leave of absence and going out to Colorado myself. See what the hell is going on."

Michelle was against it of course. "Please Matthew, I know how it must be for you, but let the police do their job. Your mother has faith in the two detectives."

"Those two lard-asses! I sure don't."

Bérénice had sensed the man's hostility towards her. It flashed in his eyes and in his tone the few times he spoke to her directly. Only God knew what terrible things Larry had said about her, including that she was now a nun. Bérénice was grateful that neither brother had shared the information with the rest of the family.

On her first night in New York, she had stayed with the younger Schmetterlings. She lay in one of the boy's beds, a body in motion: flat on her back, and then she rolled over onto her right-side, then her left, then on her back, and then flat on her stomach with a pillow over her head; then she'd submerge beneath the bed covers, and then kick them off — over and over and over. Late night gymnastics where the *symptom* and not the *cause* of why she could not fall asleep; it was a menagerie of conflicting emotions that had played bumper-cars in her head that barred the Sandman from her front door. She had once loved Larry enough to think her future might be as his wife and mother of his children — until she realized that her true calling lay in service to the Lord and His people.

In the very beginning, making love with Larry was an ecstasy she had never felt before and far surpassed anything she'd ever experienced at prayer or in church. A future yoked in body and spirit to Lawrence Schmetterling would be their own private heaven. And to bear *his* children — to practicing Catholics like themselves that meant many, many, many children — was to fill the whole earth with peace and love. Their offspring would perform many wondrous things in the name of the Lord.

Sister Bernice turned off I-80 West and onto Route 7 South. No way could she drive straight through to South Bend; she was emotionally and physically drained. Her intention was to spend the night at The Sisters of the Immaculate Heart Convent in Steubenville. Accommodations at the convent where clean and inexpensive; it would be good to rest once again in the arms of the Holy Mother Church. Sister Bernice would continue her journey back home tomorrow morning after an early breakfast.

Although there were other fine convents much closer to I-80 where she could spend the night, the one in Steubenville was where her spiritual advisor and close friend Sister Sophia nee Maggie Nutzall resided. Sister

Bernice was in dire need of advice and comfort. She smiled as she pulled off of Route 7 at Steubenville. Sister Sophia had always lifted her spirit. Whereas Sister Bernice had only briefly flirted with the outside world, the time she'd spent with Larry, Sister Sophia nee Maggie Nutzall had long been a willing passenger on that wild ride before becoming a nun. Maggie had been a wild child of the 1980s, and a failed lead singer for a punk rock band.

"My epiphany came when I finally realized that my voice was an abomination even unto myself," she had told Sister Bernice with a giggle. "Praise be to God when He finally opened my ears so that I, too, could hear how awful I sang. My voice was something between a heavy smoker and a saw on wood."

With all the sex, drugs and rock and roll Maggie had done, one day she found out that she *might* be pregnant. An abortion would be out of the question and for one of the few times in her secular life Maggie had prayed to God, "Please spare me, Lord, I'll be a lousy mother."

After He spared her from pregnancy, she decided to dedicate her life to serving Him and His church. As for sex, drugs and rock & roll — good riddance!

Now she sat across from Sister Bernice stiff and erect on a high-back chair with her hands folded in her lap. Sister Bernice sat on the edge of an equally uncomfortable 15th Century-like couch; a dark brown coffee table set with tea for two and snacks laid out between them. It seemed to Sister Bernice that her once free-spirited mentor had thrown off the last vestiges her kind and humorous self and become stern and severe. The fact that she was now Mother Superior of this convent might explain the change.

"Men a weak," Sister Sophia began. The ex- punk rocker spoke as if she knew this inconvenient truth as a matter of fact. "They're slaves to their prurient natures. It's we women who must be strong, resist."

"I know that, Mother," said Sister Bernice, "that's not why I've come to you. It's my own failings that brought me here."

The older woman's intent was clearly to pontificate rather than listen. She continued, "And it's we Sisters who model ourselves after the Blessed Mother who set must the standards for purity, chastity, and humility for all women."

It had been Sister Sophia's idea that Bérénice enter the world, find a good man, and then see if marriage and family would be what she really wanted. As it had turned out, marriage and family was *not* it. The advice of Sister Sophia had been sound, but now, listening to her go on and on about the world's wickedness, Bérénice wished she had stayed at a closer convent off I-80.

Bérénice disengaged her mind as Sister Sophia prattled on and on. Her thoughts drifted back to when she and Larry made love — and those sweet memories put a wistful smile on her soul.

His sweet kisses sent tingles up and down her spine, and curled her fingers and toes. The feel of his warm skin against hers was like two bodies melting into each other such that it was difficult to know where she ended and he began. His gentle touch was like a down comforter that said, *You are loved and protected.* Their musky, comingled scents were orgasmic. Listening to his rhythmic breathing when she lay beside him in bed eased her into her own deep, contented, sated sleep. When they made love, their physical conjoining was as powerful as their spiritual union.

"Sexually, men are primitives," said Sister Sophia nee Maggie Nutzall. "Women feel; men experience." These few words broke through the fog of Sister Bernice's memories. Then the mother superior added as if stating a universal truth: "A night spent in deep meditation and deep prayer can be just as ecstatic as a night of dirty sex with a man." The former Maggie Nutzall's face reddened as she turned away and mumbled, "Or even dirtier sex with a woman."

As for the first part of the Sister's pontification, sex with a man,

Poop! thought Sister Bernice nee Bérénice Sans-Tache. As for the other part, sex with another woman, yes, that was disgusting. She also strongly suspected that Maggie Nutzall had stepped out from behind the curtain of Sister Sophia to speak from experience. There was no doubt in her mind that the promiscuous Maggie Nutzall of the 1980s, had undoubtedly experimented with sex with a woman.

How dare she preach at me!

In the very beginning, whenever Bérénice and Larry slept together they would stop just short of copulation. They followed the same moves they'd *always* performed in foreplay. She would climax, but she knew that he always came up short. When he excused himself to go to the bathroom, although she could hear the water running in the sink, she knew what he was really doing. That he had to finish the job by pleasuring himself — this was a mortal sin that she had forced him to commit.

Guilt!

Enough toying with this poor man's feelings: "Come to my apartment for dinner this Friday night, Larry. I shall cook you a very special French meal. And then…" The smile she gave him left no doubt: Friday night they would finally *Go All the Way*.

The bottle of French red wine her parents had sent her for Christmas, *Chateau Mouton Rothschild*, would be opened. If a $500 bottle of wine could not loosen Bérénice up, then she was hopeless.

Poop! I'll drink the whole bottle myself if I have to!

Since it was Friday, and calling upon an old tradition no longer practiced except during Lent, Bérénice decided to prepare a feast of fish for them. Since they were both hardcore Catholics this was an especially poignant gesture. Although red wine did not go well with fish, Larry, not a drinker and having been raised on macaroni and cheese, and corned beef, he'd hardly know the difference. As for Bérénice's more refined palate, a red wine with an alcohol per volume content of 13.5% was required. A white would be too weak to do the job.

Bérénice had only one morning class to teach, so that left her the rest of Friday afternoon to carefully prepare a magnificent feast for the man she loved. Larry's last teaching class ended at six, so she knew he would be famished. He had a healthy appetite, but somehow never put on weight no matter how many carbs he stuffed into himself.

The first course would be a tourin soup made with garlic, onions, flour, water instead of chicken stock, and egg whites and egg yolks.

The main course would be grilled (in the oven) flounder meunière with lots of browned butter, fresh lemon and parsley. The red wine would murder the fish on Bérénice's palate, but she would endure. For dessert she would serve crème brûlée and an aperitif Banyuls AOC that was guaranteed to fortify her as well as the grapes from which it was made.

***

"You are a very lucky young woman, Sister Bernice," said Sister Sophia. "You have loved a man yet still remained chaste." The Mother superior gave her a fond smile as if she could claim credit.

Poop! "No I'm not, Mother," Sister Bernice casually replied. Her knowing smile ripped the smugness right off the older woman's face.

A moment to reset her shocked look, then: "More credit to you, Sister."

A snarky, "But of course," Sister Bernice replied, as her mind slipped back into the past. She was hardly aware that uncomfortable cone of silence had settled over the not so superior mother superior anymore.

***

When Bérénice sensed that Larry's heightened state of arousal was at its peak, she instinctively took him inside her. When she felt him explode her legs around his waist tightened as if to squeeze every last drop of his essence into her. And then both their sweaty bodies shuddered. And it was more than good, it was great.

Laying there in bed on their backs staring up at the ceiling, Larry said, "Two rookies like us... Who knew?"

She smiled and snuggled into him.

When she woke the next morning, her heart felt like the hills were alive with the sounds of music. In her mind, she twirled around and around like Julie Andrews surrounded by the stunningly gorgeous foothills of Austria under a sunny, cloudless sky. Bérénice offered up a silent prayer thanking God for having blessed all living creatures with the gift of procreation.

Neither she nor Larry had taken any precaution about bringing a new life into the world. They both decided whether or not a baby was created would be left His divine will. Besides, as they well knew it was against Church teaching to use contraceptives. They were young and in love, so the possibility of creating a new life assuaged some of their guilt for breaking another Church teaching against premarital sex.

"How an expression of love between a man and a woman be a sin?" Bérénice had said.

"It's not," Larry casually replied.

The certainty with which he sometimes spoke about what God wanted annoyed her — a lot! "We're human beings, Larry, how can we possibly know what pleases or displeases God? Sometimes you sound like a Protestant."

Back in the real world where hardly anyone believed the silly dogma of Sister Sophia, she sat having tea and pastries with another fool who dared think *she* knew God's will.

A chastened Mother Superior finally asked, "What convinced you, Bernice, to serve the Lord as His bride rather than the bride of Lawrence Schmetterling?"

A difficult question, one she'd rather not answer, but Sister Sophia had been an old friend who always had Bernice's best interests at heart. She deserved to know the whole truth.

Bérénice and Larry had continued to make glorious love together on an almost daily basis. She discovered that an entire shelf of new feelings had been hidden away in a back cupboard for far too long. Her spirit soared to such heights that she could hardly breathe. But Bérénice Sans-Tache had always been the kind of person to overdose on a good thing — luckily for her she had never been into drugs or alcohol. She easily could have become a drunkard or addict. Eventually, what went up came down.

The thrill was gone.

Sex as practiced between Bérénice and Larry had always been a game of chance: but when no baby had blessed their union, she took that as a sign. The Lord was telling her life must be dedicated to Him and not him.

Sister Bernice's heart began to pound harder and her breathing more labored when she told Sister Sophia, "I'll never forget the look on his face when I told him this." Her face reddened and her lips trembled as she held back her tears: "Like I'd ripped his heart from his chest."

Sister Sophia covered her mouth with her hand and sucked in a deep breath.

Sister Bernice began to weep — "And now this, a coma that could last for decades." That turned into an all out flood: "I did this to him, a man I once loved! How can I ever forgive myself?"

Sister Sophia reached out her hand across the coffee table. Sister Bernice clasped it tightly. Both women closed their eyes and fell into silent, weepy prayer.

Chapter 24

Body and Soul

Early in the morning on Palm Sunday, Tracy's eyes had shot open as if spring-loaded. She rolled onto her side and looked at the clock on the night table. The hands read, 3:25. The fog of sleep had disappeared in a flash. She knew exactly where she was, who she was with, and what she had done: Abomination! Fornication! With Tony Magee! *On Palm Sunday!*

She rolled onto her back again. His face was snuggled up against the side of her neck; she felt his warm moist and rhythmic breaths on her skin. His arm lay across her torso and her legs were locked in his. She felt like a slab of meat that had gratified a wicked man's sexual appetite. He who proclaimed he had been born-again had used Tracy's loneliness and yearning to defile her body and soul.

Hypocrite!

Tracy slipped out from beneath him and stood by the foot of the bed observing his blissful, sated sleep. She remembered the DVD they'd watched together, Mel Gibson's *The Passion of the Christ*, a horrid Jesus snuff film.

You've witnessed our Lord being brutally scourged; then hung on a cross where He suffered a slow and agonizing death, and what do you do? You fornicate with me!

For the handsome Mr. Magee the wages of sin would be deep penetration.

Tracy looked behind her. Her eyes followed the trail he'd left behind: white sweater, black jeans, white sneakers, a sleeveless T-shirt that had highlighted his bulging biceps, and boxer shorts. They lay on the floor exactly where he'd dropped them in his mad rush into her bed. She felt shame and guilt when she saw her own trail lying on the floor co-mingled with his: shear black blouse, short black skirt, heels, skimpy panties and bra.

Magee still lay on his side. Careful not to wake him, she nudged him onto his back. Then she propped his head up with another pillow. He smiled and mumbled some sweet nothings. He lay with one arm across his gently rising and falling chest. Seeing him lying there so peaceful turned up the burners on Tracy's rage. She opened the night table and retrieved the little .32. Many times she held its small weight in her hand, and each time she felt awed by its power. It could spit out a projectile that could deliver a punch that would snap a man's head back with more force than a blow from a heavyweight boxer. Its power was her power. Like a god, she could deliver capital punishment whenever and to whomever she pleased. She stood at the foot of the bed and leveled the gun at Mr. Magee. She aimed for her favorite kill spot: the bridge of the nose and between the eyes. She paused; the damn cracker from Mississippi had to know what was about to hit him.

"Wake up, Tony," she said with deliberation. But his sleep was as deep as death. She slapped at his feet that stuck out from under the covers; "Wake up, Mr. Magee!" but he would not return from the Land of Oz. Damn this horrid man!

As she began to squeeze the trigger, it offered a resistance so slight that only someone as intimate with the weapon as she was would notice. Never before had it defied her will. In its backward slide to engage the firing mechanism it hit a snag; however, its weak resistance was not enough to stop her. Just a little more pressure and the bullet would be sent on its way to rip into Magee's face. Then, from deep within, that strange voice called out to her again:

Look, Tracy, look! It's your clothes on the floor too. You couldn't wait to jump into bed with him. You dressed to temp and tempt you did. Men are weak. You knew exactly what you were doing, Daughter of Eve. You used HIM!

Tracy had let Satan into her soul via a most intimate road. Tony Magee had been merely the vehicle of The Evil One's deliverance. And like her, he'd also been tricked by the Trickster. The voice was right.

I failed You, Lord Jesus. Please forgive me.

She lifted her finger off the trigger. "Bang," she said softly.

She quietly slipped out of the bedroom. She went down to the basement, taking the .32 with her. Tracy felt as if her soul had been raped. In a moment of weakness, she had opened herself up not just to Tony Magee, but to Satan himself. Now she lay splayed out on the basement floor with her forehead once again numbed by the hard press of bare concrete. In her special room, a temple of atonement, her sins pressed down on her like dead weights.

My flesh is weak. Give me the strength, O Lord, to resist temptation. I try to please You, Lord. Do Your bidding. I've given You my love, my life, my soul. Why won't You lift this burden from me? My anger, my rage burns hotter than the flames of Hell!

As for the slumbering giant upstairs in her bedroom, Tony Magee had no idea how lucky he was to still be alive. He'd wake up wondering where she'd gone. Best if he'd simply let himself out. If not, if he came down here to her special room looking for her, then she'd either have to kill him or herself.

***

After spending the morning prostrate before the Lord in her special room, Tracy's soul had been as numb as her forehead. Whatever feelings for Tony Magee that dwelled inside her were now frozen in deep ice; she was through with him. Once at work, however, that glacier of which she was a part began to move. She felt like a great boulder that had been picked up and carried away. When the ice melted, it had deposited her here, to stand defiantly against the corrupt world of Women's Wear in a vast wasteland known as Wallmans-Shop-A-Lot.

It's Palm Sunday and does Wallman's celebrate our Lord's triumphant entry into Jerusalem? No, they throw a damn sale!

Her scorn also included all of humanity with the exception of Mr. Tony Magee. She had given him a bite of the apple; she would gladly carry the burden of his sin on her shoulders.

Men, ruled by their things! It's women who must be strong, must be resolute, must protect their purity.

She did not know the best way to disengage herself from Mr. Magee; so today, when he asked her to lunch, she took an easy way out: "I'm not feeling well, Tony. I might go home early."

"Is there anything I can do, Tracy? I can bring ya some dinner tonight?" Smiling, "I'm a great cook. My ma taught me."

She smiled back and shook her head, no. Then she placed the palm of her left hand on his right cheek. "You're a kind, sweet man, Tony, but you and me, we—" The pain and confusion in his eyes raked Tracy's heartstrings in dissonant chords. She turned and walked away so he could not see the tears in her eyes. Anger had always ruled her emotions and she'd struggled mightily against it. As for sorrow, it was new to her and left Tracy at a complete loss.

The strange voice inside her chipped away at Tracy with its pickaxe: *Stupid woman! That kind, sweet man is in love with you! Why can't you give in to your true feelings? You know damn well you love him, too. So you slept with him, why is that so wrong? Since when is loving someone a sin?*

Surrounded by the hustle of busy shoppers, "Miss," said a woman shopper, demanding Tracy's immediate attention. "I'd like to return this blouse."

Flatly, "Returns are over there," she replied, flapping a hand in the general direction of the courtesy desk.

As if preparing to do battle, the frump headed off without so much as a thank you. Ordinarily, such slights would turn up the gas on Tracy's front burners, but not today. She walked over to a pants rack and absently began rearranging them by size and style.

You think you've dedicated your life to God. Let me clue you in: He doesn't want you! Doesn't need you! One day when—

"Excuse me, Miss." The frumpy shopper had returned. "The girl at the desk said I need your signature on this return slip. She told me I damaged the blouse." Mrs. Frump held it up for Tracy's inspection; then a belligerent, "Do you see any damage? I don't."

The blouse looked like it had been worn dozens of times. "Then you must be blind," snapped Tracy. "Gimme the damn thing!" She snatched it out the startled woman's hand. She scribbled her name on the receipt and tossed the blouse over Frump's head. Then a snarky, "Have a nice day."

"Well excuse me!" the woman said, uncovering and, turning on her heels, she stalked off in a huff.

If you lose this job, Tracy, what will you do then?

"The Lord will provide," she said out loud; too loud. Three women by the coat rack turned around and stared.

Keep your voice down, do you want everyone to know how crazy you are?

"I'm not crazy!" she said.

The women who had been watching slowly drifted away.

You listen and listen good, one day, when you're a bitter old woman living alone in that Hill House of yours, you'll look back and curse God. You'll blame Him, but it was you who messed up your life!

Alone now in Women's Wear, Tracy demanded to know: "Who are you? Are you a demon sent to tempt me?"

Ha! You'd like to believe that, wouldn't you? You really think you're special, don't you? Of all the souls on this earth, do you really think God speaks only to you? Why should He? You're nothing, a nothing person going nowhere.

Tracy felt a tap on her shoulder. It was Joanne George, the manager for the entire floor. Her voice was official when she announced, "I've had a complaint from a customer. That you were rude to her." Then a concerned, "What's wrong, Tracy?"

"The prices we charge and people expect courtesy, too!"

Stiffening, "I think you should take the rest of the day off, Miss Millen."

"Gladly, Mrs. George! The store owes me sick days. I'll take off tomorrow, too!"

***

The Palm Sunday service at His Holy Tabernacle ended at 2:37 p.m. In the parking lot behind the mini-mall, Karen exchanged greetings with the congregation. The faithful seemed satisfied with their new, fill-in preacher.

"You were wonderful," a tall, elderly woman told Karen. The woman held out a pale, blue-veined hand.

The old Karen would barely have been moved to touch such a bony relic, but the new Karen smothered the old lady's hand in both of hers. "Thank you, Miss Shannon," she replied, smiling. "This church, its people are so important to Larry."

A tall, lanky man in his early forties wearing a cowboy hat, cowboy boots, string tie and western suit approached. "Never heard no lady preach before, ma'am," he said, "but you sure are makin' a believer outta me. You're doing a mighty fine job, Miss Stone." He smiled at her, and so too did his tiny blonde wife and two blonde, teenage daughters.

"Thank you, Dwight. But this is only until Larry comes back. Pray for him, will you?"

"Sure enough, ma'am, we pray for him every day." Dwight turned his face away, trying to hold a tight rein on feelings that *real* men of the *real* West carried on their backs like a loaded pack.

Karen remembered Mr. Dwight Bruce well. He was a recovered alcoholic. Larry had provided a small business loan out of church funds so the man could set himself up in a carpentry business. She had adamantly opposed the loan.

"The man's a drunk," she had warned Larry. "I don't begrudge helping people, but only those who can also help themselves. He'll never amount to anything; a waste of money."

"Why are you so cynical, Karen? You give a man honest work and tell him you believe in him, and he'll get his dignity back. Dwight Bruce will succeed, you watch."

That was two years ago, and Mr. Bruce had proved Larry right and her wrong.

"Thank you, Dwight," she said. "Larry told me how proud he was of you and your continuing success."

Karen choked up and even Dwight looked on the verge of tears. Then she shook hands with Dwight, hugged his wife and daughters, and all headed off to their respective vehicles. As she was about to get into her cherry red BMW, a deep voice sounded directly behind her: "Miss Stone? Are you Karen Stone?"

She turned around to see a rather large, balding man in his late thirties. His voice and the overall look of him told her exactly who this stranger was.

"I'm Larry's brother, Miss Stone. My name is Matthew Schmetterling. I'd like to speak to you if you don't mind. Can we have lunch tomorrow?"

Karen stepped away from the car. "Of course, Mr. Schmetterling, I'd be happy to meet you tomorrow." She wanted to hug him, but he seemed a bit standoffish. She remembered that Larry didn't much care for hugs either.

"That's very kind of you, Miss Stone." His words were polite, but clearly his emotions road on a saw-toothed wave.

Trying to smooth them out a bit, she said, "Please, call me Karen."

"OK, Karen. Please call me Matt."

Rummaging in her pocketbook, Karen took out a pen and one of her business cards. Writing on the back, "Here's my cell number, Matt. Please call me tomorrow morning. We'll decide on where to meet."

Matt thanked her, and gave her the phone number of the motel where he was staying. "Oh, I almost forgot: may I also have Mr. Frothe's number?"

"Sure. I'll ask him to join us tomorrow."

He smiled tightly and nodded.

Karen watched him walk back to his little rented gas-saver. Even his steps were angry. A big man needed a bigger rental. When he banged his head getting into the compact car his profane rage shot across the lot and all the way back to her ears. Then he growled, rubbed the right side of his head, and slammed the door shut.

***

Frank had no time for church. He prided himself on *not* being a C&E (Christmas and Easter) Catholic. He belonged to that branch of Catholicism that never ever went to church — the vast majority. But Mama Giavone not only insisted he join her, but that he bring his two sons with him. His boys weren't happy either, but as he and his sons knew, no church meant no big Italian Palm Sunday feast this afternoon and the same thing next week on Easter Sunday.

"I'll throw you all outta the house," she threatened. "Go eat at

McDonalds!"

Frankie's mom knew exactly where her boy's soul hid: in his belly. But he'd gotten up late, picked up the boys late, gotten to Mom's late, and, therefore, they all got to church late. At least a kindly young guy did give up his seat for Mrs. Giavone. Geez, if she had had to stand during the Mass, then she'd really be in a bad mood.

Back home that night, an antsy Frank tried to get into an old Hope and Crosby road movie on DVD. Then he looked over at the clock and did the math: 1:42 a.m. his time was 11:42 her time. He sat up, grabbed his cell, and hit speed dial.

"Karla, Frank. Got some news on the Schmetterling case."

"Yeah, I know all about the brother, your boss called my boss," she said.

"That's not what I called about. But what's with the brother?"

"Mr. Matthew Schmetterling is one nasty dude. Tell me something, Frank: are New Yorkers born ornery or is it the environment y'all are raised in?"

"Both. What happened?"

"Schmetterling is not only rude, he's angry, angry at the world in general and at two NYPD detectives in particular; fellas who won't return his calls and who aren't making any progress in the investigation."

"He told you that?"

"Yeah, his exact words were, 'The only thing the fat guys are good for is eating.' "

"He's just a little upset, that's all."

"More 'n a little, Frank; this fella strikes me as being unpredictable, maybe even a little dangerous."

Frank remembered how tightly wrapped the guy had been when they first met. "Can you handle 'im?"

"He's a king-size pain in the butt, but, yeah, I c'n handle 'im. If he gives me any more guff, I'll hogtie 'im and ship 'im back to you C.O.D."

"So what did he do to get a li'l ole country gal like you so worked up?"

She chuckled. "Li'l ole country gals like me get riled up not worked up." Then she told him what had happened when she confronted Schmetterling at the airport:

"He'd just gotten off the plane and was waiting by a carousel for his luggage. He had a look about 'im: so damn focused he was hardly aware of any other passengers. When asked him if he was Matthew Schmetterling, he says, 'Yeah, that's right. So who're you, lady?'

"I flash my badge in his face and he goes, 'So?'

"When I said his wife is worried about him, and that the CSPD doesn't want him getting into any trouble out here, he snickers and tells me, 'Like what kind of trouble?'

"I tell him, 'Like poking around places where you don't belong, sir. This is still an ongoing investigation.'

"That's when he tells me the police — he means you and your bud, Frank — 'Got squat!' Now I don't know exactly what squat is, but I c'n guess. Then he tells me no one better be telling him what he can and can't do. So I step into his personal space and tell 'im, 'I know you're upset, sir, but—'

"And then he cuts me off with a 'Good evening, Detective.' He brushes passed me and walks away. My Captain wants me to follow him to see he stays out of trouble. I didn't join the police department to babysit an ornery moose. He's one of yours, so why am I stuck with him?"

"I apologize for that, Karla. What's he been up to?" Frank said, worried that now that they were so close to collaring Millen and her brother Frothe, this new Schmetterling might screw up everything.

"Nothing good. He arrived Saturday. This morning he went out to that mini-mall church of theirs. After the service I saw him talking to Karen Stone."

"What about Frothe?"

"He wasn't there."

"You still gonna question Frothe's sister tomorrow?"

"Yeah."

"Y'all be careful now."

"I heard you the first time, Karla," he snapped.

"Don't be getting your boxers in a bunch, Frank," she shot back.

A humorless, "I wear briefs, Karla."

"More 'n I need to know, Frank."

CHAPTER 25

World's End

A bolt of lightning streaked across the sky followed by an explosion of thunder so loud that every hair on Tracy's body shot straight up. Outside thick, black clouds blanketed the horizon from north to south, east to west so that not a single beam of sunlight dared penetrate such a furious mass. Rain battered window panes. Winds slammed against exterior walls and sounded like waves crashing into dykes. Loosened vinyl siding flapped and slapped, and water surged through gutters and came out of downspouts as if they were fire hoses. Wind driven rain assaulted the roof like millions of tiny pellets.

Tracy knew the ferocity outside was God's wrath aimed at her; so she headed down the stairs to the basement to her special room. Laid out on her back the concrete walls did little to dull the howling calamity outside. The brand new red carpeting that now insulated her back from the cold cement floor offered little comfort. Here in her most private, most sacred space she stared at the ceiling praying that it might crash down and crush the life out of her. Only in death would she finally rest in peace. As for the storm that roiled inside of Tracy, its cause was Mr. Tony Magee. He had made her feel alive again. Her body craved his gentle touch.

She longed to hear his sweet innocence as expressed in a comforting Southern drawl. Instead, every day at work she had to bear witness to his hurt and bewilderment.

He would beg her, "Talk to me, please, Tracy. Tell me what I done wrong. Whatever I done, I'm sorry."

"We've committed a great sin, Tony."

"OK, so we sinned," he finally admitted. "We'll never do it again. I promise. I c'n wait. I love you. I wanna marry you, if'n ya'll will have me."

"I've been married, remember? I'm better off alone. Forget me, Tony. I've dedicated my life to God. It's He whom I serve, He whom I love." She wanted to desperately fortify these words, but each time she spoke them aloud, she felt less and less convinced of their truth. Tony Magee had been saved by faith alone! Why did God demand so much from her?

Outside, the Lord's wrath continued to smite Tracy where she lived. Inside, that strange voice said unto her: *Stupid woman! You serve a Lord and Master who doesn't give a damn about you! Tony loves you. He wants to yoke his life to yours. And you reject him? Tracy, you've had more pain in your life than Job. Don't be a fool like he was!*

"I know!" she cried aloud and sat up. To God: *Why did You choose me? I never asked for this! I'm weak, unworthy. I WANT TO LOVE!*

Forget Him, the Voice said. *He's abandoned you.*

Tracy shook her head again and again in disbelief. "No, I've displeased Him. Look outside."

The storm? You think God sent it to punish you? The Voice laughed. *Don't flatter yourself. It's raining all over Long Island. Maybe even the entire Northeast. Not everything is about you, Tracy.*

Over the din of the world coming to an end outside, suddenly she heard the front door's chimes ring. Tracy's senses were more acute when she was in a state of hyper-awareness.

Forget the door! the Voice commanded. *It's two in the afternoon. It can't be anyone important.*

"It could be Tony!" she told the voice. Tracy, her long black hair in a ponytail, climbed the stairs wearing a white terry-cloth robe, pink T-shirt, gray sweats, and faded pink bunny slippers. She was not wearing a bra. She looked like a mess but did not care.

When she reached the top of the stairs, judging from the incessant ringing and pounding at her front door, whoever it was wasn't Tony Magee. Clutching the robe tight to cover her chest, she opened her door and came face to face with four large men hunched against the storm. The one holding up a badge said, "I'm Detective Danny Fanuele, Suffolk County Homicide. These other guys are Detectives Giavone and Goldberg, and Officer George. They're from the City. Do you mind if we come in and ask you a few questions, Miss Millen?"

Detective Fanuele was a rather nice looking, blond thirty-something with a boyish grin and in fine athletic shape. As for his pals: Officer George had a compact body and a hard edge about him; and she didn't much care for the way he was trying to stare her down. Sizing up the other two, Tracy wondered: *These fellas ever hear of Weight-Watchers?*

"Yes I do mind," was her terse reply. "I'm not properly dressed."

"It'll only take a few minutes, Miss Millen," the tall, dark, fat one added in a friendly tone; then without waiting for an invitation, he forged ahead and deposited himself, along with a puddle of dripping water, smack in the middle of Tracy's living room. Looking around, "Nice place you have here, Miss Millen."

In disgust, Tracy widened the door so the rest of the herd could tromp in.

"Mind if we have a seat, Miss Millen?" Fanuele asked.

"You won't be here that long, remember?" Tracy replied looking down at the stains their wet shoes left on her beige rug.

"Excuse me, but I gotta bad back. And I think much better sitting down." The tall, fat one plopped down on the sofa and pulled out a notepad.

Tracy's eyes fluttered at his gall and downright rudeness. "From the looks of you, Detective, it seems to me that you already do too many things sitting down."

He laughed. "That's a good one." Then he jotted something in his pad.

Fanuele sat down next to him. "Helluva storm out there, isn't it, Miss Millen?"

"Did you come here to discuss the weather with me, Detective?" Tracy sat down on a chair across from them. She crossed one leg over the other, and held her robe closed with her left hand. "So, what can I do for you?" Tracy said, eyeing the young, mean one. He stood off to her right with his feet spread apart and his arms folded across his chest. The short, fat one wandered the room, poking his nose here and there. Annoyed, Tracy invited him to have a seat.

"Don't mind standing, ma'am. Like my pal here, I sit around too much, too."

Extremely rude! These police officers had tramped into her home without so much as a *By your leave.* And they hadn't even bothered to take off their soaking wet topcoats. Rude and odd and, *They've ruined my rug and turned my living room into a lake!*

"Miss Millen, do you know a man named Larry Schmetterling?" the tall, fat one began.

Calmly, "No, should I?"

"He's a business associate of your brother, Curtis Frothe."

"Sorry, but I'm not my brother's keeper."

"I take it you're not close to your brother?" asked Fanuele.

"I didn't *say* that," she snapped back.

"Didn't you know that your brother is the Chief Financial Officer of the HHT Holding Group and Mr. Schmetterling is its Chief Operating Officer?" the tall, fat one continued.

Forcing a smile, "First of all, Detective, Curtis is *not* the chief-whatever of anything. He works for a church in Colorado. He's helping to spread the Gospel of our Lord, Jesus Christ."

"Which is a pretty good business," snickered the short, fat one. "Your brother says he pulls down about eighty-five G's a year, but me and Frank think it's a helluva lot more." Shooting a wry smile at his partner, "Maybe we should find religion too, huh, Frank?"

The one called Frank smiled and nodded. Then to Tracy, "Did you know that, in addition to being the CEO of the HHT Holding Group, that Mr. Schmetterling is also a reverend and pastor of His Holy Tabernacle, the church your brother also works for?"

"No, I'm afraid I didn't know. What's this—" Suddenly, Tracy turned her anger on the short, fat one who was now poking through a shelf of her holy knick-knacks: "I'd appreciate it if you looked but did not touch, Detective!"

"Leave 'er shit alone, Howie!" said the one named Frank. Then, "Miss Millen, the church your brother works for and the corporation he's Chief Financial Officer of, the HHT Holding Group, are joint ventures. Did you know that?"

"No I did not. What difference does that make anyway?" Her voice steadily rising, she let go of her robe and leaned forward in the chair: "Why are you people in my living room with your coats on and tracking mud all over my carpet? And why are you wasting my time asking me questions I know nothing about when I should be in my special room, praying?"

Detective Fanuele perked. In *Gotcha* mode: "What *special* room?

Is that your *bedroom*, Miss Millen? That's where I say *my* prayers." He exchanged grins with the other cops.

Behind her the young, mean one snickered. Then she noticed his eyes peeking down at the slightly ajar collar of her V-neck robe. Not a line of sight she wished to give him or any of these other pigs. She leaned back again and held her robe closed tight.

"We're here because somebody shot Mr. Schmetterling," said the one named Frank, "and we think your brother had something to do with it."

Tracy would not be so easily baited. Calmly, "That's ridiculous my brother would never shoot anyone, Detectives. He doesn't even own a weapon. And would not harm a soul either."

Pastor Larry does not have a soul, so he doesn't count.

The one named Frank was quick to pounce: "Who sez anything about you, Miss Millen? Nobody's accusing you 'a nothing."

"You know my history, so don't be coy."

"Yes we do, Miss Millen. Anyway, we'll know for sure once the results from ballistics come back." To Fanuele, "You said you'll have it by tomorrow?"

Looking Tracy straight in the eyes, Detective Fanuele said, "Yeah. We're gonna match the slug you guys took out of Schmetterling to one we took out of the late Mr. Elmore Millen. If we get a match, then it looks like we got our man — excuse me," a wry grin, "woman."

A silent stare hid her true feelings. Rage in Tracy coiled slowly, building in intensity until when finally unleashed it struck as quick as a snake. But unlike a cobra or rattlesnake, there would be no warning hiss, no warning rattle. In silence she fumed; and there would be deadly silence when she struck. Then the phone rang.

Tracy excused herself and went into the kitchen to answer. She looked at the caller ID. The number was unknown but not the area code: 719, Colorado Springs. She committed the number to memory and picked up. In a low voice so the cops in the other room could not hear, "Curtis. The police are here. Call you right back."

Tracy returned to the living room and told the cops, "This is a personal call. If you don't mind, I'd like to take it in my room."

"Your special room?" asked Detective Fanuele, arching his brows.

"You do seem to be fixated on that, Detective, but, no, I'm speaking of my bedroom upstairs. As for my special room, since you're so curious, why not have a look for yourselves. There's a door just off the kitchen; it leads to the basement."

Tracy had skillfully set the trap.

If you go through with this, the voice in her head whispered, *they're going to kill you. Is that what you want?*

The Lord will protect me, Tracy's mind replied, *but if He calls me home to Him, I'm fine with that too.*

***

Karen met Larry's brother at one of Colorado Springs' finest and most elegant places to lunch. Formalities where exchanged: Karen asked how Larry was doing, and his brother's mechanical reply was, "No change." Then he asked, "Where's Mr. Frothe?"

"Curtis sends his regrets, Matt. I'm afraid he's taken the, uh — the incident badly. He hardly ever leaves his office."

"We all have our ways of coping, don't we, Karen? So I take it that Mr. Frothe and my brother are friends?"

"Yes. Both being from New York, they're quite close."

He gazed absently out the window and almost smiled. "It's beautiful out here. Back home I heard there is a big storm over the entire Northeast. The storm is so big it's a freak." He ran his rather large hands down the side of his face and sighed. "Sorry Karen. We're not here to discuss the weather."

Karen caught a glimpse of the man's humanity that lay hidden under beneath layers of anger. She unfolded her cloth napkin and placed it on her lap. "What can I do for you, Matt?"

He asked her to tell him everything about his brother's life out West; so she told him about how the three of them came to found their church. Then she had some questions for Matthew. She knew so little about Larry's life back in New York that she had to wonder how close the family was.

"We were, but once he left seminary we hardly heard from him. I suppose that was because he thought he'd let my parents down. Not me, I never thought the priesthood was right for Lars. When the police told us that he was the pastor of a fundamentalist church, the family was — it's like we never knew him." Matthew threw down his napkin and took a swig of beer. "If he was unhappy, why didn't he come to *me*?" A pause while he pushed against the tears that threatened swamp his eyes. "When we were growing up, *I was the one* he always confided in. He knew he could tell me anything, and I'd understand."

Matthew rested his elbows on the table, and then he buried his face in his hands. The dissonant chords inside him strummed sad notes on Karen's heartstrings. She waited until he had composed himself before she gave him the complexity of Larry the Good, the Bad and the Ugly. She'd always believed that those who thought they knew someone best, like family, in reality knew that person the least. *A prophet in his own town,* was the biblical paraphrase that jumped into Karen's head as she gave her summation of Pastor Larry.

After she'd finished, Matt said that he appreciated her candor. Then he added, "I gather from what you've just told me that you have a rather intimate understanding of my brother. Are you two lovers?"

The question, so pointed, temporarily tied Karen's tongue into a knot. Finally, "We were once, Matt," she replied without looking him in the eyes. "But we've grown apart since."

He nodded like a man familiar with these things. "It happens sometimes. My wife and I — never mind."

"I want you to know that I still care about your brother very, very much. I never realized just how much until this tragedy." The once hard as a rock Ms. Stone began to weep.

Matthew changed the subject: "The police don't seem to be getting anywhere in their investigation; they made all kinds of promises about solving the case, and now they won't even return my god-damn phone calls!"

After they finished eating, the waiter placed the check face down on the table; both Karen and Matt reached for it. He was a bit quicker.

"Matt, please. I said that lunch was on me," said Karen.

He hesitated, then, "OK… Please tell Mr. Frothe that I'd like to speak with him, too."

"I will but I can't promise anything. Curtis has been like a zombie ever since the — you know what."

"The shooting, Miss Stone, the shooting," he growled. "It happened and is what it is." Then to himself out loud: "I hate it when people prance around the obvious."

He stood to leave. "Thank you for lunch, Karen." Then he gave her a forlorn look: "I'm sorry if I was rude to you at times. When I get angry I take it out on the wrong people."

"I understand," was her soft reply.

***

Tracy's sweaty palms slid along the banister. She struggled to put one foot in front of the other. Step by step she ascended the stairs leading to the bedroom. She glanced out the bedroom window. No let up in the storm. Shivering as if the room temperature had suddenly dropped forty degrees, Tracy sat down on the bed. She took one, long deep breath and held onto it tightly to calm herself. Once the police matched the bullet from evil Elmore with the one taken from evil Schmetterling she'd be back on a gray/green bus headed to Mattawan. Unless, of course,

Time to do penance, Tracy, the Voice said. *Confess. Turn yourself in to the police.*

"Who are you!" she demanded to know.

A part of you with only your best interests at heart.

She picked up the receiver on her princess rotary and, with a shaky finger, dialed the Colorado phone number she had memorized. Then she began to weep because she knew she would never see Tony Magee again. Once, just once, she wanted to say to someone who did *not* transcend all human understanding, "I love you."

Between sobs she told Curtis about the ballistics test. Silence on his end of the line. "Curtis? Are you there? Did you hear what I just said?"

"I heard you, Tracy. Lemme think for a minute."

While she waited, her temples throbbed, and she was barely able to breathe.

"You didn't do anything, Tracy. It was me. I aimed you at Larry. I practically pulled the trigger myself. I'm going to the police. I'll confess. I'll tell 'em you had nothing to do with it. What did you do with the gun?"

"It's right here in my drawer."

"Get rid of it! No gun, no fingerprints, nothing to connect you to the crime."

A defeated, "The bullet will connect me to the crime, Curtis."

"I'll tell them that I shot Larry with your gun. How are they going to prove otherwise?"

"You're a good man, Curtis. The Lord knows none of us are perfect; in His infinite mercy, He'll forgive us both." She turned her attention back to the storm still raging outside: "The world is an evil place. I can see it right now, it's outside my window. It's people like you who make it better. I can't let you sacrifice yourself."

There was only one way out for her. In a voice that resonated through the fiber optics and soared unto heaven like a prayer, she said, "I am not worthy, Lord, to stoop and loosen the thongs of Your sandals. Forgive me for doubting You." Building in crescendo, "I have been baptized with water; soon You will baptize me with fire!"

Alarmed, "You're talking crazy, Tracy!"

Her lunar module temporarily returned to planet earth long enough to tell her brother, "You know I hate that word, Curtis!"

"They'll put you back in Mattawan."

"I know that! I'm not stupid!" Then, stepping back into a loftier tone, "It is a far, far better thing I do than I've ever done before. You will stay behind to do the Lord's work. My time has passed."

"Tracy! Tracy!"

She hung up the phone.

***

In the 18'x18' space in the basement of Millen's ranch-style home the only illumination came from a metal matrix of blue-cupped candles. Smoky fingers of burning incense curled towards the ceiling as if scratching for a way out of this hellhole. Even the gray/green walls chanted gloom and doom.

Simultaneously, "Creepy," said a wide-eyed Two Names, and "Whoa!" seconded an equally astonished Detective Fanuele.

Said Howie to no one in particular: "What's that stink?"

Two Names answered, "That's incense, Howie." He went to Catholic Church regularly.

"Look at them candles all over the place," noted Frank. "This dump is a fire hazard."

Detective Fanuele pointed at the candelabra. "Bet she stole that from a church."

The three detectives continued to gawk at the altar, their backs to the stairway. Two Names, at a far wall to the left of the steps, stared at various depictions in art of the Suffering Savior's sad face. He was the first to see Tracy coming down the stairs, the others being too caught up in the madness of the scene. She had changed out of her house clothes and into a bra, red sweater, blue jeans, and gleaming white sneakers. He noticed she was not wearing a raincoat. Then he saw the .32 caliber semi-automatic in her right hand.

Two Names watched, momentarily frozen in place, as she raised the weapon and aimed at his face. "GUN!" he screamed as he dove for the floor.

Crack! went the first shot.

Frank, with his back to the action, saw out of the corner of his left eye the bullet explode a statue of the Blessed Mother. In those first few microseconds, it still hadn't registered with him that they had come under fire. Then — *Crack! Crack!* — two slugs smacked into his back. Although the bullets stung, their impacts were not forceful enough to knock him off his feet. Nevertheless, instinctively he spread his arms out in front of him and dove into the middle of Tracy's altar. Hot wax and burning incense scattered in all directions.

Crack!

Another slug hit Howie square in the spine. His body went completely numb and he collapsed in a heap.

Meanwhile, Two Names, who had fallen onto his left side, struggled to reach across his chest with his right hand to draw the 9mm in the shoulder holster under his left arm, the arm he now laid upon. Detective Fanuele, being the last sitting duck in Tracy's line of fire, had turned halfway to face her; he reached for his own Berretta when — *Crack!* — a bullet ripped into his left arm just below the elbow. The bullet passed through leaving a searing, white-hot trail and broken bones in its wake. Fanuele fell on his good side and screamed. In agony, he rolled onto his back, feet facing Tracy, and somehow managed to get off two rounds — *BAMM! BAMM!* — but instead of putting two gaping holes in Tracy, they shattered a ceiling tile.

Howie, floundering on his stomach like a beached whale, tried to shake some feeling back into his arms and legs. Frank, his adrenaline rushing so that he couldn't feel a patch of burnt hair and scalp that had scorched his head, rolled over onto his stomach. He drew his .38 revolver and fired through the smoke and flames that was slowly engulfing them all: *BANG! BANG!* Two slugs winged passed Tracy's body, producing two holes in the stairwell.

Two Names, also on his stomach, fired his 9mm in her direction — *BAMM! BAMM! BAMM! BAMM!* — but there wasn't much to shoot at. Tracy was partially hidden by a stairwell wall and his angle on her was bad. He had 15 rounds in his magazine, so he might get lucky and hit her. But even if he didn't, he might draw her fire away from his more exposed partners.

Even the holiest of martyrs were bound to get unnerved when on the receiving end someone else's deadly projectiles. Tracy had sent many a round winging at targets, but this was the first time she'd ever been on the receiving end of unfriendly fire. She had only three shots left. *Crack!* — she sent another bullet blindly into the smoky haze.

I CAN'T SEE! I CAN'T SEE! her mind screamed.

WE HAVE TO GET OUT OF HERE! demanded the voice in her head.

The flames spread faster now, jumping from the altar to the drapes to the lace curtains. When the rug finally ignited the whole room would burn like an inferno.

Hacking coughs rang out everywhere. No one in this fierce gun fight could see who they were shooting at because of the thick, black smoke

— no one except Frank. He crawled towards the stairwell on his belly, beneath the rising smoke. He could see Tracy's sneakers and lower legs less than ten feet away. With both hands on his weapon, he projected upward to where he thought her body would be and fired again — *BANG!*

Tracy sensed a bullet had just whizzed by her right ear. Suddenly her desire to rest in the arms of her Lord faded away. Coughing and choking, she felt like she was drowning in a lake of smoke. Her eyes filled with tears and an animal instinct to survive took hold. Tracy had to get the hell out of there; let the Lord's holy fire consume these wicked cops.

BAMM! BAMM! Two more rounds whizzed in front of her. They came from her left, from the young, mean one. With her body still facing the altar, she lifted her right hand and, to cover her retreat, she sent her last two rounds winging in that direction: *Crack! Crack!* Unleashing those parting shots turned out to be a mistake, a fatal mistake.

BANG! a shot came from head-on. The round had found its mark, lifting her off her feet. It drilled hot and deep through her kill zone, entering her abdomen and exiting between her shoulder blades. Tracy felt herself sailing backwards until the stairs slammed into her. The bullet's wake convulsed her. A fire had been ignited inside her and reflexively she felt like heaving her insides out. Mercifully that sense of total regurgitation did not last long. Her eyes glazed over, her head rolled back, and her jaw dropped open.

Outside, the rain suddenly stopped. Tongues of fire were now free to cleanse everyone and everything in a burnt offering.

CHAPTER 26

A Sea of Lost Hope

Even as it feasted, the fiery demon roared for *More! More! More!*

Yellow and red flames blasted through the roof and spiraled into a gray sky. Crawling, crackling fire rendered the house a perverse burnt offering unto itself. Flames swirled furiously behind windows like dancers at a mad ball. Hot gas and smoke exploded through of the front door like frenzied lovers escaping a party anxious for their trysts. Flames alighted off eaves and gutter lines. The exterior walls and roof finally gave way and only a charcoal skeleton remained standing. The demon had been sated. The home of the late Tracy Millen was reduced to a smoldering compost of ash and rubble.

Half-block a away, in that no man's land that lay between the fire and the fire trucks, and police, EMS vehicles and the neighborhood lookie-loos, Frank felt the blaze's intense heat. He sat on the curb, his topcoat and bulletproof vest lay in a heap next to him. The smell of smoke clung to him like a cheap aftershave; with both hands covering his mouth, all two-hundred thirty pounds of him shook as another series of hacking, raspy coughs erupted. Coughs that seemed to well up from his deepest parts; coughs that burned through his lungs and throat before bursting out of his mouth; coughs so raw that it felt like a toilet bowl scrub brush was being run down his esophagus. When the hacking stopped, he collapsed onto his back in the wet grass and laid an arm across his face. What he wanted now was to leave his gun, badge and vest where they lay and get the hell out of this wacky city forever. Maybe settle in that pretty little town nestled in the shade of the Rocky Mountains. Someone special lived there.

Then he felt a hand on his shoulder. “How ya doing, Frank? You all right?” Captain Graham had arrived on the scene. Graham helped him into a sitting position.

A raspy, “I’m OK. How’re the rest of the guys?”

“Two Names went with Howie and the Suffolk cop to the hospital.”

Although the house had been burned away, fortunately, the flames did not consume any persons, either living or already dead. While Two Names and a wounded Detective Fanuele dragged Howie from the blaze — the bullet’s impact had done temporary nerve damage to Howie’s spine despite the bulletproof vest he’d been wearing — Frank had hoisted Tracy’s dead weight on his broad back and carried her body up the basement steps and out of the house.

Staring over at the EMS vehicle where her covered body now lay in state behind closed doors, “I just couldn’t leave her there,” a shivering Frank told his boss.

A cold drizzle began to fall; that and his own nerves did a number on Frank’s body. Graham called to a Suffolk cop who then draped a blanket around Frank’s shoulders. Then the Captain told Frank an arrest warrant for Curtis Frothe had already been faxed to the Colorado Springs PD. He and Two Names would be heading out west tomorrow.

As Frank and Captain Graham headed to Graham’s car, a short, plump, dark-haired woman broke passed the cops that had been holding back the lookie-loos. She ran up to Frank.

"My name is Christine DeVito," the terrified woman said. "I'm Tracy's neighbor. Is she all right? What happened in there? I thought I heard shots, but with all the noise from the storm I'm not sure."

Frank sensed the woman was not just another ghoul looking for ghoulish details. This woman was someone who had once been a friend and neighbor to the late Tracy Millen; this woman confirmed that Frank had killed a person not a monster. He decided to let the local PD break the news.

In silence, Frank walked on by.

When he and the Captain got to the hospital, they found Howie sitting up in bed. Between fits of hacking coughs, he was dropping enormous amounts of graceless, tasteless hospital food down his gullet. The way Frank figured it, there wasn't much else for Detective Goldberg to do except cough, stuff his face, and feel sorry for himself.

"I hate this place!" growled a hoarse Howie. "And the food's crap!" To Two Names, "Thanks kid for pulling me outta that fire." Then to Frank, "Good idea you had about wearing them vests."

The idea was due mainly to Karla's concern for their safety. Not that Howie needed to know that.

Howie continued, "Geez, who coulda guessed the whacko would go all whacko and shoot it out with us."

Said a smug Captain Grame, "That's what whackos usually do, Goldberg, go whacky."

Howie's nostrils flared when he added, "My whole career I never got to shoot at a bad guy, then this happens and I still didn't get a shot off!" Taking a closer look at Frank, he slid back into his jolly old self: "Hey, Frank, you look kinda cute with that bald spot on the side of your head. Chicks are gonna love you." He laughed and coughed, and laughed and coughed while a self-conscious Frank ran his fingers through a barren patch where hair used to be.

Graham told his men how truly sorry he was about the death of Miss Millen. "The poor woman was sick. She couldn't help herself."

When Graham mentioned that Detective Fanuele would be getting a citation from his department, Howie went ballistic. "How about a citation for us!"

Said Graham, "I'll see what I can do." On that note, he quickly left.

Grumbled Howie to Frank and Two Names: "Don't hold your breath."

A citation from the NYPD — and Frank wasn't holding his breath — meant nothing to him. The tissues in his throat and lungs would heal a whole lot faster than the soft tissues of his psyche. For the first time in his career he had fired his weapon at something other than a dark silhouette on a white poster. This was the first time he'd killed something other than a fly on a wall. When he'd shot Tracy, he swore he could hear the bullet smack into her chest and the life blow out of her. When Two Names and Detective Fanuele dragged Howie up the stairs and out of the basement, they trampled Tracy's body as if it was a pile of garbage. But Frank, following close behind, was stopped by dark, lifeless eyes staring up at him.

Don't leave me here, they pleaded. So he didn't.

***

Yesterday morning Curtis had sat at Larry's desk in the office suite of the HHT Holding Group. As soon as he dropped the phone receiver back into its jack, he knew his sister would soon be dead. Sacrificing himself to the police to save Tracy was no longer an option. He had to get out of town. But where? He drove out to Black Forest and spent the night hiding in the basement of His Holy Tabernacle. All night long survival wrestled the tag team of guilt and penance and quickly overcame both. This morning, Tuesday, March 18th, he had left her a note on the dining room table of his condo.

Curtis needed to find a place where he could be alone to think; then he remembered that the HHT had cabins in Woodland Park, a hamlet northwest of the Springs. Since this was Easter week the cabins would be unoccupied. Like Jesus who had gone into the wilderness to purge Himself, Curtis would stay at this remote camp until he figured out what to do next.

He headed north on Highway 24. He threw the 4x4 into a lower gear as the Bronco climbed higher and higher into the mountains. Highway 24 wound through crevasses of carved canyons dug deep into red sandstone cliffs. He drove passed snow-capped pines set atop ridges of sheer rock. Like a living beast gaining strength, the engine growled as it sucked in cold, thin air. Worries about Tracy and the cops chased after him. Looking in the rear-view mirror — always looking in the rear-view mirror — Curtis worried more about what might be coming up behind him than what lay ahead. With no flashing lights and sirens on his tail — yet — he turned on the local Christian radio station. The music did nothing to calm his nerves. His mind kept turning back on itself, back to Tracy. Was she dead? Was she alive? He knew his sister was crazy, but was she suicidal? In a shootout with the cops she had to know that she was born to lose. Hopefully, she'd have the good sense to surrender. But what if she played the martyr?

This whole mess was *Larry's* fault! He had to get on TV! Maybe his sister was right? The world did not need another false prophet who used the Word of God to satisfy his own selfish needs. Then there was a momentary breakdown in that part of Curtis' brain that blocked thoughts from slipping onto his tongue: "Kill them all!" he screamed, pounding the steering wheel.

What am I thinking? What am I saying? I'm as nuts as my sister!

Highway 24 leveled out briefly and then dipped. The Bronco picked up speed. Curtis moved his foot from the accelerator to the brake pedal. He slowed the vehicle down. The last thing he needed was to be stopped by the state patrol for speeding. The Bronco assaulted another incline, one not as steep. Off to the left was a beautiful wall of green pines rising from the foot of a rapid stream, March's runoff.

His Holy Tabernacle, not his! Damn you, Larry! May you rot in Hell; but not Tracy, she couldn't help herself. She's sick. Please God, have mercy on my sister. And me too. No one needs it more than me right now. I'm so confused. Where did it all go wrong?

With Larry, he's where it all went wrong! Him and his damn ego! But what about me, what's going to happen to me? Am I innocent? Maybe not, but I couldn't help myself. We're all sinners. Imperfect, but You still love us, right? Just have faith, right? You forgive all that come to You truly repentant, right?

The Bronco finally turned off Highway 24 onto Dung Beetle Boulevard; then onto Shining Path Road. It led straight to the retreat center. Larry had named the road himself. Curtis had complained about the name, he thought it sounded Buddhist.

As Curtis suspected, even the caretakers were gone for Holy Week. He parked the Bronco behind the retreat center where it would not be seen from the road. Inside the center, the first thing he did was go to the small chapel to pray. At Larry's insistence the pews had kneelers. Curtis had also complained that kneelers were too Catholic. But did Larry listen? No!

Rather than kneel in a pew Curtis sat: *Please, Lord, light my way. I don't know what to do.*

***

That night, the horrors of the day chomped down on Frank's brain with its sharp teeth. He had not had a migraine in a long time, but at home tonight he had a whopper. With his head in such agony he couldn't sleep. Tracy Millen was a sad, sick human being, but someone must've loved her, cared about her. And he killed her. He'd heard the bullet hit her; he'd heard her last breath. Sitting on the lumpy, torn sofa in his cramped living room, he sipped beer and hoped the mindless sitcom on the TV would dull his throbbing head. Then he looked at the clock on the wall: 10:43 his time was 8:43 her time; would she be home or on a date with the kiddy cop?

He keyed in the number. She came on the line, and he immediately hung up. Seconds later his phone rang.

"Caller ID, Frank. I heard what happened. How are you?"

In a raspy voice barely audible even to him, he said, "Don't know what to say. I'm not so good with words." Then he coughed.

"OK. Try and get some sleep. I'll be picking y'all up at the airport Thursday."

Another cough, then he cleared his throat and asked, "Find Frothe yet?"

"No, but we did find Schmetterling's brother. He's been playing cat and mouse with us. We brought 'im in and invited him to get the hell outta Dodge or else."

"So what happened?"

"He laughed in our faces. Said we had no grounds to hold him. We're watching 'im real careful, though. He so much as spits on the grass, we're gonna lock 'im up for safekeeping."

"Know what I wish, Karla? I wish I could'a asked the Millen woman, 'Why'd ya do it? Why'd ya shoot Schmetterling?'"

"We'll ask her brother when we collar 'im."

Frank turned off the TV and went into the kitchen to fix a sandwich. After two bites, he threw the damn thing in the garbage. Sitting at the table and staring at the digital clock on the kitchen radio, he watched seconds slowly blink into minutes. Time passed, slower now than ever before. Despite fatigue, it wasn't just the hacking coughs or guilt that kept him from his bed. To hold onto consciousness meant to keep an iron grip on life itself. As long as he stayed awake, he knew he was still alive. At forty-four years-old, most of the continuously flowing stream that was Frank Giavone's life had already passed under the bridge. As he moved closer and closer to the day when it would trickle into that final dry hole, he thought of his father, dead almost ten years now. He could see the man again in his mind, a living, breathing, walking, talking, and laughing person he so closely resembled. That the lifeless body of his father now lay buried in the ground looking like something out of *Tales From the Crypt* gave him the shakes.

Howie's lust for life could best be quantified by the maximum number of calories he could cram into himself at one sitting; as for Frank, he was evolving into a more complex being. At 12:17 a.m., he finally returned Susan Ferro's phone call. She didn't say much only that Millen's death had been a tragedy. She was glad no one else had been hurt.

"If you need to talk, Frank, come over." Her voice was like fingers gently stroking a sad chord.

"Thanks, Sue, but maybe some other time."

After hanging up, he knew there would never be a "some other time." All he wanted to do was jump back into his old life and throw the covers over his head. But he'd killed a woman today and same old same old was gone forever.

***

On Thursday, at 9:13 a.m. M.S.T., a great titanium bird swooped in from the east. Like a raptor in search of prey, eyes looked down as the plane circled the city of Colorado Springs. Frothe was down there somewhere, and Frank and company meant to get him.

Detective Karla Libbee met the Double Gs and Two Names at the gate. After a quick stop at the motel to check in and dump their luggage, Karla drove them all to the condo Karen Stone had once cohabitated with Pastor Larry. They were all seated around Stone's dining room table. This time the Double Gs were not hungry. When Karla told Karen about Mr. Curtis Frothe's complicity in the shooting of Pastor Larry, as well as the death of Frothe's sister, Miss Tracy Millen, Ms. Stone's face went from shock to sadness in less time than it takes to say, *Omigod!*

With both elbows on the table, Karen covered her face with her hands. "This is so hard to believe. I didn't even know that Curtis had a sister."

"Did Larry know about the sister?" Karla asked.

When Karen Stone uncovered, her eyes were afloat in tears. Barely able to get the words out: "Neither of us knew. Curtis never said much about his family."

"No wonder," snarked Howie to on one in particular.

Frank asked, "What *did* Frothe say about his family?"

"That his father had died years ago, before Larry and I knew him. He died of a stroke, I think. His mother died a year later of breast cancer." She paused. Karen Stone looked like a woman desperately fighting to keep her head above rising tides of emotion that threatened to swamp her. Then clearing her throat: "We thought he was alone."

"He is now," grumbled Howie.

"When was the last time you saw Mr. Frothe, Karen?" Karla asked, gently.

"We had dinner here Sunday night."

Frank, the one doing all the writing, asked for clarification: "Would that be last Sunday, the 16th?"

"Yes. Palm Sunday. I cooked."

Karla asked, "Please tell us about the last time you saw Mr. Frothe, Karen."

***

Dinner with Curtis, unlike dinner with Larry and his constant jabber mostly about himself, had always been a quiet almost solemn affair. But on Palm Sunday, Karen sensed that the cart that held all of Curtis' tightly packed apples had rolled over. A frown etched deep into his sunken face. His eyes were vacant and their focus inward. Karen's own sharp eyes caught tiny tremors in his hand as he pushed his food around the plate with a fork. Slowly and unenthusiastically did the meatloaf she had prepared for him go from his fork into his mouth.

Putting on a smiley face, "How was your day, Curtis?"

"Terrific," he grumbled.

The dainty approach had not worked. Karen, never one for subtlety anyway, "Are you sure you won't come with me when I meet Larry's brother for lunch tomorrow?"

"Sorry, Karen, but I'm just not up to meeting his brother right now."

"Stop looking so guilty, Curtis. I've told you over and over, Larry and I are finished. The shooting has not changed my feelings towards him." Softer, "Or you."

She reached across the table for his hand, but he pulled it away. He asked her not to tell Larry's brother about the two of them. She promised she wouldn't. After clearing the table, she dumped all the dirty dishes in the sink; she'd wash them tomorrow morning. Karen made one last appeal to Curtis who now lay stretched out on the sofa, a forearm lay over his eyes.

"It's going to be difficult for me, too, Curtis. Are sure you won't come with me? The brother said he'd like to talk to both of us. It's the least we can do."

A forlorn, "Sorry, Karen, I just can't."

With her pot close to boiling over, Karen said, "I really need you there with me, Curtis."

"I said I can't!"

Off flew her lid, "You're just like him! Stupid me, why do I keep getting involved with men who are only involved with themselves! You're selfish, Curtis, just like Larry." She plopped down next to him on the sofa and pushed his arm away from his face. "Look at me, damn it! I need you with me tomorrow."

"I'm sorry, Karen. I don't mean to be so — I'm just scared, that's all. I'm the weak one, remember? You and Larry, you're the strong ones."

"Spare me! You don't fool me one bit. You're far more decisive than you let on."

"I'll make it up to you tomorrow night," he said, "dinner at my place. We need to talk."

"Let's talk now. What's bothering you?"

"I need some time."

"Time for what?"

Curtis swung his long legs passed her and sat up. "Maybe I need some time away from you! Away from everybody! To think. Off by myself somewhere. To purify myself like Jesus did when he went into the wilderness."

To the world, Karen had always appeared to be a rose with a toughened stalk and extra sharp thorns. But she'd recently lost Larry, and now it looked like Curtis might dump her, too. She asked in a small voice, "Does it have anything to do with us?"

In a kinder tone, "No, Karen, it's not us. The problem is with me. So is the solution."

Karen knew instinctively when to leave well enough alone. "I just want you to know that I love you, Curtis, and I'll be there for you whenever you're ready to talk."

"For what it's worth, Karen, I love you, too. I just wish things could've…"

He hugged her tightly. Then he stood to leave.

"I'm determined to hold all we've worked for together," Karen said as she followed him to the closet next to the front door. "Not just for us, but for the people, too. What do they have besides our church? His Holy

Tabernacle is such an important part of their lives; without it, they would be lost, a people adrift. The church is their shelter island in an angry, uncaring sea."

Curtis snickered, "A sea of lost hope."

Although Curtis had been acting strangely of late, Karen had been far too busy to give him much attention. Besides running the church, she'd been scouring Larry's notes and scrupulously reading the Bible every day: once in the morning after breakfast and again at night before bed. She had also been watching televangelists performing their small-screen miracles in order to pick up pointers and improve her technique. The net result: Karen's sermons got better with each passing week. She had gained confidence but knew she wasn't all the way there yet. She told Curtis that she could not save the church by herself. She needed him.

"Isn't it a bit late to be finding religion, Karen?"

"What are you talking about?"

"Never mind."

***

"When I arrived at Curtis' place for dinner Monday night, he wasn't home." Karen stood up, went into the bedroom, and came back holding a slip of paper. She laid it on the table in front of Karla. "He left me this."

Karla read it; then she pushed it over to Frank. The note said:

K,

Will be back in a few days. Need time to think. I'll explain later.

God Bless, C.

"And you haven't heard from him since, Karen?" asked Karla.

"Not a word."

Karla signaled to Frank and the others the time had come for them to leave.

As they all settled into Karla's Saturn — Frank up front with her, and Howie and Two Names in the back — Howie said, "Stone said something about Frothe going to the wilderness. Any places like that around here?"

Karla snickered. "This is Colorado, bud. We're plum full of it."

Back at the motel, as Detective Goldberg and Officer George got out of the back seat, Karla grabbed onto Frank's left arm. "Hold on a minute, Frank."

Frank rolled down his window and told Howie and Two Names he'd meet them back in the room.

"How about you and I grab a bite, Frank? I know what you're feeling right now."

How dare this damn woman assume *she* knew how *he* felt! "No you don't."

A firm, "Yes I do. I also had to take a life in the line of duty."

That dropped Frank's lower jaw.

CHAPTER 27

Knock, Knock, Knocking on Heaven's Door

Larry awakens standing in front of a full-length mirror. He is being confronted by a full-length reflection of what he used to be: a young man in prime health and on the verge of something great. That this image of his former self also happens to be sans clothing, not even bikini briefs to cover his asset, has him thinking that Hell has reduced him to a cliché.

Yeah right, like I'm about to face the bare, naked truth about myself.

It's just Larry and the mirror in a gleaming white void. Tentatively, he reaches out to touch the glass, but his fingertips feel nothing. It's as if the mirror is a mirage. He pushes the rest of his hand into the mirror. It disappears, and Larry is now joined arm to arm to a reflection of himself. If there's another side of this mirror, what's there? He tells himself, *Through the looking glass, Alice.* Whatever is there has to be far more interesting than here. Larry steps through and finds he has returned to his senior year at St John's University. He's taking an elective called Cosmology for Poets; not an especially rigorous course. Professor J. Moody, a non-tenured and perpetually tired man of forty-three, teaches the class. Here students wrestle with multiple-choice questions as demanding as: What is the definition of a light year?

Once Moody confided to Larry, “What I want more than anything else, Schmetterling, is to teach real physics to real students of physics.”

Larry, in turn, told Moody that the study of astrophysics had been one of his passions. “I feel closer to God every time I look up at the stars. Sitting in church rarely makes me feel the same way. That’s why I registered for this course, Professor.” To which he tacked on a self-aggrandizing coda: “I am a seeker of truth.”

To Larry’s dismay, Moody replied, “Physics *is* truth, everything else conjecture. If it’s truth you seek, Schmetterling, change your major.”

Although this event must have occurred eons ago, at the moment he has a more pressing matter to attend to: Larry sits at a desk in a class with twenty other people still naked. Although it seems his nudity is of no consequence to anyone else, nevertheless, he keeps both hands cupped over his No-Peek Zone. Even in death, modesty prevails; therefore, any hand raised in this class will not be his.

The subjects of today’s lecture are black holes and neutron stars. Larry recognizes that given the limitations of the gray matter gathered around him like tiny puddles of off-colored mud, Moody has to begin in the simplest of terms: “Our sun is a star that measures some 870,000 miles in diameter. It has a surface temperature of 10,000 degrees F; therefore, it appears yellow.”

Moody pauses; so far so good, the bards-to-be appear to be following right along with his muse. Then the professor holds out a hand. He makes a small spread between his thumb and index finger. “Imagine I’m holding a yellow marble, one inch in diameter. Picture this yellow marble next to a big red balloon that’s five feet in diameter. That’s how big our sun is when compared to a red super-giant, a massive star approximately 60 million miles in diameter.”

A hand shoots up. At the root source of that arm is a brooding, intense young man with long stringy hair and a goatee. He always dresses in black. His name is,

"Thomas?" says Moody.

Thomas Aquinas Rota, who fancies himself the incarnation of Dean Moriarty, asks, "Will this be on the test, Professor?"

Larry often wondered about the pretentions of parents who would name their bad boy son after Thomas Aquinas; hard-core Catholics, no doubt.

From Moody an annoyed, "Yes, Thomas, this will be on the test; so pay close attention."

In life, on Larry's *People I Hate* list contained very few names; but at the top sat Thomas Aquinas Rota. That the girls preferred a freethinker like Thomas to a spiritual young man like him was incomprehensible. But because Larry's living body lacked armor plating, he avoided activities that might lead to its being physically damaged. He led a life of non-violence not just because he was against doing harm unto others, but also because of harm others might do unto him. *Punch not, lest ye get smacked too!* had been his creed. But here in the realm of dreams and visions, Larry is sorely tempted to remove his hands from deep cover duty and go smash a fist into Thomas's face.

Meanwhile, Moody continues: "A red super-giant consists of a helium core surrounded by outer layers of cooling and expanding gases. For the next few million years, layers of differing chemical elements will be fused around the super-giant's core, a core that consists mainly of iron. By the way, that core burns at anywhere from 5 to 9 billion degrees F."

"Wow! That'll burn your pizza!" someone snarks, and the poets chuckle.

Then the hand, the one sleeved in black wool, arises once again.

From Moody a weary: "Yes, Thomas."

Profundity must be displayed properly, so Thomas, about to say something truly profound, takes a beat to rearrange his sharp features.

Then he says, "A pizza baking in an oven is tangible, Professor. When we bite into a slice, we can taste its hot, creamy texture. It burns the roofs of our mouths. According to *Pizza Hut* a pizza cooks at 600 degrees F." Thomas pauses to allow the class another chuckle. Then, "I have a sense of what that is. As for millions of billions of degrees the magnitude of these numbers are beyond human comprehension."

"No kidding, jerk!" Larry the Nude blurts out.

Thomas ignores Larry the Nude's outburst and asks, "Will this be on the test, Professor?"

Moody ignores them both. "When the core of a red giant collapses — by the way, this occurs in less than a second, people — it causes a huge explosion that we call a supernova."

Larry blurts out, "Even a pretentious butt-hole like you, Thomas Aquinas Rota, can see just how wondrous a supernova is!"

Since neither Thomas nor Moody has reacted to his stinging commentary, Larry begins to wonder if he's an illusion unto an illusion: *Maybe they can't see me. Maybe I'm not really here?*

Moody adds, "After a supernova, if the remaining core is about 1 1/2 to 3 solar masses, it becomes a neutron star. Thus, after a super-giant with a diameter of 60 million miles goes supernova, all that remains is a core six miles across. That would be like earth being compressed to the size of a pea in less than a second."

Without raising his hand, Larry the Nude calls out, "The core of a neutron star is so dense that one-teaspoon of its matter weighs a billion tons."

Moody smiles, "That's right, Schmetterling. Where do you think I'm going with this?"

"Uh? No idea, Professor."

"You disappoint me, Schmetterling. Answer me this, then: What happens if the core remaining after a supernova is larger than three solar masses?"

"Then the core continues contracting and becomes a quark, and then a black hole."

"Bet you know all about black holes, don't you, Schmetterling?" cracks Thomas.

Damn the nudity! It's full speed ahead. In life, Larry never struck another human being in anger. In death, he figures he's waited long enough. Larry jumps from his seat and goes over to where the pompous poet sits, hands clasped together in front of him resting on his desk. The idiot does not look at Larry, he stares at the blackboard.

Larry throws Thomas to the floor and begins to pummel him. Too bad, though, because he cannot feel the crack of his bare knuckles against Thomas's pointy face; a disappointment.

"A black hole," Moody continues to lecture the rest of the class, "is a phenomenon where gravity is so powerful that not even light can escape."

Larry has chunks of Thomas's dark, greasy hair in both hands as he begins pile-driving the bard's head into the vinyl tiles. When he's done, Thomas has been planted like a tree. He is upside down, sticking out of the floor from the neck up and with his arms and legs splayed out. Larry returns to his seat. "Somebody hang Christmas lights on that clown."

The class applauds, especially the coeds.

Geez, I've been sitting naked all this time, and they ignored me. Then I beat on a guy and they're all smiles. Women! Go figure.

Moody winds down his lecture with: "An event horizon is defined as a spherical boundary that surrounds a black hole. Once a particle crosses the event horizon that particle will collapse into a singularity. It has been postulated that a singularity is a point of infinite mass density where time and space are infinitely distorted by gravitational forces. It is, therefore, believed that a singularity is the final state of matter falling into a black hole."

Suddenly, it's as if a switch has been flicked and each and every light on each and every face, no matter how dull to begin with, suddenly goes out. Even Larry, the only bright bulb in this otherwise assembly of low wattage, finds himself straining to comprehend. Moody lets out a sigh. The professor truly detests these poets and their silly musings, although, as he once admitted to Larry, he finds them a cut above the truly dark matter of the academic cosmos: pre-med, pre-law, and business majors.

"Let me clarify. Think of a black hole as a funnel and an event horizon as the rim of that funnel. Now imagine matter falling into a black hole and spiraling downward to a point at the base of the funnel. That point is what we call a singularity."

That's when Larry notices that the rest of the class has disappeared. Moody tells him, "Undoubtedly you're wondering what all this has to do with you. Well, Schmetterling, you're about to find out."

Larry feels a tap on his shoulder. He turns around and sees Thomas standing there grinning down at him. The bard has successfully harvested himself from the floor. Suddenly Thomas's smiling face morphs into an unsmiling woman, the same woman who laid him to waste so many eons ago. And she's aiming a gun at him. Because he's already dead, she doesn't frighten him anymore. Now he finds her annoying: *Not again!*

A deadly projectile corkscrews straight at Larry's face. But this time, it's not skull and bone that the bullet smashes through; rather the Reverend Schmetterling is like a massive sun with layers of ego stretching 60 million miles across. That bullet sends him into supernova. Ego, self-righteousness, and self-delusion are blown away leaving nothing but a core, a core larger than three solar masses.

Reverend Lawrence Schmetterling *is* the black hole. He has finally crossed his event horizon where every thought, every experience, every second of every minute of his entire human existence spirals down on top of him. The enormous gravity of life choices he has made — millions of billions of trillions of tons — compress into a final singularity of truth: Larry remembers that once upon a time, a long, long, very long time ago, he walked, talked, and breathed as a human being. He had a place in the world, a future. He could've done so much for so many. Then one day a lunatic blew out his light, and everything he could've, would've, and should've been was cut short. But the murder happened eons ago, and Larry's hatred for this woman has fossilized into a lifeless husk of what it used to be, buried by sediments of time.

This is Larry's Hell. No fire and brimstone or demons sticking pitchforks into him, yet he can still feel pain. Most of the time it's a constant like a sore muscle. But sometimes it feels like a heavy object is burning a hole in his soul, like the bullet that killed him is still with him. But how can that be possible? His flesh and the worms that feasted on that flesh have gone to dust. If there's no body, how can there be pain?

The throbbing ache that plagues him builds in intensity until it explodes. The pain is gone. And then there's a change in scene so abrupt as to seem instantaneous. Larry has transcended into a place so brilliant, so shiny, and so whiter than white that he feels like a whisper blowing through clouds. But this whisper has a body.

Larry stands before an old man with a long white beard and long white hair. Larry is no longer naked; he's clothed once again in the same outfit he wore the night he was murdered: a beige topcoat, a dark Armani suite, and *Bottega Veneta* shoes. But he wore those clothes ages ago. Why do they appear so fresh in his mind?

The old man wears a white robe; around his waist is a royal purple sash even more striking because of its contrast with the wondrous whiteness of this place. Behind the old man is a large gate made of gold; what lies beyond that gate? Larry suspects that it must be a glorious place, where parallel lines intersect at the end of time and space. Has he funneled down into a different singularity, a singularity we call Heaven?

But why the gate? That's folklore not Scripture.

The old man appears to be seated on something, on what Larry is not quite sure. He reads from a scroll. Judging from the expression on the old man's face what he's reading is indeed serious. Although Larry realizes that it is best not to speak until spoken too, he blurts out,

"Are you? And is this?"

The old man raises a hand, and Larry gets the message: *Shut up*.

For the first time in multiple infinities Larry has hope. Maybe this black hole is Purgatory not Hell. And maybe he's completed his sentence. The urge to speak rather than wait proves too strong a temptation. Unable to restrain himself, he tells the old man, "Whatever sins I've committed, I'm genuinely sorry. Please forgive me. Will I be forgiven?"

A long silence as the old man runs his fingers through his beard and stares at Larry.

"I know I've done wrong. As it reads in the Bible, seek and you shall find. I seek forgiveness. Please tell me I'm forgiven," Larry pleads.

The stern look he's getting from the old man says that all is not well on this side of Paradise. Many times in these dreams Larry has felt like a man dying of thirst crawling on all fours in a desert. Then, as he comes upon one promising vision after another, his thirst only increases. Hope is out there, he sees its shimmer, its inviting reflection on the horizon. Parched, he wants to run to it and dive head-first into its refreshing coolness. But when he cups his hands to drink, hope seeps through his fingers like sand.

Has he arrived at yet another oasis with the promise of salvation only to have it slip away once again? The old man and the gates, are they more cruel jokes He continues to play on him? This is what Larry truly believes; he begins to sob.

"Who are you crying for, Larry?" the old man demands to know. "For yourself? For all those you've hurt? For those you've subverted with your self-aggrandizing preaching? Are you crying for their souls as well?"

Rage rips through Larry's spirit; from his mouth come words of fire: "Yes, I cry for me! Why not! When He was crucified He begged His Father, 'Forgive them, they know not what they do.' Whatever great evil I did, I did in ignorance. SO WHY WON'T HE FORGIVE ME?"

The old man grins and Larry wants to kick him in his pillbox, but he suspects it's empty.

"Ignorance?" he says. "You know damn well what you did, Larry. The sooner you admit it the sooner you'll be out of here."

"OK, I've hurt some people, and for that I am truly sorry. But I've helped others, too!"

"Excuses, excuses! Again I say, and try to listen this time: your only chance at forgiveness is finally recognizing the sin in yourself and your willingness to forgive those who trespassed against you. Let's start with the woman who shot you. Do you forgive her?"

"Yes I forgive her! Why she did it, that doesn't matter, anymore. I'm way past that. I don't hate her or anyone else. I pray for all souls."

The old man snickers. "Truth is you don't give a damn about her; as far as you're concerned, she can roast in Hell forever."

An image of the woman screaming while eternal flames lick her body is more than Larry can bear. "No! No! Never! There never has been, and never will be, enough hate in me to sanction such cruelty. I won't wish that on anyone. Not even her. If my forgiveness spares her such torment, then she has it."

"I believe you, Larry. But how does forgiving her make you worthy of forgiveness?"

"I don't know. Maybe it doesn't. But I forgive her anyway. We're all saints and all sinners. I preached many times."

The old man chuckles, "I'm sure you did, but were you preaching from your heart or making excuses for yourself?"

"Does it matter? I'm a sinner. We're all sinners, even you."

"Forget about me. What are your sins, Larry?"

"Too many to recall."

"Give me just one then, a big one."

"When I let Karen and Curtis talk me into misappropriating church funds?"

The old man strokes his beard. Pensively, "Mis-appro-priating," he lets the word roll in his mouth before reshaping it into a better one: "Stealing! You didn't misappropriate funds, you stole the damn money!"

A defeated, "That's harsh."

Sarcastically, "As for Karen and Curtis, the twin devils, they made you do it?"

"Well, yeah, sort of — OK, I did it! Happy!"

"No, because you still don't know the plank in your eye."

"OK, OK. How about when I broke my promise to God and left the seminary? That one was all mine, no one forced me to either enter or exit."

The old man waves him off. "Not even close. You would've made a lousy priest, anyway; too damn selfish." Then he smiles and throws his thumb over his shoulder. "What do you think lies behind me, Larry, the gates to Heaven?"

Larry takes a closer look. "I don't see any pearls, but, yeah, maybe."

"And I'm St. Peter!" The old man laughs. "See any keys on *me*, pal? When Jesus told St. Peter that he was giving him the keys to the kingdom, He was speaking metaphorically. He wasn't telling a saint to be an eternal traffic cop for the saved and the damned."

Flustered, "I didn't mean to imply — I'm certainly not a biblical literalist. What I'm trying to say is—"

"Larry, do you really think that a tired old cliché is going to save your sorry butt?"

"I don't know!" Larry begins to pace in circles. To himself out loud: "This has to be a dream, a really bad one that I hope ends soon."

"That's right Larry. I can't speak to those other visions, but this one *is* a dream. Not only am I *not* St. Peter, I'm not even close. I'm your conscience. That's who's speaking to you."

Suddenly the old man slips out of his white robe revealing the physique of a wrestling superstar. "Let's get ready to rum-ble," shouts the now buff old man. He poses like Arnold Schwarzenegger and makes a growling face.

Larry waves off the challenge. "Yeah right. How about putting your robe back on."

The old man shrugs and does as requested.

"What about those other visions, the bus ride, my first sermon, all that stuff," Larry asks. "If they're dreams, then they came from me, right?"

The old man shrugs again. "How should I know? You see those gates behind me, they're not the gates of Heaven, but I am their keeper."

"So what's on the other side? Is it a place?"

"It's not a place, Larry, it's a way."

Annoyed at the old fool, but careful not to rile him because Larry does not want to be put in a chokehold: "A way where? Tell me. Please."

"Unto the deepest, most secret parts of yourself, places where few men dare go."

"My subconscious?"

"Deeper. Those gates lead to the very bowels of who you are. It's where all the plumbing is. That's where you'll find the pipe that leaks sewage into your soul."

Larry hesitates. "It's just that I've never been one for introspection."

"Introspection is all you have left, Larry."

"It's as if my entire life is passing in front of me. They say that's what happens when someone is about to die. None of this can be happening if I'm already dead. And if I'm dying, then where's the tunnel? Where's the bright light? Where are all the long lost relatives?"

The old man shrugs. "Maybe it's different for different people?"

"My life has been flashing before me, which means that I could be in the process of dying. Which means maybe I'm not dead!"

"That's a possibility," the old man says. "You might still be lying unconscious by the side of the road. Or you might be falling backwards from the bullet's impact. You might not have hit the ground yet. Or, maybe you're suspended somewhere between life and death."

"So I might still be alive! And if I am, then I can undo all the wrongs I've done. Please Lord, give me one more chance to make things right." To the old man, "Will I live or I will die? Will I be saved or will I be damned?"

"The answer is within you, Larry. It always has been."

"I don't even know where to look! Tell me, already, how can I be saved?"

The old man thrusts out his arm and points. "Go through those gates and find out!"

Chapter 28

Death in the Cathedral

After ditching Howie and Two Names at the motel on North Nevada Avenue, Karla aimed her car south. They pulled into the parking lot of a restaurant about a mile down the road. She bragged that they served the best "I-talian" food in town. Frank had his doubts. No Italian food served commercially could ever match Mom's home cooking.

Karla ordered spaghetti with white clam sauce and a side-salad topped with blue cheese dressing. Yuck! They way Frank figured it, in an Italian restaurant and on an Italian salad, only oil and vinegar need be applied. He scanned the tasseled imitation leather menu looking for scungilli with hot sauce. The staff had no idea what scungilli was.

"Conch," said Frank.

"Oh," said the waitress, "we don't have that." She smiled an apology.

Frank looked at the menu again and frowned. He settled for spaghetti with white clam sauce same as Karla. Frank wondered if the chef's name was Chuck Wonder Bread.

Karla said that since white wine went with fish, she suggested a bottle of Zinfandel.

"Sounds German, Karla," he reminded her, trying not to sound like a wine-snob; an honest attempt that failed.

"Well excuse me, city boy. What do you suggest?" she snapped.

He scanned the wine list for an expensive white wine imported from Italy. All he could find was a pinot grigio imported from Australia. Frank had wanted to impress Karla tonight. He hoped the right wine, the right food, and the right talk might gently guide Ms. Libbee into the right mood. Romance was what *he* had in mind. Frank really cared for Karla, could easily fall in love with her, especially after that close call with death. To feel alive again, he really needed to sleep with this woman tonight.

After tasting how well the wine went with the white clam sauce, she said, "Good choice, Frank. I'll never have Zinfandel with I-talian food again." Then she gave him a cute smile.

After they finished their spaghetti dinners and polished off the bottle of wine, they turned to their salads.

"You're right, Frank, the salad is much better after the main course," she said after a couple of forks of salad. He had warned her that salad should always be eaten last because its dressing would clash with the wine, ruining the tastes of both.

"Would you like dessert?" he asked.

"No, I'm fine."

After the bus-girl cleared the table, "So," he began, "tell me about it." No need for him to explain what *it* meant.

"I'd only been on the force about two years," she said, "in uniform. My partner and I received a Code A, a man brandishing a knife." She sighed, and paused. Clearly, this was an unpleasant memory that still haunted Karla even after all these years.

Frank wondered if he would ever let go of Tracy Millen.

"He was a homeless man and obviously mentally disturbed. He was in the basement of St. Mary's — that's the dang cathedral." She paused again and turned her gaze out the window, in no hurry to pick up the ball up and run with it. Finally, "There were four of us, all scared out of our wits about what he might do and that we might have to shoot him."

"Did you guys have tasers?" Frank asked. "In New York that's how we're supposed to bring down nut jobs."

An angry, "Well this isn't New York, bud! And here we don't call them nut jobs! Here we call them sick people who can't help themselves."

"Sorry," he said, apologizing for being politically incorrect. Not that he gave a damn. As far as Frank was concerned the homeless were all skels, but he decided not to argue the point. He was after bigger game: a tall, trim, physically fit young woman.

"Anyway, back then patrol officers were not issued tasers."

"When I was a beat cop we had night sticks. Don't you guys have 'em?"

She shook her head, no.

"We all had our weapons drawn and aimed at his central mass, but this poor fella was in a world of his own. He kept stomping back and forth, waving the knife, and babbling psycho-babble. It's like he didn't even know we were there." Another pause, and then, "Training is training, and that's good 'n all. We'd been well trained, but none of us had ever experienced anything like this in the real world before — and in a dang church!"

She said a sergeant and his driver arrived on the scene. The driver also drew his weapon and aimed, but the sergeant was the one who tried to coax the man into surrendering. And again, she said it was as if the guy wasn't aware of anything else except the demons inside his skull.

"From when our sergeant arrived to end I doubt the whole thing lasted no more than a few seconds," Karla continued, "but to us, it seemed like hours. And lemme tell ya, Frank, I was never the smallest gal in gym class, but my weapon was getting mighty heavy."

She said although it was fall and the cathedral basement was cool, "My head felt like it was on fire." She must've noticed him wince, because she quickly added, "Sorry. Rivers of sweat poured from my face and sweat ran down my spine. It was all I could do to hold my arm up and aim straight."

"Service piece a Glock?" he asked.

She grimly nodded, yes. He asked if her finger was on the trigger. She nodded again and turned her face away, ashamed. "I didn't even realize it until my weapon discharged."

No need to say anymore. As they both knew, Glocks had no external safeties and short trigger pulls. Frank remembered that Two Names, who used a Glock, cited a report that said that about 20% of cops keep their fingers on the triggers in high stress situations. That was why Frank carried a reliable old .38 revolver, so he wouldn't shoot himself or someone else by mistake. Frank had a strong suspicion what must have happened.

"Suddenly, like out of nowhere, the guy turns and looks directly at me! His eyes went wild, like he was an enraged bear about to attack." She looked away again, and Frank could tell she was doing her best to fight off tears.

"I messed up, Frank," she said, her voice almost cracking. "I fired. I don't know exactly how it happened, maybe my finger twitched, whatever. You know those damn Glocks. Then the others opened up on him. We riddled the poor guy."

"Them damn Glocks are accidents waiting to happen." Then he told her about a story he'd read in the papers back in New York. "A guy took his seven-year-old son to a gun show. As they were getting out of the car, the father accidently shoots his own son. Kid died." Frank, the father of two boys, let the horror seep through onto his face.

"Thanks, but there's still no excuse for what I did," she said. "For all I know, I might've been the only cop with her finger on the trigger." Her face reddened and this time there was no holding back the flood of tears. Barely able to choke the words out: "I felt like a scared little girl."

"Did the other cops back you?" he asked.

"Of course, the other cops all swore that the guy had lunged at me. The Department wanted to give me a citation. I refused, of course. I spent the next day crying and heaving into the toilet."

Frank nodded. He understood. "I cried the night I shot that poor woman, too," he freely admitted.

The silence of shared grief hovered above them. Whatever thoughts Frank had had about a lusty night with Detective Ms. Karla Libbee jumped out of his head and ran away. Instead, he let his mind drift back to the case: specifically Frothe's statement about purifying himself in the wilderness.

"I still think he's talking about a real place, Karla."

"Sorry to disagree, Frank, but I think he was speaking in parables. Dang church people do that all the time."

"No, Frothe is somewhere in the wilderness." Frank paused, trying to conjure up an image from his past: mountains, trees, lake; in the Catskills. "A camp, a summer camp!" he blurted out.

Karla looked confused. "What's that got to do with it, Frank?"

"When I was a kid, my parents sent me to a sleep away camp for a week. It was for inner city kids and run by Catholic Charities."

"So?"

"So, maybe that church of theirs has a camp in the mountains. And maybe that's where Frothe is. You know, like a nice quiet place where he can be alone and feel guilty."

"Even if they do have a place like that, why would Frothe hide there?

That's the first place we'd look."

"From what the Stone woman was telling us, I think this Frothe guy's conscience is bothering him. He wants to get caught."

After giving it more serious thought, "You might be right," she said. "It's Easter week. If they have a place, I'll bet it's empty. I'll call Karen."

Frank settled into a quiet contentment. Sitting here with Karla, he felt relaxed. He remembered his ex-wife's constant chatter at the dinner table, mostly about herself or her day. The few times when she did have something to say about *him*, her words were often critical. But here with Karla, all that seemed like whispers from the distant past. Her eyes were more emerald than green. Why had it taken him so long to notice their sparkling beauty? Maybe it was the subdued restaurant lighting that framed her perfectly symmetrical face that made those eyes seem to jump off the canvass at him. When she looked up at him, this time he did not duck and cover. Instead, he held her gaze.

Her smile was more self-conscious and uncomfortable than curious: "What, Frank, why are you looking at me like that?"

Never much of a risk taker when it came to women, yet this new Frank was evolving. For too long he had hidden his feelings behind a curtain; but a curtain was no wall. Given the right place, the right time, and the right motive, it could be easily penetrated. A romantic dinner with Karla meant life, and Frank never felt as alive as he did tonight with her.

"You Karla, I'm looking at you. You're beautiful."

Dark bangs ran across Karla's forehead like drawer-drapes. In a barely audible tone, "Thank you." Now she was the one who dropped her eyes and stepped behind her own wall.

He had dared to show her his true feelings, and now she brushed them aside like crumbs off the table. "I said you're beautiful. Doesn't that mean anything?"

She still would not face him straight on: "Course it does." Another pause, one that seemed to last forever; when she finally looked at him: "You're going through a mighty rough patch right now, Frank. You're saying, and believing, things you don't really mean."

"Don't tell me what I mean! I know what I mean! I'm in love with you, Karla, damn it!"

Looking around at the other diners, "You're getting a tad loud, Frank. Please." Then she reached a hand across the table and covered his hand. "I care about you very much. I'm your friend. I'll always be here for you."

Blasted by the F-bomb! "Friend! Is that what I am?"

"You live in New York. Dang, Frank, you are New York! You'll never be happy anywhere else."

I'd be happy anywhere as long as it's with you. Thoughts he would not give her the satisfaction of saying out loud. Parts of the old Frank still clung to him like dead skin.

"I live here. Sorry, Frank, but I'm afraid that's all we'll ever be, close friends. A woman realizes these things a lot sooner than a man does. Eventually, you'll see it too."

Grim-faced: "Yeah, Ok, whatever." *Your loss, sweetheart!*

She sighed, then, "I'll track down Karen Stone, find out where their camp is. I'll pick you fellas up in the morning." She paused: "You listening, Frank?"

Disgusted, "Yeah, I hear you. Loud and clear." He signaled the waitress for the check.

Chapter 29

The Passion of Reverend Lawrence Schmetterling

Curtis had remained hidden at the retreat house all of Wednesday and Thursday. But after lunch today, Good Friday, he hiked a trail behind the tennis courts that ran upward to a ridgeline. Up and up he trekked; but in less than five minutes, the number-cruncher's lungs were on fire. Panting, he stopped and sat down on a boulder.

A panoramic view of Pikes Peak to the northwest and hundreds of feet below, a black asphalt ribbon cut through the trees: Dung Beetle Boulevard. Instead of climbing higher, he stood on the side of a mountain and offered up a silent prayer. Then he inhaled deeply. The scent of fresh pines filled his nostrils and the crisp air cooled his burning lungs. The sun warmed his face. Across a valley covered with patches of white and green and brown, an occasional car could be seen navigating the curves of Dung Beetle: other people living their lives oblivious to the pain and suffering of a sinner sitting alone on a rock.

Curtis looked down at the steep incline that stretched below. Only three steps from the edge. All he had to do was put one foot in front of the other, then the other, then the other and then… When Jesus excised the demons out of a man, He cast them into a herd of swine; then the swine hurled themselves into the sea. Curtis felt legions of demons and filth roiling inside him, so why not jump? Then he looked down again and he saw why not: because of all the rocks jutting out like sharp knives ready to shred and mangle his rolling body. Not only a painful death but what if he didn't die right away? What if he lay there suffering in a broken pile? For hours? For days? Then he remembered that today was Good Friday. For Curtis to kill himself on the same day his Lord and Savior sacrificed Himself for all humanity seemed blasphemous. Thus, suicide became a penance this particular sinner was not willing to make. A different act of contrition, not as painful or as final as stepping off a mountain, had to be made. He would make amends to another who had suffered; so he hiked back down to the retreat house, and keyed a number into the phone.

"Hello Mr. Schmetterling, this is Curtis Frothe. I think we should talk. Why don't you come up for dinner?" He gave Larry's brother directions along with explicit instructions not to tell anyone where he was going.

In the kitchen of the retreat house, Curtis opened cans and dumped anything edible into a pot. Strange that he, Larry's Judas Iscariot, should be hard at work preparing dinner for the self-anointed one's brother. But an offer of food seemed a civilized thing to do. Some canned meat and canned vegetables in a stew served with fruit juice qualified in Curtis' mind as proper. He always enjoyed cooking. After a long day's work, he took comfort in coming home and putting his mind on autopilot while he prepared the evening's meal. Cutting up meat, rustling pots and preparing vegetables always cleansed his mind. The tribulations of the day seemed to boil off him like the steam venting from a pot. But tonight his troubles were more like sautéed butter: still there, only in liquid form.

He looked up at the clock above the oven: 5:38 p.m. If he didn't get lost, Matthew would arrive in about an hour. Suddenly Curtis remembered that Larry had said his family had remained staunchly Roman Catholic.

Frog feathers! And here I am preparing meat on Good Friday!

Curtis dumped the stew he had prepared into the trash; he frantically searched the pantry and found several cans of tuna. He decided that he would bake a tuna casserole.

On Good Friday, Jesus was taken before the Sanhedrin. Then to Pilates, and then He was condemned and crucified. Curtis looked up at the clock again; in fifty minutes he'd be meeting his Pontius Pilates. How would he justify bringing so much pain and suffering to so many? Would he tell Matthew, *The devil made me do it?* No he would not. Curtis had finally come to terms with himself. No one made him do anything. The decision to defraud the government on his taxes, so trivial yet so defining, had been the single event that set this entire tragic tale in motion. That decision had been his. Thus the morally upright, uptight Mr. Curtis Frothe had led Larry and Karen astray. They might never have sinned had it not been for him. Curtis' act of contrition would be to admit this to Larry's brother.

If he can forgive me, then maybe the Lord can, too.

***

Larry awakens and once again finds himself in a gleaming white void. The old man — his conscience? — is gone, but those damn gates he's supposed to step through remain. Problem is, with nothing to prod him, he hesitates; Hamlet at the gates. Tentatively, he reaches out with his right hand. Then the tips of his fingers break the plain. Suddenly, other hands reach out from the far side, grab hold of his arm, and yank him through the portal. He finds himself in a narrow tunnel hewn out of solid rock. Burning torches that hang on the walls light the way. Can this be the passageway that leads to his most secret place?

Dressed only in a loincloth, Larry is being dragged by his arms, facedown, across the dirt floor by two men dressed like Roman soldiers. He feels the weight of the chain cuffed across his wrists; the rough finish of the iron bracelets is warmed and wetted by his burning skin.

Larry feels feverish and chilled. There's a pounding in his head, and he's perspiring so profusely that he fears that he might be sweating blood. He hears the labored breathing of the two soldiers dragging him. He smells their sour odors. Like sandpaper, the ground grates his flesh raw, and granules of dirt stick to wounds on his belly and thighs. The muscles and tendons in his shoulders stretch to their limits as they strain to keep his arms from being wrenched from their sockets. Larry, terrified, cries out, "What have I done? Why are you doing this to me?"

One of the soldiers passes gas — it has the fetid stink of digested garlic and lentils — and the other one glances back at Larry and snickers. The soldiers continue to haul him to the end of the tunnel. Then they drag him up stone steps producing a series of jolting pains to his knees and shins that soon fuse into one long agony. Larry screams and begs them to let him go. Finally, scuffed and bleeding, he is thrown into a small dank room. An officious man perched in an officious chair looks down on a sprawled out Larry as if he is a plop of dung.

"My name is Pontius Pilates," says the man, "Prefect of Judea. You have been brought before me on charges of sedition. Are you Greek or Jew?"

"Neither! I am an American citizen! You can't do this to me. I have rights!" Despite his pain and exhaustion Larry is defiant: *This guy's like that old man at the gate. It's just me punishing me. I'm the one in control not this clown!*

Puzzled, "What's an American?" Pilates asks the guards.

"You speak English, so you can't be Pontius Pilates," Larry adds.

One of the soldiers lashes Larry's back with a whip. He hears slap of leather on skin and feels its burning sting. He hears his flesh tear open, and then the wetness of his own hot blood rolling down his back.

Enough with this self-flagellation! I'm punishing myself for what? What have I done? NOT A DAMN THING!

"I know who I am, and I know who you are, Schmetterling!" says

Pilates. "I speak to you in Koine, the same tongue you speak!" The Prefect leans forward, his hands clasped together and his forearms resting on his knees. "Since you are an American — whatever that is — and neither Greek nor Jew, you have no right to be in Jerusalem for the Passover."

This particular Pontius Pilates looks an awful lot like Rod Stieger. He has to be nothing more than a figment of Larry's desire to punish himself. But fearful not to say something wrong and bring even more pain down on himself, Larry says, "Lord, I —"

"You will address me as Prefect. Your lord is in Rome." Pilates pauses to scrutinize Larry more closely. "You are neither Greek nor Jew, yet you grovel in the dirt; so you must be a worm. Are you a worm, Schmetterling?"

Although an illusion, this incarnation of Pilates should not to be trifled with. Slowly, Larry stands to face his accuser. "Prefect, I do not know why I am here. I beg you have mercy on me."

"You have been charged with disturbing the Pox Romana. Your words sow discontent among the people."

"They do not — ah!" The whip slashes across his bare back again. "I'm sorry. Prefect, my preaching was meant to offer the people small comforts, never to challenge them."

"And enrich yourself, no, Schmetterling?"

"No — OK, yes. But I paid my taxes, didn't I, Prefect?"

"Did you?"

"Well… Most of the time I did."

"Rome expects to be paid all of the time! But that's not why you're here, Schmetterling."

"Then why?" Larry cries out. "Tell me what I've done!"

"It's your words. Your words are seditious. Do you know how Rome punishes sedition?"

Of course Larry knows. He can't even bring himself to mouth the word: *crucifixion.*

There's a glint in Pilates' eyes when he tells Larry, "We will drive nails through your wrists and feet. We will hang you on a cross outside the gates for all to see. When your apostles see you hanging here," says Pilates, "they will wonder when we will come for them."

What apostles? Karen and Curtis?

"You will hang there in the scorching sun for days," says Pilates, his eyes shining even brighter as they go from glee to orgasmic. "You will beg for water. Your tongue will dry out, turn purple and burst in your mouth. Insects will sting your flesh. Birds will wait until you are too weak, and then they will eat the eyes out of your sockets. And finally, when you are too weary to lift yourself up to breathe, you will suffocate, Schmetterling."

Larry knows the horrors of Christ's Passion. He preached the story many times on Easter Sunday and listened to it back when he was Catholic. But why is he punishing himself? When did the Reverend Lawrence Schmetterling ever claim to be anyone's messiah?

"Is this what you want, Schmetterling? Is this what you deserve?"

"Of course not! Tell me, Prefect, I beg you. How can I be saved?"

"So Schmetterling, you wish to avoid the cross?"

"Yes! Please, yes!"

Pilates' face goes from hard into neutral. "Give me names, Schmetterling. Rome knows that you've been little more than the dupe your entire life. Affirm their guilt and you will be spared."

"What will happen to these others?"

"You try my patience, Schmetterling. You know damn well what will happen to them. They will take your place on the cross."

Larry is silent.

Pilates' tone changes to one of compassion: "Why should you die for their sins, Larry?"

That's right, why should I? Nobody died for mine, including Him!

The Prefect begins a roll call of those to be condemned in his place: "Your parents, especially your mother. She pushed you into a calling you never had. She and your father, and Sister Victoria, and the entire Church of Rome, they all used you as a means to their prurient ends."

Prurient means lewd. What's he talking about? "Prefect, I don't understand?"

"Through you, your mother and Sister Victoria lusted after their own holiness; your father lusted for money and prestige. And the Church, it lusts for enhancing its own power by using people like you."

Larry remains silent.

"Karen Stone and Curtis Frothe, they led you into temptation. They blackened your soul."

Larry senses a tiny bubble slowly ascending the viscosity that has been clogging his judgment all this time. When Matthew 7: 22-23 finally breaks the surface, it will speak truth to him; meanwhile, Larry says nothing to Pontius Pilates.

"Those simple, Christian folk of His Holy Tabernacle," Pilates continues, "you dedicated your life to them and how did they repay you? By using you! Colonel Fryd even beat you for sleeping with his daughter, when it was she who seduced you!"

The fever in Larry's head burns hotter and hotter, and his body still trembles from the chills — or is it from the awful choice he must make to save himself? By condemning his parents and the others he will spare himself an eternity of suffering on the cross.

"And those televangelists; they tried to remake you in their image. This is your last chance, Larry. Are you willing to die for their sins?"

Pilates smirks. "I think not. It isn't in your nature to sacrifice yourself for others."

A terrifying thought that has led to a morality play taking place deep within the confines of Larry's sub-subbasement. The fever in his skull is like the skin of an expanding balloon. Finally the truth within him, a truth that has always burned inside him, bursts into the open: Matthew 7:22-23:

"Many will say to me on that day, 'Lord, Lord, did we not say prophesy in your name? Did we not drive out demons in your name? Did we not do mighty deeds in your name?' Then I will declare to them solemnly, 'I never knew you. Depart from me, you evildoers.'"

"I *am* the evildoer!" he screams to Pilates. "The others are innocent! Leave them alone! The sins are my sins, no one else's!"

Pilates holds up his hands, signaling, *Whoa!* Then, "Tell you what, Larry. Since this is Passover, I shall give you one more chance to save yourself." The Prefect pauses. He smirks as if he can read Larry's most secret pages. "The woman who murdered you — if anyone deserves to take your place on the cross surely it's that evil witch."

Pilates sits back in his seat, clasps his hands across his ample belly and smiles. He knows Larry's moment of truth has finally arrived.

Larry closes his eyes, takes a deep breath, and slowly shakes his head. The truth has finally set him free. There is no hate left in him, not for the woman and not for himself. Calmly, "No, Pilates, I've failed God. The darkness has always been within me. I was destined for Hell; that woman was simply my deliverance." He hangs his head. "Leave her be."

The Prefect shrugs. "As you wish, Schmetterling." To the soldiers, "Take this fool away. And bring me Barabbas."

***

Frank, Howie and Two Names had waited all morning and afternoon for Karla to track down Karen Stone. Karla called after seven p.m. She'd finally heard back from Stone. The HHT did have a retreat house in the mountains. Karla pulled up in front of their motel at 7:33 p.m. Frank jumped into the back seat next to Howie. He shot a quick glance in the rearview mirror at Karla's face. It read: *All of a sudden you don't want to sit next to me!*

Two Names rode up front.

As they headed north on a divided highway, Frank looked through a windshield splattered with the cloudy remains of flying nighttime bugs; a narrow band of illumination lighted the way. Karla's Saturn sped headlong over an endless string of white lines reflected in the high beams. The silver-glow of ghostly pine trees skirted either side of the road, and the only sound was air gushing in through the cracked-open windows. Karla had given Officer George permission to smoke in her car. Her right thumb gripped the bottom of the steering wheel. Negotiating these mountain roads in the pitch black of night, where the only illumination came from the high beams, made Frank of the bright lights and big city hope that she knew how to hold the road — and that damn steering wheel!

"Geez!" commented a nervous Detective Goldberg, "It's dark out here. Ain't you going a little too fast, Detective Libbee?"

A casual: "Nah."

"Sure is dark up here," Howie repeated, a little louder this time. "Know what I think? I think we're lost, that's what I think."

"We're not lost, Detective," snapped Karla.

While Frank had no doubt Karla was *in* her element driving these backcountry roads, he strongly suspected that she didn't know exactly *where* in her element she was. And then Karla's cell phone rang. It was Captain Whitley. Apparently the Colorado Springs PD had just gotten a call from Matthew Schmetterling. The call came from the HHT's retreat house up in Woodland Park, the same place they were headed. Frothe was there, and Schmetterling said he'd made a citizen's arrest. A pressing urgency had Karla urgently pressing on the accelerator.

A few miles further down the white lines, "Where did it say to make that right?" an annoyed Karla asked Two Names. He'd been the one reading the directions off the GPS.

"It says to go five miles east on Bushwhacker Drive, turn left at—"

"At the rock that looks like a bear," said Howie, a comment only he found funny.

"... Dung Beatle Boulevard, go another two and a half miles, then a right on Shining Path. Think we passed it, Ma'am," said Two Names.

"No, it's coming up," she insisted. Sharply, "And don't call me ma'am."

Silently speeding to the rescue of a man who might be lying dead or dying, too bad the cavalry was lost. After arriving at the end of Dung Beatle Boulevard, she swung the vehicle 180 degrees, and they headed back from where they came.

Two Names reminded her, "Now we'll be looking for a left on Shining Path, Detective Libbee."

She glared at him. "I know that, Officer George."

On their second pass on Dung Beatle, they finally found the Shining Path, a long and winding road. Bumpy, too, Frank and Howe's heads kept bouncing off the roof. Frank felt his stomach slowly working its way up his gullet. Then when Karla sped up again, it seemed to Frank that she was aiming at every pothole she saw. Mercifully, the road to salvation was short; it ended at His Holy Tabernacle's retreat center. The car stopped in front of an enormous log lodge. Peering out the window, Howie remarked, "Looks like one of Bob Vila's jobs."

Karla and Two Names got out of the Saturn.

Still in the back seat, Frank groaned to Howie, "My stomach. Think I'm gonna puke."

"If you do, aim for the driver's seat," said Howie.

"Geez, its cold up here," remarked a shivering Officer George. He wore a stylish leather jacket, useless against the blowing cold.

"Elevation's nine thousand feet, Officer George," said Karla. "What'd ya expect, bud?"

Frank and Howie stepped out of the Saturn. Words turning into steamy wisps, Frank quietly reminded everyone, "We walked into an ambush once. Let's not do it again."

Four weapons slid out of holsters.

"Let me go in first?" Two Names offered.

"That's Ok, Officer George," said Karla with quiet determination. "This is my town, fellas. I'll go first."

The four cops approached the front door, their steps crunching loose gravel. At the door, Karla turned the knob. They all stepped into the foyer. A booming voice came from the main room, to the left and out of sight: "Is it the police? If it is, it sure took you people long enough. Did the fat guys stop for coffee and donuts?" Then Matthew Schmetterling laughed.

For a guy who had fired only once in his entire seventeen year career, Frank prayed that he wouldn't have to do it again.

Karla leaned tighter to the wall. Right behind her was Frank, then Howie, and then Two Names. That made for a lot of big bodies confined in a small space.

Thought Frank: *Geez, she smells good! Like flowers.* Then attuning his nostrils to the guys behind him: *Somebody ought 'a tell them about the joys of regular bathing.*

"*Mr. Schmetterling*," shouted Karla. "This is Detective Libbee. I want you to come out slowly where I can see you, hands behind your head."

"Whatever you say, lady."

It sounded to Frank like the guy was enjoying this. Then the bulk of Matthew Schmetterling, calm, cool and collected — and with his hands placed exactly where told — appeared about fifteen feet in front of the cops. Karla leveled her weapon at his vitals and asked where Frothe was. Given the previous incident, that made Frank nervous. Then he saw her finger was *off* the trigger. *Live and learn*, he thought.

Schmetterling smirked, and then he removed his right hand from behind his head and pointed to that direction.

Karla stepped into the main room. "I'll take 'im, Frank. You and your buds see to Frothe."

Frank, Howie and Two Names quickly moved to where Frothe was laid out on his back, arms spread on the parquet floor. Karla, also moving quickly, pushed Matthew up against a wall. To Frank: "Is he alive?"

"Barely," replied Frank, bending over the badly broken accountant. "You threw him a pretty good beating, didn't ya, Schmetterling?"

Matthew shrugged and casually informed the cops, "I made a citizen's arrest. He resisted."

Frothe groaned. His face looked as if someone had taken a hammer to it. Frank noticed that Matthew's knuckles were cut and bleeding and his hands were big as mallets. Schmetterling vs. Frothe: a mismatch along the lines of Mike Tyson vs. Pee Wee Herman.

Two Names reached down and laid a hand on Frothe's chest. "You're gonna be OK, pal."

Frank whipped out his cellular and punched in 911 with his thumb.

Meanwhile, an angry Karla informed Matthew, "You're in Colorado now, bud. We don't take to outsiders coming here and taking matters into their own hands." Yanking Matthew's hands down one at a time, she cuffed him. "You have the right to remain silent..."

"So you're really going to arrest me, huh?"

"Sure am, bud."

Matthew snickered. "I can't believe this," he announced to wall. "He has my brother shot, and *I'm* the one being arrested. What kinda wacky world is this?"

"A world of law and order," Karla growled.

Howie asked Matthew, "How'd ya find 'im?"

"I didn't. He called me, said he wanted to talk."

"What'd he have to say?" asked Howie.

"Not much. He's lucky I didn't kill him."

"Lucky for you, too," Karla replied, pushing Matthew towards the front door. "Let's go, Schmetterling."

Two Names pointed down at Frothe, "Look it! He wants to say something."

With a mangled nose and a mouth full of broken teeth, Curtis Frothe spoke: "Tell him… Forgive me… I knew not what I did." And then he lost consciousness.

Matthew Schmetterling, already out the door and in the back seat of Karla's Saturn, never heard. Frank doubted there was any forgiveness in the man anyway.

***

That afternoon, on Good Friday, while Curtis Frothe had waited for Matthew Schmetterling to show up at the retreat house, in a micro-burst of consciousness, Larry's mind had been hauled before Pontius Pilates. Meanwhile, in the real world, Reverend Schmetterling was being rushed into surgery. His brain had begun to swell again.

Dr. Bloom immediately had called the family advising them to come to the hospital. To his colleagues he sadly observed, "I think this poor man's suffering will soon be over."

Chapter 30

The Burden of Sin

On Saturday morning, the day before Easter Sunday, Detectives Goldberg and Libbee stood directly behind Frank. Officer George was on his cell phone making travel arrangements. Two Names and Howie would be on the next plane to New York. Frank would stay behind with Frothe until the man was fit to travel. Curtis Frothe, Chief Financial Officer of the HHT Holding Group, sat up in his hospital bed, his left wrist shackled to the railing. He waived his right to an attorney. Frank sensed that Mr. Frothe desperately wanted to relieve himself from a whole lot of guilt. Frank was happy to oblige the man.

With pleading eyes, Frothe asked, "Before we start, Detective Giavone, is my sister OK?"

Without missing a beat, Frank answered: "She's in custody." A partial truth: her body was in the morgue pending notification of next of kin: that would be Mr. Frothe. "You can see her when we get back to New York."

Frothe accepted that explanation without question. Frank figured him for a guy who believed what he wanted to believe. "And how's Larry?" Frothe asked.

"The same," Frank said.

"Please start from the beginning, Frothe," said Howie. "When did you and your sister hatch a plan to murder Reverend Schmetterling?"

Frothe winced on the word "murder." Then Karla attempted to soften the blow of Howie's blunt statement: "We're here to help, Mr. Frothe. Confess your sins. You'll feel much better."

***

Five months ago Curtis had gone back to Long Island to visit his sister Tracy for Christmas. He and his sister sat facing each other on folding chairs in the basement. Given the intensity of his own emotions, Tracy's special room was not the best place to be telling her about his true feelings regarding Pastor Larry, Karen and the HHT Holding Group.

"I don't like the direction he's taking our church. And me along with it." Sharply, "He's turned into a megalomaniac."

Tracy flinched. Poor phrasing on his part was like poking at an already precariously balanced mind with a sharp stick. "Sorry, Tracy;" then a resigned, "and there's nothing I can do to stop him." He rustled in his chair, ready to stand. "Let's go upstairs and open our presents."

Tracy stopped him with a hand on his knee. He looked at his sister; somewhere deep inside her, in one of those darkened, twisted corridors of mind, an internal switch had clicked and Tracy's eyes had gone dead. He'd seen this many times before, those perfectly symmetrical features turning stone cold in an instant.

"Maybe there is, Curtis."

He shot straight up from his seat. "Forget it, this is my problem. I'll deal with it. It's Christmas, Jesus' birthday, joy to the world. Let's open our presents."

He walked towards the stairwell that led out of the basement. Then he paused, his right foot on the first step. As much as Curtis loved his sister, he hated it when her sickness crawled out of its lair and into the open. But the terrible truth: she was the only person left in this world he could count on; that she was also a sociopath with whom he shared DNA terrified him. Many times he wondered how balanced his own books were.

Tracy walked over to a waffling Curtis. She led him back to his chair. "Let me pray over this, Curtis." Then she kneeled down in front of her altar. She closed her eyes, tilted her head back and held both palms out in front of her as if waiting to receive a gift. After a long moment of silence, she called to him: "He's evil, Curtis. Why do you do as he does?"

"I try to resist him, Tracy, I really do," Curtis said, "but he has me just where he wants me. If I ever cross him, he'll go straight to the IRS."

"To follow evil is to do evil," she said.

Anguished eyes shut tight as if he hoped that would block the wickedness that dwelt within him, "Yes… I know."

"God has chosen —it's our obligation to stamp out evil wherever we find it." Tracy left the altar and sat down facing her brother. "Many years ago our father's people were in bondage, a great sin against God and Man. So God sent his avenger, John Brown, to smite evil from the land. In our own times, God has selected certain people to take His vengeance on those who kill the unborn. The spirit of John Brown lives. Sometimes a sin is so heinous in the sight of the Lord," she leveled a pair of dead eyes at him, "He kills, Curtis."

Alarmed, "We're not Him, Tracy."

"No, we're His instruments. The sins that Larry will commit in the name of our Lord if he ever gets on TV are too terrible to be allowed to happen."

"What are you saying?"

"No need for me to explain. You know exactly what I'm saying. Reverend Schmetterling must die."

He frantically waved his hands as if to swat away the evil. "No! No! Waidda minute! Waidda minute! I didn't say that."

"Yes you did."

Curtis had acted foolishly by bringing his sister into this. It was as if he had taken a gun and put live ammunition in it. So why was he shocked when the gun announced that she wanted to go bang?

"Let me pray about this," a shaky Curtis told his sister. "Maybe I can convince Larry of the error of his ways. Maybe there's still a shred of decency left in him. Everyone deserves one last chance at repentance."

"Let the Lord come into your heart, Curtis. He will tell you what to do, and when He does, call me."

On those rare occasions when Curtis truly attempted to post the darkness that resided on his most secret streets, the envelope always came back marked, "Address Unknown." Unknown no more; Curtis returned to Colorado knowing full well that the hatred in his heart could willingly cause the death of another human being. And death was only a phone call away.

Two months later, on Friday, February 1, Curtis drove Larry and Karen to the airport to catch his flight to New York. He made one last plea for Larry to abort his unholy mission. And when Larry flat out refused, Curtis' fingers tightened around the steering wheel; then he conjured an image of Tracy's menacing face in his mind. And her words, too: *Let the Lord come into your heart, Curtis.*

Curtis awaited the Lord's guidance, but He remained silent. Curtis knew in his heart that Larry had to be stopped, there were already enough false messiahs on the airwaves twisting the Word; however, was killing one of them the only answer? There had to be a better way.

With Larry safely on a plane, the Bronco headed home at speed.

"You're driving like you're trying to kill us, Curtis," said an uneasy Karen.

He snickered, "Where's your faith?"

Sharply, "I don't have any, remember?"

"I tried to reason with him, but he never listens, does he?" growled Curtis.

"Who cares, he's our sacred cash cow — that was a red light!"

"It was yellow."

"It was red! Please slow down."

When Curtis shifted into a less aggressive driving mode, Karen finished her thought: "Without Larry the church is nothing." Then on a more positive note, "Will I be seeing you tonight?... Oh drop that guilty look! Wasn't he the one who stole me from you in the first place? An eye for an eye and all that crap."

"Your quotes from Scripture are as wrong as they are selective, Karen."

"I know. That's what I've always liked about the Bible, it's so damn ambiguous. What about tonight?"

"I'll be there at eight. I don't like sneaking around behind his back like this. And I especially don't like doing it in his apartment while he's away. It makes it all seem so..."

"Sinful?" she snickered. Karen always kept a dagger hidden, ready to stab him where he was most exposed: his faith.

"We really should tell him about us, Karen."

"*No we should not.* I don't want to upset him. Not when we're on the verge. For the sake of the business — I mean church — I'm going to let his male ego down gently."

"You *always* know what's best, don't you, Karen." This last remark came out sounding every bit as snarky as he'd intended.

That night he had dinner with Karen in Larry's condo. By 11 p.m. they were lying in the same bed she also shared with Larry. Curtis felt like he was fouling another man's nest.

"He's not evil, Curtis. He's just... *Larry*."

"He's evil, Karen. Look at what he's done to me."

Rolling on her side to face him, "He's done nothing to you." Jabbing an emphatic finger into his rib cage, she poked each second person singular home: "*You* stole money from the collection; *you* cheated on your taxes; *you*—"

"I didn't steal from the collection," he shot back. "I just—"

"Admit it Curtis, you were as eager as me to get Larry's mug on television. And do you know why?"

"Because I was weak, I allowed myself to be talked into it."

"No hypocrite! Why can't you just admit that you love money as much as Larry does, as I do, and as much as everyone else in this whole damn miserable world!"

"And why can't you admit that you don't really love me! You never did. You're just sleeping with me because in that twisted mind of yours you're hurting Larry."

"I hate you, Curtis!" Karen jumped out of bed and reached for her clothes. "Wait a minute! This is *my* house. You leave!"

"Glad to!"

Driving back to his apartment, Curtis stopped and parked in the lot of a 7-11. He turned on his cell phone and stared at its tiny screen. Once he made this call, he'd be setting something into motion that could not be stopped. He put the phone back in its holder. He went into the store and came out with a can of soda and a package of *Twinkies*. He sat there quietly sipping, munching, and procrastinating. Then he spilled some coke on his crotch.

"Frog feathers!" He noticed that the liquid had also worked its way down onto the Corinthian leather bucket seat leaving a foul brown stain. He yelled out a tirade of obscenities, pounded the steering wheel, and threw the can out the window. He silently cursed the *Coca Cola Corporation* along with the day of Larry's conception.

The sugar rush he was now experiencing compounded his nerves. He turned on the radio. The tuner was permanently locked onto a local Christian station. Curtis listened; hopefully the inspirational music would somehow make him feel more Christian. It did not. With no glad tidings towards Larry (or Coca Cola), Curtis turned off the radio. As he lifted himself off the leather bucket seat, he saw that the stain was darker and larger than he'd first thought.

This is gonna cost a couple of hundred bucks to clean!

Someone was going to pay a price! He got out of the car and turned on the cell phone again. He dialed.

11:23 p.m. M.S.T. was 1:23 a.m. E.S.T. A groggy Tracy picked up. "Hello?"

"It's me… Curtis."

"So? What's it gonna be?"

"……"

"Curtis?"

"Do it."

"Are you sure?"

"……"

"It's the middle of the night here, Curtis. I haven't time for this nonsense. I said, 'Are you sure?'"

"I'm sure. Do it. I hate him! Do it! Kill him, Tracy, kill him!"

Calmly, "Happy to oblige, big brother, and don't worry, little sister is going to take of everything. I might even come out there and do the woman, too."

The following Saturday morning and Curtis, alone in office suites of the HHT, stared at a bright red # 1 blinking on the answering machine. He knew who it was, a dead man talking. Finally, he pressed the play button.

"This is Larry. Met with my producer friend today. He loved my tapes! Wants to take me national. Isn't it great! I'm so happy that I'll be going to Mass at St. Patrick's Cathedral tomorrow morning to give thanks. Can you believe it? See you both soon. Hope you two have been playing nicely while I'm away. Christ's love to you both; that's right, you too, Karen. Maybe this'll make a believer out of you. Bye."

Curtis stabbed the delete button with his index finger.

Egomaniac! My producer! My tapes! Take ME national! Everything's always about him!

***

"So Reverend Schmetterling and your sister never met?" Frank asked.

"No. He didn't even know I have a sister."

"How did your sister know what he looked like? Did you send her a photo?"

"I gave her a general description. He left a message on our machine saying that he'd be going to service at St. Patrick's Cathedral. I told Tracy to look for a guy who thinks he's the Second Coming. My sister disguised herself. She said she saw him refuse communion, and then walk out of the church."

"So how'd you set up their" — borrowing an idiosyncrasy from his boss Captain Grame, Howie made scratch marks in the air with his fingers — "*chance meeting*?"

"There's a jazz club on the Upper Eastside Larry mentioned he wanted to check out when he got to New York. After Tracy saw him in person, she could wait for him to show up there."

The case against Mr. Curtis Frothe for the attempted murder of the Reverend Lawrence Schmetterling had been wrapped up. But there was still the matter of an assault and battery.

"Tell us about Larry's brother, Matthew," said Karla. "What did you hope to gain by confronting him?"

Curtis winced painfully. When he said that Matthew had arrived on time and didn't get lost, Frank shot Karla a wry grin. She fired an, *It Was Dark!* look right back at him. Then she asked what happened when Schmetterling got there.

"I offered him dinner, but he apologized and said he wasn't hungry. Then we went into the hall and sat down. He started asking me a lot of questions about Larry. I answered as honestly as I could. Then I told him. Everything." Curtis paused. "I asked him to please not hate my sister, that she is a sick woman and that it was all my fault."

"Then what?" Howie asked.

"First he looked shocked; then confused. And then he gave me a look of hatred that's hard to describe. The last thing I remember was him coming at me. After that, it's a blank."

Karla tried to talk him into filing a complaint against Schmetterling, but Curtis steadfastly refused. Then searching out and looking directly into Frank's eyes: "You seem like a good man, Detective Giavone. What about my sister? I've done all you've asked of me, so please tell me the truth. What happened to her? Is she…?"

Howie and Karla melted into the walls leaving Frank alone and exposed. After a few agonizing seconds he finally answered: "Yeah… She's dead." *And I was the one who killed her.*

Curtis closed his eyes tight, but not so tight as to stem the flow of tears streaming down his cheek. In a pitifully weak voice he asked, "May I be alone now, please?"

Back at the motel, Frank found a message from Detective Susan

Ferro. He returned her call, and she said that Schmetterling's brain began to swell yesterday, Good Friday. It looked like he was going to die, and then he miraculously stabilized about an hour ago.

After hanging up, Frank told Howie and Two Names, "Guy just refuses to quit. Gotta admire that."

"Admire what?" Howie shot back. "He's a Mr. Potato Head. He don't know what the hell's going on anymore."

Frank shrugged. "Yeah, I guess."

CHAPTER 31

Tree of Life's Rotten Apples

Instead of being crucified, Larry's heart explodes with great joy as he awakens into a new reality: the dry scents of desert and sage wafting with the gentle wind and the sun warming his body. It's as if the radiance of Heaven has ascended onto the land as a special blessing on him. Larry finds his complete self — head, limbs, torso — standing by the side of a divided highway. On either side of the road sits a boundless prairie of golden grass and scrub brush. Tumbleweeds blow across the landscape. The warm breeze on his face is strong like the breath of a living being. Its life force rustles in his ears, telling him:

"You're alive, too, Larry, alive!"

There's clarity to the elements that surround him: white lines distinct from bleached asphalt, a clear demarcation of road from ground, patches of weed from dirt — all in high resolution! These are not images of things; they *are* the things themselves. Nothing is nebulous in this new reality except the white wisps floating high above in a bright blue sky.

Larry shakes one leg, then the other. He feels muscles tensing and the friction of bone in joint. He stretches his arms straight up over his head; sleeves of clothing slide against his skin. He steps back to look at himself more closely. He's glad to see that he's nattily attired in a black leather jacket, a burgundy sweater, black jeans and black *Reeboks*. Yet he's also bewildered. Subconsciously, he reaches up to scratch his head. Fingernails rub against his scalp, a sensation that has Larry on the cusp of believing that he's a creature of a new reality. Have the superfluous elements of his old life been blown away? Is he in the final phase of a rebirth?

Larry, once a voracious viewer of nature programs on TV, remembers his old life when he crawled along the earth like a caterpillar greedily devouring every delight in sight. That was when he damned himself. Then one day, like a caterpillar who stops eating and hangs upside down on a twig to spin itself into a cocoon, a woman murders him and he is cast into a black hole. Inside that black hole Larry transforms from caterpillar to chrysalis, and finally by God's grace and the miracle of metamorphosis radically transform him into his German namesake a butterfly.

Larry is struck with the irony that the butterfly is also a symbol of Easter.

Although Larry knows he is very much a new being, this new reality looks a great deal like an old reality. He wonders how much time has elapsed between his old life in Colorado and now. But instead of trying to make sense of any of this, he tells himself to just go with it.

Your will, Lord, not mine.

Larry walks up to the edge of the road for a better look. He turns his head left and feels a crick in his neck. On the horizon, the road leads to a range of majestic, snow-capped mountains. They remind him of the mighty Rockies. He turns right and sees a straight as an arrow road coming at him from across wide-open flat ground. This all looks a lot like the high plains of eastern Colorado just outside of the Springs. Isolated, he is the only living creature on a lonely prairie, Larry wonders why there are no sounds from birds or animals. All he hears is the breeze. And why aren't there any insects buzzing and biting at his neck? This lack of life is like a witch's brew to Larry's soul. Old fears bubble at the surface. Too many times he has been teased by hope only to have it evaporate at the very last minute like steam from a cauldron. Yet what can he do except stand by the road? Sooner or later something will happen. So he waits… And waits… And waits. Back when Larry was a caterpillar crawling along the lower branches of existence, to wait a New York minute for anything was intolerable. Instant gratification was what he demanded of time. No more. In this world, time is irrelevant. Situations evolve as they choose.

Maybe I'll just sing a song or compose an opera? Cats! I'll sing Memories!

Before he can put these newly found musical gifts to use, talents he never had back when he was a caterpillar, his attention is drawn to the right: off in the far distance, at the farthest visible point on the road, a light pulsates. It's coming towards him from the plains. He assumes it's a car.

He laughs to himself: *Maybe I should stick out a thumb?*

As the light draws nearer, he sees that it's a vehicle running with its headlights on in the daytime. Closer and closer it gets, a vehicle larger than a car. Closer still: it's a yellow school bus, the kind that used to take him to Our Lady of the Snows elementary school. The bus stops across the road from him and parks with its engine running. There are no markings on its side, but the yellow body and black trim look freshly painted.

A lot nicer than the old jalopy I used to ride in as a kid.

He crosses the road. The doors spring open, and Larry's hopes are ready to pile inside like happy school kids at three o'clock on a Friday afternoon. And then he sees who's driving.

Oh, no! Saul the bagel-man?

Once again, Larry feels the victim of a cruel hoax. The cruelest yet;

how will he ever recover? He won't. He'll never be the same after this; he'll spend all of eternity a madman trapped in a black hole.

His mind screams: *AGGGHHH!!!*

The Irish half of Larry's lineage came from Flatbush, Brooklyn. When he was a young child, he and Matty often stayed with their grandparents on weekends. Every Sunday after church his grandmother would take them to Saul's Bakery for bagels and bialys. Little Larry loved the smell of fresh baked goods. He also loved Saul the Bagel-man, the personification of kindness with the brightest, most engaging smile he'd ever seen. Even his grandma, with plenty of anti-Semitism baked into her crust, loved Saul.

"He's the best Jew I ever met," she would always say to the boys when they left his shop.

One time, twelve-year-old Matthew, always the smart-ass, replied, "You mean besides Jesus, right Grandma?" To which he received a smack to the back of the head.

Later, Lars asked his big brother, "I like Saul. What was that all about?"

"Grandma's a bigot, Lars. She thinks Jesus looked like an Irishman and was Catholic."

"But she likes Saul, right?"

His brother shrugged. "Suppose so."

The Driver of the school bus does not look Irish; nor does He look like the portrait made flesh of the smiling Savior that hung on the wall in Larry's office. This particular Man-at-the-wheel has a round smiling face, curly black hair and beard. He looks an awful lot like Grandma's *Best Jew I ever met*, Saul the Bagel-man from Flatbush.

He's wearing a clean white dress shirt rolled up at the sleeves. His arms are tanned and muscular. His pants are black chinos. Larry looks more closely at the pants expecting to see traces of white flour, but they are spotless.

Larry staggers backwards and falls on his knees. Hands on thighs and eyes shut tight he lifts his face to the sky. From deep within his primitive, animal self — a place where neither words nor thoughts but only feelings dwell — a wail erupts. It's as if his entire entrails are slowly being pulled out of him.

Again his mind screams: *AGGGHHH!!!*

With his guts emptied, he hoarsely whimpers to an invisible God, "I've admitted my sins. Why must I continue to suffer? Please, Lord, from dust did I come, to dust let me return. Blow me away on this beautiful prairie so I can never be put back together again."

The Driver looks stricken. "Get up, Larry," he says softly.

He remembers that other bus ride when he sat next to Sonny, the Aryan Jesus. That was not real; therefore, neither is this. For the husk that was once Lawrence Schmetterling, all he can do now is respond to commands. So he stands. A long silence passes between him and the Driver. What does one say to an apparition, anyway?

Reading Larry's mind, the Driver says, "You're right, that other bus ride wasn't real. And that wasn't me sitting next to you."

An apparition of God, even one created in his own mind, to hear Him speak so tritely instead of in a voice that could fill a cathedral with just a whisper, Larry tells the Driver, "You're not real, either. Please go away and leave me in peace and let me enjoy what little time I have left in this place."

"No, Larry, I am real, and I've come for you."

Larry turns and walks a few steps further away. With his back to the Driver, he folds his arms across his chest and stares out at the open prairie. "When will I be thrown back into that bottomless pit."

"You're not going back there. Please turn around." The Driver's voice is gentle, caring, just like Saul's was.

"If you really are who you say you are, then you're a cruel, vengeful Being. I want nothing to do with you." Sharply, "Get out of here!" Larry has no sense of movement; it's as if the prairie spins while he stands still. Once again he finds himself face-to-face with the Driver.

"Neat trick, Trickster," says Larry. "Jesus driving a school bus — come on! Where's that in Scripture?"

The Driver pauses to deliver unto Larry a deadpan look. "Would you have preferred I showed up riding an ass?"

Larry will not give Him the satisfaction of even a small grin; nor will he back down. Suffering has made him stronger. "I believe you. You're real. You're Satan himself finally showing his ugly face." Larry has gladly welcomed the Devil out of the shadows. "My apologies to the Almighty for mistaking Him for an asshole like you."

"I've taken no joy in watching you suffer, Larry. By the way, there is no devil. Pain is something people inflict upon themselves or upon each other. People of faith usually blame their troubles on a devil, on someone else, or they blame me. The unbelievers also blame me by claiming that because evil exists, I don't. Such people are as fundamentalist in their beliefs as those they mock."

Larry's mind skips passed that hint at divine enlightenment. "What happened to me in that black hole, you mean that was me punishing me?"

"That was you searching for a truth you refused to face."

Larry's anger drains away. The Driver makes sense. Satan could never be so enlightened. "Was I in Purgatory, Lord?"

"Sorry, Larry, Purgatory was a marketing gimmick meant to finance a basilica."

"Amen. Is the bus you're driving a gimmick, too, Lord?"

The Driver smiles and nods, "In a way, yes, it is." The Driver sits with His left arm resting on the steering wheel. He turns slightly towards

Larry. “This bus,” He says, slapping the wheel, “it has a deeper meaning. I’ve always known your heart, Larry. Despite some of the stupid things you’ve done, you’re a good person. So here’s your choice: you can get on this bus and come with me. Or you can turn around and go back into the world.”

Larry‘s eyes bulge like they’re ready to leap from their sockets. He wants to turn around and run off into the boundless prairie hopping and skipping and shouting, “I’m alive! I’m alive!” Instead he kneels against the first step. Hands clasped in prayer, he begs, “Please, Lord, I want to live! Please let me live!”

“I want you to live, but I want you to think carefully before you make a mad dash back into the world.”

Larry speaks his thoughts aloud: “If I go back into the world, then I can lead others to salvation. But the world is such a hard place; pockets of cruelty, man’s inhumanity and all that. Not to mention the temptations, a constant assault on one’s morality.”

“Unfortunately, that’s also true. Life’s a drama, Larry, but that’s what makes it worth living.”

“But if I go to Heaven instead of back into the world, especially after all I’ve learned, that would be selfish of me, wouldn’t it, Lord?”

“Yes it would be. But that’s how I made Man, to be selfish. It’s those who transcend their own selfishness that are my most beloved.”

To be counted among those most loved by God, suddenly what should be an easy decision isn’t so easy anymore.

“I still don’t know what to do. Please, Lord?”

The Driver smiles, “Are you petitioning your Lord with prayer, Larry?”

Larry nods. “Like the Doors, yes, Lord.”

And then from out of nowhere, the pain that has been Larry’s constant companion while in that black hole pierces his skull like a jet of blue flame. Larry throws his arms across his head and begs, "Please, Lord, make it stop!"

"It's gone, Larry."

And so it is.

"Just a small reminder: pain and sadness, happiness and joy, all go with being alive."

"And if I go with you?"

"Then you can forget about pain and sadness. Forever."

"You make being dead sound good, Lord."

"It is. So is being alive. It's the in between that's most difficult: the terror of dying."

Larry's first intimate experience with death, other than his own, happened when he was ten. While his ninety-six year-old great-grandfather was going through the process, Larry remembers listening to the relatives gathered around the hospital bed consoling each other:

"He's suffered for so long… He's had a long life… Soon he'll be at peace."

Selfish platitudes; Larry can still picture the old man stubbornly clinging to life. Tell him that he's suffered for so long, that he's had a long life, and that soon he'll be at peace, tell him that and he'll spit in your eye! Even back then in Larry's child-mind, he recognized Om-pa's terror. Deliriously he would call to his children as if someone could miraculously tear through the shroud of death that was slowly enveloping him.

"I can see you're still undecided," the Driver says, "and while I don't like to micro-manage, I want you to remember this: all is vanity. If you go back, you'll be blind."

"Is that my punishment? To never see a Colorado's purple sunset, the innocence on a child's face, or a pretty girl's smile? To be in darkness?"

"Back when you had eyes, Larry, you still could not see," says the Driver. "What that black hole has given you is vision. And that's how you will go back into the world, blind of eye but you will see with more clarity than you have ever seen before."

Instinctively, Larry turns his head to the right and stares at a reflection in the bus' side view mirror. He is horrified.

"Is that me, Lord!? Is that what I'll look like back in the world!?"

There's a scar and a noticeable indentation just above the bridge of his nose. His milky white, dead eyes are pushed in as if one is watching the other.

"I'm hideous! Blind and hideous! Why, Lord, why?"

"You were shot in the face, remember?"

"Geez, Lord, I can handle being blind, but being ugly?" Larry whines to his Savior, "You cured lepers, cast out demons, healed the sick, conquered death, so why can't you give me my old face back?"

"Because I don't want to."

Just like Moses and that damn rock! There's always a catch with this Guy!

Sternly, "Watch it, Larry. Remember I know your head as well as your heart."

Larry humbly apologizes, noting that he'd better keep his thoughts pure while in the Driver's company. Then he stares long and hard in the direction of those far off mountains. For Lawrence Schmetterling there really is no choice because, for him, vanity is all. He stands about to plant his foot firmly on the next step when he suddenly freezes. He senses that he's being stared at. He turns his head and looks to the back of the bus. He sees another passenger, a young black woman. The sad, painful look on her face fills him with pity.

"Who's that woman?" Larry asks the Driver.

"Who do *you* say she is?"

"Wait a minute! That's her! The woman who shot me!"

"That's right. Her name is Tracy Millen. She's Curtis' sister."

"Curtis' sister? I didn't know he had a sister. Is she coming with us, too?"

"Yes she is, Larry."

"Oh, God, now I know where this bus is going!" Trembling, Larry falls to his knees on the first step again and begs, "Please, Lord! Forgive me for all the wicked things I've done!"

"Get up, Larry. I'm not running a taxi service for the damned. And like I said before, you've been forgiven." Nodding His head in the direction of the woman in back, "You forgave her to Pontius Pilates. You did not nail her to the cross in your place."

"But why did she shoot me?"

"Go sit with her. You two have a lot to say to one another."

Suddenly Tracy calls out to the Driver, "Lord, Lord! Tell me, please. What of Little Larry? Will he be OK now that I'm gone?"

Larry lets a loving smile reach out to her. Softly, "I'm fine. Thank you, Tracy."

"Not you, a-hole!"

From the Driver: "Lose the attitude, Tracy!" To Larry, so as not to be overheard, "People like her," nodding in Tracy's direction, "they do put my infinite love to the test sometimes."

Tracy has been chastised, "Yes, Lord." To Larry, "I'm sorry, Pastor."

Larry asks the Driver, "Who was she talking about, Lord? Who's Little Larry?"

"Let's just say that sin has consequences; for everyone."

Before giving himself over completely to the Driver, "But she's a murderer. Even murderers go to Heaven?"

"Yes, and cats and dogs too. My patience, though eternal, is beginning to wear thin."

"I can see you have a dark side, Lord."

"I'm complex."

"So how do I know you're not Satan playing tricks on me?" Pointing, "And how do I know those mountains over there are Heaven not Hell?"

Slowly, a wry smile works its way across the Driver's face. "You don't. It's called faith, Larry. So, what's it going to be? On or off?"

***

With gravity forcing all two-hundred and thirty pounds of skin, bones, internal organs, and blubber down on his arches, a free-standing Frank Giavone was not likely to stick this one out. Like a lot of Catholics, especially those of the Christmas and Easter persuasion, he decided to leave Mass early.

Karla had arrived at the motel at eleven to drive him to the 11:30 Easter Mass at Divine Redeemer Catholic Church. Too bad Frank was still in bed. He apologized for oversleeping — most other Sunday mornings found Frank under the covers until noon — and he hurried to get dressed. They left for church at 11:25 a.m.

As Karla pulled her Saturn into a handicap zone in front of the church, she asked him, "How long does a service usually last?"

It'd been a long time since Frank last knelt in a pew, so his answer came out sounding like a question: "An hour, maybe?"

"OK, then I'll be back in an hour."

"Why doncha join me?"

"I'm not Catholic, Frank. And besides, I don't go to church, remember?" Glancing at her wristwatch, "Instead of going to a restaurant — they're always so dang crowded on Easter Sunday — why don't we go back to my place and I'll rustle up some of my fine Tex-

Mex?"

"Sounds good."

Howie and Two Names were back in New York. They'd boarded a flight yesterday. Frank would stay over another day or two until the doctors pronounced Mr. Curtis Frothe fit to travel. Then he'd take the suspect back to New York for arraignment. Karla had suggested they spend Easter Sunday together. Although he knew that they'd never break the *Good Friends* barrier, it would be nice to spend a day with her before heading back to the Rotten Apple.

Frank's bout with religion was a short one, though; he was knocked out in the first round. After promising the risen Lord that he'd make another attempt next week, he walked out before the congregation's first, "Amen."

Karla's Saturn was still parked in the handicapped zone. Her face read: *Bad news to be delivered.*

"What's wrong?" he asked.

"They just patched a detective named Susan Ferro through to my cell." She paused. "Schmetterling died about an hour ago. She said you'd want to know."

Frank stared at the great Pikes Peak. He found no comfort in that lofty mountain. Sadly, "Looks like we got Frothe for murder, now... Weird, huh? The guy almost dies on Friday, then the docs say he's gonna make it, and then comes Sunday and he's dead again. None of this makes sense, Karla."

"Tell you this much, can't say that I see the hand of Providence in any of this. Things just happen sometimes."

Frank shook his head. "So why am I feeling so bad? It's not like Schmetterling had much to look forward to even if he did recover."

"Let the dead rest in peace. What about you, Frank? How are you?"

"Me?" Opening the car door, "I'm still alive, ain't I? That's better than being dead, right? So what do I got to complain about?"

"Detective Ferro wants you to call her. She a friend?"

Without answering, he got into the car.

That old life of his, of simple routine and free of all the pain that comes with complication, might not be so bad after all. When he got back to New York, maybe he'd call Susan and finally ask her out on a date or maybe he wouldn't. Or maybe he'd keep renting Abbott & Costello dvds and spend the rest of his life watching TV, eating pizza, and drinking beer. Who needed drama when the simple life was right there in front of him, hanging like an apple on a tree?

All Frank had to do was reach up, grab it, and eat it, rotten fruit or not.

Have Hammer… Will Travel…
With Pen & Paper

Like Pastor Larry, I grew up in the Borough of Queens in New York City. There I roofed and there wrote.

In 1993, I moved to Colorado Springs. Here I roof and here I write.

Other books by this author:

CHELYABINSK: Where the Salamanders Glow
Crawdads Do Not Sing

Hell Freezes Over: Life in the 23rd Century

See: JohnPansini.com

www.ingramcontent.com/pod-product-compliance
Lightning Source LLC
Chambersburg PA
CBHW070640310726
48982CB00001B/352
9781735187372